I0670097

THE
AQUAPHOBIC
CANOEIST

Richard Butler Glenn

First published in Australia in 2024 by Richard Butler Glenn

Website: www.richardbutlerglenn.com

A catalogue record for this book is available from the National Library of Australia

ISBN 978-1-7638219-3-4 (paperback)
ISBN 978-1-7638219-1-0 (Kindle eBook)

Cover design: Word-2-Kindle
Cover Image: Canva

To my wife Virginia for her unstinting love and support, always there for me.

Table of Contents

1

Rory Colquhoun sat on the train from Manchester airport to Liverpool Lime Street glancing through a newspaper which he had picked up from an adjacent seat. He was about to turn the page when he noticed a small article at the bottom of the fourth column. He read it several times before he slumped in his seat, his face ashen.

The telephone hadn't stopped ringing since the headline and associated narrative had appeared in 'The Guardian,' describing the rescue of Ah Kum and Bo Lee, as well as that of Dr Jenny Cunningham and Alex McQualter. The story had been leaked to the newspaper by someone within Declan O'Shea's organisation, but no-one knew for sure, quite who.

Mostly the phone calls were of a congratulatory nature, but there was one from a male caller, who had asked if he could speak to Alex McQualter. When he had been told that Alex McQualter was not an employee of the organisation, he asked if he could leave a message for him.

It was Declan who had passed the message on to him, "Do you remember Rory Colquhoun?" Declan had asked.

"How could I forget?" replied Alex, "my shoulder has not yet recovered from that tackle he made on me, in practice, all those years ago. Why do you ask?"

"He left a message for you, wants you to call him, said it's about a worry he has which he would like to share with you. He would really appreciate your help and thought that you might find it intriguing," and he handed Alex a slip of paper with a mobile phone number written on it.

"I wonder what he wants," said Alex softly, "I liked Rory, the best tight-head I ever played with, tough as nails."

Declan nodded, "And not given to idle chatter as I recall."

Alex took out his mobile phone and dialled the number, a bass baritone Scots voice answered, "Colquhoun."

"Rory it's Alex, I received your message, long time no see or hear, how can I help?"

"Thanks for calling back, Alex, I want to share a worrying problem I have, with you, I'm in Liverpool currently, will be for the next few days, any chance that we could have dinner? I'm happy to come to you if it helps."

"Rory, I'm engaged to be married, my fiancée is a police officer, she is currently on a course in Chester, and I arranged to meet and take her to dinner at the Grosvenor. Why don't you join us there, say 7.30pm?"

"A police officer hey, how very apposite, I shall look forward to meeting her."

Alex met his fiancée Detective Sergeant Susan Fellingham, a little after 5.30pm, at a Cheshire Constabulary training centre on the outskirts of Chester. They embraced fondly and he took her in his car to the Grosvenor Hotel. On the way he told her a little about Rory Colquhoun, and the mysterious message he had received. She was almost as intrigued as he had been.

They had enjoyed a couple of aperitifs when a powerful looking man could be seen approaching the booth where they were sitting. Alex stood and greeted the large man warmly, "Rory can I introduce you to my fiancée, Susan Fellingham, Detective Sergeant Susan Fellingham from the Cheshire police, and Susan, can I introduce you to Rory Colquhoun, the best tight-head Prop Edinburgh University ever had."

Rory leaned forward, his giant hands accidently pinning Susan's arms to her sides, and said, "A Detective Sergeant eh, even better." He kissed her gently on either cheek, remarking how pleased he was to have met her.

"What brings you to Liverpool Rory?" asked Alex.

"I'm being interviewed for the position of, Cross Department Co-ordinator for the School of Engineering, at the University there, so fingers crossed."

The food was good, the wine excellent, and the conversation relaxed and easy. Finally, Alex said, "I found your message intriguing, what's this all about Rory?"

Rory looked serious, as though assembling his thoughts for a long discourse, eventually he began, "Alex, we never did get to know each other particularly well in Edinburgh but even if we had, I doubt that I would have ever told you what I am about to tell you."

"I had an older sister, Aileen, we were once very close, she was very good to me when I was a child and taught me to read at an early age. She was four years older than me. She was also the mischievous bane of my father's life, having strong views about the roles of women in the modern world. She once told him that he was a misogynistic dinosaur, and he was totally nonplussed that she even understood the term."

"She, of course, resisted at any attempt he made to either reform her or bring some of his discipline into her life. This usually took the form of deliberately ignoring any man of whom our father approved. She once ensured that she was seen, by some of my father's friends, arm in arm with an Indian Naval officer, knowing full well that my father would be informed. When he failed to challenge her about it, she began to leave travel brochures on India around the house, which he also ignored, infuriating her even further, as you can well imagine."

"She was a bright student though and I was not at all surprised when she was offered a place at the International College of Economics (ICE) despite her strengths being in languages rather than commerce. I've always believed that she only applied for a place at ICE because she had once heard a close friend of my father's describe it as the seat of festering communism."

"It was largely due to this particular choice that my sister and I began to grow apart. She only ever came home to see our mother on her birthday each year, and she rarely stayed in our house. I used to receive a birthday card from her each year but even they ceased to arrive after she met Ramiro Morales, an Argentinian and one of her tutors at ICE."

"My mother and I were the only two members of our family who were invited to her wedding when she married Morales. My father was not invited, which angered him, and I had to argue with him to finally agree that my mother could attend."

"There were two things that most surprised me at the wedding. The first was the large number of young females present, nearly all of whom were fellow students at ICE, but not friends or invitees of Aileen's, but of Ramiro's. The second was the almost instant and pathological dislike that Ramiro and I had for one another. Which is most unlike me, as you probably remember, it normally takes me about two years before I can decide if I like someone or not."

Rory grinned at Susan, "Not you though Susan, I fell in love with you the moment I saw you," and the three of them shared in the laughter.

"I am not at all sure that Aileen was even happy on her wedding day," continued Rory, "she had obviously sensed the unpleasant atmosphere between Ramiro and me, and she apologised to me by saying, 'He's not quite as obnoxious as he first appears.' Even my mother was unconvinced that Aileen was doing the right thing. Her comment was simply, 'I do hope she eventually finds happiness.'"

"My mum and I found a kindred spirit in Catriona, Aileen's Maid of Honour. She sensed our discomfort and made it her business to ensure that we enjoyed ourselves. She was witty and although she was happy enough to regale us with stories of Aileen's and her exploits, she could not be drawn to offer any comment on Ramiro Morales."

"She offered to keep in touch with me and I accepted. It is largely through her that I know something of Aileen's life after the wedding."

"Apparently, approximately three years after Aileen's graduation from ICE she established a business. I thought, at first, that it had been by both of them because Morales, and his father had been involved in the Argentinian aviation business. The new business was centred on sourcing and selling aircraft parts, both new and reconditioned, to all manner of clients, from large commercial passenger aircraft to small freight aircraft companies. It was, evidently, a thriving industry. Aircraft ownership has been growing, almost exponentially, over the past few decades. I was extremely surprised to learn that Morales had only entered the business several years later than Aileen. In particular, because by the time Morales joined, Aileen had reverted to using her maiden name."

"Aileen set up the business, her first office and factory, not far from here, in Macclesfield, which gave the easy access to Manchester airport. Catriona told me that she was noticeably becoming very successful and quite rich. She lived in a large house in Prestbury, a most affluent village north of Macclesfield, much favoured by professional football players of both Manchester football clubs."

"She started to see less and less of Aileen, only aware of her busy lifestyle from the frequent postcards she received which featured photographs of exotic places around the world. Occasionally she would receive a phone call from Aileen, in the beginning they were always cheerful, they would, almost always, end with a promise to meet for coffee and, equally invariably, be cancelled several days later."

"She rarely received anything except postcards from Aileen but sometimes, a momentous event in Aileen's life would prompt a letter and some photographs. One such occasion was when Aileen gained her pilot's licence. A grinning Aileen appeared in front and centre in the photograph, with a single prop aircraft in the background. There were never any photographs of Morales nor any mention of him in the letter, but for reasons that Catriona was never able to explain, she did not believe that Aileen and Ramiro had divorced."

"Things continued like this for several years, but after the photograph of Aileen graduating as a jet pilot on small jet aircraft, Catriona received no more letters, as the phone calls became less and less frequent. In the interim Catriona herself had married, to a widowed GP, named Ian Wilson, she had met at a charity ball in London. He was a Partner in a small country practice in Market Drayton in Shropshire and she had moved to this country town following their marriage."

"It was during a weekend when her husband's brother, Robert and his wife, Elaine were guests of theirs, that Catriona first heard news or gossip, she knew not which, regarding Ramiro Morales. During dinner on the Saturday evening, she had mentioned her time at ICE, her friend Aileen, and the fact that Aileen had married one of their tutors. She had gone on to say that they had both become very successful in the aircraft parts business."

Robert Wilson, who was a flight engineer with British Airways had smilingly asked, "What's your friend's husband's name?"

When Catriona had replied, "Ramiro Morales," Robert's face became extremely grave."

"Do you mean Ramiro Morales from Avnav Parts and Services Ltd?' he asked.

"I think so," replied Catriona, "but I'm not altogether sure if that is the name of their company, why do you ask Robert?"

"Are they based in Macclesfield?" asked Robert again as if by explanation to Catriona's question.

"Yes," came Catriona's reply.

Robert, still grim faced asked, "What would you say the odds are that there are two men in Macclesfield, in the aircraft parts business, named Ramiro Morales?"

"About a million to one," replied his brother.

Robert had now captured everyone's attention, "There is a high level of suspicion in the aircraft maintenance business that Avnav Parts and Services have made their recent fortune, and quite a considerable fortune at that, from supplying illegal or incorrectly certified aircraft parts. Their name has been linked to several fatal air disasters in the last few years, but nothing has ever been proved. The name of the individual which has always appeared in the investigations following these disasters has always been the same, Ramiro Morales."

"Catriona was horrified," continued Rory, "she tried to contact Aileen but either Aileen never received or chose not to reply to her calls. Catriona than decided to call me and told me this story and asked if I could contact Aileen. I tried and met with the same results as Catriona. A year ago, I decided to drive down to Prestbury and confront her, or her husband, Catriona provided the address."

"I discovered that it was not their house, but her house, and the house had been sold. According to the Estate Agents who handled the sale, the owner had relocated overseas, she thought, to her husband's place of birth. I also visited Avnav Parts and Services Ltd in Macclesfield. They then owned and occupied a significantly large building in the industrial park in Macclesfield. I have no idea if they still do. The Manager there informed me that neither Mr Morales, nor his partner, were in the country but he was unsure exactly where they were."

"As I was leaving, he said to me, 'Did you say that your name was Colquhoun?' and when I replied that it was, he asked, 'Are you her brother?' When I told him that I was he said, "That's the name she uses, Aileen Colquhoun, is she actually married to that shit, Morales?'

"Last week I was on a train from Manchester to Liverpool and I picked up a local paper lying on an adjacent seat. I just happened to notice a small article at the bottom of one of the newspaper pages, it totally stunned me. It reported that. Aileen's body had, the previous day, been recovered from the Trentabank Reservoir in the Macclesfield Forest. An overturned canoe had also been recovered. Securely fastened inside the bow compartment of the canoe was a handbag. The contacts of the handbag contained credit cards in the name of Aileen Colquhoun and there was a laminated business card with her name and the company she worked for. The company's name was Avnav Parts and Services Ltd and her position was listed as consultant."

"The local police had contacted the company and a spokesman for the company had made the following announcement," Rory handed a newspaper cutting across to them, 'The Board and Management of Avnav Parts and Services Ltd have to sadly announce the demise of one of their most valued employees, Aileen Colquhoun. Aileen, a keen canoeist, was holidaying yesterday, in her canoe on Trentabank Reservoir, when her canoe overturned, and she was drowned. The Board and Management of Avnav Parts and Services offer their most sincere condolences to Aileen's family and friends on their tragic loss.'

Rory looked at Alex and Susan and said fiercely, "That statement was total and utter horseshit. Aileen was, and always has been, a chronic and total aquaphobic. She wouldn't have gone within a mile of Trentabank Reservoir or any other body of water for that matter. Someone killed her or had her killed. Will you help me to find who did, and why they did it?"

2

Susan was the first to respond, "I'm so sorry to hear about the loss of your sister Rory, it must have been devastating news." Rory smiled quietly and thanked her.

Susan continued, "Of course we will do whatever we can to help, Trentabank Reservoir is within our patch. I take it that there has been an autopsy carried out and a Coronial investigation, is that correct?"

Rory nodded, "Death by misadventure, was the conclusion, but then no-one there knew that she was aquaphobic."

"We will need to take a statement from you, I can try to arrange an interview with my boss, Detective Chief Inspector Warbrick. He is an excellent detective; we worked together on the last case which has received so much publicity. Would you be able to come over to Wilmslow police station either tomorrow or the next day?"

"I have two interviews tomorrow morning, one at 9.00am and the next at 11.00am but I would be able to come over in the afternoon tomorrow. I'm not sure about the following day, it rather depends on the outcome of tomorrow's interviews," responded Rory.

"Good," was Susan's response, "let me have your mobile number and I'll text you a time and the address. Are both your parents alive, and do you know of any school friends that Aileen might have had who would be contactable. Also, the name of the school or schools that she attended as a child. It will be important to have as much information about Aileen's health and phobias if we wish to re-open the investigation. I don't suppose you know the name of her GP or any specialist physician that she was seeing, do you?"

"Not in recent years," replied Rory, "there was a psychiatrist that she was seeing when she was about fifteen and our family home was in Inverness. I think her name was Matthieson, Dr Audrey Matthieson, and she was based at New Craigs Psychiatric Hospital in Leachkin, but I have absolutely no idea if she is still to be found there."

Susan wrote the name down and looked up again at Rory, "It would be helpful Rory if you could write down anything that you can remember about your sister. Anything and everything. For example, did she have a close relationship with your mother or any other members of your mother's family. Similarly, her relationship with her father, I know that you have told us that they did seem to lock horns occasionally, but do you know the origins of that, perhaps fractured, relationship. Were there other members of your family who she had problems with, or conversely, had a good relationship with. Any information you can provide us with could well help us to catch her killer."

Rory threw his giant arm around her, grinned and said, "I think that I have come to the right place, I'll put together everything I can remember about my sister."

Susan was extremely quiet, deep in thought as Alex drove her home," Penny for them," he said.

She laughed, "Oh it's just me, probably making mountains out of molehills again, I mean, why would she revert to her maiden name after several years of using her married name. Rory did say that didn't he?"

"I don't think that he actually said that, but he did imply it," replied Alex.

"And then," continued Susan, "all these female students invited by her husband-to-be, at her wedding. That would really have pissed me off."

She turned to Alex as he was driving, "I sincerely hope that you are not entertaining any plans to invite the female members of the Alex McQualter fan club to our wedding?"

He laughed, "To the best of my knowledge there is only one member of the Alex McQualter fan club, female or otherwise, and she has a starring role in our wedding."

She was quiet again, "I'm a bit intrigued by the relationship she had with her father, in my experience most teenage girls sort of dote on their fathers. That is until they reach the age where they have developed a strong interest in a potential future partner. But the bickering between Aileen and her father seems to have begun at an early age. Did you ever meet either of them?"

"I never met Aileen; remember she was four years older than Rory and therefore probably me. I met his dad a few times, he frequently attended our inter-Varsity rugby matches. Rory once told me that his dad had been picked to play for Scotland in an international match. A few weeks before the scheduled match, he was playing against an English club which had several huge Kiwis, South Africans, and Australians in their side when the scrum collapsed, and his dad suffered severe injuries to his spine. He never played competitive rugby again."

Alex continued, "My impression of Rory's father was that he was the epitome of the dour Scot. I never saw him become emotional on the touch line and he was parsimonious with his praise of his son. There was one game, against Dundee, when Rory had almost single handedly demolished their pack and I think we beat them 65-6. His father's comment was, 'You were responsible for both of the infringements which gave them their penalties, do you not understand the rules of the game, laddie.' I think that he would have been a hard man to live with, irrespective of your gender."

"Coming back to your earlier comment," continued Alex, "did you dote on your dad?"

"I still do," came the reply, "maybe I'm not ready for you yet," and her hand moved playfully on the inside of his thigh.

By way of response, he slid his own free hand between her welcoming thighs, "Oh, I think you are."

3

DCI Lindsay Warbrick listened attentively to DS Fellingham's account of her meeting with Rory Colquhoun, "I thought that there was something very odd about this death when I first read about it."

"Why was that Sir?" she asked.

"Several things," replied Warbrick. "Firstly, United Utilities, who are responsible for the management of the reservoir, are not the easiest organisation to deal with. It is extremely difficult to obtain a permit to simply go walking around the reservoir and, although I don't know for sure, I would have believed it to be almost impossible to obtain a permit to go canoeing."

"Secondly, I read the coroner's report. The examining pathologist put the time of death as being between 10.00pm and 2.00am. Now, tell me, who would go canoeing in the middle of the night?"

"Thirdly, there were three rangers on duty for five days before the 'accident occurred'. Apparently, there had been reports of someone stealing eggs from the heronry. Trentabank Reservoir is the site of the largest heronry in England with twenty breeding pairs, and United Utilities are most vigilant in their monitoring of the site. The rangers were rostered on, two during the daylight hours and one overnight. Despite this, no one, I repeat no one, reported seeing a canoe on the reservoir at any time during those five days."

"Please ask Mr Colquhoun to meet me here at 2.30 this afternoon. I would like you to be in attendance as well Detective Sergeant, and please ask DC Gary Proud to attend also."

"Certainly Sir," replied Fellingham, "is Dr Moretti at your house Sir?" Warbrick nodded.

"Would it be OK if I called her, I would value her opinion on something that has been troubling me since my conversation with Mr Colquhoun?"

"If you must," sighed Warbrick, "if you must," and Fellingham left his office to text Rory Colquhoun and call Dr Gina Moretti.

She sent a text to Rory and dialled the number for Gina Moretti. Gina was pleased to hear from her, and they chatted for a few minutes before Gina said, "I know you didn't call me to exchange pleasantries so how can I help?"

Fellingham repeated Rory's account of the relationship between his sister and their father.

"What's the father's relationship like with his son?" asked Moretti.

"A bit weird as well," replied Fellingham and she went on to recount Alex's story about the rugby match between Edinburgh and Dundee Universities.

"It sounds to me that Colquhoun senior simply has a problem with children, particularly his own. He may have had a difficult childhood, been orphaned, or badly treated himself. Not every man is capable of showing love to his children or even to his wife. It seems to be a particularly British thing. I wouldn't get overly excited about this attitude Susan if I were you. You probably come from a very loving family, adored by all, but you would be among the more fortunate. The attitude you describe is more common than you would think, particularly in these islands. Don't ignore your suspicions but don't try to build a case on it. Does that help?"

"Yes Gina, thank you, I didn't want to raise it with DCI Warbrick before I had spoken to you about it. I'll keep it to myself for the time being. Thank you again."

"No problem," replied Gina, "call me again if anything else comes up, on this subject, or anything else for that matter. Take care."

Rory Colquhoun arrived promptly at 2.30pm. He had taken Susan Fellingham's advice of the night before and put together an account of his sister's life to the extent that had been possible for him given their estrangement. He also had made several copies and gave one each to Warbrick, Fellingham and Proud.

He went through the previous evening's story that he had shared with Alex McQualter and Susan Fellingham.

Warbrick was initially puzzled as to why Rory had not been notified of his sister's demise, perhaps not fully understanding until that day, that brother and sister shared only one common contact. That of Catriona Wilson, nee Macleod, Aileen's Maid of

Honour on her wedding day, but no longer a regular contact of Aileen's.

Rory had a list of four women who had been girlfriends of Aileen when she had been at school in Inverness. He had also contacted Dr Audrey Matthieson who still practised at New Craig Psychiatric Hospital in Inverness. He had told her about Aileen's death and the circumstances surrounding it. She had been as nonplussed as he had been that Aileen would have ever, voluntarily, gone to a reservoir, less alone canoe on one. He had told Dr Matthieson of his forthcoming appointment with Cheshire police and the likelihood of them wishing to contact her. She had assured him that she would do anything she could to assist in the case. He also had brought his parent's address and phone numbers and explained his suspicions to his father but not to his mother.

They spent over an hour together, Rory giving as much detail as he were able about each of the girls that he had identified as being former friends of his sister, from her childhood. He had been impressed with the thoroughness of DCI Warbrick and felt that the combination of this trio of detectives would be just what was needed to bring the truth surrounding his sister's death, to light.

For his part, Lindsay Warbrick had been equally impressed with Rory Colquhoun. His shear physical size demanded attention, he would have hated to have faced him on a rugby field, but there was something thoroughly dependable about him. Warbrick found himself liking this softly spoken and quietly shy Scot.

He looked sympathetically at Rory, "Where is your sister's body now, Rory?"

"Oh, it is still in the mortuary which I believe is in Leighton Hospital, but I have no idea where that is. I have yet to talk to mum and dad about the funeral arrangements, but I wasn't happy with the coroner's report and wanted to have a second opinion before I did, which is why I contacted Alex. Why do you ask Detective Chief Inspector?"

Warbrick continued, "The lady I am soon to marry happens to be the best forensic pathologist I have ever met. She is now retired but I could obtain approval to have her appointed to re-examine your sister's body. I don't actually need your approval to do it but, as a courtesy, I would like to ask?"

"Please do," responded Rory, "In fairness to the pathologist who carried out the first autopsy, he or she would not have been aware of my sister's chronic phobia, so I would welcome a revised examination with that knowledge in the forefront of the examining pathologist's mind."

"My thoughts exactly," continued Warbrick, "I will arrange for the re-examination, we must have the coroner's permission to re-open the enquiry in any event, and I will request a second autopsy as well. The coroner is normally very accommodating in such matters. The forensic pathologist's name is Dr Gina Moretti."

They both stood and Warbrick shook hands with Rory as they parted, "Will you be returning to Edinburgh soon Rory?" he asked.

Rory smiled, "It seems that I have made it into a shortlist of two at Liverpool University. I have another interview tomorrow morning, so, if my luck holds, I may be moving soon to somewhere much nearer here."

Warbrick thought privately, 'Luck would have had nothing to do with it if he were any judge of character,' but he said instead, "I wish you all the very best for your forthcoming interview, who knows we may be seeing more of you."

Rory then asked, "Is Trentabank Reservoir far from here. I would like to see the place where Aileen died?"

"Not far at all,' replied Warbrick, "Just south-east of Macclesfield town in Macclesfield Forest. DC Proud, would you be able to access a pool car and take Mr Colquhoun to United Utilities office in Macclesfield Forest, explain the purpose of your visit and who Mr Colquhoun is. You can tell them that I will be re-opening the enquiry into Aileen Colquhoun's death and tell them to have all their papers associated with the earlier enquiry available for mine or Detective Sergeant Fellingham's convenience. You might add that I will be wishing to interview the three Rangers who were on duty during the five days preceding the event."

DC Proud leapt to attention, "Yes Sir," he said.

Rory Colquhoun was surprised but grateful, "Thank you Detective Chief Inspector, that is exceptionally kind of you."

"Not at all," replied Warbrick, "United Utilities would not let you near the place if you had arrived unaccompanied. I would be interested to hear of your impressions of the people you meet today."

"Certainly," replied Colquhoun.

DS Fellingham then re-entered the conversation. "Alex will be picking me up at about six, why don't we take you to dinner tonight Rory in return for your generosity last night. Would you and Dr Moretti like to join us Sir?"

Warbrick looked surprised, "That's very kind of you Detective Sergeant. My normal response to such invitations has been to decline but my wife-to-be tells me that I need more work on my anti-grumpy campaign. So, I will accept on behalf of us both. I will give her a call. She will be delighted, but totally surprised that I have already accepted without first consulting her."

DC Gary Proud was pleased to be driving this giant of a man and highly regarded rugby player on this trip. Gary had played rugby himself, for a local team close to where he lived in Altrincham. He was not at all surprised to find that this giant was exceedingly modest and interested to learn of Gary's playing days. The drive to Macclesfield Forest passed quickly.

The receptionist appeared flustered when Gary flashed his warrant card at her and then awestruck as this giant of a man loomed up at her desk. The Manager at United Utilities was a Mr George Stubbins. Both Gary and Rory could hear his snapped, "I'm busy, what is it?"

"There's a policeman to see you Mr Stubbins and another man, and they tell me that it is urgent."

They could hear again his snapped, "Bloody pest, what does PC Plod want this time, I suppose they had better come in."

Rory was impressed with DC Proud's maturity as they entered Mr Stubbins' office. "I'm here on behalf of Detective Chief Inspector Warbrick of Cheshire police. This gentleman with me is the brother of Ms Aileen Colquhoun, the lady who died in the reservoir recently, he would like to see the spot where his sister was found."

Stubbins made to interrupt but before he could do so DC Proud continued, "DCI Warbrick wishes me to inform you of his intention to re-open the enquiry into Ms Colquhoun's death in light of new evidence just to hand. He requires you to have available all your documents that were presented to the previous enquiry. These documents will be examined by DCI Warbrick, Detective Sergeant Fellingham, and myself. He also instructed me to inform you that he will wish to interview the three Rangers who were on duty for the five days prior to the event. Now can you either take us or direct us to the place where Aileen Colquhoun was found?"

"What new evidence?" stammered Stubbins.

"I am not at liberty to say Sir," replied a confident DC Proud. "Will you take us yourself Sir?"

"I suppose so," grumbled Stubbins, "as if I didn't have enough to do."

After a short drive in the United Utilities' Land Rover, they found themselves in a clearing in the forest at the edge of the reservoir. Stubbins began in a voice flat with disinterest, "The overturned canoe had been blown ashore here and her body was found, floating face down, a few minutes later. She had been dead for some time. She should not even have been here. She did not have a permit to canoe on the reservoir and we have no records of her ever applying for one. She would not have received one even if she had applied. We do not permit canoeing on the reservoir." Stubbins, clearly, had no sympathy for Aileen Colquhoun as he said all this, nor for that matter, did he have any for her brother.

As DC Proud drove Rory back to Wilmslow he turned to him and said, "Stubbins is an obnoxious prick don't you think?"

Rory Colquhoun nodded thoughtfully, "Yes, and I think that he is afraid of something."

A somewhat amusing incident occurred at the conclusion of an enjoyable meal shared by the six of them, Lindsay Warbrick, Gina Moretti, Susan Fellingham, Alex McQualter, Gary Proud and Rory Colquhoun. Rory had been the last to leave the restaurant having visited the toilet before doing so. He emerged onto the street behind a dilapidated old Ford Granada car containing two youths who were hurling abuse in the direction of DCI Warbrick whilst revving the engine to make a fast getaway. Rory came up quietly behind the car, he effortlessly lifted the car off its rear wheels and called out, "Would you care to get out of the car and repeat that?"

Two red-faced and stammering youths emerged, took one look at the giant who was so easily holding the rear of their car off the road, and began bleating their apologies. DC Gary Proud stepped forward, took their personal details, and those of the car, exclaimed, "Oh this car appears to be unregistered." He then examined the one licence that they held between them, and that was held by the passenger, turned to the driver, and handed him a pink slip, "You have three days to produce your licence at any police station, that is if you have one." He then stepped round to the driver's side of the car, removed the ignition keys, and threw them to the passenger saying, "You had better drive laughing boy home."

Rory lowered the car back onto its four wheels and the two youths drove away far more sedately than their earlier performance would have suggested.

Warbrick burst out laughing as the youths disappeared, "Rory, that was classic, the funniest thing I have seen in many a long year, a perfect end to a lovely evening, thank you all very much."

4

The following morning DCI Warbrick, DS Fellingham and DC Proud met in DCI Warbrick's office. Warbrick began, "I have been in contact with the coroner's office and applied to have the Aileen Colquhoun enquiry re-opened. The coroner wasn't best pleased, said he found it difficult to believe that no one present at the earlier enquiry had been aware that Aileen Colquhoun suffered from aquaphobia. He has agreed to re-open the case on condition that I supply him with medical certification of this fact. DS Fellingham, could you please contact this Dr Audrey Matthieson at New Craigs Psychiatric Hospital in Inverness and have her fax us a copy of such a certificate?" Fellingham nodded her receipt of the instruction.

Warbrick continued, "I think that we have a natural division of the research we need to carry out on this case. DS Fellingham, will you please follow the Aileen Colquhoun trail, contact her family and all her friends. Try to visit them all personally. I know that this will be expensive, but I believe that we will gain a much better appreciation of Aileen Colquhoun the woman, from face-to-face interviews. Keep me posted about anything that strikes you as being remotely suspicious." Fellingham nodded again.

"DC Proud, I want you to follow the Ramiro Morales trail and the Avnav Parts and Services trail. I was greatly impressed with the research work that you carried out on Erik Bahruz/Eric Baker history. I expect the same level of thoroughness on this."

DC Proud grinned, "Yes Sir," he said smartly.

Fellingham and Proud left the DCI's office, DS Fellingham turned to the young detective constable and said, "Another big chance for you to impress Gary, I suspect that the Morales trail will be a difficult one to follow and you will probably need to find one or two journalists who specialise in aviation news to learn about Avnav Parts and Services. I don't know of any, but I do know a couple of journalists on the national daily newspapers who could help to point you in the right direction. Let me know if you want me to contact them on your behalf."

"Thanks Sarge," Proud replied, "I almost certainly will need to talk to these specialist journos in the aviation field, so if you could help with a couple of names that would be great."

Fellingham nodded, "I'll get onto it today and get back to you."

They went their separate ways, Fellingham to her office and Proud to a larger area which was large enough to accommodate three detectives but he, currently, was the sole occupant.

Fellingham's first call was to Dr Audrey Matthieson. She was obviously expecting the call having heard from Rory Colquhoun the previous day. She was friendly but cautious, "Detective Sergeant, "she said, "I'm sure that you are aware of doctor/patient confidentiality issues. Could I first ask you to send me a fax, on your office letterhead, clearly stating what it is you require of me. I am more than happy to help but need to be sure that I am dealing with who you say you are. I will call you back on the telephone number listed on your letterhead."

"Of course," replied Susan, "I'll do that now."

Twenty minutes later she had a copy of Aileen Colquhoun's medical history identifying her long-term problem of aquaphobia. Dr Matthieson had also sent her a copy of a report from a psychiatrist in Edinburgh to her GP in Inverness also confirming Aileen's condition. There was also a copy of a more recent enquiry made to Dr Matthieson by a psychiatrist in Manchester requesting a copy of Aileen's medical history and advising that he was now treating Aileen for the same condition.

DS Fellingham's phone rang, it was Dr Matthieson, "Did you receive the information that I sent?"

Susan replied that she had.

Dr Matthieson continued, "Detective Sergeant, I want to repeat what I said to Aileen's brother yesterday. There is absolutely no way that Aileen Colquhoun would have travelled voluntarily to any body of water and had she been forcibly deposited there she would undoubtedly suffered an acute stress disorder. This is a condition which is caused by the release of excessive adrenaline and norepinephrine into the nervous system. These hormones speed up a person's pulse and respiratory rate, dilate pupils or temporarily mask pain. It would have been impossible for her to take any action to defend herself, or to extract herself from that situation."

"Would you be prepared to make that statement in court," asked Fellingham.

"Of course," came the firm reply, "I treated Aileen for this condition from when she was seven years old until she left for university at eighteen. I have also discussed her case with colleagues who were subsequently treating her, and I can assure that there had been no improvement in her condition. The opposite may well have been true but of course I cannot swear to that."

"Thank you, Dr Matthieson, that has been most helpful," concluded DS Fellingham.

"If I can be of further assistance, please let me know," continued Dr Matthieson. "Have you had the opportunity to speak with Aileen's parents yet?"

"Not as yet," replied Susan, "I was about to call them next; do you know either of them?"

"I know both, particularly her mother, Isla. They would both often come with Aileen when I was treating her," replied the doctor.

"Is there anything that you can tell me about them without breaching any confidentiality concerns, the last thing I want to do is cause them any further distress," continued Susan.

"Yes, you do need to tread carefully Detective Sergeant, Isla has taken the news of Aileen's death very badly. Her father, Duncan, gives the impression of uncompromising toughness, but don't be fooled by it detective. There is more marshmallow than granite to that man. He adores his family and is fiercely proud of his children. He has always encouraged both Aileen and Rory to speak their minds, but more so Aileen, he has always believed that Rory's sheer size would be his greatest protection."

DS Fellingham was confused, "I gained the impression after talking to Rory that Aileen had a problem with her father, that she went out of her way to irritate him and that she rarely came home after she began at ICE."

Audrey Matthieson laughed, "Many people have made that same mistake. No doubt Rory told you the story of Aileen calling her father a misogynistic dinosaur?"

"Yes, that and a racist misogynist," replied Susan.

Audrey laughed again, "Rory probably never mentioned that when Aileen called her father a misogynistic dinosaur, she was only eleven or even ten years old. He asked her if she knew what such a person was and when she gave him the correct answer, he was so proud of her. He used to say to her, your brother has the brawn, you must use your brain and your tongue to protect yourself. He would add, women have been timid for too long, timidity brings servitude, you must always stand up and speak up for what you believe in."

"But she rarely came home after she commenced at ICE, isn't that correct?" continued Fellingham.

"That was because her father met Morales and disliked him intensely, and it created a gulf between father and daughter. They had a serious falling out after Duncan made a surprise visit to London and met Morales at the flat, she shared with two other girls. I don't know the details of what was said, by whom, to whom, but Duncan returned to Scotland gravely concerned about the safety of his daughter. You need to know that Duncan believes that Morales was somehow involved in Aileen's death. You should try to have him tell you why he thinks that, when you meet him, but do tread carefully. He is an exceptionally private man; he doesn't indulge in gossip, and you will need to gain his confidence to encourage him to open up to you. You do have one significant advantage though, he admires intelligent and forthright women, and he will be encouraged to know that you are working on the case."

"You really like her father, don't you?" Fellingham asked.

"Yes, I do, but not for the usual reasons why women like men, he has not only been an amazing advocate for me, it is not easy for a female doctor, specialising in psychiatry, here in Scotland but I admire him so much for how he has taken care of Isla and raised his two children, virtually unaided."

"Isla developed considerable difficulties when she was carrying Rory. He was such a large baby. Not only did the delivery take in excess of sixteen hours but she also developed postpartum eclampsia and suffered serious and prolonged depression and psychotic episodes following the birth. She also suffered damage to her liver and kidneys. He will be especially protective of her when you meet them, so again, you will have to be careful."

Fellingham was grateful for the frankness that Dr Matthieson had displayed. She was now absolutely convinced that a meeting, in person, with Aileen's parents was essential.

Before she called Aileen's parents, though, she considered it best that she tried to track down some, if not all, of the four girls, they would be women now, who Rory had identified as schoolfriends of his sister. She studied the four names: Alisson Macdonald, Fiona Bruce, Sheila Guilfoyle, and Mary Stirling. They could all, of course, be now married and known by different surnames. She decided to start with the school where they had all known one another; Inverness Royal Academy on Culduthel Road. She thought about her questions to the school personnel, Alex and Declan were both 34 years of age, assuming Rory was about the same age that would make Aileen approximately 38. It would also mean that her high school years would have been between 1995 and 1999, or thereabouts. She wondered if any of her teachers remained at the school.

She discovered that the principal at the school was called the Rector, and the current incumbent was a Mr Nigel Engstrand. She sent a fax to his office, on the police letterhead, introducing herself and asking him if she could call him later in the day to discuss one of the school's former pupils, Aileen Colquhoun, now deceased. She also added that she would wish to speak to any of Aileen's former teachers who had also taught any of the four girls Rory had identified, and she listed them.

She had her reply within half an hour advising that Mr Engstrand was currently available to take her call. She called him, he was reserved but polite, advising that he personally did not know any of the four girls mentioned but that Aileen's former Guidance Teacher, Mrs Gillian Davies, continued to teach at the school. He advised DS Fellingham to call his office again, during the lunch break between 12.30 and 1.00pm and he would ensure that Mrs Davies would be available to take the call. That was in an hour and a half's time.

She decided to use the time to call her contacts on the Guardian and the Observer newspapers. Sandy Woodhead was the most informative of the two. She hadn't realised that he owned his own Cessna light aircraft and was a keen pilot. He gave her names of journalists on Aviation News UK and Aviation News Magazine, Flyer, and Pilot magazines as well as the name of the editor of Aviation News Back Issues. That should keep Gary Proud occupied for a while she thought, and she gave him a call to give him the names.

She called Mr Engstrand's office again; Mrs Davies was awaiting her call. Despite the Welsh name, Mrs Davies had a delightful lilting highland's accent. "Yes, I knew Aileen Colquhoun very well, I was her Guidance Teacher for four years. I have only recently heard the news of her death, but there must have been a mistake in the report for it said that she drowned whilst canoeing. There is no way that Aileen would have gone near a canoe or a lake or wherever it was she allegedly drowned. She was, quite literally, terrified of water."

"Yes, we have only just learned of that ourselves which is why we have reopened the investigation into her death," replied Susan. "What else can you tell me about her, Mrs Davies?"

"Och well, she was very bright, probably one of the two brightest students at the school at that time. She didn't suffer fools gladly though, and she had a tongue on her that could reduce anyone to tears. She generally reserved her most acerbic remarks for members of the male sex, not that that, in any way, excuses them of course. At the same time, she was extremely kind-hearted, particularly toward girls who were being bullied or had been subjected to racist abuse. She loved all animals, she volunteered, every year, to trek into the mountains looking for sheep that had been lost in a blizzard. The crofters loved her, I heard one of them once remark that she should have been beatified as the patron saint of crofters."

"Did she make many friends at school, some who I could speak to, to learn more about her? Her brother, Rory, gave me four names, Alisson Macdonald, Fiona Bruce, Sheila Guilfoyle, and Mary Stirling. Are any of them still living in or near Inverness?"

"Let me see now," continued Mrs Davies, "now that you mention those names, I seem to remember Aileen being friendly with all of them. Mary Stirling was the other very bright girl when I said that Aileen was one of the two brightest. There was a great deal of rivalry between them of course, but there was also a good deal of respect between them as well. I understand that Mary has taken silk and is a Queen's Counsel, Solicitor Advocate and is now located in Edinburgh. I can probably find her contact details if it would help."

"Fiona Bruce married very young, to a Canadian Air Force pilot if my memory serves me correctly. She moved to British Columbia shortly after her wedding and I've lost touch with her. She has never attended any of our reunions."

"Alisson Macdonald continues to live in Inverness, she is now married to a man with the name of Finlay Fraser. Fraser is one of the most common surnames in Inverness reflecting the fact that Clan Fraser of Lovat was one of the more prominent clans in this part of Scotland. I don't believe that there is any direct lineage between Finlay Fraser and the Clan Chieftain, however. I also have her contact details as well; do you wish me to send you Mary Stirling and Alisson Macdonald/Fraser's contact details?"

"That would be most helpful," replied DS Fellingham.

She next called Mr and Mrs Colquhoun, a sombre, "Hello," in a deep male voice greeted her.

"Good morning," Susan Fellingham began, "is that Mr Colquhoun, Mr Duncan Colquhoun?"

"It is, who is that speaking?" came the terse question.

"Mr Colquhoun, my name is Detective Sergeant Susan Fellingham of the Cheshire police, and I am involved in the re-opening of the enquiry into the death of your daughter Aileen. I am calling to make an appointment to meet with you and Mrs Colquhoun at a time convenient to you."

"Yes, Dr Audrey Matthieson called me and told me that you would likely be in touch, when are you thinking of coming to Inverness?" Mr Colquhoun continued.

Was she dreaming it or had Mr Colquhoun's voice softened, just a little. "I would like to come as soon as possible," Susan replied, "but I really would like it to be at a date and time that best suits you."

"Shall we say late morning, two days from now?"

"Perfect," replied Susan, "Your son Rory has given me your address," and she read the address from her notebook, "shall we say at about 11.30am?"

"That would be fine," replied Mr Colquhoun, and he hung up.

A few minutes later she had another fax from the Inverness Royal Academy with the contact details of both Mary Stirling and Alisson Fraser nee Macdonald. She decided to call Alisson Fraser first. Alisson herself picked up the phone. It became quickly apparent that Alisson had lost contact with Aileen almost immediately following the completion of their secondary education. Alisson had not gone on to tertiary education, she had been employed in her aunt's haberdashery shop and had not seen Aileen again. She had not heard about her friend's death and was clearly distressed when Susan told her the news, without any of the details surrounding it.

Susan next called the office number for Mary Stirling. An efficient sounding female voice answered, which quickly told her that Ms Stirling was in Court and would be all day. Susan gave the receptionist her mobile telephone number with the request that Ms Stirling contact her, as soon as possible, at any time, night, or day.

DS Fellingham was a little surprised then when her mobile phone rang shortly after 2.00pm. It was Mary Stirling. "Detective Sergeant," she began, "I'm so pleased that you have contacted me, I have wanted to speak to someone in the police force ever since I learned of poor Aileen's death a few days ago. Aileen and I were very close, we have become considerably closer over the past few years. I know a good deal about her life and its downward spiral in the last few years. When can we meet?"

Susan Fellingham felt her pulse quicken. "I must be in Inverness the day after tomorrow, to speak with Aileen's parents. Do you have any time tomorrow?"

"I'll make time," came the reply, come to my house, far fewer interruptions than my office," and she rattled out an address in Morningside, which Susan knew was one of the more affluent areas of Edinburgh. Mary Stirling continued, "I'm an early riser so come as early as you like, I think that the first shuttle from Manchester arrives a little after 7.00am. I'll be expecting you," and she hung up.

Great, thought DS Fellingham, another 4.30am start.

5

DC Gary Proud began his research into the background of Ramiro Morales in his typical thorough manner. Everything that he researched he cross referenced with other research items that he had carried out on this enquiry and noted everything in his own neat handwriting.

He began his research on the ICE website and in particular any reference he could find regarding the appointment of Ramiro Morales.

Ramiro Morales was born In Buenos Aires on 17th February 1965 to an aircraft mechanic father Agustin, and a seamstress mother Isabella nee Rodriguez. He attended the University of Buenos Aires between 1983 to 1986, when he graduated with a bachelor's degree in economics.

After a brief spell with his father's aircraft repair business, he relocated to New York city and completed his post graduate master's degree in economics at Columbia University in 1990. (DC Proud's note in the margin, 'Appears to have left in something of a hurry' FRR.) FRR= Further research required.

From 1990 to 1994 there is little known. FRR.

First appears as a Tutor at ICE in September 1995. This was before the advent of social media, Proud finds that the student newspaper is called 'The Hive.'

Began search on The Hive (published fortnightly) from October 1995 and the UK's Criminal Register also from October 1995.

First comments appear in the Hive in December 1995 about the "dishy tutor in economics bringing exciting relief to a boring subject.'

More comments appear in February 1996 issue of the Hive under the heading, 'I know the Mr who I want my valentine to be this year, if you will forgive my satiric misspelling' with a reply in the following edition, 'you and three hundred others just like you'.

In February 1996 the following comment appeared, 'Feeling tired, listless, all that cramming getting you down, try learning the Argentine Tango from the smouldering master, our enticing economics tutor, Ramiro Morales.'

By the end of May 1996, toward the end of ICE's summer term, an add appeared in the Hive, 'Want to become fitter, why not join the Latin dance classes taught by Ramiro Morales and friends during July and September, write to GPO Box No 5452 Waterloo.

The first appearance of Ramiro Morales' name in the national crime register was in December 1996, 'Mr Ramiro Morales, a tutor at the International College of Economics (ICE), appeared in Westminster Magistrates Court today charged with the sexual assault on one Rita Velasquez, a student at ICE and a

Spanish citizen. Mr Morales has pleaded not guilty to all charges.'

Then again in January 1997 when Ms Velasquez withdrew all charges against Mr Morales.

A quick scan on the succeeding months on the crime register revealed no further mention of Ramiro Morales' name so DC Proud returned to "The Hive.'

He had not previously thought of himself as being particularly sharp sighted but as he quickly scanned the pages of subsequent issues of the Hive, the name, Rita Velasquez, caught his eye in the second issue in April 1997 of the paper. It was a tiny notice at the bottom of the 'Comment' section of the newspaper. A sub-heading entitled, 'Goodbye my Dearest Friend' led the reader to the tiny, sad paragraph, 'Rita Velasquez. Departed this world 19th April 1997. A better friend no-one could ever have. Desconsa en Paz Preciosa Nina.

DC Proud was instantly on full alert. He immediately accessed the autopsy reports for April in the London Metropolitan Region and quickly found the one he was looking for, 'Rita Velasquez, death by suicide whilst the balance of her mind was disturbed, service to be held at 10.00am 29th April 1997. No flowers please. Send donations to Suicide Watch UK.'

He also made a note to try to find someone who had been at ICE at the same time as Rita Velasquez and who was perhaps her friend. Who had posted that tribute to her in that second issue of the Hive in April 1997? He needed to find out.

London's Metropolitan police have a highly sophisticated data base. For example, if you are looking for suicides in a particular suburb you simply supply the filters, suicide, and suburb name. Similarly, you can do the same by nationality. Gary was unsure if you could do the same by Institution, he was not surprised that he couldn't. He typed in suicides, females 18-30 years old, 1995 -2010. There were several hundreds of them, he then subdivided them, 18-22; 23-26; 27-30. There were 141 in the youngest category, 84 in the next category and 163 in the oldest category.

He initially concentrated on the 18-22 category. He knew that over 50% of ICE's female student body were foreign born. He then added the nationality filter. The largest number was in the British category, they amounted to 72. He then categorised the remaining by nationality and in descending order by number, the following table emerged.

Mexican	7	German	3
Colombian	6	Brazilian	3
Spanish	6	Argentinian	3
Guyanan	6	Georgian	2
Chilean	5	Latvian	2
Swedish	4	Finish	1
Italian	4	Irish	1
South African	3	Danish	1
Jamaican	3	Lithuanian	1
American	3	Dutch	1
Kenyan	3	Hungarian	1

He then put together a series of postcodes that gave him an area with a radius of five miles of ICE.

Then another one of suburbs between five-to-10-mile radius of ICE

The first gave him a result of 18 names of foreign-born nationals between the ages of 18-22 who had suicided between 1995-2010. The second added a further 8 names to that list.

By the time that he had examined these 26 suicides he discovered that over 40%, or 11 of them had been attending ICE between 1995 and 2010. He decided that he needed help. He called DS Fellingham and asked to see her.

He took her through his research and where he had got to. She was, once again mightily impressed. "The problem I have Sarge is that I haven't even started on the foreign nationals who might have lived outside those two circles, and I haven't even looked at the British born suicides in the same period. Do you think that it would be possible to enlist the help of Sergeant McIver and her team."

"I also think that we need to be in touch with whoever was the Editor of the Hive in April 1997 to discover who posted the tribute to Rita Velasquez." He showed her the tribute.

"Let's go and see the boss,' she said. DCI Warbrick was similarly impressed with DC Proud's work and picked up his phone. He called Sergeant McIver to his office. He also called Uniformed Inspector Johnson and once again requested the assistance of Sergeant McIvor's team. Fortunately, his relationship with the uniformed Inspector was excellent and Ken Johnson cheerfully gave his consent.

Sergeant McIver arrived, and DCI Warbrick asked his Detective Constable to explain what it was that he needed help with. This he did and Sergeant McIver had that determined look about her when he had finished. "I will be more than happy to help you with this Detective Constable, my sister's wee girl overdosed in her first year at Strathclyde University, over some low life member of the academic staff."

DCI Warbrick asked his Detective Sergeant to remain behind as DC Proud left with Sergeant McIver. "He's a bright lad our Detective Constable, isn't he?"

"He most certainly is Sir," Fellingham replied.

"I think that you should be talking to him about taking his sergeant's exam and while we are on that subject, when are you considering taking your Inspector's exam, Detective Sergeant?"

Susan asked, "Do you mind if I sit down and talk to you about that Sir?"

"Go right ahead Susan."

"Well Sir, what would happen if I took it and passed? I mean would it result in my being transferred away from here. If so, I don't want to take it. I like working with you Sir."

DCI Warbrick smiled at her, "If anyone at this station heard you say that they would think that you had taken leave of your senses. What would happen would be up to Detective Chief Superintendent Speers, he would seek my advice though, I expect. Susan you should be aware that I am now seriously thinking of retiring. Gina, amazingly, has agreed to marry me and we both would like to do some travelling together whilst we still have the energy. We are thinking around the end of this calendar year but not before we conclude this current case of Aileen Colquhoun."

"It would be my honest wish that you take and pass your Inspector's exam and take my place here in Wilmslow. You don't need to be a Chief Inspector to do that. Speers was fulsome in his praise of you and the way you handled the situation when I fell apart. I also think you and young Gary Proud work well together. So, give it some thought eh!"

"I will Sir, and I'll also talk to Alex about it. I'm not sure what he expects of me as his wife so it's probably high time that I find out."

"You're off to Edinburgh tomorrow, early start I understand, you're meeting with a friend of Aileen Colquhoun's I believe."

"Yes Sir, Mary Stirling, and I think that she may have a good deal to tell me. I am then travelling up to Inverness to meet Aileen's parents. The psychiatrist, Audrey Matthieson has completely altered my opinion of Aileen's father, and she has known him for many years."

"Yes well, a very good friend of mine, Detective Superintendent Murray Ross is based in Edinburgh, and he called me yesterday. He tells me that Mary Sinclair QC is loathed and feared by all of the villains in Edinburgh. So much so, that the police have installed a state-of-the-art security system on her home. They also maintain a highly vigilant, plain clothes monitoring of her house. A few days ago, someone attempted to break into her house, whilst she was in Aberdeen on a case."

"They failed of course, but the security system took some excellent photographs of the two men involved. They are being watched and followed as we speak. It seems that they are employed by an aircraft parts company with a highly dubious reputation in the aircraft maintenance and repair industry, Avnav Parts and Services Ltd. Be exceedingly careful Susan."

6

It would be fair to say that DS Fellingham sleep-walked her way aboard the 6.00am shuttle to Edinburgh. She had been studying hard at the training college, working late into the night on the criminology subjects she was endeavouring to master, and then the last few nights had all been a late finish as well. The passenger in the adjacent seat, another woman, obviously felt the same, her one remark during the whole flight came when they had first sat down, "Why do early mornings have to come at such an inconvenient time of the day?"

Susan caught a cab to the address in Morningside Mary Stirling had provided. She had the door open before Susan could ring the bell, "Come in, come in, it's a wee bit braw this morning," was her cheerful, welcome.

Mary Stirling was not a large lady, in any dimension, and by any stretch of the imagination, but her blue eyes were like lasers. When they focused on you, you had the distinct feeling that she was seeing far more in you, than you would have cared to reveal. Excellent eyes for a barrister or a Solicitor Advocate as they were known in Scotland, thought Susan.

She had hot croissants and an endless pot of coffee ready for both of them and Susan could have hugged her. "I have a good deal to tell you Detective Sergeant, or may I call you Susan? Please call me Mary."

"Please do," replied Susan.

"Well before I do, why don't you begin by telling me how you became involved in this case and where you have got to?" began Mary.

Susan took her through the meeting that she had had with Aileen's brother Rory and her fiancée Alex. The origins of the relationship between Rory and Alex. Rory's belief that his sister had been murdered and his request for help to re-open the investigation. She continued by describing the meeting with her boss DCI Warbrick, Rory, DC Proud and herself and the outcome of that meeting being the request to the coroner to re-open the investigation.

She told Mary of her discussions with Dr Audrey Matthieson, Mrs Gillian Davies and Aileen's father, Duncan. The mention of Gillian Davies brought a smile to Mary's lips.

"Gillian is a wonderful woman; I doubt that a wiser soul ever walked the planet. She rescued so many girls from oblivion, including this one, pointing to herself. I tried to persuade Aileen to talk to her when she was going through all of her pain, but she was too embarrassed, or perhaps too ashamed to do so. I told her that Gillian would never have judged her, but that she seemed to possess a font of wisdom that is beyond most of us, but Aileen could not bring herself to do it."

She continued, "Anyway Susan, thank you for bringing me up to date, before I begin would I be correct in assuming that your office uses an asymmetric encrypting system for the electronic transfer of documents?"

"Yes, we do," replied Susan.

"Then in that case, you need only make supplementary notes as I will be sending you a copy of all my files about Aileen Colquhoun by encrypted e-mail. You just need to give me your public key access."

Susan nodded.

Mary began, "As Gillian Davies probably told you Aileen and I were fierce competitors at school. We would rotate the top of the class position, seemingly, at the end of each year, but although we were competitors, I honestly believe that we were good friends as well."

"We went our separate ways after school, I to read law in Cambridge, and Aileen economics at ICE. I must confess to being a little surprised when I learned of Aileen's choice, I would have thought that her strengths lay in a similar direction to my own, or perhaps towards international journalism with her extraordinary language skills."

"She attended the first couple of re-unions at Inverness Royal Academy but after that we lost touch with one another. A total blank canvass for the next nine years. Then, out of the blue, she telephoned me. I was delighted when I heard that she was on the phone but as soon as I picked up the receiver, I could hear the distress in her voice."

"She asked if she could come to see me, and I readily agreed and told her that she would be most welcome to stay with me if it suited her. She asked if she could think about that."

"Anyway, she came, to say that I was shocked to see how she looked would be a massive understatement. She had always been much prettier than I, more confident than I, in so many ways, but the young woman I saw before me that day was a shadow of how she had once been."

"I could see that she was in a great deal of emotional pain, and I persuaded her to stay with me. The first few days of her stay I asked nothing about her current life. I simply concentrated on our girlhood rivalries and friendship, and I think that it helped her to relax. Her family were all good people, I had never heard any member of her family swear or blaspheme so I was stunned when she said on about the fourth day, "Mary, I have so fucked up my life.""

"The flood gates opened then. It transpired that in her first year at ICE, she met and was attracted to, an Argentinian tutor with the name of Ramiro Morales. He was not only a Tutor, but he also gave lessons in the Argentinian tango and other Latin American dances to many of her peer female students, who appeared to be extremely willing participants. She rejected his advances throughout her first year, but early in her second year she received a letter from him that deeply touched her, and she began dating him. It quickly became a sexual relationship, and she told me that he was clearly very experienced in such matters and was constantly asking her to adopt various positions in their love making which she found neither enjoyable nor particularly arousing."

"It was toward the end of her second year, and she was in his studio. They always used his studio for their lovemaking as she shared a flat with two other girls. He had told her that he used the studio for his dance classes. There were also, always, many cameras set up in his studio. He told her that the location of the cameras was so that he could record the dancing technique of the many students which helped him to correct their mistakes and improve their dance technique. He had always assured her that these cameras were switched off whenever they used the space for their amorous liaisons, so she was horrified when she suddenly found herself watching a video of herself and Ramiro, in what she described to me as a thoroughly disgusting porn movie with her as the female star."

"She asked him to destroy it, and he laughed at her, she tried to find where he had it hidden and he told her that he had over thirty other videos of her in similar style which were probably worth a considerable sum in the porn movie market. She told him that she would report him to the University Governors, and he grabbed her by the throat and told her that should she be that stupid, he would send copies of all thirty plus videos to her parents, her brother, and the teachers at her old school."

"She told me that she came extremely close to suicide at that point and also considered dropping out of university all together. Only his threat to send copies to her family and her old school, kept her at ICE."

"She returned to ICE for the beginning of her third year. She had not seen nor attended any of the tutorials that Morales held, since that awful night when she had seen the video. Then she heard from one of her flat mates that Morales may be leaving ICE as he was having a problem with his resident's visa over some issue that had arisen from his time at Columbia University in New York. This was where he had obtained his master's degree in economics."

"Whilst on holiday at the end of year two, an anxious two months spent in Inverness, she had read 'The Art of War' by Sun Tzu and learned of his expression 'keep your friends close but your enemies closer,' and had wondered how she might be able to use such a strategy to her own advantage. She now thought that she might have a way in which to neutralise his threat and his hold over her."

"She wrote to him, it took all her self-discipline to prevent her from breaking into expletives in every second sentence, she kept it as simple as possible, it read; 'I hear that you have a problem with your residency. There may be a solution. If you wish to discuss, meet me at the Cellarium Café and Terrace at Westminster Abbey at 3.00 pm Friday 23rd October 2001. Aileen Colquhoun."

"She prepared her notes, and she reserved a table with the greatest separation between the seats. He arrived, he attempted to sit next to her, but she ordered 'Sit there, or I leave' indicating the seat furthest away from her. He complied. I have a solution for you, it is not for negotiation or amendment. Take it or leave it, is how it must be received. He clearly did not like being dictated to and tried to argue. "I'm leaving,' was all that she said, and he sat down again."

"The solution is, that you marry me, you become a UK resident through marriage. I take and use your name as my married name for as long as it suits me or until the whole of your, and your successors, video library is destroyed. The same condition applies if you seek to obtain a divorce from me. Prior to the marriage you will agree that any video material containing any images of me will not be distributed to my family, friends, educational institutions, employers now and into the future, nor any professional bodies to which I belong. You also acknowledge that this is a marriage in name only, that no co-habiting is anticipated, nor permitted. That the marriage comes with no conjugal rights between the marriage partners. After the wedding ceremony we will go our separate ways, who you go with, is entirely up to you. It neither concerns nor interests me. You also accept that this will be agreed by way of a pre-nuptial agreement, prepared by a person or organisation legally qualified to prepare such a document, and signed by both of us prior to the marriage."

"The marriage to take place on the weekend following my graduation from ICE. Following the wedding you acknowledge that I will be leaving London and that I no longer wish to be contacted by you on any matter extraneous to these conditions which we will have agreed."

"Should you not respond to this offer by mid-day on Friday 30th October 2001 then this offer is withdrawn, and no further discussions or correspondence will be entered into."

"She handed him a copy of the document which had been prepared by a lawyer frequently used in pre-nuptial agreements and said, take it or leave it. A simple Yes or No in an envelope addressed to me will suffice."

Mary broke away from her narrative on Aileen's life and said, "Had she come to me with this document I would have strongly advised her against it. Instead, I would have prepared a document for the Home Secretary, alleging blackmail and demanding money with menaces, and advocating that Morales be deported as an undesirable alien and refused permission to ever reside in Britain again. Had she, and we, done that, she may have still been alive today."

"Returning to Aileen's story, Morales accepted her offer. At the wedding he attempted to humiliate and embarrass her by insulting her mother and her brother, and having in attendance, all the other students at ICE that he was having sex with. He succeeded in creating more stress on her increasingly fragile relationship with her family."

Aileen left London and hid herself away in Manchester. She began her post graduate life as a bookkeeper handling that aspect of a real estate agent's business in Alderley Edge. She became friendly with the principal of the business, a middle-aged lady with no family of her own. She discovered that she had a 'nose' for good property deals and began to make money from her buying and selling transactions. It culminated in her befriending an elderly, childless widow with a property in Prestbury, outside Macclesfield. This elderly lady had sensed the pain and sadness within Aileen and gently, she coaxed Aileen into telling her, her story."

"The widow did two things for her, she left her house and its contents to Aileen, and she introduced Aileen to an old friend of her deceased husband's, Ken Stockdale who had a small aircraft repair factory based in Macclesfield. Ken was a good mechanic but had absolutely no idea on how to run a business. The reason for the widow's introduction of Aileen was that she believed that Aileen could introduce some organisation and good business practices into Ken's business."

"In this, she was absolutely right. The business had the potential to be highly profitable. Ken had an excellent reputation, was as honest as the day is long and was happily welcoming of Aileen's suggestions on improving the business. It wasn't long before Aileen was working full time in the business and Ken had employed an additional mechanic, who he had known for some years, and an apprentice."

"She gained an interest in flying and began taking flying lessons. She told me, years later, that her instructor had become attracted to her, but that she doubted that she would ever become romantically inclined with a man, ever again."

"Her relationship with Ken had blossomed, he was almost like a second father to her. On a couple of occasions, he had said to her, 'I sometimes see a look on your face that tells me that someone has hurt you, very badly, in the past. If you ever want to talk about it, you know you can with me,' but it was a long time before she did."

"The business continued to grow as did her proficiency in flying. Ken was becoming anxious, he was concerned about his age, he was now well over sixty. We need some younger blood in this outfit if we are to continue to grow, he would say, or how would you feel about an additional younger Partner. Aileen was now the Managing Director of the business and Ken the Operations Director."

"One day he came to her, there's a fellow I know, not well, but he seems to have a good reputation, based down in Stanstead. His business is about the same size as ours except that he has a larger proportion of the big passenger aircraft on his books than we have. How would you feel about having a chat with him?"

"Can't do any harm,' she remembered replying.

"The guy's name was Trevor Byford. They met and the personalities seemed compatible. Aileen went through Trevor's accounts, clearly her and Ken's company was worth a good deal more than Trevor's, but she thought, might be a nice way to give Ken a golden handshake."

"When she mentioned this fact to Trevor, he didn't disagree with the numbers but explained that it meant that he would have to raise some capital to complete the merger. He talked about borrowing from the bank, but the bank's condition was that they would want to place one of their people on the Board of the new company, which didn't sit well with either Aileen or Ken. Trevor then raised the question of a 'silent' partner. Aileen was worried about how silent a silent partner would be, given the size of the potential turnover of the enlarged business."

"Let me show both sets of accounts to this guy that I know who might be interested, Trevor had asked, and they had all agreed to that approach. A little while later Trevor came back, in a very excited state. My guy is very interested about the prospect but believes that we also need an increase in working capital if we are to replace some of our smaller and aging equipment to cope with the expansion. He proposes that he injects two million pounds after which he expects that the value of the new company to be 3.5 million pounds. Ken is to receive 450,000 pounds for the sale of his shares and the future shareholding in the new company would be, R M Espanto, my guy 55%, Aileen Colquhoun, 25%, Trevor Byford 20%"

"Where does Mr Espanto live?" Aileen had asked.

"Mostly in Mallorca I believe," Trevor Byford had replied.

Aileen had been unsure, but she could see the look of relief in Ken's eyes, he would be able to enjoy his retirement. She had agreed to the deal as did Ken and Trevor, Mr Espanto was as good as his word and the two million pounds arrived.

The Company, now named as Avnav parts and Services Ltd, was already incorporated and the shareholding confirmed. Mr Espanto did not attend this first meeting. Instead, Trevor Byford read out a statement from him. 'It was necessary for me to use a proxy in the acquisition of this company, that of RM Espanto. The actual shareholding will be held in my real name that of Ramiro Morales.'

Aileen had screamed, heartbreakingly sobbed "No, oh please God no."

She had turned to Trevor Byford and hissed, "You bastard, who the hell are you, and collapsed across her desk."

Ken Stockdale had looked horrified, but Trevor Byford had simply smiled.

Mary looked sadly at Susan, as they broke, for a mid-morning coffee.

7

DCI Warbrick had had more than a little explaining to do when he had arrived home after his meeting with Rory Colquhoun. He had realised, too late, that he should have obtained Gina's consent before offering her services on the second autopsy. He rather sheepishly confessed his omission, when she had asked, "Why the long face," as he came through the front door.

She had looked at him sternly, put her hands on her hips, and said, "You obviously think that I am not making a large enough contribution toward the cost of my upkeep if you are offering my services to all and sundry?"

"It's not that," he blurted, "I just thought……," and he looked up to see her laughing eyes and the huge grin as she enjoyed his discomfort.

She gave him a hug, "You are a silly Detective Chief Inspector sometimes, of course I don't mind doing the autopsy, it will be good to keep my eyes sharp and my brain functioning. When do you want to have it done?"

"We need to receive the coroner's consent first, I'm pretty sure that he will want to have the pathologist who carried out the first autopsy, present, as well. Her name is Kathleen Tebble, young I believe."

"Oh, I know Kathleen; she has been present at some of my lectures and I think that she attended one or two of the autopsies which I conducted. I'm sure that she won't be a problem."

The coroner's consent to re-open the enquiry came two days later. Warbrick wasn't best pleased when he received the request asking, "Did the police investigate this incident at all, they knew who she was, she had all of her identifying documents with her, surely it could not have been that difficult to find out that she had a history of chronic aquaphobia?"

All good questions thought Warbrick, he thought about his counterpart at the Macclesfield police station which would have been the station contacted when her body was discovered. Charlie Warburton, he knew was the DCI there. Poor old Charlie, only two months away from retirement and in the middle of a domestic murder case involving the death of the mother and her three children. They had been trying to find the father ever since but with no success. No doubt the Super and Chief Constable had been on Charlie's back with the 'domestic.' Yes, he felt sorry for old Charlie.

The second autopsy was carried out in the mortuary at Leighton Hospital, a little over twenty miles southwest of Wilmslow. Kathleen Tebble was there, ahead of Gina Moretti. She looked extremely sheepish as she greeted Dr Gina Moretti, "I did try to have the police carry out further enquiries," she said by way of both an introduction and an apology, but

DCI Warburton just told me in no uncertain terms, "To get on with it."

Gina was all smiles, "No need to apologise at all Kathleen, I know what it can be like when you have a grumpy DCI breathing down your neck. I'm about to marry one you know, put it down to a pathologists attempt to humanise the police force," and Kathleen laughed.

Before the body was removed from its cadaver rack, Gina spent some time reading the various pathology reports, taking an extensive interest in the toxicology report. They removed Aileen's body from the body storage racks and laid out on the mortuary, operating table. "I see that you had the water you took from her lungs analysed against the sample from the reservoir and found a match?" Kathleen nodded, "Well done," said Gina.

She brought the satellite lamp next to the main theatre light down to within close proximity, firstly one upper arm, and then the other. "Ah, see here, see the puncture mark in her upper left arm, that's where they injected the barbiturate, Nembutal, if I'm not very much mistaken."

Kathleen looked closely at Aileen's upper arm, she blushed, "I completely missed it doctor," she confessed.

"Very easy to do my dear, particularly with that grumpy DCI applying the pressure, was he here in the mortuary with you?" Kathleen nodded again. Gina Moretti snorted, "I think that all policemen should be banned from autopsy rooms until at least they are able to demonstrate a rudimentary knowledge of forensic pathology and the unhindered concentration that it requires."

Together, they rolled Aileen's body over onto her stomach. Gina lifted her long hair back over her head and held it in place with a series of clips. There was a prominent bruise in the centre of the back of her neck and several others, either side and extending around the side of her neck. These bruises were far fainter, so much so that they were extremely difficult to see clearly. Gina brought more light onto the region of Aileen's neck and took a magnifying glass from her kit.

She nodded, "See here, the bastard had a large cushion or at least some padding around her neck as he, or she, most likely, pushed her head beneath the water and held her there. The clear bruise in the centre of the back of her neck is where he had placed both of his thumbs," Gina place both of her hands around Aileen's neck to illustrate the position that she was describing. "My God, that poor girl must have just about gone out of her mind prior to her death, with the chronic phobia that she suffered from."

"There is not a shadow of a doubt in my mind now, that Aileen Colquhoun was murdered, do you agree?" asked Gina.

"Yes, I most certainly do, and I am so sorry again that I got this so hopelessly wrong, I feel that I should resign immediately," came the anguished response from Kathleen Tebble.

"Don't be so ridiculous," snapped Gina, "if I had resigned every time, I made a mistake during an autopsy I wouldn't have lasted a year in the job. You were a very bright student Kathleen, and now you are a very bright forensic pathologist. If you are going to take anything from this experience, take this, never, ever, undertake an autopsy under duress or any external pressure. Quietly and politely, ask any unwelcome observers to leave, otherwise you will not commence the autopsy and STICK TO YOUR GUNS. It would take an extremely brave, and in my opinion, extremely stupid, policeman to ignore such a request from a qualified forensic pathologist. I will type this advice as a statement which I will call, 'The First Rule of Dr Gina Moretti, and I will send it to you. If you wish you can have it affixed on as many walls as you like in the mortuary. OK."

"Thank you doctor," responded Kathleen Tebble softly.

8

DC Proud was surrounded by statistics, every working surface was covered in papers reflecting changes in the student population at ICE from 1995 to 2000; from 2001 to 2009; and from 2010 to 2018. Similarly grouped were the changes in the male to female profile during the same time frames.

Additionally, there were countless sheets and reports of suicides by females, between the ages of 18-30, in the Greater London area, between 1995-2010. These were further subdivided into three categories of suicides by females; Ages 18-22; Ages 23-26; and Ages 27-30.

He now knew that at the time that Ramiro Morales commenced at ICE in 1995 there was a total of 8518 students enrolled at ICE, of which 4344 were male and 4174 were female. A 51% to 49% split in favour of the men, At the time Aileen Colquhoun commenced her studies at ICE in October 1999 there were 9029 students enrolled at ICE of which 4424 were male and 4605 were female. A 49% male to 51% female split, reversing the percentages from male to female ratios to those to be found in 1995.

By 2010 the total number had risen to 10,112 but the ratio had increased in favour of the female numbers with just 4753, or 47% of male students and 5359 or 53% of female students. The ratio between UK resident students and overseas born students had remained approximately the same with just about 70% of all students having been born outside the UK.

Eileen MacIver and her team had also been extremely busy. They had taken the information that Gary Proud had provided and examined the data that related to the UK born students aged from 18-22 who had suicided between 1995 and 2010 and then reproduced Gary's chart, which became known as Table A. They had then broken this summary chart into six supplementary charts covering the periods; 1995-1996; 1997-1999; 2000-2002; 2003-2005; 2006-2008; 2009-2010. These had been identified as Charts B-G.

Gary had then summarised these findings into the narrative of his report and attached the various tables as Appendices.

He had similar charts for suicides of females between the ages of 23-26, and for those between the ages of 27-30, but his primary focus to date, had been on the youngest cohort of female suicides.

This was largely due to the fact that the majority of the students seen by Ramiro Morales were in this youngest group. There were some female post graduate students that he also had access to, but these were far fewer in number, and he reasoned, more likely to also be in an intimate relationship with one other person and therefore less likely to be seduced by Morales. He would not ignore this smaller number, but he believed, he was much more likely to be able to demonstrate a conclusive pattern to Morales behaviour by concentrating on this youngest group.

In 1995, the of Morale's appointment to ICE, the population of Greater London was a little over 7 million made up of 3.6 million females and 3.4 million males.

By 2001, this number had risen to a population of 7.35 million made up of 3.75 females and 3.6 million males

By mid-year 2009 the total population was just under 8 million, at 7.95 million. With 4.1 million females and 3.85 million males.

Eileen MacIver and her team had then spent a considerable amount of time analysing the suicide data for the whole of the 1995-2010 period, or all 141 suicides. Each time there was an indication that the victim had been a student at ICE, they would pass that particular case to DC Proud, and Proud would dig.

He also sought DS Fellingham's permission to enlist the assistance of a demographer based at Manchester University. His request was approved, provided that the demographer had the approval of both the University and the Police and agreed to sign a Confidentiality Agreement. DC Proud was also instructed to remove any references to ICE and to Ramiro Morales so that only raw numbers were presented to the demographer. The request for assistance was simply covered by the innocuous heading, 'Comparative Suicide Statistics between OECD Countries.'

The total number of ICE connected suicides that had been forwarded to him by Sergeant MacIver's team, had grown to 32 out of the total of 141 suicides of females between 1995 and 2010. Although the MacIver team had identified an ICE link it did not necessarily involve Ramiro Morales, and Proud had to examine, in detail, all the information available surrounding the suicide from police and/or newspaper cuttings. He then needed to cross reference each case with articles in the 'Hive' magazine, checking for items of relevance.

He also tabulated the names, nationalities, and years of attendance at ICE for all of the 32 suicides he had now received from Sergeant McIver. The final column on this table was blank, apart from the heading which was 'Friends.' He wasn't absolutely sure that there would be a benefit in tracking down any possible friends of the poor unfortunates who had taken their own lives, but it was certainly worth a try.

He decided to work backwards from 2010, for no other reason than the thought that Morales had been at ICE for almost seventeen years by then and may have grown sloppy in his behaviour. There was no mention of him in 2010 or 2009 but in October 2008, at the beginning of the Michaelmas term there was a notice under the heading 'Cancellation' in the first October edition of the 'Hive'. "Due to the sudden departure of our Economics Tutor, Mr Ramiro Morales, for personal reasons, his Latin American dance classes have been cancelled. No indication has been given as to when, or if, they will resume. Mr Morales has been replaced in his position as Economics Tutor by Mr Bartholomew Quinn, effective immediately."

Sounds like he was given the push, thought DC Proud, I wonder why. He could find nothing further in the 'Hive' but, he had learned, that the editor of the magazine from 1998-2010, had progressed to joining the Financial Times. He contacted the Times, Mr Winston Macauley continued to be employed by them. He sent a text message to DS Fellingham asking her to contact him.

While he was waiting for a response from Manchester University regarding the demographer he did some crude calculations of his own. He knew that ICE had approximately 4000 female students throughout the period 2004-2010. The actual numbers were less than 4000 in 1995, but more than 4000 in 2010 and he felt that using an average of 4000 would be close enough for his purposes. He also knew that 50% of this total number would be undergraduates and the other 50% would be postgraduate. The undergraduate degree at ICE was a course of three years and clearly the great majority of 18–22-year-olds would be undertaking an undergraduate degree.

He calculated that every year of the 17 years from 2004 to 2010 would see a fresh intake of a third of the undergraduate students plus the original 2000 giving a total of 13,333. He rounded that up to 14,000 as a contingency. 32 deaths amongst 14,000 students over 17 years amounted to one death in every 438 students, or 1.9 deaths every year. This can be extrapolated to reflect a suicide rate of 0.095% of the 18-22 female undergraduate body every year.

He then calculated the suicide rate across the female population of Greater London, which he knew to be regularly in the vicinity of 4 million. He realised that he only had a proportion of the total female population reflected in his suicide data, namely 18–30-year-olds and over a 16-year period, 1995-2010. Would it be stretching an assumption too far by assuming that the 18–30-year-olds would only represent about 25% of the total female population? He knew that the demographer would put him straight on that point, but he needed to develop some kind of line in the sand.

He assumed that the 18–30-year-old cohort of females amounted to 25% of the total, that is 1 million. If he divided the total number of suicides, 388, amongst females aged 18-30 by the number of years, 17, over which those suicides occurred, he arrived at an annual suicide of 15. 15 suicides amongst 1 million females extrapolated to 0.015 of that female population. Six times less than the rate amongst ICE female undergraduates.

He was either dramatically wrong in his assumptions, highly likely he thought, or there was something extremely untoward, for females, in undertaking an undergraduate degree at ICE, between 1994 and 2010.

9

Susan Fellingham interrupted Mary Stirling's narrative by asking, "When did this occur, this re-emergence of Ramiro Morales?"

"In May 2009," replied Mary.

Susan nodded, "Sorry to interrupt you, please continue."

Mary resumed, "Ken Stockdale was extremely concerned about Aileen's state of mind and attempted to take her into Macclesfield Hospital, but she refused. She told him that it had been the shock of hearing the Ramiro Morales name mentioned that had caused her collapse. She then told Ken the full history of her relationship with this Argentinian."

"Ken was distraught, believing that he had been responsible for causing this considerable grief to the woman he had long looked upon as the daughter he had never had. His first reaction was to insist that they cancelled the deal, but as Aileen pointed out, it was far too late for that. He asked her what she would do, and she replied by saying that she needed time to think. It was then that she contacted me."

"I explained the legal position to her, which was not good, she was now a minority shareholder with little or no control over the business. I then asked her why she had married this man; she replied by telling me that he had once told her that his mother in Argentina was deeply religious and active in church affairs in Buenos Aires. She believed that by taking his name through marriage, she could bring similar shame to his mother if he were ever to release the videos to her family. That was when she told me that she 'wanted to keep her enemies closer'. That gave me some food for thought."

"I made some discreet enquiries, and I recruited the assistance of a private detective in London, recommended to me by a legal colleague. I did not mention this to Aileen, initially. I learned, quite quickly in fact, that Morales had been forced to resign his position at ICE, the previous year, 2008. This had been due to a number of his students at ICE, complaining, en masse, of his attempts to either, permit him to photograph them either naked or semi-naked. In some instances, they had produced evidence that he had done so, without consent. Two of the students also separately reported that he had filmed them whilst they had been having sex with him and believed that he was engaged in making pornographic films, using unwitting female students."

"The authorities at ICE were, naturally, highly concerned that such behaviour on the part of one of their Tutors, could do serious harm to the University's reputation. They sought discreet advice from a senior member of London's Metropolitan police. I learned of this from my legal colleague in London, who also asked me to keep him informed of any information that came to my attention, regarding Ramiro Morales. He also advised me that he was aware that the Metropolitan Police had commenced discreet enquiries regarding the international behaviour of Morales, through a number of police agencies, overseas."

"I subsequently received an invitation to meet with a Detective Chief Superintendent Goddard when I was next in London, which I did the week following Aileen's arrival at my house. He told me that he had taken over the case in 2007, when he had been contacted by a Board Member at ICE and became subsequently aware that Morales had made a considerable fortune from the pornographic market throughout South America. He told me that the Met. had nothing, yet that would bring about a conviction of Morales in the UK, but he warned me, this Morales is thoroughly unscrupulous and evil. You can bet your house on this fact, whatever Morales gets into again, will be highly profitable, irrespective of its morality or legality."

'Aileen spent several weeks with me. During this time, I received several anxious calls from Ken Stockdale enquiring about Aileen's health. Each time I did she always told me that she was not yet ready to speak to him. I had the sad duty to tell her that whatever value she thought that she had with her shares in Avnav Parts and Services, in reality, they were probably worthless. Morales would see to that. She asked me if I thought that she should resign her role as a Director of Avnav and I replied that I did, but not before we had worked out a comprehensive strategy."

"We spent a whole weekend, with me asking and her answering, all of my questions about her knowledge of the aircraft maintenance and repair business. It transpired that she had both considerable knowledge and contacts in the industry. I made a few discreet enquiries, it was also evident that she was highly respected in the industry, both for her integrity and her great customer relations. All of what I learned gave me the beginnings of a plan."

"I suggested to her that she did not attempt to sell her shares in Avnav, it would only provide Morales with a further opportunity to humiliate her. I also suggested that she avoided seeing Morales, for similar reasons, if that was at all possible. Instead, I suggested that she deal with Trevor Byford."

"I thought that she should present Trevor Byford with two options. One, that she resigns her position as Director and employee of Avnav Parts and Services. In which case she would advise all of her contacts and friends in the business that she had been the victim of a hostile and disreputable takeover and believed that it would be impossible for her to work with 'such' people."

"Or, two, that she resigns her position as a director but continue as a contracted consultant, for a guaranteed minimum period of five years, at a salary of UK pounds 100,00 per annum, plus the reimbursement of all travel and associated expenses. In which case she would continue to use her extensive client base to help grow the business. I added that she should then emphasise that it mattered little to her which choice they opted for, it was for the Board of Avnav Parts and Services to decide."

"Aileen was initially horrified at my option two, telling me, in no uncertain terms, that she wanted nothing further to do with the evil bastard who had caused so much pain and shame."

"I reminded her of her own, 'keeping her enemies closer,' philosophy. I told her that I thought it fairly certain that Morales would take the business down the most profitable path he could imagine, without regard for morals or finer legal points. I emphasised that she could use her time as a Consultant, to collect proof and information regarding his activities. I added that she may be able to persuade Ken Stockdale to also help her, confidentially, of course."

"It was then that she decided to speak to Ken Stockdale and I suggested that she invite him to Edinburgh where the three of us could discuss the plan that had begun to germinate in my mind. I also informed her that I was on quite friendly terms with a lady who owned a bed and breakfast establishment in the adjacent street, and that I felt confident that she would be able to offer Ken some accommodation."

"She rang Ken, he was relieved and delighted to hear from her and readily agreed to come to Edinburgh to meet with both Aileen and me."

"I was surprised to discover, following Ken's arrival, that he had snow white hair and looked distinctly much older than the 63 years of age Aileen had said that he was. He repeated, several times, that he believed that he had been responsible for causing Aileen her most recent episode of grief and Aileen had done her best to console him."

"I could see that in his current state of mind he would be unable to focus on the formation of the plan that had been germinating in my mind over the past week. I decided to use some of my father's home spun philosophy on Ken in the hope that it would help ease his mind even if he didn't quite grasp the relevance of this philosophy."

"I said to him, my father was an extremely keen boxing fan, and he was forever quoting small boxing quips whenever he felt that I needed encouragement. I've always believed that he would have been far happier had I been born a boy instead of the girl that I am, but no matter. One of the things he would say to me was, Mary lassie, life is a fifteen-round contest, and you're only in round two or three. I calculated very early on in my life, that one of his boxing rounds was the equivalent of about five and a half to six years of human life. He would then add, so you may be behind on points the noo, but there is a long way to go in this contest. The other thing that he would say that was intended to comfort me but always made me cry was, remember lassie, I'll be in your corner with the bucket and sponge."

"Ken chortled happily at this last remark, your dad sounds like quite a man, maybe not with the most highly developed sensitive or feminine side, but quite a man. I would like to meet him one day."

"It seemed to do the trick, and he listened avidly to the outline of my plan, nodding, with increasing vigour, as I raised each point."

"You're absolutely spot on about all of those things, he said, it has become an increasing problem in the industry with the growth of aircraft ownership. Many of my colleagues are extremely worried about it and would be most willing to share their concerns with me, citing specific instances, confidentially, of course."

"Then over the next two days the three of us will develop a comprehensive plan, designed to bring retribution to Mr Ramiro Morales. To quote my father, we are only at the end of round five, maybe behind on points, but to paraphrase that famous Scot, John Paul Jones, we have not yet begun to fight."

Mary continued, "The next couple of days were highly productive and when Ken left us, he was in a much brighter frame of mind than he had been when he had arrived. His final remark to Aileen was that together they would find a way of making Morales pay for what he had done."

Susan gratefully thanked Mary as she packed her brief case for her taxi journey to Edinburgh airport, only to find that she had an hour to wait for her flight to Inverness. She had read, when she had been a schoolgirl, about the scenic splendour of the train journey from Edinburgh to Inverness, but she had no time to enjoy that now. Anyway, she thought, I'd much prefer to make that trip, the first time, with Alex.

She had booked herself into the Royal Highland Hotel on Station Square in Inverness and it was pleasant enough, with large sized traditional rooms but modernised to include en-suite bathrooms. The bistro was up-scale though and she enjoyed her meal there despite having to rebuff the interest of several large and hirsute highland men.

She had arranged to meet with Duncan and Isla Colquhoun at 11.30 that morning and with Mrs Gillian Davies, Aileen's former Guidance Teacher at the end of the school day, at 4.30, at her home in Torbreck Rd, which was a short distance from the Royal Academy. She decided to utilise the free time in the morning to prepare herself for, what she expected to be, a difficult and emotional meeting with Aileen's parents.

She took a taxi, ensuring that she arrived at the Colquhoun home at precisely 11.30am. The door was opened by a tall, ramrod straight, elderly man, with iron grey hair and piercing blue eyes which reminded her of Mary Stirling's eyes. She introduced herself. "Thank you for being so punctual Detective Sergeant, I have always appreciated punctuality, won't you please come in?" He was trying to emphasise his politeness, but his manner conveyed more of an instruction, than a request.

She had to take a firm grip of herself as she was introduced to Isla Colquhoun. This diminutive and frail, elderly lady appeared to be many years older than her husband, but Susan knew that she was in fact, three years younger. She struggled to stand despite Susan imploring her to remain seated. She grasped Susan's hand, her own hand was ice cold and seemingly devoid of any flesh, so prominent were the bones. She looked into DS Fellingham's eyes and spoke with the soft and lilting accent of the highlands, "Thank you so much for coming all this way to speak with us Detective Sergeant, Duncan and I greatly appreciate it, may I first offer you a cup of tea," she paused, "or would you prefer coffee, we only have the instant kind, mind."

"Tea would be perfect," replied Susan.

Duncan indicated that he would make the tea, but she scolded him, "Awa wi ye man, I'm no such an auld bliddy that I cannae make this sweet lass a brew," and she shuffled past him into the kitchen.

"Please take a seat Detective Sergeant," continued the struggling Duncan, clearly unused to hosting strangers into his home.

Susan attempted to relax the situation, "I've met your son Rory, Mr Colquhoun, a fine figure of a man I must say. My fiancée attended Edinburgh University with Rory; I believe that they played in the same rugby team."

"Is that so?" enquired Mr Colquhoun, his bright blue eyes now alive with interest, "Which position did your fiancée occupy?"

"Fly half, I believe," replied Susan.

"Och yes, the orchestra," responded Colquhoun, "I may have seen your husband-to-be play on two or three occasions. Tell me lassie, was there a mon playing scrum half who had an Irish name?"

Susan smiled, the smile her father had often told her, that could charm the birds from their trees, he was warming to her, "Yes, his name is Declan O'Shea and he and Alex, my fiancée, are good friends."

"Alex, you say your fiancée's name is Alex, is he a Scot, is he from these parts?"

Fellingham laughed, "I'm sorry to disappoint you Mr Colquhoun, he is an Irishman, with the bizarre surname of McQualter, bizarre that is for an Irishman," she added hastily.

Colquhoun slapped his knee heavily with the palm of his hand, "I saw them both play, I told Rory, many times that without those two his team would have been 'grannied' (pointless) more often than not. They were so good to watch."

Isla had returned with the tea, or rather the tray with the teacups and saucers, "Ah cannae manage yon pot Duncan," and Duncan quickly responded by bringing the teapot and the large ceramic pot of shortbread.

Duncan had now greatly warmed to Susan, she must remember to thank her rugby star of a fiancée, he began, "Detective Sergeant,"

Fellingham interrupted him, "If you prefer it would be fine by me if you called me Susan?"

Isla beamed, appreciating this suggestion.

"Susan," Duncan Colquhoun began again, "how can we help you with your enquiries into the death of our daughter?"

"By telling me as much as you can about her, Rory has told us a good deal, but his perspective is that of a younger brother. I would love you both to tell us how you each felt about her, her strengths, her weaknesses, her dreams, her fears, her friends, I have already met with Mary Stirling, but really, anything at all."

"I understand that you, Mr Colquhoun, met the man known as Ramiro Morales and did not like him. I would like you to tell me why?" Susan paused before continuing, "I can't begin to fully understand how much you have suffered since you received the dreadful news of Aileen's passing. Please take your time when responding to my questions, if it becomes too painful to answer, please just wave at me to stop. The last thing I want to do is add to your anguish."

To Fellingham's surprise it was Isla who began, "She was our firstborn, and she was beautiful. We quickly learned that she was also very bright, and we could not have been prouder. I always worried that she could sometimes be quite short in her responses to people that she did not like or did not respect, but Duncan believed that she needed whatever the good Lord had provided in order to defend herself in 'this man's world,' those were his words, Susan. She excelled at school. Following Rory's birth, I became quite ill, Aileen took it upon herself to help me in any way that she was able. Don't forget that she was only a wee lassie when all this started."

"As she developed into a teenager, she and Mary Stirling became fierce academic rivals, but to both girl's everlasting credit, this rivalry strengthened their friendship rather than detracted from it. I do believe though that Gillian Davies at the Academy had a significant part in ensuring that this was the case. Duncan and I were both surprised that she chose ICE for her undergraduate studies. She had an amazing ear for languages. She became fluent in French,

Italian, and Spanish, before she was seventeen years old, and in her final year at the Academy, she was learning German. She had applied for undergraduate courses at the University of Parma in Italy (Modern Foreign Languages and their Civilisations); The Universidad Europea del Atlántico Santander in Spain, (Translation and Interpretation); Ecole de Traduction et Interpretation, Uccle in Belgium (Translation and Interpretation); and our University of Stirling (Modern languages)"

"When we asked her 'why ICE' she had replied far more vaguely than she usually did, saying that the Universities in Italy, Belgium, and Spain, were too distant, whilst Stirling was too close. She also said she thought economics might provide a bigger challenge as she had always found languages quite easy. Neither of us were satisfied with that answer. We have since learned that the real answer lay in the boy she had met during her final year at the Academy. He had told her that he was hoping to study engineering at the University of London. As in so many of these things, it did not come to pass. She learned after being accepted at ICE that the boy's father had been offered a position in the United States and the whole family were to move there."

Isla Colquhoun paused, deep in thought, contemplating whether or not to continue. "When Susan softly asked, "Is there anything else that you wish to add, Mrs Colquhoun?" she looked first at Susan, then at her husband.

"Aye lassie, there is, but I've no doubt that you'll not believe me." She looked again at Susan who smiled her encouragement to continue. "When ah was so poorly after delivering yon Rory, I came close to dying. I was told this later by the doctors. but I knew afore they told me. Ah was in ma hospital bed when I saw a fight between God and the Devil. They were both trying to claim my soul for I had done enough wrong in my young life for the Devil to believe that he could claim me. The fight seemed to last for a long time and there appeared to be no obvious winner, until I heard the Devil whispering in my ear that I had cheated him. The doctors and my dear husband have told me that I was hallucinating but I don't think so. I think that the Devil came back to take our Aileen from us, as my punishment."

She looked up at Susan, her deeply set eyes reflecting her soul in torment and she whispered, "If I could just go back, I would beg him to take my soul and leave my Aileen be."

Her husband crossed the floor to be by her side, but there was nothing he could do to assuage her guilt and her grief.

He then spoke, "I have tried to tell Isla that she was hallucinating, but one thing I am sure of, that I can tell you, is that the first time that I met Morales in London, he tried his best to charm me, but I saw through him as though he were made of glass. I seized him by the throat, and we argued, Aileen begged me to release him, which I did, and we continued to argue. The argument followed us out onto the stairwell, just the two of us, and his persona changed. He was now extremely angry and when he looked at me again, it wasn't a human face that I saw but the grotesque features of evil, personified. I tried to take Aileen from him at that point, but I failed, and I wasn't hallucinating Susan. I am so sorry now, that I released the grip on his throat. I wish I had choked the life out of whatever he is. I would gladly serve a life sentence of imprisonment if it would bring our child back to us. Please find him Detective Sergeant Fellingham, and if at all possible, bring him to me. The punishment must be made to fit the crime, of that, I am certain."

DS Fellingham left the home of Aileen's parents feeling sick to her core. She had looked into the faces and heard the voices of two honourable, child loving, law abiding, God fearing, people, and she had been able to say or do, nothing, to relieve their torment. She remembered the voice of one of her police training instructors, telling her that she should never allow a case to become personal, that it would destroy her if she did. But how could she not, it had become personal, and she defied anyone with any decency not to become personally involved if they had witnessed the amount of suffering she had seen within the family of just one of Morales' victims.

She bought a ham and cheese roll from a local take-away and moved into the Botanical Gardens to eat it. She reviewed her conversation with the Colquhoun parents. Susan didn't believe in the devil appearing in human form, she was not sure that she believed in God and the Devil at all, but there was no doubting that the Colquhoun's did, both of them. Aileen's mother's explanation was understandable if not entirely plausible, but her father, with his down to earth, no nonsense, highlanders approach to life, was somewhat harder to dismiss as imaginary, and it troubled her, deeply.

Susan took another taxi to Torbreck Rd arriving there, punctually again, a minute or two before 4.30. Gillian Davies looked exactly how Fellingham had pictured her following their telephone call. She had an open, smiling, face, a round highly intelligent face and perceptive eyes which immediately confirmed their talent when the first words out of Gillian Davies' mouth were, "Oh my dear young lady, you look absolutely drained, please come in, come in and tell me all about it."

DS Fellingham did as she was bid, by entering the home, and then continuing her response to the instruction, found herself asking, "I'm sorry Mrs Davies do you believe that God and the Devil are physically present on this earth?"

Gillian Davies sat her down, "Well my dear before I attempt to answer that, why don't you tell me about the context in which this question has arisen?"

Susan recounted her visit to Aileen's parents, automatically trusting in Gillian Davies' integrity. She gave Mrs Davies the details of the conversations that she had held with both Mrs and Mr Colquhoun. Gillian Davies knew them both of course. She had made yet another pot of tea whilst she considered her response to Susan's description of the earlier events.

"In my years as both a teacher of children and as an adviser to their parents I have learned that a deeply troubled mind sees things that cannot be seen by those with either a lesser troubled, or totally untroubled mind. That is not to say that those things seen by a troubled mind, do not actually exist. The best comparison I can give you is that between the hearing abilities of humans with those of animals. As I am sure you are aware, animals can clearly hear sounds at a much higher frequency which are beyond the capability of humans. Another example I would give you is that I have often witnessed students who have lost one of their senses, sight for example, to find that some, if not all, of their other senses, sound, smell, touch, have mysteriously been enhanced. I believe that it is entirely possible for the same phenomena to occur when someone is deeply troubled."

"The difficulty arises when you try to filter out the conditioning that we have all been subjected to throughout our lives. That is particularly true of religion, it is religion that has given God, and the antithesis, the Devil, human form. Most of us have experienced this, none more so than those of us raised in the highlands and islands of Scotland. We then have the imagery of the ancient world, take Medusa for example, with her hair consisting of venomous snakes and the body of a serpent, she could turn men to stone by simply looking at her. To many people the image of Medusa is the embodiment of evil."

"In all of my years in Inverness I have never met a nicer family than the Colquhoun's'. They have been described, many times, as the pillars of this community, and that is an accurate description. They have suffered the greatest tragedy that any family can be forced to endure, the loss of a precious child to a violent and unlawful death. I can well imagine the torment that those poor people are going through and my heart breaks for them."

"What you really need to understand Detective Sergeant, and I suspect that you already do, is that there will be no release, no closure, for Duncan and Isla Colquhoun until Aileen's foul killer has been caught and punished, appropriately."

Fellingham looked at her, a question half formed on her lips, but Gillian Davies wagged her finger, "Don't ask, Detective Sergeant, you already know the answer or should I say, the wrong answer."

10

Detective Sergeant Susan Fellingham returned to Manchester with renewed determination, Aileen Colquhoun deserved justice, oh how she deserved justice. She had met similar men to Ramiro Morales during her training, not as totally bereft of any morals as Morales clearly was, but with a similar predatory sexual nature. She had also recognised the sense of outrage that had consumed Mary Stirling over the manner in which her friend, Aileen, had been exploited and humiliated. She would like to have a female friend such as Mary Stirling herself, and she realised that these feelings were reciprocated.

DC Proud was in the police station when she arrived and clearly, was most anxious to discuss his findings with her. Once again, she was impressed with the quality and thoroughness of Gary Proud's work. She was unable to make any valid comments on the accuracy of his hypothesis but, she felt, he was not a million miles away from the truth, and the University demographer would be able to confirm or rectify his conclusions.

His eager face was searching hers for a word of approval or a simple compliment. He so reminded her of a Springer Spaniel she had once owned when she was a child. The spaniel had the most expressive face of any dog that she had ever known. There was no doubting his mood, when he was sad, or acted the part, he could reduce her to tears, but when he was happy, his joy was infectious, and they would jump and frolic together for hours. Not that she felt like jumping or frolicking with DC Proud, that would never do.

She thought, this is as good a time as any to discuss his future with him. "Gary," she said, "once again you have blown me away with your meticulous research, this is all really first class. I don't know enough about demographics to know if your conclusions are accurate or even valid, but I sense that you are on the right track. Well done, really well done."

She continued, "Before I went up to Edinburgh, I had a conversation with DCI Warbrick. He as good as told me that this Colquhoun case will be his last case before, he retires. He wants me to sit for my Inspector's exam and, wait for it, he wants you to take your Sergeant's exam. I happen to agree with him about you, I think that you have an incredibly bright future ahead of you in the police force. Your work here has been outstanding. How do you feel about doing that?"

DC Proud was the ecstatic spaniel. His whole body said that it wanted to bounce with joy. It was only his English reserve and the fact that he was in the presence of his superior officer, his superior FEMALE officer that prevented him from doing exactly that.

"Do you think that I am ready for it Sarge?' he asked hesitantly.

"Absolutely, no doubt about it," she replied with a grin, "you'll romp it in."

"What about you, will you take your Inspector's exam?" he continued.

"I'm still thinking about that, there's a lot going on in my life just now and I'm not sure where my future really lies, but, as the wise old sod upstairs said to me, when the time comes, you'll know. You probably know about this already, but you can submit your application to sit the Sergeant's exam online, by all means use my name as a referee and I'm quite sure that DCI Warbrick would act as one as well."

"Thanks Sarge," Proud replied, "I'll do it when I have a minute, did you get my message about Winston Macauley?"

"Oh yes, the ex-editor of the Hive student magazine, yes, I do want to meet with him, but I also believe that the DCI would like to be there also. I have a meeting with him in half an hour to fill him in on developments in Edinburgh, I'm sure that he will want you there also to go through the briefing, but I'll check. Has he seen all of the work that you have done so far?"

"Yes, he has, I think that he was pleased," replied Proud.

DCI Warbrick was pleased to see her back in the office and was most supportive about inviting DC Proud into the briefing. Both men listened intently as Fellingham took them through her several days with Mary Stirling. Mary had been as good as her word and set the files covering the period from Aileen's departure from ICE, through to her marriage to Ramiro

Morales, and on up to the most recent meeting with Mary Stirling and Ken Stockdale. Fellingham had added that Mary Stirling had also promised to send her the files covering the time that both Aileen and Ken had spent investigating the behaviour and business dealings of Avnav Parts and Services Limited.

"That is," Mary had added as an ominous and parting remark, "until Aileen had almost completed the investigation which I now believe led to her death. There were circumstances surrounding that which I found suspicious. I believe that when you are ready to discuss this you should call me, and I will come to you in Wilmslow. At which time I also believe that your Detective Chief Inspector Warbrick should also be present."

"It seems to me Detective Sergeant," interrupted the DCI, "that you have a considerable amount of reading to do, but only following the two meetings which we three are to soon have."

"Two meetings Sir?" queried his detective sergeant, "I was only aware of one, with a Mr Winston Macauley, the editor of the Hive at the time of Morales sudden and unexpected departure from ICE."

"Yes indeed," replied Warbrick, "but we also have a meeting with Detective Chief Superintendent David Goddard of London's Metropolitan Police and his undertaking of enquiries into Morales' exploits, both here and in Argentina. He tells me that he thinks that we will find it illuminating. His words, not mine."

11

Winston Macauley did not look at all like Susan Fellingham had imagined. Her mind had drawn an image of an overgrown schoolboy, horn rimmed spectacles, sporting a 'Varsity' scarf, flung carelessly around his neck, one end trailing down his back, the other, down his front. Oh, and yes, given to giggling needlessly.

Instead, the giant who stood before her, reminded her immediately of Rory Colquhoun, his broken nose giving testimony that he had at some time in his past, partaken in the same sport that had endeared Rory to Alex, rugby union. As to giggling, Susan quickly gained the impression that this man rarely smiled, less alone giggle. Whether that was due to his employer being the staid Financial Times, she could not say, but he was reserved and scrupulously polite. He greeted all three police officers in a manner funereal enough to have graced the countenance of an undertaker.

"I take it that you have come to speak to me about Ramiro Morales, if so, you're a tad late, I was expecting you ten years ago." This statement was made totally devoid of any humour.

Warbrick bristled, he had scant regard for sarcasm, whether or not it was delivered deliberately. "Yes, partially, and also to discuss with you the late Aileen Colquhoun."

A reaction, a massive reaction, Macauley sat bolt upright, his face contorted in horror. "Aileen's dead, oh my God, when, …. how, …… did that bastard Morales have anything to do with it. No one told me………, someone should have told me. I knew Aileen quite well, the nicest and loveliest young lady that I ever met at ICE. I heard rumours about Morales and Aileen but frankly, I took all of them with more than a pinch of salt. Please tell me what happened."

Warbrick relented, the obvious shock that this man had suffered was no act. He was genuinely shocked, and grief stricken. "Her body was discovered in Trentabank Reservoir outside Macclesfield in Cheshire a couple of weeks ago. We are still investigating, but let's just say the circumstances were suspicious."

"Too bloody right the circumstances were suspicious, Aileen was terrified of water, do you know what aquaphobia is?"

"Yes, we do," interjected DS Fellingham, 'but how come you know, there were very few people in her life who knew anything about her aquaphobia, she kept that information close to her chest?"

There were tears in Macauley's eyes now, "She used to talk to me about it, you see I suffer from aquaphobia also, which is unusual, it mostly affects women and not men, or very few men. She first came to talk to me about it when the Hive had run an article about a forthcoming yacht cruising holiday in the Mediterranean. Her friends were trying hard to persuade her to join them and she did not want to tell them her secret. She came to see me as I had written a rather disparaging article about the dubious value of water-based holidays. I had concluded the article with a statement that read, 'Personally I find the endless rise and fall of waves as riveting as watching grass grow.' She thought that I might have been a kindred spirit, but I was more, I was a fellow sufferer."

"We became friends, but never lovers, much to my everlasting regret. I could listen to her talk, all day, and all night. She had the most delightful Scots accent. She was also extremely smart, that was the main reason that I never believed the vile rumours that began to circulate about her and Morales toward the end of her second or the beginning of her third year at ICE. She would have seen through Morales in a flash. She didn't ask me about him either, which I took as a sign that she had no interest in him. She would come to talk to me whenever she was homesick or troubled by something or someone. She would tell me if someone, a male student, or a male lecturer, were trying to become too close to her, and I would do what I could to help her. But she never mentioned Morales."

"What did you know about Morales?" asked Warbrick.

"More than I would have chosen to know, and all of it, and I really mean, all of it, was disgusting. One of the reasons I was chosen to be editor of the Hive is that I am multi-lingual. A product of a globetrotting fuel engineer father, for Royal Dutch Shell. I am totally fluent in Spanish, Italian, French and Dutch. Substantially fluent in Arabic and German and I can get by in four other languages in the middle and far east. I could understand everything that Morales was saying to his fellow Spanish speaking colleagues, a great many of whom were students, some in the same year as Aileen."

"He would gloat, to his mates, about his many conquests amongst the female student body. Despite his outward appearance of being genuinely friendly and supportive he actually loathed them all. He called them whores who were the children of whores. He never used their actual names, often preferring to describe aspects or characteristics of their pudenda to illustrate his carnal knowledge of them."

"I attempted, several times, to report him to the Academic Board and the School Management Committee but I failed to garner sufficient support for a full-blown enquiry into his behaviour. That is, of course, until those two brave girls from Argentina came forward in 2008 to describe their horror and humiliation on discovering that they had, unknowingly, been filmed during the sex act with Morales. His sole purpose being the manufacture and distribution of pornographic material featuring unwitting female ICE students."

"I was asked to attend, in camera, a meeting of the Committee set up to enquire into Morale's behaviour. I was able to provide them with copies of my earlier attempts to expose him, including the disappointing outcome of those attempts, as well as my knowledge of his description of many of his victims."

DS Fellingham interjected again, "Do you still have copies of those earlier attempts to expose him?"

"I most certainly do," replied Macauley. 'I also have a copy of the summary of statements made by each individual in the group that first brought the formal complaint about him. I am unable to share that with you without each individual's consent. I doubt, very much, that they would agree to the police being made so aware."

"So do I," replied Warbrick. "It's always the same, and who can blame them. The publicity and notoriety that follows, so often results in the victim being portrayed in the press as the perpetrator".

DC Proud then interrupted, "Mr Macauley, I am trying to track down the name of the person who placed an obituary in the second issue of the Hive in April 1997 for her friend by the name of Rita Velasquez who had taken her own life a short time earlier. Would you be able to help me find the name of that person?"

"I resigned from ICE at the end of 2010, The current editor is Felicity Marshall, bit of a Joyce Grenfell if you get my drift, but her heart is in the right place. She and I catch up every so often and we get along just fine. I know that she is in Canada at the moment so I will contact Terri Ryan, who is her assistant, and ask her to check it out. I do know that we used to keep records of the names of students who placed anything in the Hive. I'll see what I can do"

"Could you also ask this Terri Ryan to do something else for us," continued DC Proud, "if you think that this Terri Ryan is the appropriate person? I have produced this table of 32 women who were students at ICE who took their own lives between 1995 and 2008. I have listed their nationalities and the years in which they were students here. I am trying to find the names of other women who were friends of these poor girls. Do you think that would be possible?"

"My goodness you have been busy DC Proud, and I had no idea that there had been so many, suicides that is. I don't think that Terri would need to know that though, there will be nothing on our files to indicate that. Can I suggest that we handle it as an 'Where are they now' kind of project. I could ask Terri to look up the students with the same nationality who were here at the same time as these abused women and provide a list of names. We could then follow that up with an enquiry as to where those girl's might now be. I will need to clear it with Felicity first though. I have her contact details; I'll give her a call later today."

Warbrick returned to the conversation, "You have been most helpful Mr Macauley, is there anything else that you can think off that we should know?"

Winston Macauley thought for several seconds, "Morales had a colleague, another Argentinian, not on the Academic staff, nor was he a student. I'm trying to remember his name. The students used to call him Che, after Che Guevara, that's it, his name was either Guevara or just Guvara, I seem to remember that his Christian name was Carlos. He was the photographer.

The one who ostensibly took photographs during the dance classes, but he was here far too often, just for the dance classes. He and Morales were as thick as thieves."

Fellingham interrupted again, "Do you happen to know if he remained in London following Morales' departure from ICE? Do you have a photograph of him?"

"I've no idea if he remained in London, I certainly never saw him again following Morales' hasty departure. If you can find Morales, you should certainly be able to find Guevara. I don't have a photograph of him, but there may be one in the Hive's archives. I seem to remember that we did a spread on the Tango classes, more of an advertorial really, and I seem to recall that Carlos was included in that photograph. I'll raise that with Felicity also."

"Thanks again," said Warbrick, "anything else?"

"Have you seen or are you seeing anyone in the Metropolitan police?" asked Macauley.

"We will be visiting them following our departure from here. Why do you ask?" asked Warbrick.

Macauley was silent for a few seconds again. "Around the time of Morales' leaving and for a while shortly after that, there were strong rumours concerning the number of alleged suicides of female students at ICE, although I had no idea that the number was as high as 32. The link that tied them all together was Ramiro Morales. I think that someone on the Committee that investigated Morales invited the Metropolitan police to assist, or so I have been told.

I have no idea who the person on the Committee was, and I never met anyone from the police, but there were rumours of the police interviewing female students and a noticeable number of weepy female students around the place for a lengthy time following these interviews."

"Thank you again for talking to us and for being so helpful. We almost certainly wish to speak with you again, and probably Felicity also," concluded Warbrick.

Macauley returned to his stoic, humourless, self again, "I really do hope that you catch the bastard, or bastards, who did this to Aileen. If it turns out to be Morales, I have a good friend who operates a charter fishing business in the Caribbean. Morales would make excellent shark bait."

12

DCI Warbrick suggested that they break for a coffee before proceeding to meet with Detective Chief Superintendent Goddard of the Metropolitan police. "It would be helpful, I think, if we discussed all that we have just learned and clarify any questions that have arisen, for any of us, prior to our next meeting."

DC Proud raised the first question, "Why do you think it was that Aileen never discussed Morales with Macauley, I found that a bit strange, they were after all, very close. At least according to Winston Macauley's recollections?"

It was DS Fellingham who answered him, "It doesn't surprise me that she didn't, she was too ashamed. Macauley was clearly very fond of her, and she may have felt the same way about him. He became her refuge from the pain of her humiliation, as such she had no wish to contaminate their friendship with the knowledge of her shame. What do you think, Sir?"

Warbrick smiled kindly at both of them, "I think that you would have a far better understanding of that situation than I, Detective Sergeant. This old male copper's nose though tells me that you are absolutely spot on. Think about it, raised in the Highlands of

Scotland, by a caring, loving, and gentle family. She would have been completely vulnerable to the predatory charms of Ramiro Morales."

DC Proud spoke up again, "We have to find this Guevara person, the photographer, he could fill in many gaps in our knowledge of Morales' behaviour, and more about the sort of man that he was. Would you like me to do that Sarge?"

DS Fellingham laughed, "As always Detective Constable, you are one step ahead of me. Yes, please meet with this Felicity Marshall, of the Hive. Ask for a copy of the photograph of Guevara from the Hive's archives. Whilst you're doing that, I will pull out some names of prominent photographers around the London news scene. That should help you to track him down!"

Gary Proud grinned by way of acknowledgement.

DCI Warbrick smiled internally to himself, 'who would have thought that his swansong in the force could have given him so much pleasure. He was quietly proud of his young team of detectives. They were, without question, the best young coppers that he had ever had the pleasure of working with. To cap it all, he was soon to marry the highly intelligent forensic pathologist he had been in love with, and always afraid to acknowledge, for the past ten years. Retirement had never looked so rosy.'

They finished their coffees and set off to meet DCS Goddard.

David Oliver Goddard may well have loved his parents, but there must have been many times during his youth that he would have hated them. To so curse him with the initials, D.O.G, what were they thinking. There had been so many fights between him and his peers, his sheer physical size had prevented there being many more, as he reacted to the canine taunts of his fellow primary school students.

He knew now that those taunts had made him tougher, more determined, and had been of great assistance in his rise through the Metropolitan police force. He was aware that a few, very few, of his detractors continued to use that acronym but, for many more, he was revered and named with the reversed acronym of G.O.D.

He was another big man, big physically, big in personality, and huge in determination. He greeted all three of them warmly and his, 'Pleasure to meet you,' had a powerful ring of sincerity about it.

He was immediately all business, "Let me say from the outset how extremely sorry I was to learn of the death of Aileen Colquhoun. So young, so beautiful, so talented. I met her; you know. She was kind enough to meet with me in Macclesfield. She told me of her experiences at the hands of Ramiro Morales, she continued to be highly distraught, ten years after the event. Even then she was unable to look me in the eye as she related her story, so acute was her pain. I tell all three of you now, without apology, that if I could have been able to put my hands on Morales on that day, following my meeting with Aileen, I would have torn him, limb from limb."

"Her case, undoubtedly, was the catalyst for my dedicating myself to not only finding this bastard, but also to find, assemble and collate, sufficient evidence to put him away for an extremely long time. I regret to have to inform you that I have been successful in neither, so far."

"I have, however, a great deal to share with you, and my earnest hope is that, collectively, we can give Aileen, and a dozen more like her, the kind of justice that they so thoroughly deserve."

"But I am getting ahead of myself, I would like to begin from the time of my first involvement with the situation at ICE, following a request we received from the Management Board of that Institution. However, before I begin, would any of you like to have tea, or a coffee, I have organised refreshments in just over an hours' time, but it would be no trouble to provide some now."

All three visiting officers declined.

"There was a file open on the ICE within the Metropolitan Police following a report that had been received of a case of sexual abuse by Ramiro Morales on a first-year economics student. The female Detective Inspector who investigated that case had reported that it appeared that although Morales had admitted that sex had occurred, he insisted that it was fully consensual and initiated by the student concerned."

"The Met was subsequently approached, years later, by a senior member of the Management Board of ICE following two meetings that had been held between, firstly, a substantial group of female ICE students, and secondly, two female ICE students whose homes were in Argentina."

"The first group had a number of complaints all directed against the Economics Tutor and voluntary dancing instructor, Ramiro Morales. The first complaint was that many of them had felt pressurised to partake in dancing classes with Morales, either nude or semi-nude. The second complaint was that several of them had been pressurised into having sex with Morales in his dance studio, where he had become quite abusive when they had rebuffed him. The third complaint was that a few of them, four in fact, admitted to having had sex with Morales but each had had the extremely disturbing feeling that they were being photographed during sexual intercourse."

"The second meeting with the two female ICE students from Argentina was disturbing in the extreme for the representatives of the Management Board. Both of these students reported, in graphic terms, that both had indulged in sexual intercourse with Morales. In both cases Morales had insisted that they have sex with his photographer, a Mr Carlos Guevara. When they had refused, he had shown them the pornographic film that he had made of them having sex with him and threatened to send copies to their families in Argentina, unless they obeyed him. They had both capitulated, had sex with the photographer, and felt deeply ashamed thereafter."

"I sought a meeting with the Detective Inspector in charge of the case who was horrified when I informed her of these most recent complaints. Although I didn't, and don't doubt her sincerity when she expressed her horror, I did not believe that sufficient diligence had been applied on this case from the outset. Given the now much more serious allegations being made against Morales I decided to replace this Detective Inspector and took over the case myself."

"I interviewed both of these young ladies. Both were 18 years old, in their first year at ICE. Both had partaken in the Argentinian Tango classes that Morales offered on a voluntary basis, where both had been seduced. The younger of the two, by several months, was extremely distraught and needed the other girl to translate her story to us as she believed that she did not know enough English to describe what Morales had put her through."

"I tried, extremely hard, to help them to understand that they had been totally exploited by an evil and manipulative man and that if there were any shame, it was his. In this I also failed, both girls took their own lives several months later. The older of the two was afraid to go home at the end of the academic year and overdosed on barbiturates. This was of course following the dismissal of Morales from ICE.

The younger girl did return to her home in Mendoza. Following his dismissal Morales, did what he had threatened, he sent a copy of the video of this girl with him, not just to her parents, but also to the mayor of the town. The shock and shame that followed caused her father to blow his brains out and she," Goddard had tears in his eyes now, "climbed into her bath, opened her veins and bled to death."

"I had continued my investigations into Morales' behaviour. There were many rumours about previous female students who had died suddenly or had been associated with Morales in a seemingly unpleasant way. One of these was Aileen Colquhoun, who as I said, I visited. Although it is by no means complete, I have a list of at least twenty girls who have ended their lives after meeting Morales."

DC Proud was about to interrupt when Warbrick stopped him, 'later,' he whispered.

"Morales departed the UK for Argentina shortly after he was dismissed from ICE in May 2008. He returned to the UK via Panama and Taiwan in April 2009. I have his passport flagged with Immigration allowing me to keep tabs on him since 2008 until 2015, but more of that later. Aileen had told me about her marriage to Morales and the reasons for doing so, but I was greatly disturbed to learn, that for reasons that were beyond me, she became involved with him again in an aviation parts business in mid-2009."

"My problem has been, and continues to be, the reluctance of all of his victims, the ones that are still living of course, to give evidence against him. I can understand their reluctance, but it continually frustrates me that we have been unable to prosecute this animal."

"There have been some developments in the last few years which may yet lead to an opportunity to finally deliver at least a modicum of justice. First of all, we have been making some progress in, of all places, Argentina. Despite the Falklands War, the relationship between the Argentinian and British police forces, has been strong and growing stronger annually since the fall of the Military Junta which ruled Argentina between March 1976 and December 1983."

"This was the period when 30,000, mostly young people, disappeared or were killed, for their opposition to the Junta. The PFA or the Policia Federal Argentina, (Federal Police) have taken a strong interest in Mr Morales. I have an excellent relationship with Juan Carlos Hernandez, the Chief, Commisario General of the PFA. He has assured me of maximum cooperation."

"The other development has been in the relationship with Isabella Morales, the mother of Ramiro. Aileen had told me that the principal reason that she had married Morales was that he had told her that his mother was deeply religious, and she believed that if she had to, she could shame him in the eyes of his mother and his mother's Roman Catholic church. It transpires that like most things about Ramiro Morales, that position is not exactly correct."

Isabella's grandmother was an Italian migrant to Argentina, one of the many Italian migrants who came to Argentina during the last decade of the 19th century. This massive immigration programme was created by the growth of the Argentinian economy during the same period. The majority of the immigrants were Italian, followed by the Spanish and then the French. She was something of a firebrand who abandoned her husband soon after her arrival im Argentina, apparently as a consequence of his habitual violence toward her. She soon became instrumental in the establishment of a feminist newspaper, 'La Voz de la Mujer' (The Voice of Women). The thrust of this newspaper was the perceived double oppression of women,–By Bourgeois Society and By Men."

"This strong brand of feminism was inherited first by her mother, who was conceived by her own mother with a different man to her mother's husband, following her mother's abandonment of her husband. Then subsequently by her grand-daughter Isabella. Isabella discovered that life was not likely to be much different to that of her grandmother as she was badly beaten by her husband, Ramiro's father, the day following her wedding. She decided, there and then, that she would also involve herself in Argentina's long history of women's struggles. She created the myth of her deep faith to cover her attendance at the frequent rallies promoting justice and equality for women. Quite contrary to her deep religious belief, her favourite book was, 'No God, No Boss, No Husband' by Maxine Molyneux, published in 1986 which covered anarchist feminism in Argentina from the late 19th century.

"The older of the two female ICE students who took their own lives following their humiliation by Isabella Morales' son Ramiro, sent a copy of the pornographic video, with a letter, to Isabella Morales. In the letter the student begged Mrs Morales to first read her letter and then watch the video. Mrs Morales did exactly that. She was apparently outraged. A member of the feminist group to which she belonged apparently reported to a friend who was a member of the PFA, that Isabella had stated, 'I no longer have a son, what I gave birth to is the spawn of the Devil.' She then searched through her husband's belongings and discovered that he was the principal distributor of Ramiro's pornographic films."

"She called in the PFA; Juan Carlos Hernandez became aware of the case. Although there was no specific law in Argentina, at that time, which banned the distribution of non-consensual material of a sexual nature, there was a law that protected the privacy of people being exploited. The PFA seized all of the material, destroyed it, and charged Ramiro's father with the illegal distribution of offensive material. He subsequently received a lengthy jail sentence."

"It was apparent though, that Ramiro Morales had made a substantial fortune during the preceding ten years, through his illegally created pornography, and all of it had been deposited in a bank within the tax haven jurisdiction of Panama. Isabella Morales offered her services to the PFA with her desire to bring about the arrest of the man she had once called her son. She also advised that she would endeavour to discover the intended use of the funds in Panama."

"She learned, purely by accident, through a phone call to her home from a colleague of Ramiro's, that he was intending to invest in an aircraft parts manufacturing business in Taiwan."

"The realisation of her son's activities has deeply affected her. Since early 2015 she has been responsible for the establishment of the 'Ni Una Menos,' (Not a Single Woman Less) movement which has been uniting millions of women around Argentina with the intention of firmly placing the spotlight on machista violence. (male violence against women). Featured prominently in every publication that they issue are pictures, with names, of her ex-husband and son with the caption, 'Some faces of Machista Violence.' The same article challenges her ex-husband and son to 'sue her' which neither has done. This has caused considerable damage to her son's business reputation. The publication also regularly quotes the statistics which graphically illustrates the rising number of femicides in Argentina."

Refreshments arrived and they each had the opportunity to reflect on the information that DCS Goddard had given them.

Warbrick was the first of the three Cheshire police officers to speak, "You mentioned that you were able to track Morales movements, through his passport, from 2008-2015. Why not beyond that?"

Goddard grunted," We lost track of him for two years, we believed that he had obtained a passport in a different name, but we had no idea what. It was our colleagues in the Polizia di Stato in Italy who solved the problem. We had shared information with them about two of Morales' victims who are Italian asking the police to keep us informed should he cross their border. We had done the same with other police departments across Europe. A female member of their border police thought that she recognized his face on a Panamanian passport with the name Dacian Jiminez. She copied his passport photograph, and had it compared with the photograph of Morales we had sent to them."

"Mr Jiminez had provided the name of a hotel in Milan where he was staying and let's just say," Goddard coughed embarrassingly, "we were able to obtain DNA information that Dacian Jiminez and Ramiro Morales were one and the same."

Warbrick's face remained devoid of any emotion but privately he was extremely excited, "I take it then that Mr Morales is unaware that we now know that he is Dacian Jiminez?"

"Unless he has contacts at the highest levels of the Polizia di Stato, that is undoubtedly so," smiled Goddard.

"Then let's keep it that way," continued Warbrick, "Chief Superintendent … "

But Goddard interrupted him, "David, please."

"David, this has really been incredibly informative and helpful, would it now be appropriate if I had my colleagues here explain what we have been up to and where we believe we can now make positive progress?"

"Please do," replied Goddard.

Warbrick then indicated, first to DC Proud and then to DS Fellingham, to brief DCS Goddard on their work to date.

When they had finished DCS Goddard was beaming, "May I compliment both of you. You have given me a huge amount of optimism that together we might be able to bring some justice to these unfortunate women. Although I am not surprised to learn from you DC Proud that the number of suicides of ICE during

Morales' tenure now stands at 32, I am horrified by that number. That we also might bring to account Ramiro Morales or Dacian Jiminez, whatever he calls himself now, for the murder of Aileen Colquhoun, and heaven knows what other crimes he has committed in the aircraft maintenance and repair industry. Thank you, all three of you, if we at the Met can be of any assistance, you have only to ask!"

13

Susan Fellingham, on the few occasions when she wasn't focused on the case, had thought about whether she should take DCI Warbrick's advice and sit her Inspectors Examination. She couldn't deny that the prospect of becoming an Inspector excited her, but she couldn't decide if it was more important than becoming Mrs McQualter. She was absolutely decided about her love for Alex, and her desire to be married to him, but she was far less sure about a life away from the police force. She couldn't see herself ever becoming a stay-at-home mum and a life of washing nappies and domestic chores. She needed to have a serious conversation with Alex about it.

As it transpired, she had worried unnecessarily. When she had told him about DCI Warbrick's suggestion, he had simply shrugged and said, "Why are you surprised, anyone who knows you and him are well aware of how highly he regards you, I'm more surprised that he has taken as long as he has to suggest it. How do you feel about becoming an Inspector of Police in the County of Cheshire Constabulary?"

She had replied, "I must admit that the idea excites me, but I didn't know how you would feel about marrying a career focused woman. There would be considerably more responsibility for me if I were to be successful. Lindsay Warbrick has told me that he would like me to take over from him when he retires, following the completion of the Aileen Colquhoun case. He also wants Gary Proud to take his Sergeants exam so that we both could continue to work together. He also added that he would recommend that approach to Chief Superintendent Tony Speers."

He had hugged her then, "You should go for it, I'm proud of you whatever you choose to do, and having previously benefitted from your exceptional work as a police officer, how could I possibly object to the remainder of the Cheshire population also experiencing those benefits. If becoming a Police Inspector makes you happy, then it will also make me happy."

She had hugged him then and enjoyed the warm glow of happiness.

He continued, "Now tell me about this case that has you so pre-occupied, Rory is my friend as well you know, and I would really like to know how you are progressing?"

She spent the next hour telling him all she had learned about the case thus far, realising as she did, that she had been so busy, that she had told him just about nothing, following their first meeting with Rory. He was intrigued with her story and wished to know more about Mary Stirling, Ken Stockdale, and Trevor Byford. in particular.

She found that she could describe both Mary Pickford and Ken Stockdale quite well, but she realised that she knew virtually nothing about Trevor Byford and resolved to correct that.

Alex was thoughtful for a while. "An interesting nest of vipers you've found for yourself," he said softly, "and about ten times more deadly if I'm any judge, and from what that Chief Superintendent Goddard has told you. Promise me that you'll be careful Susan. You probably have this covered but listening to your description of the multiple potential sources of this man's income, and influence, I'm reminded of the simple advice that I was given when I was learning about tracing provenance of an artefact. 'Follow the money' my instructor told me, and he was right. It seems to me that if this guy is now making money from supplying dodgy aircraft parts, to various companies involved in aircraft maintenance and repair, then he has to have someone either in each of these company's maintenance departments or, more likely, their purchasing departments. Follow the money Susan, follow the money."

Susan was laughing, "There is so much more to you than a pretty face and a horny disposition, isn't there Mr McQualter, and aren't I delighted about that."

Susan returned to the station and began to concentrate on reading the reports she had received from Mary Stirling, since the development of the plan with Ken Stockdale, to move onto the front foot in their quest to obtain justice for Aileen Colquhoun.

Ken had been busy and had travelled extensively in the last couple of years, mostly throughout Europe, but he had undertaken three trips to Taiwan, the last of which had been only three months previously. He had utilised his many contacts in the aircraft maintenance industry, gained over a lifetime of repairing aircraft, in all types and sizes of aircraft. He had also endeavoured to keep pace with the rapidly changing technology involved in airframe developments, avionics, and aircraft propulsion systems. He knew his limitations though, and it was through admitting to these limitations, that he had been able to, surreptitiously, ascertain the key maintenance personnel engaged with each of the aircraft maintenance and repair companies. He had begun a file listing each of these people by name, type of aircraft experience, qualifications, University/Institute bestowing these qualifications by name and location, age if known/estimated of person, and if possible, date and place of birth. The file was now enormously thick with an electronic copy kept in the offices of Mary Stirling.

His travels to Taiwan had been carried out under the guise of wishing to learn about the aircraft built for and owned by the Chinese Airforce, but in reality, it had been about learning the ownership of a recently created entity, 'Faithful Falcon Flying School and Aircraft Repair,' registered in Hong Kong, to a Nominee Company. Ken had noted all that he could about this company and passed the information on to Mary Stirling. Mary, through her legal contacts, both UK based and internationally, had eventually tracked the real beneficial owners to be Avnav Parts and Services Ltd, of Panama.

Susan studied the files that Mary had provided. It was interesting that many of the names within the maintenance departments of the companies that had dealings with Avnav Parts and Services Ltd, or its subsidiaries, bore Spanish sounding surnames. She wondered how many of these could be traced back to Argentina or Panama. There was no way of knowing without alerting these companies to the enquiries being made, not the smartest of ideas. She mulled over Alex's suggestion of 'Following the Money.' She decided that she needed to talk to both Mary and Ken about the best way of doing this.

She then called DCI Warbrick to discuss her thoughts and seek his approval for yet another trip to Edinburgh. He told her that he had been about to call her and asked her to join him in his office. She took the stairs, two at a time, up to the next floor and Warbrick's office. He called her in and asked her to sit down.

"You go first," he said, and she quickly brought him up to speed with what Ken's files had told her and also adding the comment that Alex had made about 'following the money.'

"Always a good idea," had been Warbrick's response, before continuing, "and we may have found a way of doing just that. Susan, I have just come off the phone with Chief Superintendent Speers, following a conversation I have also had this morning with Chief Superintendent David Goddard."

"David Goddard called me to tell me that he had been contacted by a man in Trieste, who is aware of both of us, through Markus Ammon. The Italian man who also knows us is called Maggiore Cesare Sinarelli, from Italian Military Intelligence. Sinarelli had also been in contact with his friend, Signor Eduardo Roni, one of the five richest men in Italy. It would appear that Signor Roni's daughter, and only child, Izabella Constantini, (her mother's maiden name) attended ICE. She used her mother's maiden name following the advice of the Italian police and Signor Roni's security consultants. She was also one of the young women seduced by Morales, but in her case, Morales tried to blackmail her, and her father, by threatening to send the photographs and video, directly to the Italian press unless her father paid him 2 million dollars, for the material. This all occurred during Izabella's first year at ICE, and toward the end of Morales's time there."

"Her father refused to pay, Morales did as he had threatened, and Izabella was subjected to an angry, verbal humiliation from her father, for the shame that she had brought to his family. Three days following this outburst, the young Izabella threw herself off Westminster Bridge and drowned."

Warbrick anticipated the question that DS Fellingham was about to ask, "Yes, I know all this took place years ago, so why now? Why has Signor Roni taken so long to wish to contact us?" Susan nodded, "Apparently, he had originally contacted his friend Cesare Sinarelli requesting his help immediately following the receipt of the advice of his daughter's death. At that time Sinarelli knew of no-one with

UK police force and was therefore unable to assist Eduardo Roni."

"Markus Ammon has recently fully de-briefed Sinarelli on the Bahruz/Baker affair, including our role in assisting in his demise." Fellingham shuddered, she had never thought of their completed role in those terms. Warbrick continued, "Sinarelli's response to that de-brief was to immediately call Signor Roni and provide him with our and DCS Goddard's contact details."

"Since the loss of his only child and daughter Signor Roni has been distraught and consumed with guilt for not paying the ransom money. He has since wished to destroy Morales, but to do so as painfully as possible, without, as David Goddard put it, breaking too many of the laws of this country. David Goddard believes that we should both fly to Verona where we will be met, to be taken to the district of Sirminione. We will then travel, by car, to meet with Signor Roni at his home in the Villa Giustiniani. Chief Superintendent Speers has approved both the funding and the exploration of this suggestion."

"I'm not altogether sure if Signor Roni's first choice for retribution wasn't the Italian Mafia, but maybe he thought that their methods were too quick for what he had in mind. He may be interested in helping us to "Follow the money,' though. Do you have any thoughts about this DS Fellingham?"

Susan's first reaction was a mixture of anger, revulsion, and intrigue, and she said so. "I'm angry that a man who had the means to protect his daughter's life, whilst at the same time having the resources to fully expose the man who had threatened his daughter's reputation, and perhaps save others less fortunate, failed to do so. I'm revolted that now his guilt, and his money, are the tools he wishes to use to extract cruel revenge, but I'm intrigued that maybe, if we're smart, we can use his money and his anger, to help us bring this man to justice and destroy the evil empire that he has built. Those are my thoughts Detective Chief Inspector Warbrick," and she pushed herself back in her chair.

DCI Warbrick sat looking at her, his facial expression revealing nothing. Slowly, ever so slowly, a smile spread across his face until it became a beaming grin. He came from around his desk to occupy the vacant seat beside her. "I have been in this job for many more years than you and I have never heard a better summary of a preposterous proposal in my life. Susan, (he rarely used her Christian name when at work, unless it was personal) you display a maturity that belies your years, and I am grateful for it."

He continued, "Sometimes the blind Lady of Justice needs a little helping hand to help her ensure that Justice is triumphant. Why don't you and I meet with Signor Roni at his home, to see if we can guide his guilt and his anger, into the helping hand that our blind Lady so desperately requires?"

14

Gary Proud had been busy, following DS Fellingham's information on publications devoted to aircraft and their maintenance, he had contacted all of the editors of these publications and broadly discussed the information he was seeking. He had, eventually, been given the names of journalists considered to be the most likely source of that information.

The best contact though had been the Editor himself, of the Aviation News Back Issues. His name was Steve Warrington, he was also a pilot, and owned his own twin engined aircraft, and he had been in his current position for over fifteen years. Gary had now met with him on six separate occasions.

On their first meeting Steve had shook his head when Gary had outlined what he was looking for and said, "I only wish it were that easy to provide you with that information, but frankly, it is just not possible. What do you know, Detective Constable Proud, about the aircraft industry, the aircraft themselves, and the many parts that enable an aircraft to fly?"

Gary had shaken his head," Absolutely nothing," had been his reply.

"Well at least you're honest," Steve had added, "OK let me begin by giving you a brief outline of the processes involved in gaining approval for an aircraft or any of the parts that make up that aircraft. Firstly, I am sure, that even if you don't know, you must have some idea about the stresses that come to bear on an aircraft, at take-off, during flight, which can include withstanding a whole range of extreme weather conditions, and landing."

Gary nodded.

"Well, throughout the world, each country normally has an agency that is responsible for certifying the safety of all aircraft that operate within its area of jurisdiction. There is a considerable amount of information sharing between these countries, worldwide, but particularly, western countries. This has been designed to ensure that safety standards of all aircraft are, for the most part, identical. There are some exceptions to this which we may get to later."

"When a civil aircraft, engine, propeller, or appliance is designed, and a prototype is tested, the goal of the manufacturer is to obtain, from their country's respective authority, the granting of an 'Approved Type Certificate' so that the product can be offered to the market. In order for the product's airworthiness to continue, parts that are installed must conform to the previously granted, 'Type' design approval, with limited exceptions. The granting of the 'Approved Type Certificate' means that the manufacturer has successfully demonstrated that the aircraft, engine, propeller, or appliance design conforms with all applicable regulatory and design criteria. It is, in all respects, an enviable mark of approval."

"After obtaining 'Type Certification' a type certificate holder must obtain 'Production Certification,' by demonstrating that each duplicate aircraft, engine, propeller, or appliance, will comply with the "Type Certificate.' The manufacturer must demonstrate a high level of quality control and assurance to obtain this 'Production Certification.' The manufacturer has, by demonstrating that each duplicate conforms to the 'Type Certificate,' additionally, demonstrated the airworthiness of each successive duplicate."

"Among other things, the approvals thus granted presumes that all the parts that comprise the finished product have been tested, inspected, and approved and that the manufacturer's quality control and assurance standards are an integral part of the airworthiness determination for the complete product."

"It then becomes apparent that variations to this approved type, however minor, infringe upon the 'Type Certificate,' again with some exceptions, but these are mostly minor details, if you need them, I can send them to you?"

It was a question, and he looked across at DC Proud who was writing furiously in an effort to keep up with this torrent of information, all of which was totally new to him. He realised he was being asked a question and he looked up, "Yes that would be fine," he said, "if I need them, I'll ask for those details."

Warrington paused, allowing time for Gary to catch up with his note taking, "OK so far?" he asked. Gary Proud nodded and smiled across at Steve Warrington, who then continued. "There are three other certificates which you need to be aware of, the first is a 'Supplemental Type Certificate,' (STC). These are granted for modifications to the design of the original product, usually to the originator of the original design. Once again, the application for an STC must present test and engineering data which demonstrates that the modification is air worthy. The STC is then approved by the respective aviation authority before it can be issued and remains the property of the designer or the developer. It can then be licensed to aircraft owners or operators."

Steve continued, "Now this is when it starts to become tricky, parts manufactured in conjunction with an STC may, or MAY NOT be, produced by the original holder of the 'Type Certificate,' but are legitimate nonetheless and acceptable for installation on certified aircraft, providing they conform otherwise with the various regulatory schemes. However, no one may produce replacement or modification parts unless they hold, what is called a 'Parts Manufacturing Authority (PMA). In order to obtain a PMA, the alternative manufacturer is required to submit design and engineering standards to satisfy airworthiness requirements for the part or parts that they intend to manufacture. This issued PMA will then identify the part, or parts, that the holder of the PMA is allowed to manufacture. The PMA is the second of these three other certificates."

"The third of these certificates is a Technical Standard Order (TSO) which is issued by the relevant aviation authority when mandatory modifications are required, usually due to changes in safety regulations. These TSOs are regularly issued with a detailed specification on any part, or parts, required to be manufactured. The TSO will only be approved when the manufactured product has been found to meet a specific set of design and performance criteria. This approval is demonstrated as being granted by way of a letter of acceptance, or a letter of design approval, from the relevant aviation authority."

Steve Warrington paused again to allow DC Proud to complete his notes and to provide him with the opportunity to ask questions.

Gary looked up having completed his writing, "It sounds extremely comprehensive and thorough to me, always provided of course that it is policed correctly."

"Aha," responded Steve, "Exactly, the system was designed to ensure that any aircraft which had been licensed to fly had been done so because it had been designed, built, and MAINTAINED, to unwavering standards of quality in design and manufacture. Unfortunately, this has not always been the case."

As you will have undoubtedly gathered from all that I have told you so far, to obtain any of the licences I have described requires an enormous amount of time. Firstly, in research and development, secondly in the manufacture or purchase of appropriate materials capable of withstanding the extremes of heat, speed and vibration encountered in aviation, thirdly in the precision required in the manufacturing process, and fourthly, the demanding testing of the finished product to ensure compliance with the issued specification. All of this costs money, and lots of it, consequently, legitimate replacement parts in aircraft maintenance are extremely expensive."

"If then, an unscrupulous individual, or company, specialising in aircraft maintenance, were to obtain an alternative product, that looked the same, but may not be constructed from the same material, and most certainly, had not been subjected to the rigorous development required of complying parts, but was significantly lower in cost, he/it stood to improve the profit margin, quite dramatically. You would undoubtedly ask, but what about the certificates that are mandated to be shown? I would answer that by saying, sometimes through forgery, total or partial, but more often by deliberate avoidance, compounded by accidents of geography and circumstance."

DC Proud looked at him, a puzzled expression on his face, "Can you explain that to me in more detail please Steve?"

Warrington paused for a moment or two, "Let me give you an actual example of a serious aircraft incident. Some years ago, an aircraft chartered from a Norwegian company, departed Oslo bound for Hamburg. There were 50 passengers and 5 crew on board. The passengers were all employees of a shipping company who were scheduled to replace a crew, who had completed their contracts, aboard a ship, owned by the same shipping company. Later in the day, all contact was lost with the aircraft as it approached the coast of Denmark. It appeared that aircraft had gone down into the body of water known as the Skagerrak. There were no survivors and air/sea rescue teams had recovered bodies littered over an area near the aircraft's last known position. The aircraft, apparently, had experienced a sudden deceleration whilst the victims were belted in their seats."

"The aircraft in question, was a veteran of hard service in an unglamorous trade, having had at least 10 previous owners prior to the current Norwegian owner. The aircraft had a total time in service of a little under 37,000 hours and substantial sections of the maintenance records were either missing or written in Spanish, and occasionally French. Flight manual revisions and other documentation related to the various modifications that had been made to the aircraft during its life, were deficient, or also missing. As a consequence, it is highly likely that potentially unsafe conditions might not have been understood by either the flight crew, or maintenance personnel, leading to unsafe operation, loading, and the flight itself."

"The accident investigation, conducted by the Norwegian authorities took three years. 90% of the wreckage was recovered from the sea bottom of the Skagerrak. The investigation disclosed that the recovered shear bolts and sleeves from the vertical stabiliser, did not comply with material specifications because of inadequate heat treatment after fabrication, and were well below the stated and required strength of such parts. Excessive wear of these parts would have been undetectable without targeted inspection. The investigation also revealed that a decision had been made to use the auxiliary power unit (APU) throughout the flight to Hamburg, contrary to procedures in the existing aircraft manual."

Warrington stopped himself before continuing, "I should explain that an auxiliary power unit (APU), on an aircraft, is generally only used whilst the aircraft is on the ground. It supplies power to the aircraft for lighting and power, heating and cooling, a few essential pumps throughout the aircraft, including the starting of the main engines. It is generally only used in flight during an emergency, such as the loss of one or more engines."

"The accident investigation concluded that it appeared most likely, from the recovered wreckage and reconstruction of the last moments of the flight, based on air traffic control plots, flight data recorder tapes, and forensic evidence, that the immediate cause of the destruction of the aircraft, with the deaths of all on board, was structural failure, brought about by sudden and violent 'flutter' in the control surfaces of the rudder and elevators. 'Flutter,' is an uncontrollable, destructive oscillation of control surfaces which can be initiated where conditions of vibration and excessive wear exist."

"The investigation revealed that the 'flutter' in the tail control surfaces of the aircraft was precipitated by four factors which together led to the loss of the aircraft. 1) The improper airborne use of an inadequately restrained APU which could have induced a high level of vibration in the tail structure. 2) Inferior maintenance which could not, and did not, discover progressive deterioration in the shear bolts and sleeves securing the vertical stabiliser. 3) The shear bolts and sleeves themselves which were of indeterminable origin and quite evidently, defective in manufacture. 4) The APU support, which was also of suspicious origin."

Steve Warrington pushed his chair back, "So you see the difficulty here DC Proud. You have an old aircraft with 10 previous owners based in different parts of the world. You have logbooks maintained in different languages rendering them unlikely to be understood by subsequent maintenance personnel. You have at least two important parts being replaced at some time in the aircraft's past, but no record of who did so and the origins of the parts themselves, or their manufacturer.

Then you have the APU being incorrectly used during flight, with total disregard for the instructions included in the aircraft manual."

Gray Proud added softly, "And no survivors to shed light on the situation."

"Quite," replied Steve Warrington.

It was at this point that their first meeting ended, with DC Proud expressing his gratitude for the comprehensive insight that Steve Warrington had given him into the aircraft maintenance business. He hadn't mentioned Avnav Parts and Services either prior to, or during this first meeting. He did so now.

"Have you ever heard of an aircraft maintenance company named Avnav Parts and Services, Steve, I think that they are based in Macclesfield."

"Indeed, I have," replied Warrington, "and not very much of it is good. They have more bases than just Macclesfield though."

"Really where else are they located?"

"I only know of two, Buenos Aires and Panama, but there may be more, give me a little time and I'll look into it for you. I suspect that it is this company that has prompted your visit to me here today. Would you like me to unearth anything that might be of interest to the police?"

Gary grinned, "that would be fantastic," he said, and he meant it.

15

Mary Stirling was in her home in Morningside Edinburgh, it was early evening on a Tuesday and Ken Stockdale had arrived a few minutes earlier. Mary had thanked him for coming, offered him a drink, which he had declined and then she had come straight to the point. "Ken, I had a call from Detective Sergeant Fellingham yesterday advising me that she and DCI Warbrick are off to Italy early next week, to meet with the father, apparently the very rich father, of one of the other victims of Ramiro Morales, Izabella Constantini. She would like to meet with us both, prior to leaving for Italy, in order for us to fully update her on what we know, or have discovered, that we have not yet passed on to her. She is specifically interested in learning about why I believe that Aileen had discovered something substantial about her former husband's criminal activity in the aircraft parts business, immediately prior to her murder."

"What was it that made you believe that?" asked Ken.

"She told me, during a phone call when she had asked again to meet with me, that she had found a document that clearly identified the illegal activity of a company that Morales had formed in Taiwan for the sole purpose of manufacturing, duplicating, or illegally renovating replaced parts, and methods of producing 'certificates,' false of course, but capable of passing more than a cursory glance. She was planning to bring it with her, to her meeting with me, which was planned to occur on the day that her body was found."

"Was that company the Faithful Falcon Flying School and Aircraft Repair," asked Ken.

"No, it was a different company altogether, Aileen couldn't remember the name when we spoke, she had written it down and said that she would also bring that with her to our meeting. I have since been trying to find the name of it through nominee companies in Hong Kong whose beneficial owners are either Morales or Avnav Parts and Services, but so far without success."

"What do you need from me, you know I would do anything to put this bastard away and bring some justice to Aileen. There's not a day goes by that I don't regret that discussion I had with Aileen about bringing new blood into the company, and all because I selfishly wanted to retire," an anguished Ken asked.

"Stop beating yourself up Ken, we've had this discussion before, it's the most normal thing in the world to want to retire after a lifetime of hard work. We'll bring this," Mary paused for a moment, before continuing, "iniquitous Morales to justice Ken, we, in conjunction with Cheshire police. You haven't met Detective Sergeant Fellingham yet have you Ken, you will be most impressed when you do, I know that

I was. Now why don't you show me the information that you have obtained in, and from, Taiwan."

Ken opened his brief case and brought out a folder heavy with documents and other pieces of paper, "I have here," he said, opening the first document, "the names of all of the personnel employed by the Faithful Falcon Flying School and Aircraft Repair (FFFaAR) including the names of the Chief Mechanic which is Suarez who hails from Panama, and the purchasing manager named Hernandez, also born, and raised in Panama. There are several more employees of, evidently, either Panamanian or Argentinian descent, all of whom appear to be occupying positions of some authority."

"Next," he opened the second document, "I have this interesting spreadsheet comprising four columns. The first column identifies a part, with its number, and type of aircraft it is fitted to, the second identifies the name of the current PMA holder for the manufacture of that part. The third column shows the price, in 2018 terms, that the PMA holder charges, in wholesale terms, to the installing company, and the fourth column shows the cost to FFFaAR for that part. You can quickly notice the vast difference in prices between columns three and four, the figures in column three are between 5-8 times higher than the cost shown in column four."

Mary studied the spread sheet intensely, she raised her eyes to meet Ken's, "Ken, how did you manage to procure this spreadsheet and secondly, what is a PMA?"

Ken answered the second part of the question first telling Mary that, "A PMA is a Parts Manufacturing Approval, issued by the relevant aviation authority of the country holding the 'Type Certificate.' He went on to briefly explain the process involved in gaining approval for any aircraft, including the inherent parts of that aircraft, to be considered airworthy. He had previously told Mary the huge amount of potential profits any disreputable aircraft repairer could make by using alternative and unapproved parts.

Mary continued to stare at him, those laser-like eyes boring into him like a cobra surveying its prey, "And the first part of my question, please Ken?" there was absolutely no gentle politeness in the use of the functional 'please' in her request.

Ken stared back at her, chin set resolutely firm in its determination, "You really don't want to know, Mary. I have skills that fall outside of my training as an aircraft mechanic. All I will add is that I am equally proficient in all of them."

Mary continued to hold him within the hypnotic fix of her eyes, but then she smiled, "I don't doubt your proficiency for a second Mr Stockdale."

Ken reached back into his briefcase and withdrew several sheets of paper, before he showed them to Mary he said, "These documents are based on summations and guesses that I have made, following receipt of copies of several order forms produced by FFFaAR, and coming into my possession via a similar route to the spreadsheet that we have discussed."

He looked across at Mary who was wearing an expression that would have been worthy of a member of the clergy, receiving a request for forgiveness from a supplicant member of her flock.

Ken continued, "The first sheet," he passed it across to her, "is what I consider to be a list of parts that are 'Completely Counterfeit'. I say this because I believe that it would not have been possible to achieve these parts by any other way than by the complete manufacture of the part, but almost certainly not by using the correct material."

"The second sheet," again he passed this over to Mary, "I have headed, 'Parts produced by Legitimate Manufacturers outside the Chain of Accountability.' This list shows those parts made by legitimate manufacturers, but which have NOT been substantiated by certificated compliance with the regulatory scheme or distributed without authority from the certificate holder. This list is potentially the least accurate of the four as I have used my judgement in deciding which parts a legitimate manufacturer would, in reality, manufacture and distribute in this manner, given the risk that exposure would bring to the legitimate manufacturer. Generally speaking, the parts on this list, I have chosen because they are parts that are unlikely to inflict a major catastrophe, should they fail."

"The third list, headed, 'Runout, Cycled Out Parts," again he handed this sheet to Mary, "lists those parts that are damaged and salvaged after removal from service, then subsequently reintroduced into the parts pool, through the use of misinformed, deceptive, improper, unapproved, inadequate, or fraudulent repair schemes and documentation. These parts are generally those that are most difficult to inspect once an aircraft has been in operation. The certified manufacturer generally recommends these parts replacement after a specified number of flying hours. Whilst it is true that these specified flying hours are always on the conservative side, the fact is, that no one actually knows how much life is remaining in these parts, post the specified flying time, it might be a further 1000 hours, but it could be as little as 10, and the risks are huge."

The fourth list headed 'Commercial Parts,' lists those parts which have been converted to aircraft use without passing through more stringent aircraft inspection requirements. You would be surprised, and I suspect horrified if you were aware of how frequently this happens. I have personally found, during an inspection of an aircraft that I had been requested to repair, that simple car batteries had been installed by a previous repairer instead of the authorised batteries for use on aircraft. Authorised aircraft batteries have special vent caps and check valves which are included to control spillage of battery fluids under flight conditions, as well as to safely vent combustible battery gasses. I have also found that an alternator belt on an aircraft had been replaced with a belt from a well-known lawn mower manufacturer."

"The fifth list is simply a list of other illegal processes involved in the procurement and installation of parts that are un-approved. These include, a) Parts and components which have been overhauled or repaired without authorisation and marketed using descriptors such as 'Overhauled', 'Reconditioned,' or 'Like new'. b) Parts for which certification cannot be demonstrated for some unknown reason. c) Parts manufactured to military or foreign (and un-recognised) certification requirements which have been improperly altered. d) Parts which have been substituted without authority. e) Parts which have been misrepresented as meeting certification requirements. f) Stolen parts."

Mary was almost struck dumb, "My God Ken, it makes you wonder why you ever take the risk of flying anywhere. I had no idea that there were so many different ways to illegally keep an aircraft being allowed to fly. How widespread are these practices?"

Ken Stockdale looked her firmly in the eye as he said, "More widespread than you could possibly imagine and, getting worse. Fortunately, most of the major carriers have their own maintenance crew who follow maintenance procedures, by the book. I say most, but not all. Some of the larger carriers subcontract their maintenance work to organisations that they trust. I'm sure that the vast majority of these subcontractors are organisations with a high level of integrity, but there is nothing to stop a carrier from changing his allegiance from one subcontractor to another, 'more economically attractive,' competitor. The passenger carrying business for airlines, is a tough and uncompromising industry, each airline is trying to undercut the other on passenger airfares. Passengers probably think that that is great, but for my part, I know which airlines I will fly, and which I won't."

"I don't think that I wish to burden myself with more thoughts along these lines Ken, what else have you obtained?"

Ken continued, "Not a great deal more, but I have found someone who works for and is, shall we say, an intimate friend of FFFaAR's purchasing manager, Senor Hernandez. Her name is Huang Jia-Li, I understand that she is reputed to be extremely attractive and anxious to migrate to the United States to seek her fortune in Hollywood. She is 20 years of age, and I believe Senor Hernandez is 55, and recently divorced."

"I thought it prudent not to attempt to meet the Chief Mechanic of FFFaAR, Senor Suarez as I am led to believe that he is known to Trevor Byford of Avnav Parts and Services in Macclesfield. Apparently, they meet fairly frequently."

"OK," said Mary, "Let me call DS Fellingham to see when she is free this week, Thursday would be best for me, what about you Ken?"

"I can do any day that suits you two ladies, I am officially retired and fancy free."

The call was made and a meeting set for 10.00am on Thursday with DCI Warbrick, DS Fellingham and DC Proud.

16

DS Fellingham was in the process of preparing herself for the meeting with Signor Eduardo Roni the following week. She had called the number that DCI Warbrick had supplied, and a low female voice had answered, "Pronto." She had firstly apologised for her lack of Italian and then introduced herself. The low, and now musical voice, had responded, in perfect English," Please don't apologise, Detective Sergeant, I myself am English although I have lived in Italy for so long now, I often forget that I am. It is nice to speak my native tongue again, so how can I help you?"

Susan explained the reason for her call, and she was told that Signor Roni had been expecting a call from the English police. The voice continued, "My name is Vanessa Montefiore, from my father, a great improvement on my mother's maiden name, which was Longbottom, don't you think. I've always much preferred to be thought as someone who mounted flowers than one who suffered from a distended rear end." Susan immediately liked her.

Vanessa continued, "Signor Roni is currently in Pretoria, South Africa. He will be returning on Friday of this week and I'm quite sure that I can re-arrange the meetings that he has scheduled for Monday. He has an extremely full day on Tuesday with some important meetings, but I could also change a few commitments on Wednesday if that would best suit you. Monday would be the better day though if you can make it at all, I could ensure that he is free for most of that day. There is a plentiful supply of available accommodation at his villa, the Villa Giustiniani, and if you are able to travel on Sunday, to Verona, I could arrange to have you met at the airport and brought to the villa."

"May I first check with my boss, Detective Chief Inspector Warbrick, both of us are intending to meet with Signor Roni, and I will call you again once I have done so," replied Fellingham.

DCI Warbrick wasn't best pleased about flying to Italy on a Sunday, he loved his weekends with Gina. Susan Fellingham wasn't thrilled by the prospect either, she had been planning a fairly intimate lunch with her fiancée, Alex McQualter, with the afternoon free for what she knew would be the most desirable finale. Nevertheless, she knew that Warbrick would opt for the Monday, he would like as much time as possible with Signor Roni. In this assumption she was quite correct, Warbrick, in a grumbling voice, told her to go ahead and book flights for the Sunday to Verona and advise Signor Roni's staff accordingly.

She returned the call to Vanessa Montefiore and gave her the news. Vanessa seemed pleased with the decision, "I am quite sure that Signor Roni will be delighted that you will be coming here so promptly.

He is most anxious to meet with your Detective Chief Inspector Warbrick and yourself, of course. He has asked me to enquire, is it Signora Fellingham or Signorina. He does like to be precise in such matters?" Susan answered her, but suppressed the desire to add, soon to be Signora McQualter.

Susan Fellingham put the phone down and called her fiancée. His phone was turned off, it was, frequently, when he was working. She left him a message saying that she would like to meet with him that evening as something had come up which would scupper their plans for Sunday.

Whilst she was waiting for him to return her call, she walked down the corridor to the large office whose sole occupant was DC Proud. He was happy to see her and, as always, he had reams of paper that he wished to show her. Steve Warrington had been true to his word and produced a series of articles highlighting the loss of aircraft, of varying types and sizes, where there had been a loss of human life or lives, and/or the loss of valuable cargo. Attached to each of these highly graphic cuttings there was a brief typewritten attachment reading, these aircraft, serviced by Avnav Parts and Services with the date or dates when this servicing had occurred. There were 23 such articles with their attachments.

DC Proud looked up from his desk to his superior officer, "I wonder how many other aircraft servicing companies have such an abysmal record. By my accounting, some 156 human beings have lost their lives in an aircraft disaster, where that lost aircraft had been serviced at least once by this company. Surely Sarge, that's enough to begin an enquiry into this outfit, isn't it?"

"You would think so Gary, you most certainly think so, but because we don't have the full records of those aircraft, I doubt that we could instigate such an enquiry. It's frustrating I know but let's keep on with the excellent work that you are doing, and I'm sure we will succeed in our determination to provide Aileen Colquhoun's family with the justice that they deserve."

"Another thing Sarge," he continued, "Both Rory Colquhoun and I thought that George Stubbins, the Manager of United Utilities, became quite nervous when I told him that we were re-opening the enquiry into Aileen Colquhoun's death." DS Fellingham nodded. "Well, could you and I make an unannounced visit on him and put the frighteners into him?"

"What I think you meant to say DC Proud was 'should we visit him and subject him to a highly rigorous enquiry,' isn't that correct, we don't use terms like 'put the frighteners into him' on this side of the Atlantic, now do we?"

Gary Proud grinned, "No of course not Sarge, my apologies please put it down to watching too much, 'The Sopranos' on TV, but would you be up for 'subjecting George Stubbins to a highly rigorous enquiry,' any time soon?"

"Of course I would DC Proud, let's discuss it when I return from Italy next week," and she grinned at him as she left the office.

On her way back to her office Alex returned her call, "What's up," he said, "what's come up to scupper our plans for lunch on Sunday, and how can anything be more important than that?"

"If I was to tell you that I have a date with a billionaire Italian businessman on Sunday, how would you respond."

"I would respond by chaining you, naked, to your bed on Saturday and making love to you incessantly, until you had missed your booked, and all subsequent flights, on Sunday. How do you respond to that?"

"Promises, promises, promises, all I ever get from you are promises, when are you ever going to make good on your promises, answer me that, you gorgeous man?" and she chuckled happily.

"If it wasn't for the fact that I am currently examining a 500-year-old virgin, and that is a challenge in itself, I would head over there right now and make good on my promises."

"If you are trying to tell me that a 500-year-old virgin is preferable to a 20th century, slightly shop soiled, equivalent then I shall be most upset, and banish you from my boudoir for at least one week."

"I, and Signor Sandro Botticelli are distraught at your admonishment, can I seek an audience with you this evening, preferably around seven?"

"Yes, you may, but please bear in mind that whilst your ongoing examination with your 500-year-old Italian virgin, I will be dining with a 21st century Italian billionaire, but I promise to try to resist his, undoubtedly planned attempts, to examine me."

'You outrageous hussy you, I shall see you at seven, when any examinations that are to be had, will be had, by me."

"Promises again," and she laughed again and hung up.

She climbed the stairs to DCI Warbrick's office, he saw her as she entered the corridor and called her into his office. "Sorry about this Sunday thing, I hate it as much as you," he looked at her face, 'well maybe not quite as much as you. I think that it is important that we have our strategy fully developed before we leave on Sunday. Mary Stirling and Ken Stockdale are coming here at ten on Thursday to bring us up to speed on their progress. I suggest that following our meeting with them, we lock ourselves away and plan our approach with Signor Ernesto Roni. Do you have anything on Thursday afternoon that can't be altered?"

"No Sir," she replied, "there is a good deal for us to go through. There are three strands of our investigation that we need to review and develop strategies for. The first is, Morales' behaviour at ICE and the many victims who have suffered, including Signor Roni's own daughter. The second is the activity of Avnav Parts and Services, and any associated companies, in the aircraft maintenance industry. DC Proud has a considerable amount of information on that, and I won't be at all surprised to hear that Mary Stirling and Ken Stockdale do also. The third of course is the murder of Aileen Colquhoun, we have not progressed as far as I'm sure we would have liked on this strand. Both Rory Colquhoun and DC Proud believe that the Manager of United Utilities, George Stubbins, became nervous when DC Proud told him of your intentions to re-open the enquiry into Aileen Colquhoun's death. DC Proud has suggested that he and I pay Mr Stubbins a surprise visit to, as DC Proud described it, 'put the frighteners into George Stubbins. I told him that we would discuss it on my return from Italy."

"That's a great idea." responded Warbrick, "however I think it should be the three of us to visit our Mr Stubbins. I mean no disrespect Detective Sergeant, but I am probably more experienced, and have less to lose, by not just putting the frighteners in, but terrorising this bastard George Stubbins, if he has anything to do, anything at all to do, with that young lady's death." DS Fellingham looked across at DCI Warbrick's face, what she saw, frightened her, she almost felt sorry for the unsuspecting George Stubbins.

17

Thursday morning and Mary Stirling was at the Wilmslow police station by 9.30 am with Ken Stockdale arriving at 9.55. The mid-sized, of three, conference rooms had been selected for this meeting. DS Fellingham had met them both and brought them to the conference room where she introduced DC Proud. She apologized for the quality of the coffee from the canteen at the station, but Mary Stirling had dismissed her apologies with, "I'm sure it can be no worse that the mixture posing as coffee served by some of my colleagues in the legal profession."

DCI Warbrick entered the room and was quickly introduced to Mary and Ken. He was all business as he immediately began to describe the amount of progress they made thus far, but also emphasising the huge gaps or lack of compelling evidence, in all of that work. Mary Stirling was immediately impressed. She sensed the focused energy emanating from this man, together with a suppressed outrage at the violence that had been visited on the unfortunate Aileen Colquhoun. He talked for over forty minutes, not a word was wasted, not a phrase repeated, he clearly ate, slept, breathed, dissected, this case, and it was obvious to Mary that he would not rest until the perpetrators had been brought to justice.

He finished speaking and turned to DS Fellingham asking her if there was anything that she wished to add to his summary of their situation, and she had replied, "Not me Sir, but I do believe that DC Proud has a good deal of information that would be of interest to our guests, could I ask DC Proud to do so?"

DCI Warbrick nodded his agreement. DC Proud then spent the following thirty minutes showing Mary and Ken all of the information that he had received from Steve Warrington. Ken Stockdale became quite excited, "This is fantastic DC Proud, what's your Christian name, I can't go on calling you DC Proud, or you DS Fellingham by your title, I'm Ken and this is Mary," and he pointed to Mary Stirling, who was smiling.

Agreement was reached and it became Susan and Gary, Mary, and Ken. Only DCI Warbrick retained official status. Ken Stockdale continued, "As I was saying, this is fantastic Gary, there are ways in which I can supplement this data from some of my other contacts in the aircraft maintenance business, and I'll get onto it quickly."

Mary Stirling entered the conversation, "Before we become too excited, can I remind you that we are trying to put together a case against Ramiro Morales. You may well be able to construct a case against Avnav Parts and Services, but I suspect that our Mr Morales will have been far too smart to leave himself vulnerable to such an enquiry into that company."

It was DCI Warbrick's turn to speak, "Our legal colleague is absolutely spot on, I'm not saying that we should abandon the task of establishing the culpability of Avnav Parts and Services in some of these tragedies in the airline business, but I am saying that it should be secondary to our focus on the man, once known as Ramiro Morales, but now, calling himself by the name of Dacian Jiminez. Incidentally that last piece of information is highly confidential, Senor Morales/ Jiminez is not aware that we know of his change of identity."

It was Mary Stirling who now become excited, "That explains it she said, DCI Warbrick, I was asked by Susan, at one of our earlier meetings, why I thought that Aileen had some hard evidence on the criminal activity of Morales and his companies. She had told me, in the final phone call I had with her before her death, that Morales had set up an entirely new company. She was unable to remember the name of that company which had been established in Taiwan, but with a nominee company based in Hong Kong. This company had been set up, specifically, for the illegal manufacture of aircraft parts. She was planning to bring the name of that company with her to a meeting we were scheduled to have on the date of her death. I have since been trying to track down the name of that company, through legal colleagues based in Hong Kong, but of course I was using his former name, Morales. I will begin my searches again using his new name of Jiminez."

"Thank you, Mary," said DCI Warbrick, "I think that we should allow Ken and Mary to share with us everything that they have been able to gather in our pursuit of this man."

Ken talked for the best part of an hour, everyone became extremely interested in his spread sheet which reflected the huge profit margins to be gained by using illegally manufactured or altered/modified aircraft parts, and also by his summaries of the differing ways that nefarious individuals or companies, could line their pockets, in total disregard of what their activity could do to the safety of an aircraft whilst in flight.

Mary Stirling's contribution, other than her attempts to identify this newly formed company, was mostly focused on Aileen's state of mind in the weeks and months leading up to her death. She also stated that she believed that Aileen had been verging on the suicidal, on numerous occasions, when she was overwhelmed by the difficulty, she was experiencing in attempting to bring Morales to justice.

Warbrick interrupted her, "Mary I believe that you mentioned to DS Fellingham that there was something suspicious about Aleen Colquhoun's remarks when she said that she was coming to see you on that final planned meeting, what was it?"

"Yes, I did, before she hung up, I had told her to be extremely careful both for herself and the information that she was carrying. She replied that she was aware of the danger and that she would be travelling to meet me by a circuitous route. The thing is that Morales seemed to have her picked up extremely quickly. Less than three days after telling me that she would be travelling by a circuitous route her body was discovered in the

Trentabank Reservoir. I believe that he was either tracking her or he had an informer somewhere."

"I see," said Warbrick, 'that's most interesting Mary."

Mary's final comment had been, "When Aileen became despondent, I did all in my power to lift her mood by telling her that we would succeed. I have to admit, that I had privately come to the view that this was extremely unlikely. However, today, having met the three of you, I feel more encouraged than I have ever been. I just simply want you to remember that she was my dear friend, and if there is anything, anything at all, that I can do to assist you in pursuit of justice for Aileen, then you have only to ask."

They broke for a late lunch and shortly afterwards Mary and Ken said their goodbyes and returned to their respective homes. DC Proud went back to his large office and began the process of trying to link the information that Steve Warrington had given him to that which Ken Stockdale had provided.

DCI Warbrick and DS Fellingham returned to the conference room. DCI Warbrick began, "I have been giving some thought to how Signor Roni could be of most help to us. Clearly, he is distraught over the loss of his daughter and holds Morales totally responsible, whether that is fair or correct is another matter, but he wants Morales personally brought to justice. He is unlikely, at the moment, to hold much interest in the illegal manufacturing of aircraft parts. However, he has said, to DCS Speers, that he wants to 'destroy' Morales. I think that it would work most favourably our way if we were to persuade Signor Roni that destroying his business empire might bring about both of his desires."

"Susan, I want you to take the role of the exploited young woman, seduced and then abused by this man. I want you to read again all of that information that we received from DCS Goddard and Winston Macauley. I want you to describe, as a female, and as graphically as possible, what all of those young women went through. I want you to imagine being eighteen again, beginning your studies at university, consumed with your hopes and dreams, with the belief that one day they would all be realised. I want you to imagine meeting a handsome and charming man, several years your senior who sweeps you off your feet. I then want you to imagine how those young women must have felt when they realised how they had been abused. I want you to make Signor Roni live the last few weeks of his daughter's life. I want to see him distraught; I want to make him angry. Do you think that you could do that?"

Susan looked at him gently, "It won't be too hard for me to do any of that Sir," she said, "I have already been through the process, privately, myself. What will you do Sir?"

"When you have taken him through his daughter's pain and raised his guilt and his anger, I will then continue by telling him that since his activities were discovered at ICE he has moved on to another equally horrific enterprise. The murder of at least several hundred innocent people, in a series of airline catastrophes whilst in flight, caused in no small part by the failure of substandard aircraft parts, illegally manufactured by companies owned by Morales. I will go on to tell him that at no point did Morales attempt to manufacture these aircraft parts to the required standard, as it was too expensive to do so. I will then show him the spreadsheet that Ken Stockdale has so generously provided. I will also explain to him that this man's activities are not simply confined to the UK or even Europe, but that we are aware that he operates in, at least Taiwan, in Argentina, and Panama."

Warbrick paused, considering his next words carefully, "Whilst I am doing this, and throughout your description of the suffering his daughter was forced to endure, I will be watching his reactions, should he display any. Dependent on what I observe, I will then share with him other information we have gathered in our enquiries thus far about the death of Aileen Colquhoun, but I will certainly tell him about the change of name from Morales to Jiminez, stressing, of course, that this information remains, highly confidential."

The discussion was over and both Warbrick and Fellingham collected their papers from the conference room table. "We should look on the bright side DS Fellingham," said Warbrick, "here we are, you and I, about to enjoy the hospitality of an Italian billionaire at his villa on Lake Garda, I would think that you never expected to see that appearing in your job description?" and he laughed, humourlessly.

Susan was about to pack up all of her files and head home when she received a message to say that Winston Macauley was on the phone for her. She smiled to herself, she knew when she had, 'won a heart' and Winston Macauley was one such candidate. "Yes Winston, how are you, how can I help?' she said sweetly.

"Oh, I'm well thanks, just calling to say that I have that name of the student who submitted that obituary notice in the Hive, it was Olivia Montez and guess what, she continues to be in London, working for the Spanish Bank Santander, her business number is," and he read out the number.

"That's terrific Winston, thank you, any developments on those other names that Gary gave you?"

"Yes, there is, Terri has been a regular little Sherlock, or should I say Shirley, Holmes. She promises to have it completed by early next week. She is highly intrigued however, but I have told her that she will need to interrogate DC Proud if she needs further information, you might have to warn him."

"OK," and then the eternal matchmaker in her took over, "do you think that he would like to be interrogated by her."

"My word, and by 90% of the male population of Britain also."

18

Their flight departed Manchester airport at 11.15am, on a direct service to Verona. Susan settled herself against the window of the business class seat, Warbrick had the aisle seat, she opened her briefcase and began to read.

There was an interesting amount of information regarding Signor Eduardo Roni, his family, and their friends.

Eduardo Roni was the second born son of Alessandro and Cecilia Roni (nee Bentivoglio). He had been born in 1961 three years following the birth of his elder brother Salvatore.

It had been the parent's intention that the eldest son would follow his father into his highly successful and profitable business, and his education had been focussed on this intention. His undergraduate degree was in law from the University of Milan and his master's in business administration, taught in English, at the Institut Europeen d'Administration des Affaires (INSEAD) in Fontainebleau, France.

Eduardo had been allowed to follow his heart's desire studying medicine at the University of Bologna before intending to specialise in paediatric oncology, also at the University of Bologna. Unfortunately, within a month of graduating as a fully qualified oncologist, his brother Salvo was killed in a helicopter disaster whilst on a flight from the island of Skopelos to Rhodes, in Greece. There had been no survivors, and the enquiry had identified a malfunctioning main rotor bearing as the likely cause of the disaster.

Following his grieving parent's request that he assist his father in his business, he completed a second post graduate degree in Business Management at the SDA Business School of Management in Milan.

His father's lawyer and close friend was Luciano Constantini who had married his wife Sofia, (nee Lippi) one month prior to the wedding of Alessandro and Cecilia Roni and the friendship blossomed between the two families.

It was several years before Luciano and Sofia were blessed with a child and she was to be their only child. They had christened her, Lucia, after her father.

Although there had been close interaction between the two Roni brothers and the Constantini daughter, there had been no romantic indications despite, and probably because of, the overt efforts of both sets of parents. All that was set to change when Lucia attended the University of Bologna, studying economics. By the time both Eduardo and Lucia had completed their undergraduate degrees, a passionate romance had developed between them.

Lucia had set her heart on obtaining an MBA from Harvard Business School, but two months prior to her departure for Cambridge Massachusetts, they were married to the delight of four effulgent parents

Alessandro Roni, Eduardo's father, had served in the Cadore Alpine Brigade (Alpini) in the Italian army, post WW2. One of his colleagues, of equivalent rank, Maggiore, was Lorenzo Sinarelli and they had become close friends. Their unit was tasked with defending the Italian border in the Cadore region and throughout the Carnic Alps. The level of fitness required, and the intensity of the training led to the Alpini being regarded as the elite amongst the Italian armed forces.

Lorenzo Sinarelli had married his childhood sweetheart, Gina, from the Alpine village of Mazia, located in the Autonomous Province of Bolzano in the Italian Tyrol. He always claimed that she was a far better skier than he had ever been. Alessandro had been forced to agree with him after Gina had given him a head start in a slalom down a mountainside in the Carnic Alps and made him feel that he was stationary as she flew past him on her descent.

Sadly, Gina Sinarelli died giving birth to their son, named Cesare. Subsequently, Cesare was virtually raised by the Roni family becoming close friends with first Salvatore, then Eduardo, and finally Lucia. When the time came for his military service, following the completion of his law degree at the University of Milan, Cesare followed in his father's footsteps by joining the army before being recruited by military intelligence and being based in Trieste.

DS Fellingham completed her reading, learning that Eduardo's father, Alessandro, had passed away five years previously from prostate cancer, whilst his mother, Cecilia, who had been born of the Italian noble family of Bentivoglio, lived in an inherited villa on Lake Garda in Malcesine. She continued to commute, at age 80, by boat, from Malcesine to her son's villa in Sirmione, handling the 12metre power boat with all the skill of a professional boatman. Most of those professional boatmen on Lake Garda would simply cut their engines and watch, in admiration, as she thundered by.

Eduardo and Lucia were now joint Directors of the multi-national business following the passing of Alessandro, during which time they had succeeded in quadrupling the company's turnover and profits. Fellingham put down the documents, privately admitting to a newly found admiration for the family that she was soon to meet.

They were met, as promised, in Verona, by Vanessa Montefiore and a chauffeur driven stretch Mercedes limousine. They were quickly settled into the sumptuous rear seats whilst Vanessa took the centre row facing them, and with a warm and welcoming smile, began her briefing.

"First of all, a little about myself," she began, "I am Signora Roni's assistant and the daughter of an Italian man and an English mother, my father, Luigi Montefiore, was a sergeant in the Alpini serving under Maggiore Roni, and my mother was a geography teacher from Tunbridge Wells. She met my father whilst on holiday in the Italian Alps. He apparently, taught her to ski, and probably a few other things besides, as they were married nine weeks later, and I appeared on the scene less than a year from the day that they first met. My mother's maiden name was Sarah Longbottom and although I am aware that I would probably would never have had to bear the embarrassment of such a surname, I am forever grateful to my father for his salvation."

She laughed easily as she said all this and Susan knew that it was intended to be a self-deprecating way of breaking the ice between strangers, and her original liking of this lady was confirmed. "Secondly," continued Vanessa, "the Villa that is now home to Signor and Signora Roni, and where you will be staying, is the Villa Giustiniani. It was originally owned by Count Lorenzo Giustiniani and his wife ND (Nobile Donna) Roberta Soranzo. The Giustiniani is a noble Venetian family descended from, not one, but two former Doges; Giuniniano Partecipazio, Doge from 819-828; and Marcantonio Giustiniani, Doge from 1684-1688."

"Alessandro Roni bought the property from the Count approximately fifty years ago. The Count and his wife were in the process of divesting themselves of many properties that they owned, partially due to damage sustained during WW2 but mostly due to the prohibitive taxation that they were faced with. They retained the original Villa Giustiniani which is to be found near the village of Vanzo, which is south-west of Padua."

"As I am sure you are soon to discover, the Roni family are not in the slightest way, pretentious, and never have been. Alessandro had no desire to rechristen the Villa with his own surname. It had been known, for the three hundred years of its existence, as the Villa Giustiniani, and that is how it should remain, was his view. I cannot but help to agree with him."

"You will be joining both Signor and Signora Roni for dinner this evening, they normally dress formally for dinner but have asked me to advise you that they would not be in the slightest way offended, if that is not to your choosing. Please discuss it between yourselves and let me know, and they will arrange accordingly. They have also asked me to ascertain if there are any dietary requirements, gluten free, vegan, vegetarian, or any allergies chef should know about. The chef trained in Sienna and is regarded as one of the finest chefs in Italy. If you like Italian food, I am sure that you will love it."

The Mercedes crunched down the cinder coated driveway and drew up alongside a large portico. They had arrived.

The rooms that they each had been given looked out across the sparkling waters of Lake Garda as the declining sun provided it with its final burnish before setting.

Susan was immediately taken by the simple elegance of her room with its tasteful appointments. This is not the work of some interior designer, she thought, there is far too much love and care she could sense, in every aspect of the room. No, she thought, this room has been created by someone who loves this home, and she immediately thought of Signora Roni.

Warbrick's sentiments on viewing his room were somewhat similar, thinking, Gina would love it here, and then his Yorkshireman's sense of humour took over, 'I wonder if they do B&B 'he mused.

They had both been briefed on the likelihood for the need of formal dinner dress and they emerged from their rooms, at approximately the same time, DS Susan Fellingham looking stunning in a simple but well cut, black cocktail dress. DCI Lindsay Warbrick looking somewhat less than stunning in a dinner suit that had clearly been pressed prior to packing, but now bore the creases of frequent movement within the confines of his suitcase. His bow tie displayed the efforts of a man who had long since forgotten the rudiments of tying a bow tie. Susan spent several minutes re-tying his tie and doing her best to smooth out as many of the creases in his dinner suit, as possible.

They were escorted into a drawing room for pre-dinner drinks where they were met by a smiling and handsome couple. Lucia was tall, not excessively so, but her bearing, that seemingly, of a former ballerina, emphasised her height. Her dress, Susan immediately thought, 'Givenchy', was classically elegant, and framed the much younger body of a lady, now in her fifties. Her jewellery, clearly expensive, but not in the slightest way, ostentatious, paid tribute to a face, remarkable in its serenity except for the profound sadness residing in her eyes. Her make-up, lightly but expertly applied, emphasised the almond shape and colour of her eyes, and the fullness of her lips.

Eduardo kissed Susan lightly on her hand, and stood before her, a superb example of middle-aged masculinity that Hollywood has so frequently attempted to capture, and only rarely, succeeded. He was over six feet tall, slim but with the shoulders of a former rower or gymnast, dressed in a dinner suit that must have been created by Armani, it fitted him so well. Susan could feel her own pulse beginning to accelerate as he looked deep into her eyes, and she could well imagine how many women would have been captivated by that look.

There were, however, two features of Eduardo Roni that she would remember for the rest of her life. The first was the whiteness of his hair, she had seen photographs of him taken not more than a few years earlier, when his hair had been a luxuriant black or dark brown with just a touch of grey around the temples. His hair now was of a man thirty years his senior. The second feature was the agony in his eyes. As he had looked into her eye's moments earlier, she had seen the depth of his anguish and his pain, and every fibre of her female body wanted to reach out and comfort this man who was so clearly suffering. She was flustered, and her first opinion that this man must have been heartless to allow his daughter to suffer, began to founder.

Drinks were served and they were seated in the drawing room, Fellingham and Warbrick in separate armchairs whilst Eduardo and Lucia sat alongside one another on a large settee, or divano.

Eduardo began, in perfect English, with a touch of an Italian accent which Fellingham thought romantic until she took control of herself. "Firstly, thank you both for coming, so far, to assist Lucia and I in our quest for justice. We are planning to discuss our current positions in this quest during the day, tomorrow, and we are soon to enjoy what I hope will be a memorable dinner, which I have no wish to spoil by discussing unpleasant matters. I do though wish to set a few matters straight before we do so."

"I have read in a report produced by London's Metropolitan Police that I refused to pay the demands made by this man, Ramiro Morales, and that I severely castigated my daughter for becoming involved in this whole repugnant business. Whereas the first point is true, the report failed to mention the extenuating circumstances of that situation. The second point is untrue, let me now please explain;"

Before he could do so, Lucia gently interrupted him. "Per favore amore mio, lascia che ti spieghi, (Please my love let me explain). Eduardo had sadly squeezed her hand in acknowledgement.

Lucia continued, "Detective Chief Inspector and Detective Sergeant, you should first know that I was responsible for Izabella attending the International College of Economics. Izabella had undoubtedly been spoiled during her childhood, probably by us," she smiled at her husband, "but mostly by both sets of grandparents. She never went without anything that she desired, and I am sorry to say, developed an entirely unrealistic view of the world and the small matter of earning a living. Her choice of reading material was also of great concern to me, she would read only trashy romantic novels, where the hero is always tall, dark, and handsome, and where the lovelorn girl is forced to fight against the antiquated prejudices of her family, before emerging victorious, and living happily ever after."

"The first time that we received financial demands to protect our daughter's reputation was when she was fourteen. We gave the letter of demand to the local police, and they rapidly uncovered an amateurish plot by two local boys to obtain money from the wealthy 'Roni" family. The second time, when she was fifteen, was more elaborate, the letter of demand included a detailed description of Izabella's regular activities and movements, with threats to kidnap her from any one of a number of places identified in this description, unless we paid up. Once again, we used the local police and they quickly found the perpetrator who told the police, following his arrest, that Izabella had put him up to it and provided him with the list of her movements."

"The third time, was following her sixteenth birthday, when she began by demanding her inheritance to seek her fortune in the world and when this was refused, began meeting men, much older than she, all of whom were the 'love of her life.' One of these men did launch a demand for payment in order to 'avoid' physical harm to our daughter. Izabella thought this to be 'wonderfully romantic', but the man was caught a few days later. Apparently, he was a known offender who had left his fingerprints on the letter of demand."

"The fourth time we were able to end it before it began. A man came to see me whose brother works on our estate. His brother had told him to seek me out and confess. He had apparently overheard his son plotting with Izabella to kidnap her and demand five million euros for her return. He had wanted to demand only one million, but she had told him that her parents had plenty of money and then sulked that he thought that she was worth only one million."

"On each of these occasions, I can assure you both, that I held an extremely frank discussion with Izabella, in which I explained the facts of her life to her, that she would not be receiving any lump sum inheritance until she had reached an age when I believed that she understood the value of money. I told her that she would be required to demonstrate this by working for a living, and the best thing that she could do to assist her in this regard, was to obtain a degree. It was then that I mentioned the ICE, I have a degree in economics, and I thought that I might be able to help her with her studies. I also thought that London would be stimulating enough for her to experience a normal student's life. I had no idea, at that time, that this man Morales was preying on female students at ICE."

Lucia had become quite emotional at this point and Eduardo hugged her to him. She continued, "When we first received the demands for 2 million from Morales it was me who suspected that Izabella was behind it and I told Eduardo firmly, that we should not pay it. When, some days later, we received the pornographic photographs we were horrified. What made it worse was that he had also sent copies of the photographs to Eduardo's mother Signora Bentivoglio, and she had been outraged."

"Our first reaction was to demand that Izabella return home, but then we feared that might prompt her to do the opposite. Then I thought that I should travel to London to bring her home, but Eduardo was concerned that Morales might harm me in addition to Izabella. We had finally decided to ask Cesare Sinarelli to accompany me, but he was in Berlin, at a conference, and we had not been able to reach him. I can assure you both that my husband did not call our daughter and castigate her, he was far too upset for that."

"The following day we heard from Cesare, and he readily agreed to travel with me to London to bring Izabella home, but before we could do so, we received the news that Izabella's body had been recovered from the River Thames." The tears were now running freely down Lucia's beautiful face and Eduardo was struggling to contain his.

Only Lucia's sobbing disturbed the quiet of the drawing room. Fellingham looked across the room at Warbrick whose face mirrored the deep compassion that she felt. There would be absolutely no need for her to describe the suffering his daughter had gone through; he had been suffering that same pain for the past god knows how many years.

Warbrick softly asked, "Pardon me for asking, but do you still have those photographs and the demand notices made by Morales?"

His wife's pain had brought fire to Eduardo's eyes, "Yes I do," he said, "both sets of photographs and every piece of paper that animal ever sent to us."

19

Dinner had begun quietly enough, as all four of them sought tranquillity from the outpouring of emotion that accompanied the events surrounding Izabella's suicide. The dishes, as they came, were delicious living up to the expectations raised by Vanessa Montefiore. The menu, unsurprisingly, was very Italian but both Warbrick and Fellingham were fond of Italian food. The total menu comprised six courses served with perfectly timed separations between each course. Eduardo had selected the wines, and they matched the dishes superbly displaying yet another of his talents, the knowledgeable sommelier.

Lindsay Warbrick and Susan relaxed in the comfort of this lovely home, in the tranquil location of Lake Garda and indulged in the rare pleasure of enjoying the perfection of freshly sourced produce, magnificently prepared and presented. It was for Susan, one of the most memorable evenings of her life. Obviously, Eduardo and Lucia dined like this every night, she was pleased that Alex wasn't with her. He might expect her to be able to present something similar, and her culinary talents had never reached even the heights that her mother expected, let alone this banquet.

Lindsay also, despite having attended many formal evenings in some of the more revered Institutions of his homeland, had never experienced anything like it, all he knew was that his palate, so accustomed to the ingestion of basic English fast food, the copper's curse, was loving these new experiences. He savoured his Soave again; this complements this dish so perfectly he thought.

As the meal progressed and the atmosphere relaxed, Lucia Roni was fascinated by the role that Susan Fellingham had performed during their most recent case. They had now dropped the formality of their titles, and it was now Lucia, Eduardo, Susan, and Lindsay except for Susan continuing to refer to Warbrick as, Sir. Lindsay had explained to both Lucia and Eduardo, Susan's exceptional work in tracking down the kidnappers of Dr Lee's wife and child and again her ability to find the abductors of Declan O'Shea's wife Jenny and Alex McQualter. There was a little too much hyperbole in his descriptions for Susan's comfort and she could feel herself blushing frequently.

At the mention of Alex McQualter's name Eduardo interrupted, "Is he the same man who is an art adviser to the Vatican and many of the ancient religious orders and places throughout Italy and Europe?" and Susan had smiled her acknowledgement.

"He and I are soon to be married," she said, "we haven't set a date yet, but I am hoping that it will be shortly after we have brought this current case to a satisfactory conclusion."

Eduardo smiled at her, "I love to hear that confidence in your voice Susan, do you really think that we will be able to deliver justice to our Izabella?" and he squeezed his wife's hand as he said this.

Susan smiled at both of them, "That is really for tomorrow's conversation, but I know my boss and his determination, and I know my own determination. Having listened to you both today, particularly you Lucia, I sense that together we may be able to do just that, but let's continue that conversation tomorrow."

Lucia and Eduardo both agreed to this suggestion and Eduardo returned to the subject of Alex McQualter. "I am something of a philistine when it comes to the subject of religious art and I have to admit, that it has never been to the taste of either Lucia or myself. Your husband-to-be is unlikely to find any priceless works of art in our collections, but I am always willing to learn. I would welcome the opportunity of meeting him one day."

"I'm sure that can be arranged, but hopefully not on our wedding day. I have already had one argument with him this week over his obsession with an Italian virgin," but then she blushed to the roots of her hair as she realised what she had said. "I should have said a 500-year-old Italian virgin," but without any diminution in the colour of her face. Eduardo and Lucia laughed openly, but kindly, at her embarrassment and the conversation continued in lighter vein.

It was close to 11.00pm before dinner was concluded and the last of the Grappa had been consumed. Breakfast had been agreed for 8.00am with the day's discussions scheduled to commence one hour later. Warbrick invited Fellingham, into his room for a nightcap of brandy before retiring and as they settled each around their brandy balloons he asked, "What do you think, Detective Sergeant?"

"My heart breaks for both of them, I take it all back, what I said about his heartlessness, the pain that he continues to suffer is almost palpable."

Warbrick nodded, "She does also, possibly to a much greater extent than him. She attempted to bring some discipline into that foolish girl's life, and she was the one who recommended ICE, don't forget. I felt her pain as you obviously felt his. We have to get this bastard Susan, and not to see him languish in the soft hardship of an English nick, it has to be something far more permanent than that."

Susan Fellingham looked at the care worn features of this police officer that she so greatly admired. "I agree with you Sir, but I don't know how two serving officers in the Cheshire Constabulary can ever achieve that?"

"There are ways Susan, there are ways and the diligence of our Detective Constable Proud is key to it all. Follow my lead carefully tomorrow, Susan. As sure as night follows day, I'm going to get this bastard, or my name isn't Lindsay Mornington Warbrick."

Early the next morning, before Susan had risen, she received a call from Mary Stirling. As always Mary was up with the lark and her normal, conservatively soft voice was tinged with excitement. "Sorry to call so early Susan, but I have just received confirmation. The company set up to manufacture those illegal aircraft parts, by Dacian Jiminez, is called 'Intercontinental Precision Engineering' based in Taiwan but controlled by a Hong Kong based Nominee Company. I hope that proves to be of some help."

"I'm sure it will Mary," responded Fellingham, "thanks a million."

Warbrick and Fellingham enjoyed a quiet breakfast by themselves, with Fellingham confiding the latest information that she had received from Mary Stirling, they were then escorted to a large first floor room with audio-visual equipment and panoramic view of Lake Garda. Lucia and Eduardo joined them, far more comfortably dressed than dinner of the previous evening. Eduardo began, "Can I suggest Lindsay, that you take us through where exactly you are on this case, we can then tell you what we know, which is not a great deal, and we can conclude by you telling us how we might best be able to help to achieve the result we are seeking."

DCI Warbrick began, "There are three main streams of activity that we have been pursuing, and we are about to add a fourth. The first three are a) The suspicious death of Aileen Colquhoun, sometime during the past three weeks. b) the Immoral and Criminal Activities of Ramiro Morales at ICE between the years of 1995 and 2008, when he was dismissed. c) the Illegal and Criminal Activities of Ramiro Morales aka Dacian Jiminez and their associated companies between the years of 2009 and today's date, and now, d) the circumstances and events leading up to the suicide of Izabella Constantini/Roni in May of 2008."

He spoke for the best part of two hours. As he described what Morales had put Aileen Colquhoun through and how she had tried to control him to protect her parents and her former teachers, there were frequent softly whispered expletives, in Italian, from both Lucia and Eduardo, with Eduardo furiously writing notes in his large notepad.

He had then gone on to detail the work done by Gary Proud, the co-operation offered by DCS Goddard and the information held by the former editor of the Hive, ICE's newsletter, Winston Macauley. He avoided giving too much detail, he knew that it would only serve to confuse. He concluded by saying that although they had not yet obtained any definite proof, he felt fairly confident that Morales had been directly, or indirectly, responsible for the suicides of 32 undergraduate female students at ICE between the years of 1995 and 2008. As to the number of female undergraduate students he had sexually assaulted during this same period, he had no idea, but he would not be at all surprised to learn that the number was well in excess of 100.

Eduardo was livid with anger now, "How can that be, how is it that you have not put this man in jail years ago. How could the University Authorities allow him to continue to be a member of the Academic staff. It is outrageous."

Warbrick explained the difficulty of persuading the traumatised victims to come forward as witnesses against him. He explained the kind of processes these young women would be subjected to by defence counsel and how no-one had been prepared to face that kind of humiliation. They had either ended their lives or tried to forget their loathsome experiences.

Lucia took hold of her husband and said, in English, "It is the same the world over, here in Italy as well, especially here in Italy. I can totally understand what Lindsay is telling us and his frustration because of it." Eduardo looked earnestly at his wife and nodded.

Warbrick moved on, "We now come to the re-emergence of Morales into Aileen Colquhoun's life via the company that she had owned with the mechanic, Ken Stockdale. The company is called 'Avnav Parts and Services Ltd,' Morales bought into majority ownership of this company through the assistance of a third party, Trevor Byford, who Ken Stockdale had approached some months earlier, as Stockdale was keen to retire, and Byford was initially viewed as a potential replacement for him. Neither Stockdale nor Aileen Colquhoun had been aware of any association between Byford and Morales. If they had, they would not have gone within a million miles of him."

"Since that takeover, Aileen Colquhoun resigned her role as a director of the company but retained her minority shareholding. She took on a role as a Consultant to the Company, her sole objective being, the collection of evidence against Morales in order to gain a criminal conviction against him. We have since discovered that Morales' maternal grandmother was an

Italian migrant to Argentina at the turn of the $19^{th}/20^{th}$ centuries, I do not have her grandmother's name, but if you think it would be helpful, I can probably obtain it through the Policia Federal Argentina, who have been cooperating fully with DCS Goddard in London."

"We have since learned, confidentially, and via the good offices of your own State Police Force, that Morales changed his name from Ramiro Morales to Dacian Jiminez, in 2015. He now travels on a Panamanian passport, bearing that name. As far as I am aware, he does not yet know, that we know about both this name and passport change. I would like to keep it that way." He looked seriously at Eduardo and Lucia as he said this, and they nodded in acknowledgement.

Warbrick continued, "We now know that Avnav Parts and Services are registered in, at least, Argentina, Panama, and Taiwan. He has since established an additional aircraft repair business, known as 'The Faithful Falcon Flying School and Aircraft Repair' also in Taiwan and this morning we learned the name of the company which he has set up to illegally, and contrary to almost all International Aviation regulations, manufacture a whole range of aircraft parts, for a wide variety of type and design of aircraft. These parts are mostly for the light, and privately owned aircraft market, but we are also aware that he has had manufactured parts for older types of commercial fixed wing aircraft and some types of helicopters." Warbrick, aware of the circumstances surrounding the death of Eduardo's brother, Salvatore, could hear the intake of breath by both Eduardo and

Lucia, on receipt of this news. "This company's name is 'Intercontinental Precision Engineering' again in Taiwan but also owned by a Nominee Company in Hong Kong."

Warbrick now returned to the death of Aileen Colquhoun and tied that into his intended actions concerning the death of their daughter Izabella. "Aileen Colquhoun dedicated the last years of her life in endeavouring to uncover hard evidence linking Morales/Jiminez to the manufacture of illegal aircraft parts and, we believe, the installation of those parts into aircraft that subsequently suffered a catastrophic failure. We also believe that Aileen had been successful in her quest, which had culminated in her death."

"She suffered a particularly cruel death. Aileen had been a chronic aquaphobic since childhood, she was terrified of large bodies of water. I believe that Morales was well aware of that fact. He had her snatched, we believe by three men, although we are soon to establish the actuality of that belief. She was brought to a reservoir not far from our police station, where she was drugged to make her immobile, but not unconscious. She was then placed in a canoe and taken a short distance from the banks of the reservoir, into deep water, where her head was held beneath the water, until she had drowned."

"Susan here, visited the psychiatrist who had been treating Aileen for this condition since childhood. She described for Susan, the absolute terror that Aileen would have been subjected to during this episode. She did so by describing the effects of that terror on Aileen. It would have caused the excessive release of two hormones into her central nervous system, these hormones are adrenaline, of course, but also the lesser-known hormone of norepinephrine. These hormones speed up a person's pulse and respiratory rate, dilate pupils or temporarily mask pain. It would have been impossible for Aileen to take any action to defend herself or to extricate herself from her situation. What these hormones did do, was to prolong her terror."

"These three examples of human vermin, then calmly returned the canoe to the reservoir bank, overturned it, and left Aileen's body in the shallows of the reservoir, in a pathetic attempt to simulate a canoeing accident."

"We will be re-visiting the scene of her death following our return from here to Manchester, where there is an individual destined to 'assist us with our enquiries." There was a grim set to Warbrick's mouth as he said this. The expression though, was clearly recognised for what it was, by his three colleagues.

"And so, to the tragic loss of your daughter, we will ensure that we access all information held by the police and the coroner as a consequence of the police enquiry and subsequent autopsy. If you have any information yourselves then we would greatly appreciate receiving it. Similarly, if Izabella had made any friends at ICE that you are aware of, we would appreciate it if you could make them known to us. It is most important for us to speak to anyone who can shed light on Izabella's state of mind following her becoming aware of Morales' filming activity and also immediately prior to her passing."

Warbrick sat back in his chair, everyone was deep in thought, absorbing the horror of Aileen Colquhoun's death, overwhelmed by the total evil within this man known as Morales or Jiminez, but separately and collectively resolved, to deliver justice.

Lucia was the first to speak, "Lindsay, thank you for all of that, I am full of admiration for the work that you and Susan have been through, but that description must have been thoroughly draining. Can I suggest that we adjourn for lunch and collect our thoughts?"

20

Lunch was taken on the terrace on the foreshore of Lake Garda. Eduardo had taken Warbrick and Susan aside as they had vacated the first-floor conference room, "Lindsay, Susan," he said in his most courteous manner, "would you kindly excuse Lucia and I if we don't join you for lunch. You have provided us with much food for thought which I would like to discuss privately with Lucia prior to our afternoon session. I trust that you understand that I mean no offence, please forgive us?"

"Apologies not at all necessary Eduardo, I realise that I have dropped a considerable amount of information on both Lucia and you, let us not set a time for resumption of our discussions, just call us when you are ready. If necessary, and if you prefer, we could always postpone resumption until the morning, simply let us know."

Warbrick and Fellingham selected a shaded table and two chairs which provided the widest panorama of lake Garda. "I really must bring Gina here," said Warbrick as they sat down and awaited the arrival of the lunch steward.

DS Fellingham looked across at her boss, "I take it that you gave them that graphic description of Aileen Colquhoun's death in order to divert their attention from the death of their own daughter?"

"Partially yes," answered Warbrick, 'but I also wanted them to understand what a truly evil man Morales is. I need them both to be 1000% committed to his destruction, it is the only way we will fully succeed."

"I thought that they already were," added Fellingham, "committed to his destruction."

"No", said Warbrick, "that was just words, now they are truly angry and outraged, I saw Lucia's eyes as we left that room. Morales will receive absolutely no mercy from her."

They enjoyed a light lunch of poached salmon with salad, garnished with an exquisite dressing. The meal was complemented by a delightful example of the Garganega grape from Soave in the Veneto region of northern Italy. They enjoyed the relaxing ambience of the terrace and the breezes from the Lake provided maximum comfort. They had been on the terrace for three uninterrupted hours when Eduardo returned, apologising again, and suggesting that they should return to the first-floor conference room.

They did so and Eduardo began, as though having overheard Warbrick's comment that his earlier commitment had been 'just words,' "I didn't believe that I needed anything further to motivate my resolve to bring justice to my beautiful Izabella, but the information that you have shared with Lucia and

I today, has quadrupled our commitment to see this man, if not exterminated, then made to suffer the most painful of existences known to anyone."

"We have given considerable thought to all that you have told us, and it appears to us that there is a natural divide between the avenues that we should both pursue. The obtaining of illegal activity, within his businesses, leading to criminal charges, and the ultimate destruction of his business should, quite naturally fall to us. We are in a far stronger position, than the police in either of our countries, to be able to obtain the most comprehensive information, about each and every business, owned partially or totally by this man, anywhere in the world. I have extensive contacts in the international business and finance sectors. There are many people in both of these sectors who hold me in high regard, and I shall commence immediately, to discreetly use those contacts, to put together a complete portfolio and a plan of action for a pre-emptive strike against this man's empire. I expect to be in a position to execute that pre-emptive strike within three months of today's date. To assist us in this, it would be appreciated if you could provide us with all of the information uncovered by Ken Stockdale and Mary Stirling."

Warbrick nodded his assurances that this would be done before he then contributed to the discussions, "I am pleased to hear of your thoughts on the natural division of investigations and I could not agree more. I will forward the information that Ken and Mary have obtained and then I will instruct them to refrain from making further enquiries for fear of complicating your investigation."

"For our part, we will adopt a more aggressive examination of the circumstances surrounding Aileen Colquhoun's death. Similarly, we will re-open the enquiry into your daughter's death, please let us have whatever you have in that regard, and we will attempt to track down any of her former friends or colleagues. We have excellent sources of information on previous students of ICE and the Dean of Studies at ICE is now cooperating fully with us."

"One of our colleagues, in Manchester, has developed a source document identifying the countries of residence of each of the known female suicide cases which we believe are linked to Morales. We will now seek to confirm those details whilst also expanding the data to include the residential addresses of those victims, and the names of any other students at ICE who were friends with each of the deceased."

"We will also return to our quest to locate the former photographer, and rapist colleague of Morales, this Guevara or Gavara. In this regard I believe that London's Metropolitan Police will be best placed to assist us. I would also like to suggest that as you believe that you will be ready," he paused, "to launch a strike within three months, can we four meet again in six weeks' time. It may have to be in the UK though, I doubt that I shall be able to obtain funding for a further trip here."

Eduardo laughed, "My dear Lindsay, I feel that we four have already become close friends, united in a most overdue common cause. I would be delighted to arrange for your travel here if that would be your preference. Conversely, we do have a town house in Knightsbridge, maybe we should decide a little closer to the time."

Lucia interrupted, "No, I think that it should be here, you were saying last night Lindsay that your fiancée is a forensic pathologist with Italian ancestry, and you Susan, your fiancée has many connections with Italy. Why don't the four of you join us here in six weeks' time. I will have Vanessa make the arrangements."

Warbrick was whistling as he climbed the stairs to prepare for dinner that evening, Fellingham grinned to herself, it was only right that her boss enjoyed a little luxury before his retirement. God knows, he has given enough beyond the call of duty service, to the police force over the past forty years. How kind of Lucia to suggest it.

Over dinner that evening Eduardo said to Warbrick in a quiet aside, "How do you feel Lindsay in departing so far from standard police procedures, in pursuing this man. I hope that I am not causing you any embarrassment by suggesting what I have, and involving ourselves as I have?"

Warbrick thought for a few moments, "There would have been a time, many years ago, when I would have felt guilty simply by requesting your help. But over the years I have seen too many villains walk free following the intervention of a smooth-talking barrister, or worse, receive a minimal sentence for a horrific crime. That all changed when I began to have an interest in ancient Greek history and culture. Have you ever read any of Cicero's writing Eduardo?"

"Not that I can remember," replied Eduardo.

Warbrick looked up, his tired eyes twinkling, "Cicero wrote, in 60BC, 'The aim of justice is to give everyone his due,' that's all I want, is to give this bastard Morales his due," and he chuckled, but there was no humour in it.

"Did you also know that the ancient Greek word for justice is Dikaiosini, but if you research that word, you discover that it is synonymous with the ancient Greek word, Ekdikisis, which means vengeance. I think that the ancient Greeks had it absolutely spot on."

"You are a surprisingly erudite man, my friend," responded Eduardo, "I have taken solace in the words of the famous Irish playwright and critic, George Bernard Shaw when he said, 'Criminals do not die by the hands of the law, they die by the hands of other men.'"

21

DCI Warbrick and DS Fellingham returned to Manchester the following day. Warbrick had impressed upon her that she should admit, only, to the Roni's assisting in uncovering the links between the known companies owned by Morales/Jiminez, with any other companies, currently unknown to the police.

The following day, the three of them, DCI Warbrick, DS Fellingham, and DC Proud made an unscheduled visit to the offices of United Utilities at Trentabank Reservoir in the Macclesfield Forest. They had prepared themselves prior to this visit with DCI Warbrick arranging through DCS Speers for a warrant to search these offices and the homes of the Manager of United Utilities, George Stubbins, and his receptionist Gladys (she called herself Roxie) Brown.

They entered the offices, Warbrick flashed his warrant card and walked across the office to the door indicated by DC Proud. "You can't go in there," cried Roxie, 'he's in a meeting."

"Tough" said Fellingham.

Warbrick flung the door wide open, George Stubbins had been fast asleep on his couch prior to their arrival. He struggled to come awake, "What's going on, what's the meaning of all this, who the hell are you, how dare you burst in like this?"

"Wake up Sonny Jim, I am Detective Chief Inspector Warbrick, alongside me is Detective Sergeant Fellingham and Detective Constable Proud, you have already met. The death of Aileen Colquhoun is now a murder investigation, and it is looking highly likely that you are the person responsible for her death. What do you have to say for yourself?" began Warbrick.

"You must be fucking joking," spluttered Stubbins, "she died in a canoeing accident, nothing to do with anyone here."

"No, she didn't, she was rendered immobile through the illegal use of an immobilising substance and then, her head was held under water, until she drowned. She was absolutely terrified throughout this whole ghastly event. Where were you Mr Stubbins on the night of the 5th of April, this year?"

Stubbins had now turned white, "I don't know, I'd have to check, I wouldn't have been here at night in any event, I usually leave for home by 5.30pm."

Warbrick studied him with eyes that had scrutinised a thousand or more felons and were accustomed to pealing back the fabrication of lies and deceit. He said in a quiet voice hardened by accusation, "Let me help you Mr Stubbins, the 5th of April was the last of the five nights in which you had employed additional rangers to patrol the grounds surrounding the reservoir. Who was on duty that night Mr Stubbins?"

Stubbins was quivering now, "I'd have to check the roster."

"Oh, let me help you again Mr Stubbins," his voice was little more than a whisper and all the more sinister as a consequence, "we already have done, those splendid works of fiction that you provided for DCI Warburton from Macclesfield police. They clearly show that you were the nominated person for the night of 5th April. Memory a little clearer now, Mr Stubbins?"

The use of the term, 'works of fiction' to describe the documents he had given to DCI Warburton was rattling Stubbins, "Yes, yes, of course now I remember, it was a quiet night, and I used the time to catch up on my paperwork."

"Of course you did Mr Stubbins, we saw an example of that when we arrived earlier today. You also provided DCI Warburton with video security discs for the nights of the 1st through to the 4th of April, but not the 5th, why was that?"

"It must have been an oversight," stammered Stubbins.

"Of course, of course," said Warbrick, his voice dripping with disbelief, "could you please do that now."

"Certainly," replied Stubbins and he picked up his phone, depressed a single button and when it was answered said, "Miss Brown, could you bring in the video disc for the night of the 5th of April?"

They could all hear her reply, "It's not there Mr Stubbins, you remember we took them all out of their secure case and gave them to the police when they came here, the first time.

"Are you sure Gladys, the police are now saying that they don't have it, can you check again please?"

DCI Warbrick stood up, crossed to the window, looked outside for several minutes, then turned and spoke softly to DS Fellingham and DC Proud. Addressing them by their titles he asked them to leave the room, which they did.

He turned to face Stubbins, his face white with anger, "Mr Stubbins this is a murder investigation, one more lie from you and I will have you charged with obstructing police and attempting to pervert the course of justice, so fast you won't know what's hit you. I have here a document signed by DCI Warburton which clearly shows that he collected discs from the 1st to the 4th inclusive. That document is countersigned by you, and he thrust the document in the face of the trembling George Stubbins. "Now for the LAST time where is the disc for the 5$^{th\,of}$ April."

This last sentence was roared out so loudly that residents from the distant town of Cheadle may have heard it.

"I don't know where it is," he sobbed

"LIAR," roared Warbrick again. He called Fellingham and Proud back into the office and asked them for two documents.

He turned to George Stubbins "This Mr Stubbins is an arrest warrant, issued in your name and this here," he waved another document before George Stubbins, "is a warrant to search these premises and your home and the home of your lovely receptionist, Roxie, I believe you call her."

"What do you mean?" spluttered Stubbins.

"It means Mr Stubbins, that I am arresting you on the charge of accessory to the murder of Aileen Colquhoun, read him his rights DC Proud.

"No way," screamed George Stubbins.

DC Proud began, "George Stubbins you are charged with aiding and abetting the murder of Aileen Colquhoun by a person or persons unknown, on or about 5th April of this year. You do not have to say anything, but it may harm your defence if you do not mention, when questioned, something which you may later rely on in Court. Anything you do say may be given in evidence."

"This is all crazy, I need to call my lawyer," Stubbins was now a quivering wreck

"You do that, Sunshine, tell him or her to visit you at the Wilmslow nick where you will be waiting," he spoke into a shortwave radio and two uniformed policemen arrived to drag the still protesting George Stubbins into a waiting police car.

They returned to the outer office where Gladys 'Roxie' Brown was trembling in fear, tears pouring down her face. DC Proud repeated the 'rights' statement he had made to George Stubbins and Gladys Brown collapsed in her chair, "I haven't killed anyone," she wailed. She was also taken to a separate police car by two female police officers and driven back to Wilmslow police station.

The search squad then entered the offices, "Top to bottom," he ordered, "I expect you to find everything including last year's nail clippings, and if you don't, then you haven't been vigilant enough. Do I make myself clear?" There were several heads nodding in unison.

"DS Fellingham," Warbrick continued, "please take DC Proud with you and half of the search squad and visit Roxie's mother, at their home, with the search warrant. I will accompany the other half of the search squad and pay a visit to the Stubbins' home."

The two groups arrived at the homes of Gladys Brown and Mrs Stubbins, showed the occupants of these homes the search warrant, and took the search teams inside the two houses. Leaving the search squads in their separate places, the three officers returned to Wilmslow police station.

There had been at least one interesting development. Gladys 'Roxie' Brown terrified by the charge of accessory to murder levelled against both Mr Stubbins and her, had believed that she could demonstrate a perfect alibi to clear both of them. She was, of course, unable to communicate with Mr Stubbins, which is a little unfortunate, as he may have been able to persuade her to keep quiet. Instead, she asked to make a statement to a uniformed police sergeant, prior to the return of all three officers to the station.

In her statement she had sworn that she and Mr George Stubbins had spent the evening, and all of the night of the 5th of April, together in bed, in room 14, at the Hilltop Country House Hotel, on Flash Lane in Prestbury. She felt sure that the manager would confirm it because he had flirted with her questioning why she was with a man so much older than herself and offered himself as a much more suitable replacement. She had ended her statement with, 'so you see he couldn't have murdered that woman, he was in bed with me the whole time.' The police sergeant had not bothered to explain to her that they were both charged with being an accessory to murder and not the murder itself. What she had done was confirm that George Stubbins' statement, that he had been on watch at Trentabank Reservoir, was patently false.

As the evening progressed and merged into the next day, additional information came to light. Mrs Stubbins, not yet aware of her husband's nocturnal gymnastics with Roxie had been unable to explain the appearance of a lump sum of £5000 into an account, of which she had no prior knowledge, but was in the name of Mr and Mrs George Stubbins. Neither could she explain the withdrawal of 80% of that amount on the 5th of April. There had been several other deposits into this account, over the past six years, usually between the months of March and June. Each deposit had generally been in the vicinity of £500 and the combined total of these minor deposits amounted to in excess of £9000. The majority of these funds had also been withdrawn and Mrs Stubbins was unable to explain why, muttering only, that 'she had never seen a penny of it.'

Nothing had been forthcoming from the search of the United Utilities offices, not even the nail clippings that Warbrick had insisted that they find, but the search of 'Roxie's home was far more illuminating. Beneath her bed was a large briefcase, containing letters of an amorous and highly explicit nature from George Stubbins to his 'darling Roxie'. A quick glance at the dates on the letters revealed that the affair had been in existence for at least five years. There were items of moderately expensive female jewellery in the case, indicating that these were but some of the baubles that the amorous Mr Stubbins had been buying for his darling Roxie. There were also several letters which appeared to indicate that Mr Stubbins had been selling Heron eggs for quite some time which might serve to explain the source of the lesser deposits into the joint secret bank account. But the search squad had struck paydirt in one of the pockets on the lid of the briefcase. It was the security video of the 5th of April.

The video was examined in Wilmslow by Warbrick and Fellingham. It had clearly been filmed on an infra-red camera; the whole of the background was basked in a red glow. They viewed it within their conference room but although they could make out the figures of three men over the supine body of what they believed was Aileen Colquhoun, the images were not clear enough. Warbrick grunted, the Met have an excellent photographic laboratory in Lambeth, I wonder if DCS Goddard can help us. He picked up the phone and called Goddard, who was only too willing to help. The disc was on its way, that afternoon, to a scientific officer by the name of Brian Saunders, but with a letter attached which emphasised that DCS Goddard had asked for this work to be carried out as a matter of urgency.

Warbrick and Fellingham met with George Stubbins and his lawyer on the afternoon following his arrest. His lawyer protested that he had been waiting for over 24 hours for this meeting when Warbrick cut him short by saying that he should instruct his client not to lie to the police, doing so only complicates matters. Stubbins had clearly been rehearsing his statement that he had been on watch and inadvertently fallen asleep when Warbrick had abruptly stopped him.

"More lies George, did you never play that game liar, liar, pants on fire, when you were a child. The lawyer was about to interject when Warbrick continued, "Your co-accused has given us your alibi. She has told us that you and she spent the afternoon and the whole of the night, in bed, at the Hilltop Country House Hotel in Prestbury. Pretty difficult to maintain a vigilant watch on a heronry whilst at the same time ploughing your furrow, so to speak, on the delectable, if not too bright, Roxie. Incidentally George she told the desk sergeant that you were planning to leave your wife and take her to live in Rio, is that correct, you will have to sell considerably more heron's eggs to be able to do that."

"Oh shit," gasped Stubbins, "the stupid, stupid, bitch," he paused, the enormity of these facts descending on him, "Oh Jesus, my wife doesn't need to know does she, please tell me that you won't tell her?"

"Might be extremely difficult to keep it from her, George, Gladys Brown has already admitted that you were in bed together, in Prestbury. It is bound to come up in Court."

"Oh Christ, I'm toast," moaned a desolate George Stubbins.

Warbrick stood, "It may be a good time for you to have a chat with your client, Mr," he looked down at the lawyer's business card, "Sheldon, about cooperating with the police instead of lying to them."

He left them then, Sheldon shaking his head and Stubbins sobbing his heart out.

22

DS Fellingham was with DC Proud, in the large office. "More leg work for you Gary, I'm sorry to say. We need to expand the information we have on each of those 32 women who had been at ICE and had suicided largely because, we believe, of what Morales had done to them. The boss is keen to try to find addresses for all of them. I suspect that we will need the assistance of DCS Goddard, to at least open a few doors for you, and I'll talk to the boss about that. The Dean of Studies at ICE now appears to be cooperating with DCS Goddard and it may now, just be possible, for us to obtain unfettered access for you, on historical student records. What do you think?"

Gary Proud grinned, "Can't wait Sarge, do you think the boss would let me spend some time in the Big Smoke. If I could meet with Winston Macauley and his successor, Felicity Marshall, not forgetting this, Terri Ryan. I may be able to obtain more information about these victims, and Terri may have completed the list of some of the names of friends of the victims. I could also work with DCS Goddard's team on scrutinising the information that they have, in case they have addresses for the victims. Failing that perhaps the

Dean of Studies would allow me to peruse overseas student applications, addresses are bound to be there."

Fellingham laughed, "You're like a dog with a bone DC Proud. OK we'll go up and see the boss now if we can. There is one other thing that I have forgotten to mention. We now need to intensify our focus on this photographer, Carlos Guevara, or Guvara, I'm sure that the Met could help us with that. We'll raise that with the boss as well."

DCI Warbrick liked the idea, nodding frequently as both junior officers described their desired lines of enquiry. "I'll call Goddard now," was his only comment to them.

They remained in his office listening to one side of the conversation their boss was having with DCS Goddard. Within fifteen minutes Warbrick had reached some form of agreement with the Detective Chief Superintendent of London's Metropolitan Police.

"Right DC Proud," Warbrick began, "as from tomorrow am you are to commence a one-week secondment to DCS Goddard's team in London. If you need to extend that beyond one week, that shouldn't be a problem, but I need to emphasise that time is now of the essence in this enquiry and I would ask you work as diligently as I have always known you to, but also, as expeditiously as possible. Is that understood?"

DC Proud almost sprang to attention, "Yes Sir," he said.

Warbrick continued, "You need to take yourself to the accounts office, ask them for a travel warrant for a return train trip to London Euston, also ask them for an accommodation voucher for a hotel close to ICE. You could also ask for meal vouchers as well, but I wouldn't recommend it. The food normally served up with these vouchers I wouldn't even serve up to my neighbour's cat, and I dislike my neighbour's cat, intensely. You'd be better off buying your own meals, keep the receipts, and claim the expenses on your return. OK?" Proud nodded and grinned. "Off you go then, but before you leave here this afternoon, see DS Fellingham. There is something that she will need from you." Proud nodded, and grinned, again.

DC Proud turned and walked out of Warbrick's office but Fellingham had gathered that the boss wished to talk to her about something, but not in earshot of DC Proud.

When Proud had disappeared down the stairs Warbrick turned to Fellingham saying, "I had a call from Eduardo Roni about half an hour ago. He is in the process of organising flights around the world to set up a process to discreetly investigate Dacian Jiminez and his companies. He is doing this through third parties in order to avoid Jiminez discovering that he is behind these enquiries. He called me to ask me if I thought that the nationalities of Morales' many deceased victims would have any bearing on the places that he had set up businesses?"

"I told him that I didn't know, but that I didn't think so. He then asked me if I could provide him with the nationalities of victims, where a minimum of two victims of that same nationality, had suicided following their association with Morales. I told him that I would send that information to him, but I asked if he was intending to involve himself in the deaths of these young women. I added that I understood that enquiries regarding the student suicides was to be left to us. He immediately understood my concern and assured me that he had no intention whatsoever of involving himself in these deaths, he simply wanted to know these nationalities in order to avoid blundering into a territory where Morales/Jiminez was active but that we were not aware of."

Fellingham nodded, "That makes sense, it pays to be extra cautious with Morales, I like the way this man Roni thinks."

"So do I Detective Sergeant, so do I."

"I'll have DC Proud provide me with that information before he leaves for London," said DS Fellingham before she left DCI Warbrick's office.

Gary Proud tapped on her office door approximately thirty minutes later. She told him what she required before he 'had his holiday' in London.

"It will be more like a holiday Sarge he laughed; I like this sort of work and I'll be working with people that I've never met so I'm hoping to learn a great deal. I can give you those nationalities off the top of my head, I don't need to return to my office, they are scorched into my brain. Top of the list is Mexico, then Chile, then Spain. South Africa, and Argentina, are joint fourth. Then Germany, Sweden, and Italy, are joint fifth. I can give you the actual numbers if you wish but those are all of the nationalities with more than one victim."

DS Fellingham shook her head in wonderment, "I don't know where you store it all Gary, I really don't."

With a happy wave DC Proud left the police station for his home, he had much to do to prepare for his week in London. Fellingham had returned to her office reading through all of the notes that Mary Stirling had sent her. She was about to have them all copied, along with Ken Stockdale's notes, prior to sending the copies to Eduardo Roni as Warbrick had promised. She was interrupted by the soft buzz of her phone, an internal call, it was DCI Warbrick.

"Our disingenuous suspect wishes to amend his statement, I'm not altogether sure if this change of heart is due to the ministrations of his lawyer or the terror of confronting his wife with his tale of a five year long extra-marital affair. In any event he is being brought up to Interview Room 1 to advise of his amendments, I would like you to join me there."

DS Fellingham made her way to Interview Room 1 where she was joined by her boss, a few minutes later. A cuffed George Stubbins entered the room in the company of a large, and heavily muscled, constable.

"I want to know if we can do a deal?" Stubbins plaintively asked, "my lawyer said that the police sometimes do deals if the accused is able to assist them further with their enquiries." He was clearly quoting the formal words that his lawyer would have given him, particularly the, 'assisting you further with your enquiries' phrase.

Warbrick gave him the benefit of a long and withering stare, "Why would I ever consider doing a deal with the likes of you, in so much of a hurry to get away to shag your mistress that you totally ignored the plight of a young, innocent woman. Just tell us it all, and I mean ALL of it."

Stubbins collapsed, "I didn't know anything about the woman, honestly I didn't, they just gave me the money to stay away from the reservoir."

Warbrick glared at him, "So they gave you a large amount of cash to simply stay away from the reservoir, who did you think they were, Father Fucking Christmas and his Elves, I said all of it."

Stubbins shuddered under the sarcasm and began again, "A guy came to see me and asked if I would join him for lunch the following day as he had something to discuss with me." Warbrick said nothing, "I did have lunch with him, and he told me that he worked for a company who specialised in developing underwater designs for racing boats, from canoes to 18 metre racing yachts. He said that they had developed a revolutionary design, and he wished to conduct trials on a body of water as far away from unwanted eyes as possible, including mine. He asked if I would allow him to use the Trentabank Reservoir for the night of the 5th of April and the early morning of the 6th. He told me he would make it worth my while."

Warbrick interrupted then, "Who was this guy, had you seen him before, when did he come to see you on that first occasion, what did he offer you to make it worth your while?"

Stubbins reeled at the intensity of the questions, "I had never seen this guy in my life before, he gave me a business card with the name John Stone printed on it, but he didn't look English to me, there was a Mediterranean look about him. He came to see me the first time around the 15th of March, but I have the lunch date written in my diary, which you have. He offered me five thousand pounds to stay away from 5.30 pm on the 5th of April until 9.00am on the 6th.''

"So, he offered you five thousand pounds to allow him to conduct trials, on a boat, OVERNIGHT, I repeat, OVERNIGHT, and you didn't regard this as being suspicious?" Warbrick's incredulity was being stretched to breaking point.

Stubbins began to sob, "I didn't think about it, I know that it sounds stupid now, but I believed him," he paused, because he also told me that the actual trials would be at first light on the morning of the 6th, they would simply be setting up on the night of the 5th'' he paused again, "maybe I just wanted to believe him."

"Too bloody right, you wanted to believe him. OK Sonny Jim, how many other men were with him?" Warbrick snapped.

"I never saw anyone other than John Stone," sobbed Stubbins.

"What about the security video of the 5th of April, we have that now you know?"

"I never looked at it, I didn't want to know what was on it, I just hid it away so that no one could find it," a distraught Stubbins replied.

Warbrick turned to DS Fellingham and asked, "Please tell me that I am not going insane Detective Sergeant, did this man just tell us that he accepted five thousand pounds from a man he had never seen before, as payment for the use of the reservoir to conduct boat trials in the dark, and then, having believed this cock and bull story, totally avoided viewing the security video for fear of what it might show him. Is that correct Detective Sergeant?"

"Yes Sir, and you are not going insane Sir," replied DS Fellingham.

Warbrick turned to Stubbins, "I have listened to many tales over the years, where stupid men have allowed the small head of their penis to rule their larger head, that was allegedly provided to permit the function of logic. However, I have never heard such a pathetic and disgusting explanation to justify a few hours of carnal satisfaction, in absolute disregard for the obviously illegal activities being perpetrated on the reservoir that you were paid to protect and supervise. You knew that something untoward was to happen on the reservoir that night, not only did you fail to stop it, but you also failed to view the evidence that your own security cameras could have shown you. I have never known such an obvious case of aiding and abetting a murder in all my life. You may not know, so I am now telling you, in a recent change to the laws covering a case of murder, an accessory to murder now faces the same sentence as the actual murderer. Take him away constable."

The smell that now pervaded Interview Room 1 confirmed that George Stubbins had soiled his trousers.

23

Eduardo Roni had been busy over the two weeks following the return of Warbrick and Fellingham to the UK. He had been in touch with three close friends he had known over many years through several business ventures that he had embarked upon with each of them. They in turn had become quite wealthy and, without ever commenting upon it, knew that their wealth had been acquired, largely, through the contacts and advice provided to them by either Eduardo or Lucia Roni. His request to each of them had been quite simple, 'Find out everything you can about Dacian Jiminez, under no circumstances should this enquiry be traced to me.'

He had also read, thoroughly, the copied notes of Mary Stirling and Ken Stockdale which he had received five days earlier from DS Fellingham. He had been particularly interested in Ken Stockdale's comments about Gustavo Hernandez, the Purchasing Manager from the Faithful Falcon Flying School and Aircraft Repair in Taiwan, and his mistress Huang Jia-Li which had provided him with yet another reason to visit Taiwan.

Additionally, he had been in touch with his oldest friend, Cesare Sinarelli of Italian Military Intelligence.

Cesare was the only other person, besides Lucia and himself, who knew the full story surrounding Izabella's death, and the more recent fact that he had met with DCI Warbrick and DS Fellingham. His request of Cesare had been an unusual one for Eduardo but when he had explained his reasoning to Cesare, he had been only too happy to help. Eduardo was about to fly to Trieste, by helicopter, to meet this contact of Cesare's, Yevgeny Dolgopov.

Yevgeny had been recruited by Italian Military Intelligence following the covert identification of a Russian based hacker who had been attempting to break into the Italian Military's most sensitive computer sites. There had been something about these attempts, which the computer people in Military Intelligence in Trieste had believed to be a deliberate intent to expose the hacker himself. Cesare had investigated, the investigation had continued over an eighteen-month period before Cesare had been convinced of Yevgeny's genuine desire to defect. He had now been working for Italian Intelligence for close to five years and his talents had led to a vast increase in the data base of Italian Military Intelligence in respect of the workings of the most secret organisations within the modern Russia.

The flight to Trieste, in his self-piloted Bell Jet Ranger, took a little over one and a half hours and he was in Cesare's office thirty minutes later. Cesare suggested that he and Yevgeny meet in a small conference room at a nearby hotel, which Eduardo paid for. Cesare did not wish to incur the wrath of his military masters by utilising military resources, other than Yevgeny, for what was an entirely personal purpose. He had cleared the use of Yevgeny with his direct superior, who, when being given a broad outline of the reasons behind it, had endorsed Cesare's request, willingly.

Eduardo outlined what he was looking for to Yevgeny. When he had finished, Yevgeny shrugged his shoulders, "Shouldn't be a problem," he said confidently. "I'll do it all from home. I'll time my cyber 'visits' to each of these company locations to coincide with peak traffic time in each location, usually the first three hours of the working day. That way it will be more difficult for them to even notice an unauthorised 'visit'. I will be using a system, which I designed myself, to hide my identity. The encryption system is so impenetrable it is virtually impossible for anyone to discover who I am, or where I am located. Write down a schedule of the information you are seeking, if you know the location of the source information, write that down as well, if not, don't worry, I'll find it anyway."

Eduardo spent the next half hour filling two A4 pages of information that he was seeking. He handed it to Yevgeny, "How long do you think it will take?"

Yevgeny studied the A4 sheets, "Not too long I think, the longest period will be waiting for the correct time zones in each of the locations. I'll send you a message at the end of the week, if the message reads, 'your dog is ready for collection', it means that I have it all and you are welcome to come by to collect it. If the message reads 'your dog much improved' means I need a little more time. A message that reads, 'your dog has sadly experienced a relapse' it means that the cyber security system that I have encountered is far more difficult to countermand than I had first expected, and I am uncertain how long it will take me to overcome the problem. In that situation come back to Trieste and we will endeavour to find an alternative approach."

"I will be out of the country for the next four or five days, but I will be contactable either by phone or via e-mail. Please let me know should you require additional funds, and also let me have your banking details. Thank you for all your help," and Eduardo shook Yevgeny by the hand and made his exit.

His return flight took him to Verona International airport and not Sirminione. His helicopter was taken to one of the hangars used for the purpose of storing wealthy client's personal aircraft and he was driven to the main terminal to board his flight, and its first-class seat to Taiwan.

Arriving in Taiwan, he elected not to stay in Taipei but in the ancient capital of Tainan, on the opposite end of the island. Although Taiwan is known, economically, as one of the four Asian Tigers, alongside Hong Kong, South Korea, and Singapore, it is not home to the major multi-nationals found in those other three cities. Instead, its economy has thrived due to multiple medium sized businesses across the island. The owner of one such business, Chen Chin-Lung, had not just survived but flourished despite straddling the volatile divide between the pro-independence, 'Greens' and the pro-Unification 'Blues.' He and

Eduardo Roni had completed many successful dealings between themselves and become good friends in the process, Chen, in the best traditions of the inscrutable Chinese, had kept their friendship private and had never divulged or bragged about his association with the Italian billionaire. He had been an amazing font of knowledge, on all business happenings of any consequence, on the island as Eduardo had discovered many years earlier. He hoped that Mr Chen continued to maintain the same level of interest, for it was for this reason that Eduardo had chosen to come to Tainan instead of Taipei. Mr Chen lived in Tainan.

Eduardo had sent prior notice to Chen, of his intended visit to Taiwan including the name of the hotel he had booked in Tainan, the Taipung Suites on Yonghua in Anping District. He expected to find a message and an invitation to dinner from Chen, on his arrival, and he was not disappointed.

They met at Chen's elegant home where they had so frequently in the past. The routine was always the same, Eduardo would meet with Chen's gracious and now aging wife. Years before there had always been three children to inspect as well, but they had now moved onto lives of their own. After no more than five minutes of small talk, which usually included an enquiry into the health of the Pope, Chen would say something in mandarin and his wife would withdraw. They would then have the evening to themselves, to talk business.

They talked for a while about the general state of the Taiwanese economy, as they always did, with Eduardo refraining from asking, or speaking about the matter that was on his mind, until he had been invited to by Chen. Chen neither drank alcohol or smoked any substance, legal or otherwise, but he retained an excellent selection of fine wines and spirits for his guests and this night was no exception. There was an excellent, chilled, Pouilly Fuisse and a superb Pomerol available, for Eduardo, always at the correct temperature and appropriately decanted.

Finally, Chen raised his old eyes to Eduardo, "How can I be of assistance my old friend?"

"There is a company, or rather a series of companies, based here in Taiwan but owned by Nominees in Hong Kong, that I am interested in. Not necessarily to purchase, I have heard some disturbing things about them, but rather to understand if they might negatively impact on some of my other business interests," began Eduardo.

"Ah so," mused Chen, "and the names of these companies?"

"The Faithful Falcon Flying School and Aircraft Repair, and the Inter-Continental Precision Engineering Company,' answered Eduardo.

Chen looked at him for what seemed an inordinate length of time, "I have heard of these companies. Forgive me but I am surprised that you are interested in them. I have heard much talk; I have heard many say that these companies will bring discredit to Taiwan. I have heard that the owner, I believe he is from Panama, is a Piyan (an arsehole), so you intrigue me my friend."

Eduardo nodded grimly; he thought for a few moments thinking of how much to say to Chen. He was well aware that Taiwan continued to be largely a misogynistic society, where women who claimed to have suffered a sexual assault were, more often than not, regarded as bringing the problem onto themselves by either dressing or acting, provocatively. He decided to say nothing about the fate of his daughter, or any of the other students at ICE.

He now turned to Chen and answered him. "I am not surprised that this is what you have heard, I now know, that they are involved in both the manufacture and installation of illegal and unapproved aircraft parts. I understand that this practice has led to numerous aircraft catastrophes resulting in significant losses of human life. My own brother died from such a set of circumstances."

He omitted to mention that Salvo had died many years before Jiminez appeared on the scene.

"The man you are talking about is called Jiminez, he travels on a Panamanian passport, but he is not Panamanian. He is from Argentina; his birth name was Ramiro Morales, but he changed it several years ago, as the police in both Argentina and Great Britain were closing in on him."

"I am determined to destroy him and his companies, but my problem is that I don't know the extent of his empire and I need to know how far, and where it stretches, before I plan his downfall. I also need some proof of his illegal manufacturing processes so that I can notify the various Aviation Authorities about his activity and, illegal practice."

"You gladden my heart old friend," responded Chen, "I will gladly do all that I am able to see you succeed in this venture and rid our beautiful island of this egun (bad guy). What else can you tell me about this man or his businesses?"

"I can tell you of a major vulnerability in his enterprise," continued Roni, "there is a man, here in Taiwan with the name of Gustavo Hernandez. He is the Purchasing Manager for the Faithful Falcon Flying School and Aircraft Repair. He is currently having an affair with a young Taiwanese girl, thirty years his junior, with the name of Huang Jia-Li. I understand Miss Huang is endeavouring to save sufficient money to permit her to relocate to Hollywood, she apparently has ambitions in that direction. The point is that Senor Hernandez has access to, not simply all of the aircraft parts being manufactured by the Inter-Continental Precision Engineering Company, their wholesale prices, and the comparative prices of legally produced and approved parts for the identical purpose, but also the means of identifying the illegally manufactured parts as opposed to the legally produced parts, in his warehouse."

Chen smiled at Roni, "I have heard of Miss Huang and her apparently highly flexible body, she is much in demand by visiting Japanese businessmen. I have also heard that she does engage on occasions, in her areas of specialisation, with two younger female colleagues, for a hugely increased fee you understand. You may safely leave this issue with me."

24

DC Proud was welcomed into the offices of the Metropolitan Police in Agar Street, Charing Cross and immediately escorted to the office of Detective Sergeant Paul Asquith, who stood, came around his desk and shook DC Proud's hand. It was a firm handshake.

"It's Gary isn't it," he said, "DCS Goddard has apparently been mightily impressed with you, you must tell me sometime how you managed to do that, he is not the easiest man to impress. Welcome to the Met, I believe that we will be working together on this ICE business, I understand that your first task is trying to track down addresses of the victims of that scumbag Morales. We don't have them here, but I have arranged for you to be given access to past student records. The Dean of Studies, Professor Alexis du Plessis has set it up."

DC Proud was delighted, he hadn't known what to expect, half fearing that he would be treated like the provincial country bumkin on his first visit to the 'Big Smoke' but no, Paul Asquith could not have been friendlier. To find, within minutes of his arrival, that a visit to ICE to view past student records, had already been set up, was terrific, and he said so.

Paul grinned, "All part of the service," he said, "I've also mentioned to Felicity Marshall, the editor of the 'Hive' that you might wish to speak with her, but she has told me that there are plans for her to meet with you today. She has indicated that she would look forward to meeting anyone who could bring justice to all those unfortunate young women. This is her extension number at the College, you can call her from the Records office when you have finished there. Anything else I can do to help?"

"This is all great Sarge, I couldn't be more grateful, and I really hate to ask, but I am also trying to track down the photographer who worked with Morales, and who a couple of the unfortunate women identified as having raped them in addition to the rape they suffered from Morales. His name is Carlos Guevara or Guvara, and I was wondering, on my trip down here this morning, if any of the guys from your Vice squad had come across him. Would it be possible to ask?"

DS Asquith muttered, "Good thinking Gary, I've a few good contacts in Vice, I'll get on to it."

The Dean of Studies at ICE may well have believed that DC Proud could be given free access to the records of past students but the Librarian in charge of the records, a formidable woman in her sixties, was having none of it. "Professor du Plessis should know better, I can't allow any Tom, Dick, or Harry to simply wander in here and demand to see past student records, such behaviour would contravene every piece of legislation ever written to protect the rights of the individual. No young man, you give me names of the women whose addresses you are seeking, and I shall endeavour to find them for you. I don't know how long all that will take though, I understand that these women were students her over a fourteen-year period. It could take some time."

DC Proud was inclined to give this woman, he looked at the name badge on her fulsome bosom, Geraldine Withers he read, short shrift over her comment about any Tom, Dick, or Harry but he decided against it.

"It was because Professor du Plessis realised the amount of work involved in accessing this information that he believed that I could relieve you of the burden by accessing the records myself. However, if you wish to do it, be my guest. I need to remind you though that this an ongoing murder investigation and unless you have the information I require, to me, within 24 hours I shall have to ask Detective Chief Superintendent Goddard to apply for a warrant to search your entire records. The issue of such a warrant would result in approximately five police officers descending on your domain and pulling all of the files."

At the mention of a Detective Chief Superintendent and a Search Warrant, Geraldine Withers visibly deflated. "I'll do what I can," she said.

"You do that, remember 24 hours from now," and DC Proud left the records office.

He entered an adjacent office and asked the receptionist there if he could call the Editor of the 'Hive' and showed the extension number given by DS Asquith. The receptionist smiled, did not ask him to identify himself, and pushed the telephone across to him. Felicity Marshall picked up almost immediately and, hearing his name, provided him with directions to her office and said that she was free to see him as soon as it suited him. He crossed the campus and five minutes later he was in her office.

Meeting her he instantly remembered Winston Macauley's description of her being. 'a tad Joyce Grenfell 'ish' as she resembled a rather goofy looking schoolgirl whose appearance had not changed over the past thirty years except for the greying of her hair. She could not have been more friendly though and was boiling a kettle of water in order to make coffee, when he arrived.

She had been at ICE since 2016, so she had never met Morales, but she had, or rather the 'Hive' had a vast array of photographs of him which she had put together for DC Proud's benefit. She also had the completed list of friends of the victims compiled by Terri Ryan. Seeing these photographs triggered a memory in Gary Proud's mind, something that Winston Macauley had told them, "Do you have any photographs of the photographer, Carlos Guevara or Guvara, the students used to call him Che?"

"I believe so," she said, spun around in her chair and called into the adjoining office, "Terri dig out what we have on Carlos Guvara, you know the photographer of those tango classes, ASAP please."

Felicity turned to DC Proud again, "This is a terrible business, Winston tells me that you are investigating the death of Aileen Colquhoun who had been a student here and one of the victims of Senor

Morales, may he rot in hell. I wasn't here during his time, but I have made friends with some of the students who went on to do a master's degree having suffered the abuse from Morales. One of them, a South African woman was also a friend of a lady by the name of Annika Kampfert, who took her own life after Morales published pornographic photographs of them both. He also sent these photographs to her family, her father was a Minister in the Dutch Reformed Church of South Africa, and she couldn't bear the shame."

DC Proud could feel his pulse quicken, a living victim of abuse, it could provide a vital breakthrough. He tried to control his excitement, "Do you continue to keep in touch with this friend of yours, the lady who was also abused?"

"I do," replied Felicity, "not as often as I once did but at least three or four times each year."

"Would you be willing to contact her again to ascertain if she is prepared to discuss her experience with the English police. If she would prefer to speak to a woman about it my Detective Sergeant in Wilmslow would be available. Her, my Detective Sergeant's name is, Susan Fellingham. You can tell her that one of the former sexual assault victims of Morales has now been murdered, and we are of the strong opinion that Morales had something to do with it. Any help that she can provide would be greatly appreciated. What is your friend's name by the way?"

"Yes, her name is Loraina Beyers, and I will send her an e-mail this evening. How long do you expect to be in London DC Proud?" asked Felicity Marshall.

Before Proud could answer a beautiful young woman in her mid-twenties came in clutching a file. DC Proud could feel his pulse quickening again, but this time, for entirely different reasons.

"This is Terri, DC Proud, Terri Ryan. Terri this handsome chap is Detective Constable Gary Proud," and Gary could feel the colour rushing to his face.

Terri Ryan laughed, "And you've been hogging him for the past thirty minutes, it's very nice to meet you Detective Constable, here are all the photographs that we have of one Carlos Guvara, formerly of Bahia Blanca Argentina. Has Felicity given you that list that I put together of the girls of the same nationality who attended ICE at the same time as that list of girls that Winston Macauley gave me. This is all very intriguing Detective Constable; would you care to elaborate a little on why you require this additional information?" As she said this, she looked at him coquettishly, she had the most beautiful eyes, and he could feel his heart pounding in his chest.

Gary struggled to regain his composure, and with trembling hands, he opened the file that she had given him. A ferret faced man peered out from the manilla folder. There were only five in total and the clearest of them was the one he had first viewed, "Can I have a copy of this please?"

Terri smiled, she had the loveliest smile "I'll have it done this afternoon, say by three, if you want to call back then I'll have it for you."

He spluttered his thanks whilst avoiding looking into her eyes, which he felt sure were teasing him.

Felicity brought him back to the point of his visit, "Is there anything else we can help you with DC Proud?"

"Yes, to answer your question Terri, about the list that you have so kindly compiled for me, we are trying to trace any girls who were friends with the girls on that first list. The one Winston Macauley gave you. It is possible that some of them may be able to help us with our enquiries. In addition, do you have a mailing list for former students who wish to continue to receive the 'Hive?'"

Felicity Marshall nodded. "Would it also be possible to have a copy of that, I have asked Geraldine Withers to provide me with the addresses of those ICE students who suicided after their experiences with Morales, and she has promised to have it to me by tomorrow am. It would be helpful to compare those addresses with those that you have, I realise that it is most unlikely that the families of those poor girls would continue to take the 'Hive', but you never know."

Terri was the first to respond, "I'll do that for you as well, I'll also try to have that completed by three pm, will that be OK?" She then added, "In what way could they help you with your enquiries?"

Now he knew that she was flirting with him and chose to ignore the second part of her question, "That would be great," he said, "the least I can do is buy you a drink for your trouble. Will you join me later for a drink, Terri."

"Thank you I'd love to," and winking broadly at Felicity she sashayed from the office.

In order to distract himself, or his imagination, from the ministrations of the gorgeous Terri Ryan he decided to call Olivia Mendez at the Santander Bank in Regent's Place London. It took three diverting's, but he finally spoke to her. He introduced himself and then told her that he had been given her name by ICE following the obituary she placed in the Hive magazine all those years previously. He asked if she had time for coffee and she replied that she didn't. He then asked if she was prepared to answer his questions over the telephone. Her answer was a suspicious, "It depends on what those questions are?"

"I suppose that I gained the impression from the thoughtful wording in your obituary that you were surprised when your friend Rita ended her life?"

"Yes and No," came the answer. Before he could ask the obvious question, she added, "Yes because she told me that she would not let up until she had prosecuted him and she sounded extremely determined, but then, no, because I knew what she would be forced to go through in the Courts, and I figured that it all just became too difficult. I was sorry that she didn't pursue it though, that bastard Morales deserved everything that could be aimed at him, he was an absolute monster."

"Thank you, Olivia, for sharing that with me, would you be willing to speak with my Detective Sergeant, she is a woman and wishes to try to obtain justice for Rita."

"Yes, I would, but only outside of working hours, things are quite strict here."

He had managed to put fifty metres between himself and the Hives offices by walking as casually as possible, but he was excited by the prospect of having a drink or two with Terri, she really was one of the most beautiful women he had ever seen. He brought his mind back to focus on the key issues that he had learned from Felicity, and he decided to call DS Fellingham.

He told her briefly of his progress so far and the exciting news about a living survivor, resident in South Africa, who had been a friend of another South African student at ICE who had suicided. He gave the name Loraina Beyers to DS Fellingham and also told her that he had suggested that this Loraina, could contact DS Fellingham if she wished to discuss her experience with another woman. He also told her of his conversation with Olivia Mendez. DS Fellingham had ended the call with "Great work Gary, I'll let the boss know, keep me posted."

He returned to the 'Hive's offices at 3.00pm and Terri had completed the tasks that she had promised to do. There were five copies of the photograph of Carlos Guvara and the extensive mailing list of 'Hive 'readers. Terri had also cleared it with Felicity Marshall that she was able to finish early that day and she suggested that they move away from the ICE campus and visit the Harp pub in Covent Garden as it wouldn't be too busy at this time of the day. She linked her arm through his as they made their way to the pub. She was quite tall, the top of her head being level with his eyes and Gary stood at a little over six feet. She was incredibly easy to talk to and he had the strongest feeling that he should pinch himself, he was sure that he must be dreaming.

25

DS Susan Fellingham received the enhanced photograph of the man George Stubbins identified as John Stone from the Met photographic lab in Lambeth. She opened the envelope, the swarthy features of a man of Latin American origins were clear for her to see. She called DCI Warbrick to check if he wished to allow George Stubbins to confirm that this was the man he had met, before she began her troll through the international 'villains' websites. He did so but also said that he would confront Stubbins with her. 'He's not going to let up on this bastard any time soon she thought,' but she had absolutely no sympathy for the man, supposedly a senior employee of a large company, who so casually had abandoned a young woman to a terrifying death.

Stubbins was brought from his holding cell; he had now been formally charged with 'Accessory to Murder' and was due to appear in court later that day. Warbrick had petitioned that bail be refused and Fellingham had no doubt that his petition would be granted, the charge was that serious. She was also aware that Stubbins' wife had, so far, not been to see him in prison. No doubt, she had learned by now, of his long-standing affair with Gladys 'Roxie' Brown. The said Miss Brown had now been released on the minor charge of aiding and abetting an accessory to murder and was no doubt regaling other employees of United Utilities with how poor Mr Stubbins had been so badly misunderstood by his wife.

George Stubbins had now descended into the state of self-pity, and he sullenly studied the floor as DCI Warbrick placed the photograph of 'John Stone' before him. "Is that the man you know as John Stone?" demanded Warbrick.

"Yes," replied a surprised Stubbins, "where did you get the photograph?"

Warbrick and Fellingham simply stared at him in amazement and had Stubbins returned to his cell without making any further comment.

"How did that stupid prick ever get a job as a Manager with United Utilities?" queried Warbrick. He was about to say, "Roxie must have fucked his brains out," but he fortunately remembered who was with him and held his tongue.

They quickly learned that John Stone was, in reality, Juan Aiza, which is Spanish for John Stone. 'Obviously feeling so confident that they didn't need to try too hard,' muttered Warbrick as he was reading the lengthy crime sheet. He was wanted by the police in Mexico and Argentina on charges of Grievous Bodily Harm (GBH), extortion, racketeering and living off the immoral earnings of several women. There had been a charge of assault levelled against him in Taiwan some years earlier, but the charges had been dropped by the victim for unspecified reasons. There was no extradition agreement between the UK and Taiwan but there was one between Hong Kong and the UK.

"It's a long shot," remarked Warbrick, "but pass his details to the Hong Kong Authorities, if he puts his foot anywhere on their patch, I want him arrested and deported back here. I think that they will cooperate, after all he's not a Chinese national."

He read further down the notes attached to the crime sheet. "He is described here as Senior Vice President in charge of Security, I think that our Mr Stone is No2 to Dacian Jiminez, now wouldn't he make an interesting catch."

Later in the morning she received a scanned copy of the photograph of Carlos Guvara, sent to her by DC Proud. There was a note attached to it, 'A new pin-up for you, you should leave it lying around at home to give Alex something to be jealous about. I am meeting with someone from the Vice Squad tomorrow who thinks he knows the whereabouts of Senor Guvara. Will keep you posted. Cheers! Gary.

'Cheeky sod,' she said to herself, 'if I left that lying around as though I were interested, Alex would think I was desperate.'

DC Proud had also sent her the list of possible friends of some of the other victims of Morales and she decided to try to establish some links. She spent the next two hours telephoning wherever she could, which was mostly confined to the European countries due to time differences elsewhere. She also realised that she didn't speak any of the European languages that she was about to call so that she would be dependent on them understanding English or at least being able to answer the simple question of 'were you a friend of such and such a girl.'

She managed to speak to three Spanish girls who had been at ICE during the correct period, two Swedish, two German, one Italian, one Danish and one Irish. Of these ten girls only six had been friends with the relevant girl who had suicided, but of these six, two had been surprised that their friend had ended her life. They had been convinced that these women would have pursued Morales through the courts.

She gave it further thought, I believe that we need a team of interpreters to follow this up with all of these cases. I'll talk to the boss about it. I have to try to find a way of bringing Aileen Colquhoun's murderer within reach.

She pondered at her desk for a while, she decided to call Lucia Roni, she too had seen the look in Lucia's eyes when Warbrick had finished his description of Aileen Colquhoun's death, Lucia would have no mercy for Jiminez/Morales or any of his associates.

She picked up the phone and called the number that Lucia had given her. A female voice that she did not recognise answered "Pronto."

"Vorrei parlare con la Signora Roni per favore?" (May I speak with Signora Roni please.)

"Chi sta chiamondo?" (Who is calling)

"Signorina Susan Fellingham."

"Attendere prego." (please wait)

A few moments later Lucia's voice came over the phone, "Susan how lovely to hear from you, how are you, how are things at your end?"

Susan warmed to the call; she had become quite fond of Lucia Roni even though she was probably old enough to be her mother. "We're progressing," she said, "we have arrested the guy who abandoned Aileen on the night of her murder, and we have been able to identify the actual murderer. Unfortunately, he is based in Taiwan, and we don't have a repatriation agreement with Taiwan."

"That's great news," responded Lucia, "how can I help?"

"The actual murderer's name is Juan Aiza; his title shows him to be the Executive Vice President in charge of Security. We think that he is Jiminez/Morales 2 I/C. I know that Eduardo is exploring the businesses associated with Jiminez and I was wondering if he were able to come up with any reason that might force Senor Aiza to visit the UK any time soon. I was thinking that maybe something could arise with Avnav parts and Services in Macclesfield that would warrant the attention of the Executive Vice President in charge of Security."

Lucia chuckled, "I almost feel a little sorry for Senors Jiminez and Aiza, almost but not quite enough, I'm sure that we can come up with something that will cause Senor Aiza to come scurrying to the UK. I'll discuss it with Eduardo, have your Immigration Authorities primed and ready. On a separate note, have you discussed with your fiancée the possibility of him coming with you to see us again in a few weeks' time. I read an article about him in an art magazine over here. It seems that he is highly regarded by not just the church authorities but also by those who have the wherewithal to purchase highly expensive works of art, how did you meet him?"

Susan couldn't resist saying it, "He was in custody, it was the only thing that I could think of to keep him closer to me for a little longer, and it worked." She held on to the phone until the silence of incredulity was replaced with a huge giggle of laughter. She chuckled to herself, I'd better keep my eye on Lucia Roni, I've made Alex sound far more intriguing that he really is. At least I think I have, or maybe I have yet to discover more intriguing things about him.

26

Eduardo had returned to Sirminione. His study in his home was extremely large and it needed to be, every horizontal surface was covered in paper. His international business associates had not let him down. He now knew that the Jiminez empire was mostly focused on Spanish speaking countries with the exceptions of Taiwan and the UK. The aircraft parts and repair businesses were located in Mexico, Panama, Argentina, Spain, the UK, and Taiwan, but the parts manufacture was confined to only one site: the Intercontinental Precision Engineering Company also in Taiwan. He had received financial reports and company balance sheets from each of the five Avnav Parts and Services companies in Argentina, the UK, Panama, Mexico, and Spain. The single aircraft repairing company of the Faithful Falcon Flying School and Aircraft Repair in Taiwan and the single manufacturing arm of Intercontinental Precision Engineering Company, also in Taiwan. This latter company was by far the largest, but all seven companies were profitable, if somewhat erratic, in their performances.

He had learned that the companies in Central and South America had been set up with debt financing from two banks, one in Panama, and the other in Mexico. Each debt was fully secured utilising the assets of land, buildings, and equipment, owned by the five separate Avnav Parts and Services, the single entity of the Faithful Falcon Flying School and Aircraft Repair Company and the huge complex of Intercontinental Precision Engineering. His finance colleagues had told him that there were some concerns held by the two banks, that the rising level of interest rates due to inflation in both Mexico and Panama, together with the mounting provision for bad debts appearing in the balance sheet of the Faithful Falcon Flying School and Aircraft Repair company, were giving cause for concern about the ability of the group of companies to continue to service its commitments. The bank in Mexico had launched its own confidential enquiry into the reasons behind the rising provision for bad debts and were not liking what they were hearing. His closest colleagues were telling him that it was highly likely Senor Jiminez would soon be called to a meeting with both banks for what is understatedly called a 'Please Explain' meeting.

He had also received a report from the Head of Surgery at the Oncology Hospital that he owned, based in Brescia, fifty kilometres west of his home. He had purchased the hospital in order to maintain his interest in the subject which had occupied a large slice of his life and in which, he continued to be, intensely interested. He occasionally practiced there, and privately wished that he could increase this role.

He had not been surprised with the content of the report. The hospital, he had known from the outset, faced an uncertain future. Developments in cancer treatment had led to a multi-modal approach where combinations of surgery, radiotherapy, and chemotherapy were proving to be, by far, the preferred route for treatment, for all but a few, of the solid tumour cancers, such as prostate, and localised colon cancers. Even the solid carcinomas of breast cancers were now being treated with a combination of surgery and radiation therapy.

The report that he had now read reflected the declining occupancy rates and the comment from the Head of Surgery, a close friend, and the appointed Godfather to Izabella, had been apologetically stark in its forecast; 'The situation at the hospital now has reached the point where hard decisions need to be made. Although it is likely that a surgical solution to prostate cancer can be expected to continue for several more years, the treatment of solely patients such as these, cannot be expected to sustain the hospital. A change of use to a day patient surgical centre presents, as I have previously advised, the best possible future option, but I have recently received an enquiry which I had never before considered. The Polizia Penitenziaria (Prison Service) have enquired as to our interest, in providing a secure facility for prison based male patients requiring prostate surgery. The numbers they are quoting are quite staggering. I am completely unsure as to your likely reactions to this proposal, but we can discuss further if you are, in fact, interested.'

Eduardo read the report again, interesting, most interesting, he thought.

The next report he examined was from his old friend in Taiwan, Chen Chin-Lung. He always wrote in the romantic and highly descriptive manner which his classical mandarin training had given him, even though he wrote to Eduardo in English. He always commenced with, "It gives me great pleasure to advise." Even if the next sentence was to advise on the collapse of a business. On this occasion however, Eduardo was pleased with his report. Mr Chen advised that Senor Gustavo Hernandez was in high spirits, he had advised his closest Taiwanese friends that his Company had recently received multiple orders for the installation of highly expensive aircraft parts, on multiple aircraft being brought back into service by an air-freight company based in Macao. This is turn had required Senor Hernandez to place a significant order for these same parts from the manufacturers. He failed to mention that the manufacturers in this case were the Intercontinental Precision Engineering Company.

What Senor Hernandez also failed to mention to his Taiwanese friends was that the proceeds from this success would provide him with the necessary funds for extended nights with Huang Jia-Li and her two colleagues, Zheng Chia-Hao, and Liao Hui-Fang. He failed to mention this to his colleagues, but it did not matter, they learned soon enough from the mouths of Jia-Li, or Chia-Hao or Hui-Fang who regaled them with crude stories about the antics and pathetic performance of the Fankui (evil foreigner) who had paid them many US dollars for each night with the three of them. Chen had learned through his sources that Hernandez was paying Jia-Li 20,000 US dollars each night for the three, but she was only paying her two younger colleagues 1000 US Dollars each, she was therefore pocketing 18,000 dollars for each night with Senor Hernandez. At that rate, Hollywood would soon be in sight.

Chen also attached the two invoices that Hernandez had obtained. How he, Chen, had obtained them, Eduardo never asked, and would not have been told, had he done so. The first one was from the Intercontinental Precision Engineering Company to the Faithful Falcon Flying School and Aircraft Repair reflecting the prices for the parts that Ken Stockdale had previously obtained. The second invoice was from an alleged account of the Faithful Falcon Flying School and Aircraft Repair to the Macao Company. There was an 800% markup for each item on the second invoice compared to the first. The alleged Faithful Falcon account number was in fact a Gustavo Hernandez account, he simply paid the original Precision Engineering account from this and donated the proceeds to his carnal, and less than gymnastic, pleasures.

Mr Chen's final advice was to identify the location to which the purchased parts had been sent. It was never to Macao.

As Eduardo was re-reading this report from Chen he received a text message on his phone, 'Your dog is ready for collection,' was all that it said. He had arranged with Yevgeny that on receipt of this message he would reply, 'My brother is now taking custody,' which was a message to Yevgeny to send the entire volume of files by encrypted message to his home. He looked forward to reading it and developing his plans a little further.

When the file or files came, they were priceless in their completeness. Every e-mail between the various companies, particularly those between the manufacturing company and the companies involved in the subsequent installation or repair, was there. It appeared that almost every invoice, ever issued, by any of the companies was also included. It did not take a mathematical genius to calculate that the mark up between the prices for parts manufacture by Precision Engineering would increase by, in excess of 1000% for every part that was subsequently invoiced as being a genuine and authorised part.

There was a complete inventory of all parts manufactured by Precision Engineering for each of the installation and repairing companies. There had been a massive amount of production in the earlier part of the financial year, but the last several months had seen a marked downturn in manufacturing production. As Eduardo examined these numbers it appeared that several of the installation and repairing companies had grossly overestimated their requirements. This was particularly true of Avnav Parts and Services in Macclesfield UK. The erratic performances of these companies were now more clearly understood.

There was one file that contained the complaints on which the provision for bad debts was based. The major complainant was a mainland Chinese aircraft repairing company who had purchased parts via the Faithful Falcon Flying School and Aircraft Repair rather than the Precision Engineering Company. This puzzled Eduardo to begin with, but he finally worked it out that Jiminez had not wanted to risk this new client in mainland China finding out that these parts were manufactured by a Company also owned by him. In reading between the lines, it appeared that Jiminez was preparing to fold the Faithful Falcon Flying School and Aircraft Repair Company, and walk away from the claims, in order to protect himself, and the other companies. Eduardo made a note to embark on further research on this Chinese Company, he thought that they may prove to be a diversionary if not a valuable ally. There was also another complainant, this time based in Wales, with a complaint about Avnav Parts and Services based In Macclesfield England. The wording of the letters from the lawyers of this complainant, was becoming increasingly threatening. Trevor Byford had exacerbated this situation simply by ignoring the lawyer's letters.

He then reached the final file, it was in a different coloured folder, blue, to the others which were all cream. The heading on the blue file was headed 'Bluebird.' He read it with increasing but worrying interest. He spent over two hours reading it and then decided that he must speak with Lindsay Warbrick about it.

He then realised that he was missing an important document. One that would not be available from Yevgeny's detailed search of Jiminez's companies. He needed someone to carry out a detailed examination of all the aircraft parts that he was now aware were being manufactured by Precision Engineering. He thought of Ken Stockdale. Ken would be perfect. He should call Lindsay Warbrick to see if he could help set up Ken's assistance. Lucia had told him about Susan Fellingham's call. He now believed he knew of a way that Juan Aiza could be persuaded to fly to the UK.

He called Lindsay Warbrick; he was about to head off to London on a quest to track down the photographer involved with Ramiro Morales. He was pleased to hear from Eduardo. They updated one another in a general manner both men acutely aware that phones can be tapped. They avoided giving specific details for this reason. Eduardo began, "I may have a way of persuading your person of interest to come and talk to you, we can discuss details when we meet, in the meantime could you persuade Ken to come and spend some time with me at my home. I need his spreadsheet expertise."

Warbrick's heart skipped a beat, it would be fantastic if Eduardo knew of a way of bringing Juan Aiza to the UK. Warbrick would have him banged up as soon as his feet touched UK soil. He responded to Eduardo' second comment, "I'm sure Ken will be happy to help, Susan has his phone number, I'll have her phone him this evening. Shall I ask her to ask him to call you?"

"That would be perfect," replied Eduardo.

In fact, Eduardo received the phone call from Ken within half an hour of hanging up from Warbrick. DS Fellingham had called him before they left for London.

Ken was quite excited, "I hear that you may need a little help with something, if it's within my ability to do so, you have only to ask."

"Thanks for calling back, Ken, that was incredibly prompt. Yes, I do need help with a spreadsheet that I need to put together. Would you be free to pop over here for a few days, we have plenty of room. I can arrange to have a return ticket available for you at Manchester Airport and I'll have Vanessa pick you up there and bring you here."

"I could come over in the morning, is that soon enough?" asked Ken.

"Perfect, give me your phone number and I'll have Vanessa organise the tickets and call you. I look forward to seeing you tomorrow."

27

DC Proud woke up on the morning following his date with Terri Ryan, in a condition many psychologists would describe as 'emotional euphoria.' The evening had flown by, they had enjoyed several drinks at the 'Harp' before managing to secure a table at a small Italian Bistro which Terri knew, and where she was known by the proprietor. Conversation had come easily, something that he rarely experienced on the first night of a date. She was completely relaxed with him, she laughed frequently and naturally, and she appeared to have a genuine interest in him, his family, and his aspirations in the police force.

She told him that she was from Shrewsbury in Shropshire. The only daughter and middle child of an architectural draftsman father and a mother who was a high school teacher of English. She had two brothers, one older, who had taken a First at Cambridge in Civil and Structural Engineering and was now working in Scotland, and one younger, who had recently been accepted at the University of Bristol studying for a science degree in geology. When asked about herself, she had modestly explained that there was no scientific blood in her, she had completed an arts degree in musical composition at Liverpool University and had a passion for classical music.

She had thought it hilarious when he had described himself as a modern day 'Hobbit' living in a 'Granny flat' at the bottom of his parent's garden. He had a much older sister and the 'Granny flat' had been built for her when she had married Alistair, a meteorologist. They had since emigrated to Canada, where he was a meteorologist based in Gander in Newfoundland. His parents continued to live in Knutsford where they had been since they had first married. His father was a cabinet maker who was helped by his mother to run the business. Gary had told her that his father had been disappointed that he hadn't wanted to join him in the business, as he had, apparently, shown talent with his early woodworking efforts, but now seemed resigned to the fact that his son's future lay in the police force. As he related this part of his story, he realised that he had never mentioned this aspect of his life to anyone else, she was that easy to talk to.

She told him that she shared a house in Barnes with two post-graduate students from ICE. She light-heartedly told him that sometimes it felt like she was living in a railway station as there was so much coming and going of a variety of her house mates' friends. He insisted on taking her home by advising that she had no authority to refuse police protection, and, in a brief moment of seriousness, she had looked into his eyes and said, "I like the sound of that."

The only time the conversation stopped was when they arrived at her front door. Gary suddenly felt awkward, unsure of quite what to do next. She sensed his shyness, "Sorry I can't invite you in, my house mates have been known to lounge around almost totally naked, and I can't have you being swept off your feet by naked women when I've only just met you." She reached up to him then and kissed him, softly, on his mouth.

"Can I see you tomorrow?" he asked as they parted.

" You'd better," she replied with a smile, "You know my extension, call me when you know you will be free."

It had been the happiest evening of his life, by a country mile.

Undoubtedly due to his euphoria, he was in DS Paul Asquith's office a little after 8.00am. The Detective Sergeant look one look at his beaming face and said, "Who had a good night in the Big Smoke then, what's her name?"

DC Proud blushingly grinned, "That's on a need-to-know basis."

He gave a photograph of Carlos Guvara to DS Asquith. Asquith looked at the photograph, "George Clooney doesn't have much to worry about from this feller, does he, right ugly bastard? I think the best guy to contact would be Kingston Marley, he's terrified most players in the obscene publications business over the years, you'll see what I mean when you meet him."

"Where's he based?" asked Proud.

"Good question," answered Asquith, 'The Vice Squad was merged with the Human Trafficking Squad in 2014. Before and since that time, following the corruption in the Met, uncovered in the 1970's, the Met has refrained from identifying a particular unit with named officers involved in Vice, for fear of those officers being 'corrupted' by the big money involved in Vice. They now have officers who may be attached to a particular unit, but all are responsible to the Police Commander at Head Office in Dean Farrar Street Westminster. Kingston Marley was, the last time I heard, attached to the Mare Street Hackney office. I'll give him a call there."

Asquith dialled a number, Proud heard a deep voice reply, "Hackney Police."

"Marley, you ugly bastard, have you guys learned to play cricket yet?"

"Piss off, you white trash apology for a human being. What do you want Asquith, bored with nothing to do and trying to convince another lowlife that you're busy?"

Asquith roared laughing, bizarre sense of humour thought Proud, Asquith became serious, "Kingston I have a guy with me, from the police up north, who is showing me a photograph of a guy who took some really nasty pics for a truly bad piece of shit that we are trying to nail. I was wondering if you could take a look at it and tell us if you know who it is?"

"Sure," replied Marley, "are you still at Charing Cross?"

"Yes, but we could come across to you if it would help."

"No, I have to go to DF Street soon, I'll come to you on the way, I'll see you in about half an hour."

Thirty minutes later, the largest black man that Proud had ever seen off a basketball court or a cricket pitch, walked in. He walked up to Asquith, picked him up bodily and sat him on top of a four-drawer filing cabinet and said, "Now we're both at about the same height, show me."

Asquith jumped down from the filing cabinet, "Gary meet my good friend DS Kingston Marley, Kingston meet DC Gary Proud from Wilmslow police, show him the picture Gary."

Gary did so. Marley took a brief look at it and said, "Carlos Guvara."

"Yes, we know that, but do you know where he is now?"

"Last I heard he was down in Brighton, skips across to France now and again for a porn shoot for an outfit based on the outskirts of Paris. I haven't heard that he is up to anything like his shoot at the ICE though."

"Does he still deal in the UK market?" asked Asquith.

"What was that about leopards and spots, he sure does, mostly through a guy who has been my snitch over the past few years, based in Soho."

DC Proud was all ears now, "Do you have an address for him in Brighton?"

"No, but I can find one, the boys in Brighton have been keeping an eye on him ever since we informed them about ICE. They'll have his address for sure."

"It is important that we don't tip him off too soon," said Proud, "we have not been able to find his collection of the tapes or discs he took at ICE, and we would dearly like to. There are some of his victims who might be persuaded to come forward if we were able to show them the tapes or discs that he took." This last statement was not actually true but Proud was forever the optimist.

Marley looked at him, "How are you planning to find them?"

"My bosses, DCI Warbrick and DS Fellingham will be in London later today. They will almost certainly want to travel on to Brighton after I have passed on the news that you have just given me. I have been hoping, and please tell me if you think that it is a stupid idea, that once we have his address, we can put a tail on him. If somehow, he could discover that there might be a possible customer for the kind of stuff he shot at ICE, he may lead us to the place where he has the material stored.

"That could work," responded Marley. What time are you expecting your bosses in London?"

"Some time this afternoon, I have to call them very shortly. Could we all meet up with you later?" and he looked imploringly at DS Kingston Marley.

Marley laughed until his sides shook, "I bet the girls would just love that look Gary, would win em over every time. Here's my card, call me when you know when they will be here. I'll get that address for you in Brighton, in the meantime."

DS Marley then left for his meeting in Dean Farrar Street. DC Proud then turned to DS Asquith, "Thanks for your help, Paul, I have to leave for ICE now, I had a little problem with Geraldine Withers yesterday, the records office librarian, I had to threaten her with DCS Goddard and a search warrant to stimulate any cooperation. I need to find out if it worked."

"I'm sure that it would have done," replied Paul Asquith, "DCS Goddard's name does seem to have that effect on most people."

Prior to leaving Charing Cross Police Station DC Proud called DS Fellingham to give her the news about Carlos Guvara. She became almost as excited as he had been. "I'll talk to the boss; we'll try to get to London by no later than three."

She also told him of trying to track the friends of victims and six she had found that had been friends. She told him that of these six, two had been fairly convinced that their now deceased friend had stated that she intended to pursue Morales through the courts. She also told him that she intended to speak to Warbrick about obtaining the services of interpreters for each of the languages of the victims, to conduct a more thorough enquiry.

Interesting, he thought, it was beginning to look as though more than one of the deceased women had intended to pursue Morales rather than end their lives. What or who had changed their minds.

He completed the walk from Charing Cross Police station, along the Strand and Aldwych to ICE in a little over ten minutes. He arrived at Geraldine Withers office, twenty-five and a half hours since he had last been here. She was in no better mood, but sniffed, "I have completed the list of addresses you requested, I trust that that is all you will be requiring?"

"That's a little hard to say," said a smiling DC Proud, "until I've checked."

He turned on his heel and walked across to the Hive's office, a beaming Felicity Marshall greeted him, "Good Morning Sir Galahad, I take it that it is the fair maiden you are seeking and not some dusty relic," she paused, "from our library of course."

Terri came out from her small office, laughing happily, and pulled him into her office. She kissed him again, this time with a little more fervour than the night before.

"I just wanted to check," he said, "that I wasn't dreaming about last night, that you really do exist."

She hugged him, "I had a wonderful time last night, thank you, and even more wonderful dreams throughout the night."

"You'll have to tell me about them, soon," he whispered.

"They wouldn't pass the Censor," she whispered back.

His face turned sad, "I'm sorry to have to tell you that my two bosses are coming to London this afternoon, and we may have to travel down to Brighton this evening. I'll try to persuade them that I am not essential for the task, but there will be a considerable amount of leg work involved and that is usually my responsibility. I'm really sorry, but please give me your mobile phone number and I'll call you when I have some more news."

She hugged him again, "I understand, a policeman's lot is not always a happy one, please there is no need to apologise. It's a bit of a coincidence really. I was about to ask you if you would like to come with me to Glyndebourne in Lewes this weekend. Puccini's La Boheme is being performed, it is one of my favourites. Would you like to come, we could maybe stay over in Brighton or Hove, what do you think?" she was the one who was blushing slightly now.

He hugged her and this time kissed her passionately on her mouth, "I would love to come, this week is turning into one of the most fantastic weeks of my life."

He hurriedly left the Hive's office, before he lost complete control of himself, and disappeared down the corridor, to the sound of Felicity's laughter ringing in his ears.

28

The train bringing DCI Warbrick and DS Fellingham to London arrived at London's Euston station at five past three that afternoon. DC Proud had given DS Kingston Marley their scheduled arrival time and he had asked that they come directly to his office in Mare Street Hackney. They arrived at his office twenty minutes later.

DS Kingston Marley was immediately taken by DS Fellingham. No one else would have noticed but DC Proud, having witnessed the borderline jocular abuse between Marley and Asquith realised that DS Fellingham made this giant negro male, quite shy. He shook her hand so gently that she had to smile at his overt attempts at playing the gentleman.

DCI Warbrick, who had made his own discreet enquiries about DS Kingston Marley and had been impressed, was much more to the point.

"Pleasure to meet you DS Marley, heard a great deal about you, all of it good, what have you got for us?"

"Well Sir, here is the address where you will find Carlos Guvara, I haven't yet contacted Brighton police in case you have a contact of your own there, Sir. I can contact them if you would wish me to, but sometimes I have found, that any request from the Met to a provincial police force, is not always greeted in the same spirit of cooperation that we would all wish."

Warbrick laughed, "I fully understand Detective Sergeant, but delicately put. Detective Superintendent Tom Hyland in Brighton and I joined the force in the same year. We have been friends and colleagues ever since. If I may use your phone, I will give him a call now.

This was done and following the usual pleasantries Warbrick came to the point, "Tom I am currently in London with DS Marley of Vice. We are trailing a guy who was the photographer of those poor girls at ICE during the time of the pornography scandal. We have his address in Brighton. The thing is we have never been able to find his collection of filthy pics and it is now imperative that we do so. I would like to enlist your help, if you are able, to put a tail on this guy 24/7. I don't believe that it will be for an extended duration, we are in the process of setting up a Sting whereby a fictional client will be seeking pictures of the kind taken at ICE. We hope that in doing so, Guvara will lead us to his 'collection.' I believe that I will also be able to obtain compensation for your costs over this, I know that 24/7 tails can be most expensive. What do you think?"

"No problem, Lindsay," said Hyland. "I'm not that well-endowed with experienced ghosts, (a UK police term for people skilled in tailing) but hopefully your guy won't be suspecting anything. I'll put my best team on it though. Don't worry about compensation if we can crack the location in under five days. Anything longer, I may have to come back to you, OK."

"Thanks a million Tom, I'll do the same for you if you ever suspect that any of our multi-millionaire footballers are up to anything naughty that is of particular interest to you."

"Where are you staying Lindsay, are you free for dinner tonight, Mary would love to see you, it must be at least ten years since we last caught up?"

"I haven't booked anywhere yet and I would love to catch up, but I have……" he was about to add 'colleagues with me as well' when he caught sight of Fellingham vigorously shaking her head. "My colleagues are telling me that all is fine," as he noticed DC Proud joining Fellingham in the head shaking with a grin like a Cheshire cat across his face.

Tom Hyland came back, "Then please stay with us and we'll have dinner at home, a little bird has told me that you have recently become engaged, Mary will want to hear all about that. Call me from the station when you arrive in Brighton, and I'll pick you up."

"I obviously have things to discuss with you two," said Warbrick, "I'll take that address in Brighton from you now DS Marley and thank you for your excellent help."

They left the Hackney police station and Warbrick took all three of them into a local café. "OK so what will you two involve yourselves in, whilst in Brighton?"

Fellingham and Proud looked at one another but before Fellingham could speak Proud jumped in, "Well if it's all the same to you two, I have a tentative date in London for tonight, I haven't confirmed it as I thought that all three of us would be travelling to Brighton, but I really would much prefer to stay in London tonight and travel to Brighton early in the morning."

They were both looking at him open mouthed, 'Gary Proud had a date in London, how could that be, he never had a date, he simply worked the whole time. Fellingham broke the silence, "You have a date Gary, who with, how come I've never heard a whisper about a love interest in London. I'm totally gob smacked to learn that you're a dark horse?"

Warbrick grinned, "That makes two of us."

DC Proud was now bright crimson, "I've only just met her, she works at the Hive offices at ICE, and she is the most beautiful woman I have ever seen. We had dinner last night, it was magic, and I really would like to see her again tonight."

Fellingham put her hands on her hips, she was standing next to the table, "So the two men in my working life are about to abandon me in the big bad city, what's a girl to do. I know, I need a few art lessons," and with that she left the café to call Alex.

So, it was three happy police officers who enjoyed their stay away from home. Lindsay Warbrick with his old friends in Brighton, Susan Fellingham with her fiancée, Alex McQualter, who flew down from Manchester to take her to a show in the West End, and Gary Proud who breathlessly called Terri Ryan to tell her that he was free to see her again that night. Of such circumstances are happy memories made.

The following morning, on a 7.30am train, DC Proud caught up with DS Fellingham. She was looking particularly lovely this morning thought DC Proud.

This date is doing him the power of good thought DS Fellingham.

Proud was going through the list of addresses of deceased victims compiled by Geraldine Withers, he had found the address of Anika Kampfert in Port Elizabeth. He next looked up Loraina Beyers, she had lived in Stellenbosch at the time of her application. He turned to DS Fellingham, "I have these two addresses in South Africa, the first is for an Anika Kampfert who took her own life following her father's receipt, her father was a Minister in the Dutch Reform Church, highly right wing and conservative, of the pornographic material organised by Morales and filmed by Guvara. This other address is for a woman named Loraina Beyers who was a close friend of Anika's whilst at ICE. She was also a victim of Morales' pornography, and he had also sent her parents copies of the material. Fortunately, her parents were far more liberal that Anika's."

"Felicity Marshall told me, that Loraina had told her, that her parents had been hippies who had lived in San Francisco in the 60's and 70's. They totally supported Loraina throughout her ordeal."

"At the time of Loraina's application to ICE she lived in Stellenbosch, which is east of Cape Town, in the mountains, I think. I need to check with Felicity if she continues to live there. The point is, is that Loraina Beyers might be prepared to give evidence against Morales on a charge of rape if we could ever bring him to South Africa or here. She will need the photographic evidence that I really hope that Guvara still has, for the case to be certain of success. Felicity Marshall sent an e-mail to Loraina two nights ago and we are awaiting a reply."

"Fantastic Gary," said DS Fellingham, "maybe we can find similar other cases where a friend who has also suffered, but survived, might be prepared to take the stand. Let's keep our fingers crossed that we can find this horde of filth stored by Senor Guvara."

They met DCI Warbrick at Brighton police station. He was not looking anything like as bright as either DC Proud or herself were that morning. She caught herself ruminating on the cause of DC Proud's happiness, wondering whether its origins were in anyway similar to her own stimulation. She immediately dismissed that train of thought and focussed instead on the red eyes of her boss. "How many unsolved cases did you finally resolve last night Sir, you and DS Hyland that is."

Warbrick gave her the bleary look of the hungover, "I'll thank you not to gloat DS Fellingham, I only did it so that you could enjoy the company of your fiancée, in a totally unexpected way."

"Thank you, Sir," she said demurely, but her eyes were laughing at him.

Warbrick received a call from Kingston Marley, "I'm starting the Sting this morning, I'll try to let you know if and when our friend bites."

"Thank you, DS Marley, I appreciate it, we will be beginning our recce this morning in any event."

DS Hyland introduced them to the first watch of Ghosts, members of the Uniform Branch but in plain clothes, a Sergeant and two constables. The plain clothed police officers quickly departed to take up watch in pre-arranged locations and to pre-arranged activities in close proximity to the target's place of residence. The Sergeant then returned to take the three of them, in an unmarked vehicle, to the Whitehawk district of Brighton. The area had once seen better days and the house which was allegedly occupied by Carlos Guvara looked particularly unkempt. The two plain clothed constables had adopted the roles of surveyor and his mate, toting the theodolite to various locations close to the target's address but with frequent changes to the position of the indicator pole. These roles would be changed to suit the timing of the different shifts, but it was a case of becoming comfortable with the observation.

Whilst all this was happening DS Fellingham and DC Proud had occupied an office within Brighton police station and were busy tabulating the list of address and names supplied by Geraldine Withers and cross referencing with the list of Hive recipients supplied by Terri Ryan. There was nothing obvious emerging thus far, the best link had been the one provided by Felicity Marshall. She had heard back from Loraina Beyers who enthusiastically agreed to do whatever she could to, in her words, "crucify the bastard'.

Using the frustrations arising from the lists which refused to provide any connection, as an excuse, DC

Proud had taken to making frequent calls to Terri Ryan, allegedly asking her to check with Felicity Marshall about other sources of possible connections.

It was only due to Fellingham's increasing suspicions surrounding his reasons for the frequent calls to Miss Ryan that he had the brain wave. The dance lessons, those who participated in the Argentinian Tango classes, of course. With Felicity Marshall and Winston Macauley's help he had been able to correlate connections between six former students of both economics and dance, who had taken their own lives, with eight ICE students who had also taken dance lessons, but to the best of anyone's knowledge were still alive, what he didn't know was whether any of these eight had been sexually abused by Morales. He had their names and their addresses and soon maybe they would have photographs. He had no idea how Guvara would have labelled his photographs. He just hoped it was by name.

Two days later Warbrick had a further call from Kingston Marley. The Sting had been set, Guvara had expressed an interest in finding the requested material, the Ghosts should be ready. The following day, a little after peak hour morning traffic, Guvara left his house in his Ford Granada and proceeded to drive down through Whitehawk to Kemptown. He was followed by several plain clothed officers in an unmarked Ford Transit van. He clearly had no idea that he was being followed as he made no attempt to lose his 'tail'. He arrived at a lock up private garage, one of twelve, in a side street in Kemptown. The garage was fronted by a roller door and Guvara quickly depressed the remote control which opened the door and disappeared inside the lock up. Five Police Officers followed him in.

The horde was huge, it transpired that it contained over 80% of all of the pornography filmed in ICE between 1995 and 2008. It also contained a substantial amount of pornographic material filmed elsewhere, but that would only be identified through interrogation. The ICE material was bundled up and crated and shipped back to Wilmslow Police Station via a high security vehicle. Guvara was charged with the manufacture and distribution of obscene material contrary to, and the act was quoted. DC Proud had taken a brief look at the ICE material. They weren't labelled by name, but they were by initials, that would be good enough for him.

29

Eduardo took stock of where he was at. Ken Stockdale had completed his work on the comprehensive spreadsheet and Eduardo was completely satisfied with it and had made several copies. He was ready to move into phase 2 of his plan.

Several days later, at a meeting being held in Mexico City, between Board Members and Executives of BBVA Bancomer, Mexico's largest bank, with certain advisers to Carlos Rhon, a US dollar billionaire who had made his fortune from banking, there was general chatter, during a break for coffee, about events and developments occurring around the world. One attendee at that meeting was Ricardo Touché, an independent assessor on the Board of BBVA Bancomer Bank. He had heard the name Dacian Jiminez mentioned and he discreetly enquired as to the subject matter involving Senor Jiminez. He became somewhat concerned.

On a day, around the same time of the month, in Panama City, Chris Amenechi, Vice President responsible for Pricing and Revenue at Copa S.A had showered, following a game of golf with his colleague from Caja de Ahorros, a large bank in Panama.

This bank was reputed to strictly adhere to the US Department of Treasury's instructions regarding accounts held in Panama by companies or individuals, conducting business outside of Panama, but banking within it. Panama had by 2012, become known as the Switzerland of the Caribbean, and the US Department of Treasury had grown tired of the number of American companies and citizens who were denying Uncle Sam his dues in respect of taxation, by using the tax haven of Panama. The major banks in Panama had quickly fallen into line.

Chris Amenechi and his friend from Caja de Ahorros had moved into the bar for a quenching beer after their game when his friend had asked him if his company, Copa S.A. continued to manufacture aircraft. Chris had told him no, which was true, but he failed to mention that the finance arm of Copa S.A. was supporting a number of companies involved in aircraft maintenance, Chris asked his friend why he had asked this question. His friend had responded by saying that he had just wanted to give him the heads up about a brewing scandal regarding aircraft parts supply, adding that he was relieved that Copa S.A. were no longer involved in this industry.

Both of these men reported their stories to their Board member colleagues at the next scheduled Board meeting of their respective companies.

In Zurich Switzerland an eminent legal practice had received instructions from a respected client to set up a business in the name of Einzigartig Entwickelte Losungen Suisse AG, to become known as E.E.L.

Suisse AG. The English translation of this name is Uniquely Developed Solutions Switzerland AG. The instructions then clearly stated that the intention of this company was to provide secured funding for any project considered worthy by the Board of the Company.

The lawyers were than advised that standard commercial conditions, prevailing at the date of signing, were to apply to any loan granted. There was a simple addition to the conditions attached to the clauses on default and foreclosure, which specified that the beneficiary of the loan was to operate within the laws of the jurisdiction, wherever it operated, at all times.

The company was to become operative at the earliest possible date but not later than the 31st of May.

For many years, both Eduardo and Lucia had been approached, frequently, to financially support many projects. They mostly ignored the individual begging letters that they received but when a request was made by an organisation that they knew to be genuine, and where the support requested could best be described as meeting an unmet essential need, for the greater good of a large proportion of the community, they would, most times, assist. Sometimes though Eduardo, in particular, had been approached by a United Nations agency to either address an assembly where his support was thought to be most helpful, or where his expertise could bring some clarity to a complex issue.

It was through these latter approaches that Eduardo had met many political leaders throughout the world, but particularly in Europe. One such person was Emma Solberg, the Prime Minister of Norway. Eduardo placed a call to her office, advising the receptionist who he was, and requesting that she call him, at a time, solely convenient to her. He was not surprised when he received her call a little over one hour later.

They did not know one another well, but Eduardo respected her, she was one of those rare creatures, an honest and forthright politician. For her part, she admired his integrity and his quiet generosity, much of the Roni's philanthropy, both husband and wife, was carried out anonymously, and it always warmed her heart to know that such people existed.

He quickly came to the point, explaining that he needed the help of her government but that he couldn't discuss it over the phone. If she were able to grant him half an hour of her time, he would be able to explain it all to her. She quickly agreed to do that, and they agreed a time, five days hence when they would meet, in her office at 11.00am.

Having agreed that date, he blocked out a further two days in Norway, and then proceeded to arrange flights to Cologne, London, Montreal, Washington DC, and Taipei. He knew people in each of these cities, but they were not the people he needed to know there. Nevertheless, he thought that each of the people he knew, would also know how to put him in touch with the people that he needed to meet. Again, he did not wish to discuss it over the phone, and he mentioned this in each of his phone calls to the people he knew in these locations. There were five very intrigued people when he concluded his phone calls. One of these five was DCI Lindsay Warbrick.

He could now turn his attention to his hospital in Brescia. He had owned the Ospedale Oncologico di Brescia for the best part of 25 years. The Chief Surgeon, who he had known from his student days in Bologna, and his wife, a former Operating Theatre Sister, at their previous hospital together, he had recruited when they were experiencing a highly traumatic family tragedy. Their friends were being extremely kind to them, they had told him, but every expression of sympathy only served to re-open the wounds of their pain. They had needed a complete change from where they were, and he had offered them the positions in Brescia. They had both accepted and thanked him with emotional sincerity.

He decided that he would drive over to Brescia and discuss the proposal received from the Polizia Penitenziaria with them. Firstly, though he needed to discuss with Lucia all of the plans that he had been putting in place that day.

She had been busy in her office for most of the day but the redness around her eyes told him that she had been thinking of Izabella. He took her into his arms and held her there for several minutes, finally he said, "It's been a long day, and it looks to be a lovely evening out there, why don't we go out onto the terrace and have a quiet drink and maybe watch the moon rise?"

She squeezed his hand, he always knew when she was distressed, and, more importantly, how to calm her.

She listened to his plans, interrupting only when she needed something clarified. She looked into his eyes, and then noticed, the set of his jaw. She could feel the determination pouring out of him. He had never blamed her or criticised her for taking such a tough stand over Izabella. He probably had every right to, even though she knew that he had been partly to blame. He had doted on their daughter, and she had been smart enough, or cunning enough, to exploit it. He had always had difficulty in denying her anything, and she, Lucia, had told him, many times, that his behaviour was not good for their child. Although his logic had told him this was true, his defence had always been, that Izabella reminded him so much of her, Lucia, when he had first fallen in love with her. If only she could have been able to have a second child, that might have solved the problem, but it wasn't to be, and that was fate. Here they were, two good people, she thought, with more money than they could ever spend in ten lifetimes, and yet, they were unable to have the one thing that may have possibly averted their tragedy, another child.

They had been sitting there for quite some time, watching a gibbous moon rise over Lake Garda, and sipping a product of Soave, Lucia's favourite wine region. "You will take care, amore mio, won't you, I couldn't bear to lose you too, and she pulled him close to her.

The following morning Eduardo drove the fifty kilometres to Brescia. He had called the Chief Surgeon Istvan Csany that morning, prior to leaving, who had been pleased to hear of the visit. He also remarked that his wife Greta would be pleased to see him again.

Eduardo had met Istvan Csany when Eduardo had been a fourth-year student and Istvan a Registrar in Oncology at the hospital in Bologna. Istvan was different to other Registrars in that he did not assume any airs of superiority when he addressed the students and was always willing to help them with their studies in any way that he could. His family were originally from Hungary, both parents being University lecturers at the University of Budapest. They had managed to flee Hungary, with 200,000 other Hungarians following the 1956 uprising in their native country. They had sought, and been given, refuge in Austria and Istvan was born in Vienna, the following October. He had met his future wife, an Italian girl named Greta Barbieri, whilst still a Registrar in Bologna, and they had married in 1988.

Identical twin daughters followed who they christened, Lilliana and Gemma. Tragically, when their girls were just five years old, they were both kidnapped, following Istvan being mistakenly identified as a Serbian politician. A ransom had been demanded, Istvan and Greta agreed to somehow find the money, but then the kidnappers had realised their mistake and had fled Italy. Lilliana and Gemma's bodies were found three days later.

The family had been living in Rome at the time of this tragedy. Istvan working as an Oncologist at a Teaching Hospital there. Greta was inconsolable with grief and Istvan had become increasingly anxious about his wife's mental health. Eduardo had heard of the tragedy and both he and Lucia had travelled to Rome and taken both Istvan and Greta to New Zealand to provide a break from the environment which served as a continual reminder of their immense loss. Lucia had rarely left Greta's side, saying little, but seeming to know when to simply hold her close. Gradually, ever so gradually, Greta emerged from her pain, and the two families had remained close, ever since.

Before they returned to Italy, Eduardo had offered both Istvan and Greta, the positions at his hospital in Brescia, which they had accepted, with deep gratitude.

Six months later, Lucia had asked him how he would feel about Istvan and Greta becoming Godparents to Izabella. He had no problem with the suggestion but was concerned about the reaction, particularly from Greta. Lucia had gently broached the subject with Greta, and she tearfully said that they would both be honoured. They had taken their godparent responsibilities seriously and had become affectionately close to their daughter. They had been as outraged as both Eduardo and Lucia when they learned how Izabella had ended her life.

Istvan had only a short theatre list that day and was prepared for Eduardo's arrival. Greta joined them and they talked for over an hour about the Polizia Penitenziaria proposal. Istvan opened up about his reservations, and Eduardo could immediately see his point. Eduardo also added that converting the hospital to, day-case surgery only, would also be quite expensive and given that the recent Pancreatic

Oncology service in Verona had been successful, he did not believe that it would be too long before they expanded onto other areas of surgical oncology.

Istvan shared his concerns that if patients had to be diverted to other facilities elsewhere whilst the alterations were happening, they might be lost forever. Eduardo had shaken his head, "Unless we were to move into a service that no one else would want. Those potential patient numbers you were showing me were mightily impressive. Could you imagine anyone wishing to be treating prisoners, some of whom have been seriously violent in the past, because I can't."

"Put like that I'm not sure that I would want to either."

"We could stipulate that if this is to be for purely prostate cancer patients than all patients being transported to our facility should have been on a programme of Cyproterone Acetate (CPA) or some other antiandrogen, for at least one week prior to transfer."

Istvan nodded, "Yes, that could work, or alternatively a cocktail of CPA and propofol."

"The other advantage that I see is that because the security at our specialised hospital will have to meet Government standards for the protection of everyone involved in these patient's care, we could probably obtain a government grant toward the cost of the alterations. That has merit. We could also move quite quickly if they were to look favourably on the grant scenario."

Istvan then asked him when he was thinking of carrying out these alterations, assuming a grant could be obtained. Eduardo had answered, "Quite soon, this coming summer in fact." If Istvan and Greta were surprised by that, they gave no indication.

Istvan's only comment was, "I know that the Hippocratic oath doesn't differentiate between the free and the damned, but I never thought that when I entered Oncology, I would one day become a custodian of the damned. Will you contact the Polizia Penitenziaria, or would you like me to do it?"

"If you could do it Istvan, that would be extremely helpful."

Eduardo returned to Sirminione, his mind racing with the implications and the opportunities that the discussions recently concluded would mean for him, and his business. He resolved that until he heard back from Istvan, there was nothing further that he could do.

Several days later he was on a flight to Oslo, Vanessa had booked him into one of his favourite hotels, The Continental on Stortingsgaten. He was welcomed back, even though it had been several years since he had last stayed there. It was one of the things that he liked about this hotel, they always researched the history of their booked guests to determine if they had stayed, previously.

They had obviously discovered that he preferred a room looking out over the Radhaus (Town Hall) toward the Pipervika which is the name given to the bay that lies between the fortress and the Aker bridge, and which is a frequent hive of boating activity with the many ferries arriving in, or departing from, Oslo.

The view always seemed to confirm for him that Norway was a country where things that mattered, were the things that REALLY mattered. The need to arrest global warming and this country's commitment to that end. The celebration of the efforts of many ordinary people trying to improve the lives of others, reflected in the testimonies to be found here in the Nobel Peace Museum. The celebration of family, heralded by the many statues of children and families, so beautifully created through the artistry of one man, Gustav Vigeland.

Norway made him feel glad to be alive.

He met with the Prime Minister of Norway, Emma Solberg, the next day, at 11.00am. He came quickly to the point, describing the reason for his visit, watching her reaction as it crossed her face, highlighting what he was endeavouring to achieve, and articulating the ways in which she, and her colleagues, might be able to assist him in achieving this. Her response was immediate. "You must first meet with Sylvi Listhaus, she is a rising star in my government and acting, at the moment, in the position of Minister for Foreign Affairs. She will put you in touch with the man that you need to see." She picked up her phone and called someone, a few moments later Eduardo was escorted to the office of the Minister for Foreign Affairs.

Within a further 24 hours he had met the key individual whose assistance he needed most directly. Once again agreement to assist was reached almost instantaneously and within a further 24 hours, he had met the three young women who would be working directly with him. It had all been extremely professional, profoundly reassuring, and delightfully friendly.

From Oslo he flew onto Cologne to meet with long established contacts who had resided in this city for many years and were familiar with the inner workings of all areas of Government to be found in this city. He quickly learned of the names of the people that he would need to contact in the near future.

This process was repeated, with identical results, in the cities of Montreal, Washington DC, and Taipei. Prior to travelling to London, he had called Lindsay Warbrick asking if Lindsay could meet him at his townhouse in Knightsbridge. Lindsay, still highly intrigued, agreed to the meeting.

Eduardo had arrived at the townhouse prior to Lindsay. Eduardo offered Lindsay a drink, Lindsay declined and then Eduardo had said, I think that you should, you are not likely to be too relaxed after you have heard and seen what I have to tell and show you."

Eduardo told Lindsay of his links with Cesare Sinarelli, Cesare's role in Italian Military Intelligence and the fact that Cesare had been virtually raised by the Roni family. He told him that he had approached Cesare for the use of a highly skilled computer technician who could hack into the most sophisticated of computer security systems. Eduardo had asked this computer guy to hack into Jiminez/ Morales computers and secretly extract just about everything he could to do with Jiminez or his companies.

Lindsay had stopped him looking a little uncomfortable, "Should you be telling me any of this Eduardo, I am a cop you know?"

"I'm afraid I have to tell you my friend for what I am about to show you affects everything that you and I are doing. When I have finished, we can work out how to explain it to others."

"Go on," instructed Lindsay continuing to look troubled.

"The computer guy obtained everything that I asked him to, and more, he also accessed Jiminez personal files, and this is what he found."

Eduardo handed Lindsay the 'Bluebird 'file.

Lindsay began to read, twenty minutes later he looked up at Eduardo his face suffused white with shock. "My God Eduardo, there's a leak, the Met has a leak, and it has been leaking for thirteen years. It begins with that case that DC Proud told me about, the first one involving Morales and it's been going on ever since."

Warbrick was flicking through the pages of the Bluebird file. "It was going on a few months ago, if I am not much mistaken this e-mail here relates to Aileen Colquhoun's travel arrangements from Taiwan to the UK via Canada. I don't understand what Esc1 means though. I happen to know from DCS Goddard that she told him that was her intended route. With this information Aiza could have picked her up at any number of places. This is dynamite Eduardo, it is devastating, DCS Goddard will be sick to the stomach when he reads this."

"Do you trust this DCS Goddard Lindsay?"

"With my life Eduardo, with my life, I've never met a better or straighter copper in my life."

"Good, I trust your judgement my friend, we need to discuss how we came by this information in the first place, before we can involve DCS Goddard."

"Yes, but what does Esc1 mean?"

"It means that Esc1 was Morales first Scottish victim. Don't forget Morales is Spanish speaking and the Spanish word for Scotland is Escocia, Esc. His first UK victim would have probably been ReUn1 for Reino Unido, United Kingdom."

"My God this is terrible, who is this, Bluebird. As I look through this, I can see that we could have stopped Morales in his tracks long before those 32 women killed themselves. My God, I've just realised, they probably didn't, Bluebird has been tipping him off that they were planning to pursue him through the courts and he had them killed, the evil, stinking bastard."

He paused for a few moments, "But I don't suppose we can ever prove it now. My team, Susan and Gary have been trying to track down friends of the deceased, they have only yesterday asked me to approve the use of interpreters to speak to these friends of victims trying to establish the states of their minds, prior to their death. They both believe that they have found three of those friends who are insisting that the deceased had no intentions of killing themselves, that they had every intention of prosecuting Morales."

"What should we do now?" asked Eduardo.

"I have to speak to Goddard, today, before this Bluebird inflicts any more damage. OK Eduardo it is time for you to leave the country, for your own sake. I intend to tell Goddard that you were making enquiries about Jiminez's businesses to understand how widespread they were when you were given this file. I will say that I have no idea what method you were using to investigate these businesses of Jiminez. He won't believe me, but he won't want to know. You are not a UK citizen, and neither is Jiminez. How you conduct your business enquiries in Italy is entirely your affair, but you should leave the UK ASAP"

"I'll book a flight to Verona/Venice or Milan whichever is the earliest departure from Heathrow. I'll do it now." Fifteen minutes later Eduardo had a flight booked to Milan, departing Heathrow in one hour fifteen minutes."

"I'll call DCS Goddard and ask him to meet me away from his office, I don't want this Bluebird being tipped off that I'm meeting him. I'll call him on his direct line and then we will both leave."

DCS Goddard picked up on the second ring, "David it's Lindsay, please just listen, something extremely serious has just arisen which I don't wish to talk to you about, in your office. I'll explain when I see you. It's highly confidential, can I see you at your home, it's in St John's Wood isn't it. Great," he wrote down the street address, "I'll see you in an hour."

"Can I have the Bluebird file Eduardo?"

"Of course."

Eduardo returned home to Sirminione and Lucia, via Milan. He was tired, highly stressed, but generally satisfied with the progress that he had made.

He knew that it would soon be time to meet with Lindsay and Susan again, but the question of the Bluebird needed to be resolved before too much more took place.

30

DCI Warbrick took a cab from Knightsbridge to the address in St John's Wood. He was there ahead of DCS Goddard. Goddard's car arrived and he was briskly out of it and entering his house indicating to Warbrick to follow him. Bellowing "Jane," as he entered, his wife put her head around the door from the kitchen and looked enquiringly at him.

"Lindsay Warbrick's with me, but that's confidential, we don't wish to be disturbed, under any circumstances. OK"

"Whatever you say dear," came the reply from a wife long experienced in the crises that often consumed their serving officer husbands.

"OK Lindsay, what's the crisis, it's not like you to react the way you have, so out with it."

"I hate to tell you this David, but you have a major leak in your office, and you have had, for thirteen years." He handed DCS Goddard the Bluebird file.

DCS Goddard did not rush through the file as DCI Warbrick had, he methodically went through it page by page, occasionally looking up at Warbrick, the horror of what he was reading etched deeply into his face.

"This Bluebird has systematically been telling Jiminez everything we know about him, almost just as soon as we know about it. Those poor women, Bluebird was telling him that they were planning to bring charges against him, why do you think that they went ahead and committed suicide?"

"I don't believe that they did Sir, at least not all of them. I can't prove it, but I believe that he had them murdered."

"Oh my God, based on a tip off from my office. And here Bluebird is telling him about Aileen Colquhoun's travel plans, that Esc1 means Aileen Colquhoun, doesn't it?"

"Yes Sir, Escocia is Spanish for Scotland Sir."

"Yes, I knew that, Lindsay."

Another thing Sir, my team DS Fellingham and DC Proud have been trying to link some of the suicide victims with former living friends from ICE. They have found three thus far who do not accept that their friends ever had any intention of taking their own lives. I have just approved the use of interpreters, across all the languages spoken by the victims, to ascertain if there are any more. I realise that it will be extremely difficult, if not impossible, to prove murder so long after the event, but it would be helpful to have some idea."

"Yes indeed," said Goddard. "I am trying to think who Bluebird might be, my first thought was Detective Inspector Judy Sneddon, she was the DI I took off the Morales case because I thought that her work had been slipshod, but why should she. It's not likely to be a sex angle, is it? She was over 30 when she was first assigned to the case and would be well into her fifties now. Morales always liked them young, didn't he?"

"Yes Sir, he did. Is she still working on the case now Sir? Jiminez seems to be receiving the most up to date information?"

"No, she isn't Lindsay, but I can tell you who is, a Detective Constable named DC Pam Miller. When Pam Miller first entered the force, DI Sneddon took her under her wing as she told me once that she thought that DC Miller appeared vulnerable. The thing is I do believe that DC Miller continues to socialise with DI Sneddon even though Sneddon is a couple of ranks above her and now works in a different building. I am tempted to bring them both in and scare them but if I'm wrong, I could well have a constructive dismissal case brought against me by either one or both of them."

"As DS Fellingham is fond of telling me, based on advice she receives from her art expert fiancée, Alex McQualter, 'follow the money.' What do we know about DI Sneddon, where she lives, her marital status, her hobbies, travel habits, entertaining preferences, that sort of thing?"

"I'm told that she lives with her older and wealthier sister who, apparently, is partially disabled in Holland Park. Not much else I know; she always seemed a touch intense to me."

"That all sounds a tad suspicious to me, would it do any harm to have the Secret Squirrels (Special Branch) take a look. Needs to be a false trail though so that it doesn't come back to you. Possibly due to consideration for promotion, prompted through HR."

"That would work, she has been a DI for fifteen years now, been passed over a few times mostly because of me. I'll give the AC (Assistant Commissioner) in control of HR a call, ask him to identify officers who appear to have been ignored for a while and have them checked out, no more than three though. I might let it slip that DI Sneddon seems to have been at her level for quite some time."

"I'll also have DS Winifred Jacobs have a chat to DC Pam Miller. DS Jacobs is everyone's favourite Aunty. Hails from Barbados, with a smile as wide as the Caribbean. Very loyal to me though, I helped her husband through a difficult patch a few years ago and she is still trying to repay me."

"Lindsay what more damage can Bluebird do, do you have any ideas?"

"I can't think of anything, most of the enquiries surrounding Jiminez's business activities are being handled by Eduardo Roni so that's not likely to come back through you. We are trying to work a plan to have Aiza travel to the UK so that we can nab him, but that's being handled at my end, and I'll keep it there for now, so no, I can't think of anything that can cause us serious harm. All the damage has been done."

"Tell me about it Lindsay, can you leave the Bluebird file with me, I want to study it some more, see if anything leaps off the page at me.

"No problem David, sorry to have brought all this to your door."

"I'm glad that you did, have you the time to share a dram with me?"

"I thought that you'd never ask," replied Warbrick.

Several hours later a Detective Inspector from Special Branch, using his Special Branch Authority to access a whole range of personal and confidential files discovered that DI Judy Sneddon did not have an older disabled sister, she did not have a sister at all. She was an only child. He also discovered that the house in Holland Park was in the sole ownership of Judy Sneddon. There was a small mortgage of a little over 100,00 pounds but the house was valued in excess of 2 million pounds. Accessing her tax records, he discovered that there was an alleged income from an investment in the Caribbean which amounted to in excess of 80,000 pounds annually. More in fact than her salary as a Detective Inspector. He sent these findings to DCS Goddard.

The next day DS Winifred Jacobs brought her smiling face to the office where DC Pam Miller worked. She eased her heavy frame into the seat next to Pam Miller and chatted easily to her. How was she finding life in the Metropolitan Police. Reluctant to say too much to begin with she did admit that it was only her friendship with DI Sneddon that kept her there. The Met was really just a 'Boy's Club'. Look how poor DI Sneddon had been treated; she had been handling that awful case about those poor girls from ICE when it had just been snatched from her by DCS Goddard. It just wasn't fair. DI Sneddon was always asking about those poor girls, she didn't believe that any man could understand what those girls had gone through. She just wanted to know that they were OK and if it hadn't been for her, DC Miller, filling her in on the details she would never have known.

That report also went to DCS Goddard.

31

DC Proud had returned to his office in Wilmslow mid-morning on the Monday following the most wonderful weekend of his, relatively, short life. Terri and he had travelled to Lewes, a small town north-east of Brighton on the Friday evening. She had booked them into the Premier Inn for three nights and after he had collected the key they went immediately to their room. They had both behaved a little awkwardly and shy as they did so, but Gary suddenly found himself possessed of a courage that he never thought that he had, as he took her passionately into his arms. She responded enthusiastically and they made love with a hunger shared since they had first met.

He was not the most experienced of young men when it came to the art of lovemaking, but he knew that he wanted to please her, oh how he wanted to please her. The problem was that she wanted to please him also and their first coupling was over, seemingly, within minutes of its commencement. He held her close to him for several minutes following this first attempt, feeling the joy of her nakedness as he stroked, first her hair, then her back, then her buttocks. "I'm sorry," he started to say, but she put a finger across his lips and whispered 'Shush.'

They lay like that for a while and then she rolled on top of him and said, "I do really have to thank Winston Macauley when I next see him. He was the one who told me all about you when you visited him with the old Detective Chief Inspector and the beautiful Detective Sergeant. I think Winston was quite smitten by the Detective Sergeant, are you?" and she raised her head to look into his eyes.

He kissed her then, "I may have been, a little, when I first met her, but not nearly so smitten as I was a few days ago when I first met you, I still have to pinch myself to believe that having you with me like this is actually happening to me. I find it almost impossible to believe that you find me in any way attractive."

She kissed him, before moving his right hand between her thighs, "If you're ever in doubt again simply check out your own hygrometer, I hereby grant you exclusive access to it."

They made love again then, this time, more slowly, more thoughtfully, and this time he did give her pleasure, and she trembled, vigorously, against him before exploding in a paroxysm of delight as her orgasm overwhelmed her.

The remainder of the weekend was spent, mostly in bed, realising the joy to be experienced in exploring one another's bodies, and when they would fall apart from each other to recover from their exertions, they would laugh and hold each other tenderly, until the passion began to rise again.

They talked, as easily as they had on their first date, she told him more about her life, the snobbery and condescension that she experienced when she had briefly experienced life in an exclusive 'Ladies College'. Shropshire was a wealthy County and the primary qualification one needed to have to gain acceptance into the lofty corridors of "Shropshire Country Life," was land ownership, the more the better, provided that it came with a manager and 'Hands' to do the work.

She told him about her parents, how her dad was never bothered by the pretentiousness of some of the people they came into contact with. "It doesn't bother me, "he would say, "they have to live with themselves, I don't."

Her mother, she had discovered early, had a giant intellect, she could have been or done anything that she had wanted. She had 9 'O' Levels by time she was 14 and 6 'A' Levels at 16. She could have had her pick at Oxford or Cambridge, she could have studied medicine or law or hieroglyphics and mastered them all.

Instead, she helped a boy who wanted to pass his Higher National Diploma (HND) in architecture and in order to do so, he needed 'A' Levels in English and Maths. She tutored him and he achieved his 'A' level results. He also achieved a result in making her mother pregnant and they were married on her 18th birthday. Her eldest brother, Brendan, had been born five months later. Her mother had then decided to commit her life to raising a family, including tutoring her children as well, if need be. This she had done with spectacular results.

Terri had turned to him then and said, "But the best thing that she ever taught me was how to read people's eyes. From the time when I was about eleven, she would take me out saying to me beforehand that she wished me to study the eyes of the people that we might meet that day. We would then return home, and she would ask me what I had seen. At first, I was hopeless, and she would say to me, you weren't looking at that boy's or man's eyes at all, you were simply impressed that he was handsome. She would also be hard on me if I didn't study a girlfriend's eyes as well. She would sometimes ask me why I was friends with such and such a girl and If I replied that I thought she was nice, she would tell me to look into her eyes with a comment such as 'she can't be trusted that one.' The thing is, she was never wrong."

Terri then straddled him in the bed. "When I looked into your eyes in Felicity's office, I saw a good and honest man, like my father, and I love you for it," and she pushed him back into the bed and pulled him inside her again.

They went to Glyndebourne and Puccini's La Boheme. He was surprised to find that he enjoyed it, not nearly as much as Terri, but he had enjoyed it.

By the time that they travelled back to London on the Monday morning he knew that he had met the love of his life. He turned to her, "Would there be any chance that I could persuade you to travel up to Manchester next weekend, I would like you to meet my parents?"

She laughed happily, "Of course, would we have time to meet my parents also, Knutsford is not too far from Shrewsbury."

"58 miles, precisely, via the M6 and Nantwich, I looked it up secretly when DS Felling wasn't watching whilst we were in the police station in Brighton."

They parted company at Waterloo station, Terri to travel to ICE and Gary across to Euston and on to Manchester Piccadilly. "Come on Friday if you can, I'll be desperate to see you by then," he whispered as they were about to separate.

"I'll be there she sighed," as she crushed his mouth to hers.

The photographic files from the lock up had been placed in a highly secure office, the key to it being held by DCI Warbrick. There was a message waiting for him, from the DCI, that he wished to see him on his return to the office.

He made his way to Warbrick's office, knocked on the door and was told to enter. Warbrick looked at him, "I can see just by looking at you that you enjoyed yourself, down south?"

DC Proud blushed, embarrassingly so, "Yes Sir, I did, very much."

"Good, because you have some unpleasant work ahead of you, but before you begin, I need to ask you, are you feeling OK about doing this because I could ask DS Fellingham to do it if it embarrasses you?"

"No Sir, I'll do it. I've thought about it. I've decided to commence by first simply looking through the year headings and then the initials. I only intend to take out those files where we have a connection of a living victim with a deceased friend of that victim, and then to simply check that the faces of the women in those files match the faces of the same women at the time of their application to ICE. I have no need, nor any desire, to look further into the content of the files that we had brought up from Brighton."

"Good man and thank you, I know I can trust you to do just that. I want you to remember that all of these poor girls had their privacy, and their dignity ripped from them by this evil man Morales. I want this office to do whatever it can to protect whatever remains of that privacy and dignity by ensuring that no other prying eyes gain access to those files. There are only two keys to that office, and the office lock is not included in the master key schedule. I have one key, which will remain with me at all times and here is the other."

He handed the second key to Proud before continuing, "Under no circumstances is that door to be unlocked, when you have entered, lock yourself in and permit no one, other than DS Fellingham or myself to enter. Should anyone try to bully you or pull rank, call me or DS Fellingham and report them. If you have to leave the office, for any reason whatsoever, or for any duration, no matter how short, lock that door when you leave. You will leave that office, each evening, no later than 5.30pm and you will return the key to me. This is for your own protection. I will return the key to you each morning. Is that all clear and do you have any questions?"

"Absolutely clear Sir, and I have only one question, when I have 'paired' the victims who knew one another, do you wish to see each pair individually or do you wish me to complete the pairing of all those who knew one another?"

"Good question Gary, I think that as, at the moment, we have only the pair of the two South African victims where the living survivor has confirmed her agreement to testify, just bring me those two files. The remaining pairs you can complete before bringing them to me, OK?"

"OK Sir," and DC Proud turned to leave.

"One more thing DC Proud?"

"Yes Sir."

"When are you intending to sit your Sergeant's exam?"

Proud grinned, "Very soon Sir, just as soon as I have an hour or ten to spare."

Later that day, DC Proud brought the two files of Anika Kampfert (Deceased) and Loraina Beyers (alive and living in Stellenbosch) to DCI Warbrick.

DS Fellingham meanwhile was preparing to make a trip to Aberystwyth on the west coast of Wales to visit the offices of Alun Jones and Morgan, Solicitors, at 11 Northgate Street in that city. She had originally thought that she would travel by train, that way she could prepare properly for the meeting and then write her report, should a report be required, on the return journey.

She had since discovered that a train journey would take in excess of four hours, involving over a one hour wait in Wolverhampton. Aberystwyth was a little over 100 miles from Macclesfield, surely, she could drive that in two hours.

DCI Warbrick had asked to delay her trip until he had been able to discuss with DC Proud the business of pairing the files received from Brighton. This he had now done, and she was planning to leave by car, early the next morning. With any sort of luck, she would be able to return home the same day.

It was Alun Jones himself who met her, he had with him an Associate Partner in the business, Helen Childs, who was the solicitor handling the claim by a local aircraft repair business against Avnav Parts and Services of Macclesfield. Alun Jones had involved himself because, as he had explained, "It was a little unusual to find the police involved in a commercial legal dispute, particularly so when the police office involved was based in the same location as the defendant."

DS Fellingham had agreed with the solicitor's comments and began her prepared speech, "The reason that I wished to meet with you is that we have reason to believe that your client is only one of a number of clients who have engaged in a similar dispute with this defendant. One of these other clients has been in contact with us, and brought us evidence, that the part that this client had purchased from Avnav Parts and Services, whilst purporting to be an authorised and certified part, was in fact, an illegally fabricated part."

"What evidence did this other client bring you?" interrupted Alun Jones.

"The supplied part itself, which we have had checked, by an authorised aircraft repairing engineer, who has confirmed that the part supplied is from an unknown illegal manufacturer. In addition to being an unauthorised manufacture it is also manufactured from inappropriate material that would be unlikely to withstand the stresses of an aircraft in flight."

"I see," said Alun Jones, as he steepled his fingers together, "and what are you seeking from our client?"

"The actual part supplied by Avnav parts and services and if possible, the packaging it came with. Do you happen to know if your client installed the supplied part into an aircraft, and if so, which one?"

"Detective Sergeant, we are not in the business of enquiring of our clients exactly what they have done on a day-to-day basis, we have absolutely no idea if our client has installed this part, you would have to ask him."

Detective Sergeant Fellingham smiled her sweetest smile, "But Mr Jones, I am sure that you are in the business of reading the local newspaper. If that part has been installed, I am sure that you may be reading, in your local newspaper, about the loss of a locally owned aircraft, no doubt with several of your more prominent citizens aboard, maybe even other clients of yours, aircraft failures do not discern the passengers' status, prior to failure."

The smugness had disappeared from Alun Jones face, "Helen call Bryn Griffiths, ask him if he has installed that part yet, and if he hasn't, tell him not to."

Helen Childs disappeared from the office to make the call, and an oppressive silence ensued, which DS Fellingham did nothing to relieve.

Helen Childs returned, "No he has not installed it Mr Jones, he was intending to return it once he had received a refund, he asked what we want him to do now?"

Alun Jones glared at DS Fellingham, "Ask him if he is prepared to give it to the police as evidence, but also tell him that he is unlikely to receive payment unless we sue Avnav Parts and Services for damages with costs."

Helen disappeared again; this time she was gone for much longer than previously. DS Fellingham thought that the relationship between this Bryn Griffiths and the office of Alun Jones and Thomas was primarily between Bryn Griffiths and Helen Childs. When she returned, she said that Mr Griffiths had agreed to give the part to the police and would do so today. "I could take the Detective Sergeant to Mr Griffiths workshop to collect the part, if you like, Mr Jones?"

Mr Jones snorted without replying and walked hurriedly from the room, "Did you take that as a Yes, or a No?" asked DS Fellingham, sweetly.

"I'm taking it as a yes," replied Helen Childs, "I would like to talk to you on the way there?"

"Is he always like that?" enquired DS Fellingham, 'that smart-arsed old boss of yours."

'Lately yes," replied Helen, He's not been the same since his wife left him two years ago. She has most of the money you see, she caught him burrowing in someone else's garden."

Fellingham said nothing for a while before asking, "What was it that you wanted to ask me?"

"Oh yes, is it true that Bryn will not be able to receive compensation for the part he is about to give you as evidence. He doesn't have much money, and I told him that I would ask you?"

"Technically yes, it's true, but I'll see what I can do, ask Mr Griffiths for a copy of the receipt when we get there. Also, if you agree, get his bank account details, if I can negotiate a refund, I will prefer that it went directly to him and not through your offices. No doubt your charming Mr Jones would want to extract his commission if it did."

They met Bryn Griffiths, even with the grease and dirt wiped across his face DS Fellingham could see that he was a darkly handsome man with striking green eyes. She could also see that there was a lot more to the relationship between Bryn Griffiths and Helen Childs than a simple client lawyer arrangement.

32

The stretch limousine had already collected DCI Warbrick, Gina Moretti, and Alex McQualter, before it arrived at Susan Fellingham's house. She settled, comfortably under the encircling arm of her fiancée in the centre row of seats, whilst Warbrick and Moretti were similarly seated in the rear row. They were taken swiftly to Manchester airport, but not to the commercial passenger airline terminals. They went instead to the separate section dedicated to those fortunate individuals who owned their own private aircraft or were the guests of someone who did. The four boarding passengers belonged to this latter category.

The 12-seater Lear jet moved swiftly and almost silently upward from the airport until the pilot, one of two on board, banked to the left and adopted a course slightly east of south. The pilot had announced that their destination was Verona and their flying time, somewhat less than two hours. Their 'hostess' was the charming Vanessa Montefiore, who had volunteered for the role.

Gina Moretti snuggled up close to Lindsay Warbrick, "If I didn't know you better Mr Lindsay Warbrick, I would say that you're trying to seduce me," and then she whispered, "and guess what, you've succeeded. I feel as though I'm on my honeymoon."

"Make the most of it my love, on a copper's pension you won't be doing this too often."

Vanessa served them smoked salmon canapes and chilled white wine as they experienced the luxury of privileged travel. She chatted easily to Susan and Gina, but it was Alex McQualter who she turned her gaze on, with a frequency that might have alarmed Susan except that Alex seemed oblivious to this attention as he focussed on reading the technical specifications of the aircraft.

They touched down in Verona, were swiftly escorted to yet another stretch limousine whilst their luggage was collected from the Lear jet and stowed in the capacious luggage compartment. Vanessa asked DCI Warbrick and DS Fellingham if they wished her to take their guests, Gina, and Alex through the history of the Villa Giustiniani, as she had for them on their first visit, and they indicated that she should.

Gina then surprised them, by saying that she had met Count Lorenzo Giustiniani and his wife, Roberta Soranzo at a formal investiture, in her honour, when she had been presented with the Ordine al Merito della Repubblica Italiana (OMRI) (The Italian Order of Merit and that nation's highest award) for her contribution to humanitarian services.

Both Lindsay and Alex were stunned, but most particularly, her fiancée DCI Lindsay Warbrick.

It would be fair to say however, that there were four highly impressed people in that car at that moment, Lindsay, Susan, Alex, and Vanessa,

They arrived at Villa Giustiniani, Eduardo and Lucia were there to meet them. Vanessa had hurried forward to give Eduardo and Lucia the news about this most prestigious award given to Gina.

They were greeted with a warmth normally reserved for friends of long standing, but it was more a long understanding of the grief suffered by Eduardo and Lucia and the determination to see it assuaged that had provided the bond between these six people.

They moved into the house. Lucia advised that lunch would be served in thirty minutes on the terrace, but they were welcome to freshen up beforehand. Vanessa then assumed the role of guide and taken them to the two magnificent bedrooms prepared especially for their stay.

As the door was closing behind them Gina was giggling, "Never in a million years would I have dreamed that the man it took me eight years to convince that I loved, would ever be the one to give me a world I have dreamed about since I was a child, even if it is only for a couple of days. Do we have time to make love before lunch?"

All six were on the terrace, Lucia was indicating where each of them should sit. The champagne was served, Eduardo stood and raised his glass, "To friendship, and the realisation of justice. Six voices said in unison, "To friendship and the realisation of justice."

The table was set for six, the seating arrangements were, Eduardo at the head, then clockwise around the table, Susan, Lindsay, Lucia at the foot, then Alex, and Gina. DS Fellingham thought to herself, I see that Lucia has positioned herself next to Alex, but then she realised that she had been placed next to Eduardo, she couldn't really make a fuss could she.

Lunch was light but again excellent, as it was drawing to a close, Eduardo asked the question that he had the previous time, would their preference be casual or formal attire for dinner. It was Susan and Gina who had simultaneously answered, 'formal'.

As they broke away from the table, Warbrick approached Eduardo and asked if he could meet with him privately. Eduardo had nodded, "We can move into my study now if you wish?" and Warbrick had agreed.

What has he got up his sleeve, Susan was thinking, but before she could put too much thought into it, Gina had moved alongside her, "Why don't you show me the garden Susan, Lindsay says that you loved it when you were last here.

"Sure," smiled Susan, thinking, damn that will leave Lucia with Alex.

Lindsay Warbrick sat in Eduardo's study, "There are a couple of things that I believe that we should speak about privately, "he said, "concerning senor Morales that I would prefer that DS Fellingham did not know about until after the event."

Eduardo smiled, "And there are a couple of things I would prefer that Lucia did not know about until after the event also."

"Firstly, how good are your contacts in South Africa?" asked Warbrick.

"Excellent," replied Eduardo, "particularly in Pretoria and Cape Town."

"Does that include the police force, the legal profession, and the judiciary?"

"As a matter of fact, it does, and I think I can see where your thinking is heading, there must be a reason for this?"

"Yes, there is," and he took out the files of both Anika Kampfert and Loraina Beyers and handed them across to Eduardo.

Eduardo began to look at them, his face becoming more horrified with every turning page. Finally, he could look no more. "They're disgusting, what an animal."

"Yes indeed, the point is poor Anika Kampfert is dead, by her own hand after Morales sent those pictures to her father, who was a Minister in the Dutch Reform Church."

"Madonna, he would have killed her if he could have brought her home."

"Yes indeed, the second set are the ones of Loraina Beyers, she is not dead and, this is vital, she is prepared to take the stand against Morales in South Africa, if we can get him there and if we know the appropriate police officers, prosecuting council and possibly a judge so as to ensure a conviction. We both know what would happen after that."

"Madonna Santa, Lindsay, this is absolutely bloody brilliant, this is what I have been looking for, for the past countless years. Don't worry about getting him there, I'll do that. Can you give me those two files or will copies suffice?"

"You will need the originals, any defence counsel worth his salt will have those photographs analysed, if they're copies, he will claim they have been doctored, but I need photographs for the police records, where, in fact, these came from. Do you have a way of having them copied?"

"They would have to be done here, there is no way I can give these to anyone else. I have the equipment, it's a little slow though, as it is several years old. I would need everyone out of the house for several hours tomorrow morning, including Lucia. I wonder if our artistic colleague Alex could be persuaded to take them somewhere?"

"Leave that with me, I think that I may know of way of having him help us, unwittingly."

"I'll put these photographs in my safe now and I'll give you the copies tomorrow to take back with you. Leave the South African end to me, I have to return there shortly in any event, I'll simply bring it forward."

"Now what can I do for you," asked Eduardo.

"I have a guy locked up in Manchester that I have charged with accessory to the murder of Aileen Colquhoun. We also found a copy of a security film that was taken on the night that Aileen was murdered. The guys that were responsible for her death had been told by the guy I have in gaol that he had turned the cameras off, but there was no way that he could do that without alerting his Head Office. His primary motivation for this lie, was that he wished to take possession of the money they were offering him."

"We have had the film footage enhanced and the man responsible for her murder has been clearly identified. His name is Juan Aiza, and he is the Executive Vice President in charge of Security, but he is based in Taiwan, and we have no extradition arrangements with Taiwan. We know that Avnav Parts and Services is being threatened by a firm of lawyers acting for an aircraft repair company in Wales. Susan collected the part from that aircraft repair company, which is the reason for the dispute, a few days ago. We have had it checked, we have discovered that it has been manufactured illegally from non-approved materials, but we have no way of knowing where it was made, we suspect Taiwan. What we need to do now is put the frighteners into Avnav Parts and Services in Macclesfield, to such an extent that Senor Aiza comes across to the UK to sort it. The moment he sets foot in the UK, I will have him, and I now have a fairly solid case to obtain a conviction.

Eduardo thought for a while and then smiled, "I think that I know how to ensure Senor Aiza takes a trip to the UK."

Lindsay then turned to him and said, "There was something you were wanting to tell me that you did not wish Lucia to know about."

"Ah yes," said Eduardo. I have arranged for three Norwegian girls to entrap Senor Jiminez/Morales whilst he is in Zurich. Lucia does not approve of my using women in such schemes, she believes it to be too dangerous."

Warbrick said nothing but did not believe a word of what Eduardo had just told him. He had seen the look on Lucia's face at the conclusion of his account of the fate of the female students at ICE. He knew that Lucia would stop at nothing to avenge her daughter. Like so many of God's species that occupy this earth, the female is far more deadly than the male when it comes to protecting or avenging her own. He also knew that Eduardo had a much more sinister plan for Senor Jiminez/ Morales, he could sense it. It did not bother him, in the slightest, that Eduardo did not wish to share that with him. There are some things that are best for a policeman, not to know.

Had he known it, Eduardo was having similar thoughts, I'm sorry not to have been totally frank with you my friend, some things must be kept on a 'need to know basis.'

They returned to the terrace, Alex was explaining the work that he had carried out in Italy over the past several years, to Lucia. She appeared to be fascinated. She looked up as Eduardo and Warbrick returned, "What have you two been up to, plotting if I am not mistaken, I can always tell when Eduardo has been plotting, he scratches his forehead". Sure enough there were scratch marks across Eduardo's forehead.

"Alex has been telling me about his work here in Italy. I do believe that he has seen more of Italy, and he certainly knows more of the history of Italy, than either you or I Eduardo. I suddenly feel that I have been living in this treasure house of history and have been too blind to see it. Thank you, Alex, it was truly fascinating."

"Will you please excuse Eduardo and I for a few minutes, I need to talk to the chef about dinner and I need Eduardo to check our stocks in the wine cellar, we will just be gone a few minutes."

Whilst Warbrick had Alex to himself he said, "Why don't you suggest that you take us all on a tour of somewhere special, say the Cathedral in Venice, it is not too far away you know. It would be a nice way in which we could thank Eduardo and Lucia for their hospitality. Maybe tomorrow morning?"

"Will there be sufficient time? I sometimes become a little carried away with these sorts of tours and I understood from Susan that you were here to work."

"Eduardo and I have just agreed a strategy to bring things to a head, I really believe that they brought us here to enjoy a break, rather than work incessantly. Perhaps it is time for Lucia to discover more of her native treasure house," and Warbrick did look contented when he said it.

Alex raised it with Susan as they were preparing for dinner, "It sounds like a terrific idea if we have the time, Lucia is not the only one who loves to hear you relate the fascinating history of Italian art. First it was Jenny O'Shea that you were cosying up to, with descriptions of sunrises and sunsets and Giotto and Caravaggio and Botticini and next you are huddled together with Lucia no doubt discussing the relative merits of 500-year-old virgins."

"Detective Sergeant Fellingham, I do believe that you are jealous, how many times do I have to tell you that the only work of art that I am truly interested in, is you," and he came from behind her, spun her around, and kissed her.

"Oh, I'm sorry, I just never seem to have time to be with you by myself, first DCI Warbrick is demanding my attention and then when I think that I will have some spare time Gina is asking me to show her the garden. I'm not jealous of the women, I'm just jealous of the time they have with you," and she sulked.

"Maybe I could suggest that we have a latish start to our sightseeing tomorrow, that way we could make love with Lake Garda as our only witness, what do you think?"

"I think that sounds wonderful," she was chuckling, "did you hear the noise next door before we went down for lunch, do you think Gina and Lindsay were 'at it'?"

"Good luck to them if they were," replied Alex. "I obviously have some catching up to do."

"Indeed, you do, and by my watch there is still 35 minutes before dinner."

Dinner was, once again, an excellent repast. Eduardo had been the perfect and charming host. Before the meal was served, he announced, "I have been checking the list of previous guests at our Villa, and although there have been five men who were recipients of the prestigious Order of Merit award, who have stayed here, I am delighted and honoured to announce that Dr Gina Moretti is the first lady, who has received this award, to have done so. I believe that is worth celebrating."

The company was relaxed, the wine flowed, and each course consumed with considerable praise directed toward the chef. Gina, in particular, seemed to be enjoying herself immensely. She had many humorous anecdotes of her life as a forensic pathologist which she delivered with a tact, and sense of timing, which ignored the gruesome nature of her training, and focussed on the ridiculous. Eduardo and Lucia clearly enjoyed her company, and she even succeeded in telling some amusing stories about her failed attempts to seduce Lindsay Warbrick before the fateful day when she had come to examine the cadaver of the edifying John Doe.

Lindsay Warbrick was clearly feeling a little nonplussed about all this hilarity, which made his failure to understand Gina's not so subtle hints, all the more amusing. He took it in good spirits though.

As the evening was drawing to a close, Alex tinkled the side of his wine glass with an item of cutlery and when he had everyone's attention said, "I was thinking, that being this close to the Bassilica Cattedrale Patriarcale di San Marco in Venice, and if you can spare the time, I would like to suggest that I take you all on a tour of this magnificent Cathedral. It truly is one of the gems of Italy. Would anyone like to do that?" The three ladies immediately cried yes, with Gina looking at Lindsay and asking, "Is there time?" Warbrick nodded and said that he would also like to participate, only Eduardo had not answered.

He looked at Lucia, "Sadly amore mio, I need to travel to South Africa next week, and I have much to prepare, but you must go, perhaps Alex, we might be able to find time in the future, when we could make a further visit."

Fortunately, he had mentioned to Lucia, when they had been briefing the chef and checking the wine cellar, that he had received a call requiring him to travel to Pretoria and Cape Town, so she was unsurprised that he would not be able to make the visit to Venice.

Alex continued, "There are just a couple of additional points, the Cathedral is always exceptionally busy on a Sunday morning, and I would appreciate a couple of hours to prepare. I would like to suggest that we plan to leave here around 11.00am and return in time for dinner, is that OK with everyone?"

It was and Eduardo and Warbrick exchanged a brief smile between them, which no one noticed, not even the eagle-eyed Susan Fellingham.

33

Dacian Jiminez/ Ramiro Morales was angry, the banks in Mexico and Panama cities were turning the screws. It had commenced, mildly enough, several weeks ago, when the first letters had enquired, politely, if he would kindly make arrangements to visit the bank to discuss both his personal and business accounts. He had not bothered to reply.

It had seemed to him that both banks were displaying a singular lack of patience when, a week or so later, he was receiving letters which began, 'Due to your failure to respond to our earlier correspondence it is now imperative that etc, etc, etc.' Typical of banks he had thought, give you an umbrella when the sun is shining only to demand its return at the first sign of rain.

It was then that he began making enquiries about alternative sources of funds to get these Central American banks off his back. It would be helpful to be able to escape their clutches for other reasons also. Interest rates throughout this region had been rising alarmingly due to the economic uncertainty prevailing in this part of the world at that time and he had been thinking about replacing these loans as a consequence.

He simply had not had the time to do so due to other pressures of business.

His enquiries about alternative sources of funds were being handled by both his business accountants and his lawyers. His accountants were based in Taiwan, but his lawyers were based in Panama. It was his lawyers who were the first to notify him of the possibility of replacing his loans through an organisation based in Switzerland with an unpronounceable German name but with the acronym E.E.L. (Suisse) AG. He liked the sound of Switzerland; interest rates were much more reasonable there. He instructed his lawyers to make further enquiries.

Jiminez had been based in Taiwan when these banking issues had first arisen and these irritations had been compounded by several calls from that pathetic creature in England, Trevor Byford. There had been many times over the past years when he had regretted ever getting into business with this man. He always seemed incapable of making even the most basic of decisions without first contacting himself. If an issue had even the slightest degree of difficulty or complication about it, such as this problem with some tin pot company in Wales, he simply went to pieces. Now it seemed that this Welsh organisation was threatening to report Avnav Parts and Services in the UK to the Civil Aviation Authority in that same jurisdiction.

He called his second in command Juan Aiza to come to see him. "Juan, I may have to travel to Switzerland, at short notice, over the next few weeks, whilst I'm away, you'll be in charge. I'm having a little difficulty with the guy who runs my business in the UK, Trevor Byford, who is about as much use as tits on a bull. Apparently, there is some hiccup with a company based in Wales who have been making threatening noises to Byford. I'm about to try to sort it but I may need your help. If Byford can't make this problem go away by himself, I may need you to pay one of your trademark visits to this peon in Wales and provide him with a close encounter with something that he should never recover from. Take the Torres brothers with you again, they did as you asked during your recent visit to Macclesfield, did they not?"

"Si Senor Jiminez."

"It may not be necessary, but should the problem continue whilst I am away in Switzerland, I am authorising you to make whatever arrangements are necessary for you and the Torres brothers to visit Wales and put an end to this problem. I will send you a file with all the necessary details, later today, understood?"

"Si Senor Jiminez."

Several days later Jiminez received a bulky document from Switzerland. It contained application papers for a secured business loan. The attached letter of introduction was on the headed notepaper of Einzigartig Entwickelte Losungen (Suisse) AG, the English translation of which, Jiminez read, was Uniquely Developed Solutions (Switzerland) AG.

Two days from the date that Jiminez received his loan application forms, and nine thousand miles to the west, Trevor Byford received an ominous letter.

It advised him that the dispute between West Wales Aircraft Repair and Avnav Parts and Services Ltd had now been passed to a debt collection agency and unless payment, in full, was received within 28 days, an application to the Court would be made for the seizure of assets owned by Avnav parts and Services to the full value of the outstanding debt, plus costs. Trevor Byford dialled the number he had for a business in Taiwan.

Jiminez had completed the application form and despatched it. He instructed his lawyers in Panama to write to the banks in Panama and Mexico, advising that arrangements were being made, for all outstanding loans from the banks, to be discharged in full, via the re-financing of the debt through a bank in Switzerland. The letter went on to request the cooperation of the two banks, in the transfer of all securities held by those banks, to the bank in Switzerland, in order to expedite the approval of the new loan and the discharge of the existing loans with the two Central American banks.

This letter was sent in order to buy time, Jiminez had not yet had his loan application approved, and he realised that by sending this letter he was playing one of his final cards. If his loan application was declined, he knew, that the Central American banks would foreclose, and he would be ruined. He was not aware of any alternative to the one he was now clinging desperately to in Switzerland.

The call he received requesting him to attend an interview with E.E.L. (Suisse) AG in Zurich was manna from heaven. He prepared for his visit to Zurich advising Aiza that he had no idea what length of time his visit to Switzerland would take but that he, Aiza, had his full confidence.

Aiza then informed Jiminez that he had taken a call the previous evening that had been diverted from the office phone to his own, which had been from Trevor Byford. Jiminez had muttered 'Useless prick'. Aiza had then told him of the content of the call, clearly the Welsh problem now needed to be resolved, permanently, but was Jiminez comfortable with Aiza being away from Taiwan whilst Jiminez was in Switzerland?

Jiminez thought about it, "You say that they have given us 28 days to pay up in full," Aiza nodded, "well plan your visit to Wales two weeks from now, I may have completed what I need to in Switzerland by that time, if not, I should not be away much longer, I'm sure that the business can manage without us both for a few days, put your best man in charge whilst you're away."

34

Lindsay Warbrick, Gina Moretti, Alex McQualter, and Susan Fellingham had returned to the UK, by Lear jet, having thoroughly enjoyed their weekend In Italy. It was impossible to single out any one thing or event that had been the highlight. Yes, the visit to the Cathedral in Venice had been spectacular and Alex's obvious knowledge and effort that he put into his guided tour, amazingly impressive, but it was a minor detail compared to the warmth and generosity of the hospitality they had received from Lucia and Eduardo. It had been truly and heart-lastingly wonderful and as they had embraced one another in the forecourt of the Villa Giustiniani prior to their departure, there was no doubting the admiration and respect that now existed between the six of them.

"What were you and Eduardo cooking up together?" enquired DS Fellingham of DCI Warbrick as they resumed work the following Monday.

"He was looking for ideas as to wedding presents," lied Warbrick unconvincingly.

DS Fellingham placed both hands on her hips, "Never stray from the straight and narrow Sir, that is the most pathetic explanation for a suspicious act that I have ever heard."

He looked at her, "You really think so, how about, I was fascinated reading Alex's notes for the forthcoming trip to Venice, I didn't realise that I was late for breakfast."

She blushed to the roots of her hair and his smiling face only added to her discomfort. She decided to beat a hasty retreat whilst she retained any shred of dignity.

DC Proud had completed his 'pairing' of deceased and surviving victims of Ramiro Morales. He had supplied DCI Warbrick with six further pairs of files for his consideration. All remaining files were securely locked in two large trunks and placed in the evidence room. The key to these trunks could only be accessed with the explicit written approval of DCI Warbrick, or his appointed nominee.

What DC Proud had not been able to establish was the existence of a friendly and trusting relationship between the survivor of the pair with the deceased. This would only be possible through the direct contact with the survivor and DC Proud was unsure if DCI Warbrick wished to follow this course of action. He had asked DCI Warbrick, and he had replied by saying that 'He wished to think about it.'

DCI Warbrick was thinking about it now. All six of these additional 'pairs' were from Latin American countries, predominantly Spanish speaking, with the exception of one pair from Brazil whose native language was Portuguese. The five remaining pairs were two from Mexico, and one each from Colombia,

Chile, and Argentina. He pondered the problem. Contacting the surviving person of each pair would undoubtedly re-awaken the pain and humiliation that they had suffered, before ever discovering if there had been a close relationship between the survivor and her deceased 'pair.'

Secondly, he had strong reservations that the police and the courts of these countries would respond, as they should, given that the perpetrator, a male, was from the same region as the victims. Was it not more likely that the systems in these countries were unfairly biased in favour of the male. In which case all he would achieve would be further humiliation of the victims rather that achieving the justice that he was seeking for them.

In the end he decided to simply put all of his eggs in the South African basket and trust to God that through him and Eduardo, and the justice system in South Africa, that justice would triumph. He was well aware that South Africa had recently become far more robust in its prosecution of rape cases due to the high incidence of that crime, in that country. It just needed the prosecution of the case to be handled aggressively and with complete resolve. He knew that he was totally in Eduardo's hands in this latter regard, but he smiled to himself, he knew of absolutely no one better equipped or determined than Eduardo Roni.

DS Fellingham was sitting quietly in her office, reflecting on her bosses' comments and obvious awareness of the true reasons for her late breakfast on Sunday morning. Her embarrassment was fading.

Although it was not a deliberate act, she knew that she was inclined to reflect her joy of the sex shared with Alex McQualter, in a boisterous and yes, noisy manner. She shouldn't have been embarrassed, sex with Alex was everything she had always hoped sex would be. She was delighted that it was. She was proud that it was. She vowed never to be embarrassed about her sex life, ever again.

DC Proud entered her office, "Sarge I'm thinking that now the heat of the investigation is subsiding, I might try for my Sergeant's stripes, online. Is it still OK for me to use your name as a referee?"

"Absolutely Gary, better still why don't we both go and see the boss now, tell him that you are about to sit your Sergeant's exam and I'm about to do the same with my Inspector's exam and ask him to be a referee for both of us. I'm sure that he will be delighted."

"Great," said DC Proud, "I'm really pleased that you're going for Inspector, I think that you will be a shoo-in. One other thing that I would like you to know before we see the boss, but promise me that you will keep it to yourself for now, I've asked Terri to marry me and she has said yes, can you believe it?"

Gary Proud then received the first, and only, kiss on the mouth from DS Fellingham, that he would ever receive. She had beautifully soft lips, but he resolved not to mention that to Terri.

DCI Warbrick was delighted to hear the news of their intended actions in their quest for promotion and he delightedly endorsed both applications. He also privately resolved to speak to DS Tony Speers about his preferred option for the future running of the Wilmslow Detective base. He went home that night to Gina to tell her the good news. "I think that it is now time to set the date for our wedding, do you have any thoughts?"

"Tomorrow," responded Gina cheekily.

They finally agreed on the third Saturday in September because it was important, for both of them, that Gabriella, Gina's daughter would be able to attend. The Michaelmas term at Oxford University commenced in early October.

Warbrick privately believed that he would not be able to retire by that date in September. He doubted that the case would be fully wound up by that time, but his own involvement should be greatly reduced, he believed.

He certainly was not about to try to change their wedding date. He had been wonderfully happy, if just a little surprised, to see the joy in Gina's eyes when they had set the date. He could hardly wait for his retirement; his future had never looked brighter.

35

Dacian Jiminez arrived in Zurich on a late, but surprisingly warm, spring day. He had booked himself into the Hotel Baur au Lac on Garnischstrasse. It was expensive, but he was feeling positive, as well as which, it was located around the corner from the Adler PrivatBank on Claridenstrasse, where his interview was scheduled to occur.

He settled into his room and read again the copy of his loan application which he had brought with him. Most of the information contained within his loan application was not entirely true, but difficult to prove that it was so. The only exception to this was where he had stated that the aircraft parts that his company manufactured were all approved and authorised by the relevant Aviation Authorities, but he had failed to include licence or certificate numbers. His response to any question that might be asked in this regard was simply to state that such information was commercial in confidence, that may be of benefit to a competitor. He would also offer to supply such licences or certificates if required, and here he would be bluffing 100%.

The referees he had nominated, all existed, albeit not in the capacity that he had indicated, but the addresses were generally correct. The people he had nominated as referees were all on his payroll, although that was not a generally known fact. They all could be relied upon to provide him with the most glowing of references.

The interview was held two days later, three middle aged men conducted the interview on behalf of E.E.L. (Suisse) AG. He thought that he had handled the interview quite well, only one of the Interviewers, a Herr Mauser, had asked any penetrating questions about the manufacturing process of the aircraft parts. He had asked why such parts were being manufactured in Taiwan when the majority of the original licences and certificates would have been granted by authorities based in either North America or Europe. Jiminez had been forced to lie stating that his company had originally commenced operations in North America, when the licences and certificates had been first issued, but had been forced to relocate to Taiwan due to the high labour costs of North America. This answer had appeared to satisfy Herr Mauser.

At the conclusion of his interview, he was asked if he could remain in Zurich for a further three days as a decision would be made on that third day. In the interim a copy of the contract would be sent to him in addition to the papers that required his signature for the transfer of the mortgage on his company's assets from the banks in Panama and Mexico to Adler PrivatBank.

The Jegertroppen, (Hunter Troops) are members of Norway's armed forces. They are, in fact, part of Norway's Special Forces. In such capacity they are not markedly different from the SAS, SBS or Royal Marine Commandos in Britain; the Navy SEALS, Green Berets or Ranger Regiment in the USA, or any other of the Special Forces Command in Russia, Germany, or France, or for that matter almost anywhere in the world where Special Forces have been deemed essential.

Their training is generally the same, they are extraordinarily fit, tough, talented, and ruthless. The only difference between the Jegertroppen and other Special Forces is that the Jegertroppen are 100% female. They can outrun, outswim, outshoot, outfight, 99% of men on the planet. They are also trained to kill with their hands and countless other improvised weapons and carry their equivalent bodyweight in materials and weapons in backpacks over a 25-kilometre run.

They are the only 100% female Special Forces Unit in the world.

It was to recruit three members of this troop that Eduardo had visited, first the Prime Minister of Norway, Emma Solberg, then the Acting Minister of Foreign Affairs, Sylvi Listhaus, and finally the Commander of Norway's Special Forces, Colonel Frode Kristofferson. He had explained the reasons for his request and all three had given him their 100% support. He had met the three selected Jegertroppen troops in Zurich, several days before the arrival of Jiminez in that city.

The three selected troops were, Tonje, 22 years old, Venderla also 22, and Mari aged 20. All three were typically Norwegian, blond haired, blue eyed and attractive. The most attractive of the three was probably Tonje, who in addition to her many other talents was a champion cross county skier.

Although in normal operating circumstances she was covered in camouflage gear, she did possess a magnificent body. The contours and firmness of her body were now being vividly displayed, in the tightest of leather short shorts, the skimpiest of tiny and low-cut tops, as she stood on the corner of Dreikonigstrasse and Glarnischstrasse studying a map of Zurich with a perplexed look on her face, as Jiminez returned to his hotel from his interview.

She took his breath away; she was a goddess. He approached her, "Are you lost?" he asked in English.

"Ja," she replied, "I am looking for the ferry for the lake where I am supposed to meet my friends, do you know where it is?"

"No I don't, I'm a stranger in Zurich also, but I could help you find it."

She looked him up and down, "Nei tak, no thanks, I will find it myself."

"Why don't we ask at the hotel, this is the hotel where I am staying?" and he pointed to the entrance doors of the Baur au Lac.

"Nei tak" she said again and began to walk away from the hotel down Glarnischstrasse.

He ran after her, "Why don't we have a drink together or a cup of coffee, what is your name, my name is Dacian, I am from Panama." hoping curiously, that being Panamanian might stimulate some desire in her.

"Nei tak," she said again and increased her walking pace down the street, anxious to move away from him.

"You are the most beautiful woman I have ever seen in my life, please don't go, where are you from."

She laughed then, a musical kind of laughter, but she continued to walk away from him, "Norge," she said, "Norway."

"Please don't go," he called after her, but it was too late, she was gone.

Jiminez couldn't stop thinking about her, she really was one of the most beautiful women he had ever seen, what wouldn't he give to have her horizontal beneath him, begging for more.

He really must try to see her again, where would a young female tourist from Norway stay in Zurich, probably in a backpacker hotel. He asked the concierge at his hotel where the backpacker hotels were in Zurich. The concierge sniffed, took a street map of Zurich from the pad of street maps that are always present on concierge desks worldwide. He circled several, "Try these, will you be checking out sir?"

Jiminez simply glared at him. He had nothing else to do in Zurich so, for the following 24 hours he walked the area where the majority of backpacker hotels were to be found. There was no sign of her.

The contract arrived for him to examine with a note to say that the mortgage documents should arrive the following day. He read the contract, pretty standard stuff, except for a rather heavy clause about having to comply with the laws of which ever jurisdiction he operated in. Probably a Swiss Government requirement. He had read how stuffy Swiss bureaucracy could be. He would sign the contract in any event if his application was approved, he really had no other choice.

It was the following day when he saw her again. He had taken an afternoon walk from his hotel, along Glarnischstrasse toward Dreikonigstrasse where he had turned right along the Borsenstrasse. He had just noticed the Schweizerishe National Bank when he saw her, looking in the window of Tiffany's on Bahnhofstrasse. She had two friends with her, they were also nice but nowhere near as beautiful as the girl that he had first seen.

He hurriedly crossed the road again, "Hello beautiful lady from Norway," he called.

She looked up, first appearing to be puzzled, then she recognised him and said something to her two friends. They had laughed.

He was now next to her again, "Would you like to introduce me to your friends?" he said.

She looked him up and down again, clearly still hesitant about him, "She then said, this is my friend Venderla, and this here is our baby Mari," Mari had lightly punched his goddess on the arm following this comment.

"And what is your name," he said looking into her eyes, which stared fearlessly back at him.

"My name is Tonje. "She did not elaborate with surnames or where in Norway she was from.

"Well Tonje as I told you two days ago, you are the most beautiful woman I have ever seen in my life. Are all three of you from Norway."

"Yes," said the one introduced as Venderla, "What is your name and where are you from?"

"My name is Dacian Jiminez, and I am from Panama, and I am at your service, "and he bowed slightly from the waist.

This brought a laugh from Venderla and Mari but not from Tonje.

He persevered, "And what are you three ladies from Norway doing in Zurich, Switzerland?"

"Looking for three millionaire bankers from Switzerland," laughed Mari in reply.

"Would you settle for one millionaire businessman from Panama?" he quickly asked but with a smile on his face.

"It would depend on the stamina of the millionaire businessman from Panama," was Vederla's smiling response.

"Why don't we have a drink somewhere where we can discuss my stamina and…… your willingness?"

That brought another laugh from Venderla and Mari but still nothing from Tonje. All four of them did, however, move to a bar around the corner.

The three ladies chose beer to drink. They could not be persuaded to take anything stronger. He bought himself a Cuba Libre, "The national drink of Panama," he said, but it wasn't, legend has it that it was first created in Havana, Cuba.

"Where are you ladies staying?" he asked, after their third or fourth beer and his similar number of Cuba Libre's.

"Oh," said Venderla, "we have rented a little chalet just outside of town, very cosy, lovely views and large comfortable beds."

"Whereabouts out of town?" he asked.

"Just out of town," said Tonje abruptly. It was the first thing that she had said since they had entered the bar.

"Why don't you want to tell me?" asked Jiminez in a pained voice. "haven't I paid for all your drinks?"

"I thought that you said you were a millionaire," said Tonje in the same abrupt voice, "Surly a few beers wouldn't break the bank or are you a peseta millionaire?"

He almost lost it at that point, she might be gorgeous, but no bloody woman could speak to him like that and hope to escape unharmed. His eyes blazed with anger, but she held his look with the same unafraid eyes. He looked away, he would make her pay, my word would he make her pay.

Venderla then played the role of peacemaker. "I think Tonje believes that you are attempting to rush us. We won't be rushed, you see Dacian, we do everything together, and I mean everything. We three need to talk about this between ourselves to see if we agree. Maybe we should meet again here in a couple of days after we have had time to talk about it, what do you think girls. All three girls nodded."

"OK Dacian?' it was a question, "is that OK with you?"

"What do you mean you do everything together, what exactly do you mean by that?"

It was Mari who spoke up, "Oh you're a big boy Dacian, I'm sure that you can work it out. It's either the three of us, or none of us."

Dacian Jiminez was trembling with excitement, these three women, including his goddess, in bed with him simultaneously. He simply couldn't dream of anything better. "OK" he said, I'll see you here, this time, in two days."

The following day the mortgage documents arrived, he tried to concentrate, but his mind refused to refocus from the images it continued to create of a naked Tonje and her two naked friends doing the most wonderful pleasurable things to his body. He took another cold shower. He tried again to concentrate on the mortgage documents, and again he failed. Oh, they're probably correct and he signed them anyway.

He received a call on the afternoon of the third day. His loan application had been approved. If he would care to return to the bank, sign the contract, hand over the signed mortgage documents, the Adler PrivatBank would discharge his mortgages with the banks in Mexico and Panama and deposit the residual of his approved loan into his nominated bank account. He had done it. He had escaped the clutches of the banks in Central America, and he now had sufficient funds to pay off that irritating Chinese company, transfer all of the expensive machinery from the

Faithful Falcon Flying School and Aircraft Repair Company of Taiwan to the Intercontinental Precision Engineering. He could then shut down the Faithful Falcon Flying School and Aircraft Repair Company, walk away from the bad debts on the balance sheet of that company and to hell with his creditors.

Two hours later he returned in a euphoric state of mind. It had been tedious; he had had to initial every page and alteration on the contract and the mortgage documents, but it was now done. What would make it perfect was if Tonje were to enter his room and give herself to him. He would have to wait.

The next day, at the appointed time he returned to the bar. The three girls were not there, and he was suddenly afraid that they would not show, but then he saw them coming. They entered the bar, Tonje smiled at him, she actually smiled at him. Venderla was the spokesperson. "We all agreed that you appear to have the stamina to cope with the three of us. Our car is outside, and we will take you to our chalet."

It was about to happen, he thought, it's about to happen, he was almost delirious with excitement. They drove to the chalet. Venderla and Mari were the first out of the car, Venderla called out, "Tonje take Dacian to the chalet while Mari and I bring in the shopping, we've bought enough for a week, do you think that you'll be able to cope Dacian?"

Jiminez didn't bother to reply. As Tonje led him into the chalet he thought, 'I might just have a little entrée with my goddess before the others arrive and he reached forward to grasp Tonje's breasts. He heard the break in his arm before he felt the pain and then that pain was suffused by the impact of his face on the wall. She now had him by the throat, "This arsehole, is for the 32 women who took their own lives after suffering rape and sexual abuse from you," and she withdrew a hypodermic needle from her handbag and blunged it deep into his unbroken arm.

"That was quick," said Venderla as she entered the chalet devoid of any shopping, with Mari close behind, also without shopping bags.

"Too quick," said Tonje, "I wanted the bastard to really suffer. I would love to have chopped his balls off and stuffed them down his throat, but I believe there are other plans in store for him. Where is it we are to take him?

"Just to Lucerne," said Mari "where we will be met by an ambulance, and from there I believe, by private jet to Oslo. Oh, I do hope the pilot is handsome."

36

Juan Aiza and the Torres brothers, Emilio and Pasquale boarded the China Air flight for the short hop to Hong Kong. From Hong Kong they were then booked on a Cathay Pacific flight to London via Dubai. DCI Warbrick had organised with the police and Immigration in Hong Kong to advise him if anyone with the name of Juan Aiza boarded any flight out of Hong Kong to London or any other British or European destination.

He received an e-mail before the flight had departed Hong Kong that Juan Aiza had checked in for a Cathay Pacific flight to London. There were two other men with him, both with the same surname Torres. Warbrick quickly e-mailed a return. Request photographs of two pax with name of Torres, if at all possible, may also be on wanted list, exercise caution.

Juan Aiza and the Torres brothers were in the business class lounge enjoying a pre-flight drink when they were approached by a pretty hostess. "Mr Aiza, Mr Emilio Torres, and Mr Pasquale Torres, I am delighted to inform you that you have been upgraded to First Class, may I please have your boarding passes and passports. It will only take a few minutes to complete the paperwork.

There were grins all round as the hostess departed with boarding passes and passports. She returned minutes later with the passports and now, First Class boarding passes. If you would care to follow me gentlemen, I will take you through to the First-Class lounge.

Warbrick received the photographs within minutes. He compared the passport photographs with the security photograph taken on the night of Aileen Colquhoun's murder. "Bingo," he said, "we have a winner."

He called DS Fellingham to his office and she arrived five minutes later.

"Take a look at these passport photographs and the security camera photograph from Trentabank Reservoir," he said.

She did and suddenly gasped, "It's the three of them, all three of those animals that murdered Aileen Colquhoun, where are they now?"

Warbrick smiled, a deeply satisfying smile, "They are on their way to London's Heathrow airport courtesy of Cathay Pacific. Round up DC Proud Susan, we three are going to London, both you and young Gary deserve to be in on the collar."

The flight arrived, Senors Aiza, Emilio and Pasquale Torres were required to queue in the line headed 'Other Passport Holders,' their passports being either Panamanian or Argentinian. They were brought together at the Immigration Officer's desk who studied the three passports, probably because we are first class passengers now, mused Aiza.

"Welcome to Britain," smiled the Immigration Officer, "would you care to step this way?"

They followed him quickly down a short corridor and into an office where they were greeted by several armed police officers, armed with either X26 Taser electroshock stun guns or 9mm Heckler & Koch submachine guns. Despite a brief attempt by the Torres brothers to resist, they were quickly subdued by the sight of multiple stun guns and several of the more deadly Heckler & Kochs pointed at them. Their arms were unceremoniously pulled behind them and their wrists handcuffed.

Warbrick, Fellingham and Proud were there to witness it. All three greatly enjoyed the moment.

DCI Warbrick stepped forward and introduced himself. He then addressed Juan Aiza. "Senor Juan Aiza, also known as John Stone, I am arresting you for the murder of Aileen Colquhoun on the night of 5th/6th April of this year at Trentabank Reservoir in Macclesfield in the County of Cheshire," he went on to read Aiza his rights before moving on to each of the Torres brothers.

Each brother was charged with Accessory to Murder and also read their rights. They were then led through a series of corridors, away from the public's view to a waiting, armoured and secure police van with two police officers, and secured inside the van. They were then driven to three high security cells in the remand centre in Manchester to await the preliminary hearing.

On arrival at the remand centre in Manchester Aiza asked permission to make an international phone call. It was granted and he called the mobile phone owned by Dacian Jiminez. There was no answer, and there never would be.

When the prisoners had departed and within earshot of the armed police officers who had assisted the arrest, DCI Warbrick proudly announced, "This has to be one of, if not the, most satisfying day I have had in my 40 years as a police officer. Detective Sergeant Fellingham, Detective Constable Proud I am now about to take you for the best meal that this city has to offer because you thoroughly deserve it. The work of both of you on this case has been nothing short of stupendous, and I thank you for it."

The assembled and armed police officers cheered loudly and clapped enthusiastically. It doesn't happen often enough that perpetrators of violent crime are so comprehensively 'collared.' Neither does it happen often that serving policemen in the lower ranks will hear a Detective Chief Inspector deliver such fulsome praise to his junior offers. It had given everyone present a huge 'lift'.

Before they did sit down for that special lunch DS Fellingham asked if she could make one phone call, he smiled at her and simply said, "Of course."

A telephone rang in a small house in the Scottish Highland's city of Inverness and an elderly man answered it.

"Is that Mr Colquhoun, Mr Duncan Colquhoun?"

"It is," replied the voice.

"Mr Colquhoun, this is Detective Sergeant Fellingham of the Cheshire police, we met a few months ago."

"Aye, we did that, I remember."

"I am ringing to tell you that we have just arrested the three men who were responsible for the actual murder of Aileen in Macclesfield."

She heard the sharp intake of breath and then his loud cry to his wife, "Isla, Isla, it's Detective Sergeant Fellingham, she has just told me that the police have arrested the three men responsible for the actual murder of Aileen, isn't that wonderful?"

Isla was obviously saying something to Duncan, but DS Fellingham couldn't make out what it was.

Duncan came back to the phone, "Detective Sergeant, can you please wait a moment, Isla wishes to speak to you?"

The voice of a frail elderly lady spoke, "Susan," she said, there was no formal title, this was a conversation between two women, one who had suffered so much grief and anguish and the other, who had understood and tried diligently to help. "Susan, thank you so much for letting us know, I knew from the moment I met you, that you would find them, you remind me so much of my Aileen, so clever, so determined. Thank you again."

DS Fellingham was crying silently now, "I'm just so pleased that we were able to do it. Please take care of yourself Mrs Colquhoun."

"Tush lassie, it's Isla, my name is Isla, and you have given me the tonic that no doctor could ever prescribe. Hang on for a wee minute more, Duncan wishes to speak with you again."

Duncan Colquhoun came back to the phone, "Aye and my name is Duncan, no more of this Mr Colquhoun nonsense d'ye hear, it's Duncan and Isla Colquhoun from here on. Do ye mind if I ask ye another question?"

"Go right ahead Duncan."

"Is there any news of that evil devil Ramiro Morales?"

"Yes, Duncan there is, there is an international hunt on for him now, we don't have him yet, but we're closing in."

'Good God lassie, is there no end to the brightness that you bring to our lives, wait till I tell Isla, she has gone for a wee lie down and a good cry. Please let us know when you do nab him as I'm sure you will. Please call us anyway and bring that man of yours up here to meet us. We would love that."

37

The International carrier UPS delivered several packages on the same day to a number of cities across the world. The individual who was the nominated recipient was different in every case of course, but the organisations on the delivery address were unsurprisingly similar.

The recipients were:

European Aviation Safety Agency, in Cologne Germany,

Civil Aviation Authority London United Kingdom,

International Civil Aviation Organisation (ICAO) Montreal Canada,

Federal Aviation Administration Washington DC,

Civil Aeronautics Administration Taipei City Taiwan.

The packages were quite large. In each package and the first item to be found, was a copy of the spreadsheet produced by Ken Stockdale on which the first column showed a significant number of the parts requiring maintenance or replacement in the most common types of light aircraft or older commercial passenger/cargo aircraft. A second column then provided the relevant licence/ certificate numbers for authorised parts. A third column reflected the wholesale price of legitimate parts, current as of three months earlier. The fourth column, the wholesale price of the counterfeit parts manufactured by the Intercontinental Precision Engineering Company of Taiwan. A fifth column showed the name of the Company and location of the anticipated installation. In each and every case the company's name shown, was either Avnav Parts and Services Companies in Mexico City Mexico; Panama City Panama; Buenos Aires Argentina; Bilbao Spain; Macclesfield UK or by the Faithful Falcon Flying School and Aircraft Repair Company in Taiwan.

Each package contained, for the most part, the same examples of the illegal parts manufactured by the Intercontinental Precision Engineering Company, complete within the original packaging with the coded identification of the manufacturer highlighted on this packaging. These illegal parts had all been obtained as a consequence of the excessive sexual appetite of Senor Gustavo Hernandez, Purchasing Manager of the Faithful Falcon Flying School and Aircraft Repair Company, of Taiwan.

The response was immediate and comprehensive, within 48 hours the Avnav Parts and Services companies in Mexico, Panama, Argentina and Spain had been raided, all parts, both legal and illegal, seized, the Company Directors charged with fraud and the employees made redundant.

It was a similar situation in Taiwan except that the operation against the Intercontinental Precision Engineering Company took considerably longer given the size of the organisation and the huge volume of its illegally manufactured stock needing to be transported to a secure police warehouse pending further examination. The Directors of this company, Senors Dacian Jiminez and Juan Aiza could not be contacted. Both were known to be overseas, but then the Taiwanese police were notified that Senor Aiza had been arrested by the UK police on a murder charge. Senor Dacian Jiminez, believed to be in Switzerland, could not be contacted. He failed to respond to frequent calls to his mobile phone.

He had apparently travelled to Switzerland for a business meeting with Adler PrivatBank and that organisation was contacted requesting that they advise Senor Jiminez to contact the Taiwan Police as a matter of urgency should he be in touch with them. The Adler PrivatBank, sufficiently alerted and concerned, commenced their own private investigation.

The raid on the Faithful Falcon Flying School and Aircraft Repair was rather more productive. Senor Gustavo Hernandez, seeing the arrival of such a fleet of police vehicles, immediately believed that they had come for him, so prominent in his mind, was his guilt. He was fearful of the police, but he was absolutely terrified of Juan Aiza and his two gorillas, the Torres brothers.

He attempted to take his own life by considering jumping off the platform of the aircraft observation tower, but he lost his nerve when he saw how far below the ground appeared from this lofty platform. He was found by the police, a huddled and weeping wreck, against the windows that made up the external wall of the observation room. His confession poured out of him, and he was led away, quite willingly, to the police station where he made and signed his statement prior to being charged with fraud. He was aware that this would lead to a prison sentence, but that would mean he would be safely secure from the Torres brothers.

He did not yet know that he would be safe from the Torres brothers and Juan Aiza, forever.

Trevor Byford was in his office early; he was becoming increasingly anxious as the days ticked away on the 28-day deadline for the compulsory removal of his company's assets. Aiza had told him that he would fix the problem, but Byford had heard nothing from him other than being told that Aiza was due in the UK anytime soon.

His anxiety reached palpitation levels as a series of police vehicles swept into the forecourt of his offices and factory. Several uniformed policemen and women dispersed from the vehicles and began to surround the building with blue and white tape that depicted a crime scene. Several minutes later, uniformed police officers entered his offices, ignored him and went immediately into the warehouse. They began to emerge, minutes later, carrying quantities of aircraft spare parts. This process would continue for a further hour.

A tired looking plain clothed police officer who introduced himself as Detective Inspector Hunt, addressed him, "Trevor John Byford, you are charged with the installation of illegal and unauthorised aircraft parts, in full knowledge of the facts that these aircraft parts were both illegal and unauthorised. In so doing you contravened regulation 17/62 of the Safety of Aviation Act 2007 and as amended by paragraph 4 sub-section 3C of the Amendment to Aviation Act 2011. Additionally, you, knowingly and deliberately, put at risks the lives of many, as yet unknown, people and you are cautioned that further investigations will now ensue, out of which may lead to further charges being brought against you. How do you plead?"

"I don't know."

"Do you plead Guilty or Not Guilty," insisted DI Hunt.

"Oh Christ, Guilty." and then, "May you rot in hell Morales, I'm sorry I ever met you."

DI Hunt looked at him, contempt so clearly obvious across his face, "Take him out of my sight Sergeant" and a uniformed Sergeant stepped forward, locked the handcuffs on Byford's wrists and led him outside to the waiting police car.

38

There was an ambulance waiting at a small airfield on the outskirts of Lucerne for the arrival of the three Jegertroppen troops with the drugged Dacian Jiminez/ Ramiro Morales. Eduardo Roni was in the ambulance. He stepped out from the ambulance and opened the rear doors. Two paramedics exited. They removed the recumbent Dacian Jiminez and lifted him into the ambulance ensuring that he was safely secure for the winding road trip to Brescia. The name on the side of the ambulance was, Ospedale Oncologico di Brescia.

Eduardo approached the three women. "I cannot express my gratitude sufficiently for all that you have done for me over the past week. I know that there must have been many occasions when you were disgusted. I am truly sorry that I had to ask you to do this, but I do hope that you understand that it was the only way that I could be sure to capture him. Please accept this small gift as a token of both my appreciation of your help and my admiration for everything that you each are," and he handed them each a thick envelope.

He personally drove them across to the parked Lear jet remarking, "There are plenty of refreshments on board, I trust that you have a pleasant flight." He returned to the waiting ambulance, climbed aboard, and the ambulance drew swiftly away. The vehicle that the Jegertroppen troops had utilised, would be collected later that day.

Venderla, Mari, and Tonje, entered the aircraft. The pilot one of two, both of whom were indeed handsome, asked, "All set ladies?"

'Yes," they responded and settled into their seats which had been refigured into a club formation so that they could talk between the three of them. Venderla was the first to open her envelope and her colleagues quickly followed suit. Venderla whistled, "Faen i helvete (Fucking Hell) there's twenty grand in here."

"Mine too," added Mari.

"And mine," said Tonje.

Venderla smiled, "Now that's a man I would willingly honour and obey."

"You'd have to fight me first," grinned Tonje.

The drive from Lucerne to Brescia took a little over four hours. Eduardo said little en-route pre-occupied as he was with what he was about to have done. He had thought about it many times over the past several months, ever since, in fact, that the idea first occurred to him. He wasn't a religious man, but he honestly thought of himself as an honourable man, if he was such an honourable man how he could contemplate doing the disreputable thing that he was planning to do.

It had been Istvan, and, he had been surprised to find, Greta who had helped him to come to terms with his intended actions and his conscience.

They had decided to proceed with the proposal put to them by the Polizia Penitenziaria in relation to the surgical treatment of prisoners suffering from prostate, testicular or localised colon cancers. They had received a grant, and work had commenced on the alterations to the hospital in Brescia to ensure that it met with the standards of security required for the treatment of male prisoners. It was not yet complete but there was now an area at the hospital, free from other patients, where he would be able to carry out what he was planning.

At no stage had he discussed his plans with anyone, not Lucia, not Lindsay Warbrick, and not Istvan and Greta Csany. He had then decided that he was not being fair to them by involving them in something to which they may feel strongly averse. He had asked them both to meet him, in the office he kept at the hospital for his own purposes, on a Saturday morning.

He had begun by requesting that they first hear him out, totally, before commenting. He had talked for two hours; he gave them the full history of Ramiro Morales as he had heard it from DCI Warbrick. Previously they had only known about Izabella, the abuse and humiliation that she had suffered and her tragic suicide. He now quantified the extent of the pain created by Ramiro Morales, 32 suicides and a suspected number of rape and sexual abuse victims reaching a number in excess of 100.

He told them how he had come into contact with DCI Warbrick and DS Fellingham and the plan that he and Warbrick had concocted together but without Warbrick knowing, fully, what he, Eduardo, intended. He told them of the incredibly detailed work done by Warbrick's support team in Cheshire. He told them of DCS Goddard's attempts to utilise the Argentinian police to prosecute Morales which had been to no avail, and he then told them what he intended. He didn't have to go into detail, they knew exactly what was involved.

Both Istvan and Greta were deeply sympathetic, but it was Greta who comforted him. "I am a catholic Eduardo, and I believe that I am a good catholic. I do not and cannot believe that my God put such an evil man on this earth deliberately. But no matter that I am a good catholic, I cannot and do not believe that such men are worthy of redemption. They are not just an insult to God, they are also an insult to all good men such as my husband, and yourself Eduardo. Morales' mother was correct when she described him as the spawn of the Devil, and she disowned him. I truly believe that this woman would have cut the heart from his chest if she were in a position to do so. I know that I would do so if he were my child. My God is a compassionate God, but he is also an angry God. I believe that he is extremely angry as he has listened to your story today, Eduardo. I say punish him Eduardo, punish him with the instruments of his own evil and then, exterminate him."

The ambulance arrived at his hospital in Brescia. Morales was brought, still unconscious into the operating theatre in the vacated section of the hospital. Istvan and Greta were both scrubbed and ready. Istvan was to be surgeon, Greta the theatre sister and Eduardo, the anaesthetist. It would not be an excessively long procedure. The procedure is known throughout the surgical fraternity as a Radical Inguinal Orchidectomy.

The general anaesthetic was administered with Eduardo carefully watching the machine controls and the monitoring of the patient. Morales was supine, the ipsilateral, inguinal, and lower abdominal region shaved and cleaned. A square sterile drape was positioned to expose the ipsilateral inguinal region and hemiscrotum, with the penis pulled away from the surgical field.

A traditional oblique incision was then made by Istvan parallel to the inguinal ligament. The ilioinguinal nerve was then identified and dissected free from the external spermatic fascia. The ilioinguinal nerve was then retracted from the surgical field. The spermatic cord was then gently mobilised, and the cord encircled with a drain to create a tourniquet and secured with a clamp.

Applying gentle traction to the spermatic cord the testes were pushed into the surgical field. A triple clamp technique was then used by Istvan to divide the spermatic cord. Both testicles and the spermatic cord were then removed and non-absorbable sutures applied to the divided cord, Istvan then applied suture ligation to avoid ties slipping off the retracting spermatic cord.

The ilioinguinal nerve was then placed on the floor of the inguinal canal followed by routine closure of the subcutaneous fascial layers and skin to complete the procedure.

Senor Ramiro Morales was now a eunuch and was highly unlikely to sexually abuse any other unfortunate female, in the future.

Recovery from the procedure would take approximately two weeks, during which time Morales would be maintained in a semi-comatose state. The only hospital staff that he would see would be Istvan, Greta or Eduardo. He was fed a special diet containing a high content of Cyproterone Acetate and which was fed to him by Greta. He did attempt to speak to her, first, in his poor Italian which she genuinely didn't understand, then in English, at which she shrugged her shoulders, then in Spanish, at which she smiled, and shrugged her shoulders.

Eduardo had taken it upon himself to stay overnight at the hospital, to give Istvan and Greta a break and to ensure that Ramiro Morales remained closer to unconscious rather than conscious.

Finally, the two weeks were complete, sutures removed, and wounds healed, and Morales being prepared to face the full force of the law and the distressed voice of a victim he could scarcely remember, nor care about.

39

Detective Inspector Judy Sneddon arrived at her place of work with London's Metropolitan Police at her normal time but totally unaware of the events that lay before her that day. She had recently heard that she may, finally, be considered for promotion. She knew that she had been passed over several times in the past and she was fairly sure that the old bastard Goddard had been responsible for that. She wasn't sure anymore that she wanted to be promoted. She was now comfortably off, her house almost paid for, but she knew that the additional income that she had been receiving from her former lover, would not continue for a great deal longer. Those days were coming to an end.

Perhaps it was time for a change of occupation, but she had no idea what that change might look like. She was about to find out.

She arrived at her office where a uniformed female police officer was waiting for her, "Detective Inspector Sneddon, I am instructed to advise you that your presence is required in Conference Room 3, immediately,"

"Very well constable, you have so instructed me, you may go now."

"I am instructed to escort you to Conference Room 3, Detective Inspector."

The first spasm of alarm ran through her, she looked to her left and right along the corridor. There were two other uniformed female police officers stationed at either end. Shit. What is this.

She was escorted by these three police officers to Conference Room 3. She entered the room. There were three Senior police officers seated along one side of the table, In the centre was Detective Chief Superintendent Goddard, to his right sat her boss, Detective Superintendent Thompson and to Goddard's left, the arch witch who had always hated her, Assistant Commissioner Walker, the only female who was also in uniform. There was a single seat on the opposite side of the table from these three. She was told to sit, there were no pleasantries.

DCS Goddard began, "Detective Inspector Sneddon," he breathed deeply as though trying to retain control, "or should I simply address you as Bluebird."

She cried out, her hand flew to her mouth and one word escaped "How?"

Her first instinct was to flee but the two constables who had entered the room with her pushed her back into her seat.

DCS Goddard produced a file, a blue file, opened it and began to read, her e-mails to Ramiro, his replies to her, the names of the students she had advised him about, his description of the sluts who had offered their bodies to him. They had it all. How in God's name did they get it. Ramiro must be dead; she hadn't heard from him for over a week. Oh God he must be dead. She was shaking in terror now and the tears came.

It was the rapier-like voice of Assistant Commissioner Angela Walker which said, "All of it from the beginning, and we really do mean all of it."

The flood gates opened then, from the beginning when she had first visited ICE to investigate the claims of Rita Velasquez that Morales had sexually assaulted and then raped her. Her meeting with Morales when he had charmed her and convinced her that he was but a stupid male who could not resist the pleadings of an attractive young woman, to comfort her. How she had been convinced by his charm. How within one week of meeting him she herself had become sexually involved with him.

She told them that he did not wish her to visit him at ICE, it would arouse too much suspicion, he had said. He had suggested that he visit her in her home where they would meet, twice weekly, to begin with, but not for any great length of time, because he was too tired from his tango classes. He had started to give her money later in that first year. There had been a couple of other complaints, from other students who had thrown themselves at him, and when he had rejected them, they had fabricated stories of his assault. He had asked her to keep him informed of any other complaints that the police might receive because he was anxious to protect his integrity with the University Authorities.

His financial contributions had increased, and she had become used to them, and so after he stopped having sex with her in the third year after they had met, he continued his payments because she had become his loyal friend, and he trusted her.

He had told her about Aileen Colquhoun who, she said, had blackmailed him into marrying her after she had reported his visa expiration to the Immigration Authorities. She had also claimed that he had raped her and photographed her naked, but she was just another one who he had rejected. He had told her, Judy Seddon, many times that he loved her, even though she was so much older than him, and she believed him. She loved him with every fibre of her being and the fact that he was so often too tired for sex made her believe that his interest in her was only because he loved her.

Then there had been that conspiracy by all those tarts from Central and South America that he had also rejected, who had then conspired to have him sacked from ICE. She had been heartbroken when he had been forced to leave and flee the country, but then he had contacted her again about a year later. Didn't that prove that he truly loved her she had plaintively asked the three judging police officers.

DCS Goddard had taken her off the case, which had upset her, so she had befriended DC Pam Miller on DCS Goddard's team, who kept her informed of other students from ICE who were trying to harm him. They had set up their e-mail link in the late 1996, where she had adopted the Bluebird name and logo as her username. She had thought it appropriate as she was a serving police officer.

He had told her that he now no longer worked in the education sector because he had to work at a place where there were no young women who would try to seduce him. He was working on top secret installations in the aircraft defence industry, and she needed to keep him informed of any emerging complaints because he feared for his job if there were to be any scandal.

As an illustration of that fact, she told them about the woman who had blackmailed him into marrying her was now hounding him again with more lies and threatening to report him to his employer, and the aviation authorities in the UK. Pam Miller had learned of that woman's plans and travel arrangements from Taiwan to the UK via Canada and she had passed that on to Sneddon, who in turn had passed it on to Morales. She added that he had changed his name to Jiminez to protect himself from further slander.

She continued to cry when her dissertation had finished. DCS Goddard was completely stunned and was trying to frame his response when A/C Walker leaned across the table toward Sneddon and in a voice dripping with sarcasm said, "And when did you have your lobotomy, you have forgotten to mention that. You must have had one, or at least one, to even begin to believe that bizarre fantasy you have just insulted us with. How did you ever make Detective Inspector, I have heard more logic expressed from patients suffering from end stage dementia. Please tell this imbecile what she has done Detective Chief Superintendent.

Goddard was angry, extremely angry and the words that this woman Sneddon had so recently uttered had done nothing, absolutely nothing to alleviate this anger.

"Is this an attempt on your part to establish your insanity should a charge of murder be brought against you? Tell me, is it, because if it is I must tell you that it will fail. Your sanity and intellect have only recently been assessed as part of the processes undertaken when a candidate is being considered for promotion, and I must tell you, you passed with flying colours."

"Murder, what do you mean murder?" the colour completely drained from Sneddon's face at this point.

"You have been responsible for the grossly untimely death of 32 women between the ages of 18-22, the sexual assault and rape of in excess of 100 more women of a similar age and the murder of a woman in her thirties, another victim of Morales, who was murdered in Cheshire less than one year ago after you provided Morales with her travel arrangements."

"No" cried Sneddon.

Goddard then hit her hard and repeatedly with the tales of Morales' victims. "Beginning with Rita Velasquez who was planning to take Morales through the courts on a charge of rape and sexual assault which YOU, ONLY YOU, believed to be consensual. Did Maria Olivares' family consent to her overdosing on barbiturates after she was raped by Morales and photographs of her being raped by Morales sent to her family. Did the mother of Juanita Mendez consent to her husband blowing his brains out and her daughter climbing into the bath, opening her veins after Morales had sent them photographs of him raping Juanita. He also sent them to the mayor of the town where she lived. Did Aileen Colquhoun's family consent to her being taken to a large tract of water, something which totally terrified her, and having her head held beneath the water until she drowned by men operating under the instructions of Ramiro Morales. Would you like me to go on?"

"No please no, I can't believe it, he wouldn't do that."

"Then I'll go on until you do, I can also bring the photographs to show you, of your beloved Morales, with his grinning face between the legs of some incredibly unfortunate 18-year-old girl. Would that convince you?"

A low moan escaped her mouth, "Take her to a cell somewhere, have a doctor visit her, but take her out of my sight."

She was picked up by the two constables and taken from the room.

40

Amongst the many papers that Dacian Jiminez/Ramiro Morales had signed that afternoon at the bank but had not read, were several related to his forthcoming trip to South Africa which had been slipped into his bundle of papers, but in his distraction over the beautiful Tonje, he had not noticed.

There was an internal note on Intercontinental Precision Engineering letterhead to his secretary (she was his mistress in Taiwan) requesting that she arrange for his flights to, and accommodation in, Cape Town and on to Buenos Aires. There was a letter to an aircraft repair company also in Cape Town signed by both Dacian Jiminez and the Manager of the Adler PrivatBank advising of his interest in securing a contract with the Cape Town company for the provision of certain aircraft parts, and a third to a Commercial Real Estate agent in Cape Town expressing an interest in viewing industrial complexes suitable for the erection of warehousing.

He was taken to Manchester Airport with his suitcase, which had been removed from the Baur au Lac Hotel in Zurich, where he boarded an extended range Lear Jet with no Company markings and flown to Dubai where the aircraft refuelled. He then flew on to Cape Town in South Africa. He slept almost the entire distance from Manchester to Cape Town.

At Cape Town airport he was met by a driver of a taxi who was holding a board with his name written in chalk on it. He was only partially aware of a young woman wearing a British Airways Air Hostess uniform, who was already in the cab. The taxi pulled into the Radisson Blu Hotel in the Victoria and Alfred Waterfront area of Cape Town and the airline hostess asked him to wait whilst she obtained a wheelchair from the hotel. She returned a few minutes later and helped him into the wheelchair and wheeled him inside the hotel.

The hotel staff were most concerned. The hostess, she said her name was Paula, did her best to settle everyone down by saying that Mr Jiminez was OK, he had taken a bad turn on the flight from London, he had now been checked by a doctor who had administered a sedative but otherwise described Mr Jiminez as well enough to travel. The hostess had helped to check him into the hotel and then requested assistance to escort Mr Jiminez to his room. A bell boy was summoned who carried the suitcase and brief case whilst Paula pushed the wheelchair.

He was taken to a room on the fourth floor overlooking the waterfront, where Paula made a fuss, in full view of the Bell Boy, of ensuring that Mr Jiminez understood that she had returned his passport and the unused section of his airline ticket. His boarding pass from London was also with his passport and ticket. She checked again that he was feeling OK and then, thanking him for flying British Airways, she wished him well and departed.

The following morning Dacian Jiminez awoke, he was feeling pretty ordinary. He lay in bed wondering where the hell he was. His most recent memory was being hit by that Norwegian woman, he thought that she had broken his arm, he looked at his arm, it was still encased in plaster. His face felt sore also, he stood groggily and examined his face in the mirror. It was heavily bruised.

Where the hell was he, he looked for the hotel stationary, he was in the Radisson Blu Hotel in Cape Town South Africa. What was he doing in South Africa, he had no recollection. He looked for his passport, yes there it was, stamped yesterday for admission into the Republic of South Africa. He found his boarding pass for the Business Class seat from London. He couldn't remember boarding that flight either.

He went through his papers, he could remember none of it, not asking Wei Ting to make the airline and hotel bookings, not even remembering flying from Zurich to London. He was reading through the remainder of his letters, becoming more and more confused as he did so, when he felt a discomfort in his groin. He dropped his underpants, there was a small healing scar in his groin. He had undergone an operation recently and he couldn't remember why, what for, or where it had been carried out. There was something different about him. He reached down to feel his scrotum, his testicles had gone. Some bastards had removed his testicles, and he didn't know who. He began to panic, what did that mean, did it mean that he couldn't get it up anymore. Oh my God, I've been castrated. Those Norwegian bitches, they must have somehow done it.

The hotel Manager called to enquire after his health. He replied that he was OK but couldn't remember arriving at the hotel the previous day. The Manager then informed him that he had been brought to the airport by an airline hostess, he thought from British Airways.

"Did she leave a card" asked Jiminez.

"No" replied the Manager, "but she looked after you extremely well."

"My face appears to be bruised," said Jiminez, 'how did that happen?"

"Apparently you had some kind of episode on the aircraft, and you fell," replied the Manager.

Jiminez hung up without further comment.

He was dressed and sitting in a bucket seat in his room becoming increasingly depressed when there was a heavy banging on his room door.

He opened the door, there were three men, three large men standing outside. One of them, the one at the rear flashed a warrant card, Captain Andre Coetzee, South African Police, "Can we come in?"

Jiminez walked into his room without commenting, the three policemen followed him in.

Coetzee continued, "This is Sergeant Friedrich Potgieter, and this is Constable Johan Pienaar.

"What do you want," snapped Jiminez.

"You arrived in South Africa yesterday?" asked Coetzee.

"Apparently," another blunt response.

"Are you aware that you are wanted for fraud in Taiwan, that your businesses, worldwide, have been closed down, your stock impounded, your employees made redundant and your fellow Director Juan Aiza and two other employees Emilio and Pasquale Torres, are in jail in England having been charged with murder."

"We are also aware that you are about to be pursued on bankruptcy charges in England, Mexico, Panama, Argentina, Spain, and of course Taiwan."

Jiminez turned white, "You must be fucking joking."

"Not at all," continued Coetzee, "whereas most of that is of no interest to us, only insofar as that it helps us to understand what kind of," he paused, "person that you are. We are not here for any of that."

"We are here to arrest you for the rape and sexual assault of one Loraina Beyers of Stellenbosch in 1996. The rape and sexual assault are alleged to have occurred in London whilst she was an undergraduate student at the International College of Economics and where you were a Lecturer in Economics at that same Institution. At that time, you were employed in your birth name of Ramiro Morales of Argentina which you changed in 2012, along with your nationality, to Dacian Jiminez of Panama. How do you plead?"

"You must be fucking joking,"

"No Mr Morales or Jiminez or whatever the fuck you wish to call yourself, I am not fucking joking. How do you plead."

"Not guilty,' whispered Morales, but the light had vanished from his eyes.

He was taken handcuffed and an obvious prisoner of the South African Police, to a Remand Centre in the centre of Cape Town. The hotel attempted to charge the credit card Paula had extracted from his wallet at the time of check-in, but payment was declined.

He was remanded to face a hearing the following day where preliminary evidence would be presented to determine if sufficient evidence existed for him to face trial.

Rape and Sexual Assault had been a significant problem in South Africa for many years. In a major survey conducted some two years earlier, 35% of women between the ages of 15- 35 had admitted to being raped at least once, usually by someone known to her or her family. One in four men had admitted to raping a woman at some time in their past.

The consequences of this survey were several-fold. Firstly, sentences for men convicted of rape and sexual assault were toughened considerably, with the maximum prison term being increased from 8 to 18 years. Secondly, victims of rape or sexual assault could apply to have their case heard in Chambers, or in Camera in Court, where the press and members of the public were not permitted entry. This simple change to the act alone, had quadrupled the number of cases being brought before the Court. Victims of rape and sexual assault could no longer be forced to endure the humiliation of an aggressive defending Counsel, and then read about it in the next morning's newspapers, alongside millions of other South Africans.

Loraina Beyers had applied to have her case heard by jury in Camera and her request had been approved.

Prosecuting Counsel was to be one Yvette Botha, a highly experienced prosecuting Counsel with a formidable reputation for obtaining convictions in such cases and almost always demanding the maximum term of imprisonment possible. She, again, almost always, succeeded in obtaining it. She had in her possession the file of photographs, taken without the victim's knowledge or consent, graphically showing the many instances of rape and sexual assault, inflicted on Loraina Beyers by Ramiro Morales. His laughing face appearing frequently in the photographs.

The remand hearing was a formality, and the trial was set for six weeks hence.

Morales, now devoid of funds and without access to any, was granted legal aid. A junior Counsel, a male, 12 months out of Law School, was appointed to defend him.

41

The Directors of the Adler PrivatBank were quite distraught. It had all happened so quickly. When the Senior Partner of the Legal firm with whom they frequently did business had approached them saying that he had a wealthy client who had a desire to invest in a business, but not directly, they were, naturally, interested. The proposal was, that the wealthy client would deposit a substantial sum of money, confidentially, of course, to provide security to the bank, as encouragement for them, to enter into a formal secured loan arrangement with the business that the lawyers' client held an interest in investing. The Senior Partner had detailed the situation by explaining that the business in question was experiencing some short-term cash flow problems, and its current mortgagees, two banks, one in Mexico City, the other in Panama City were insisting that their mortgages be discharged.

The securities that the business owned, and were now mortgaged to the Central American Banks, were the land, buildings, and machinery, involved in the manufacture of aircraft parts. The lawyer's wealthy client believed that these assets would be sufficient to secure, initially, the loan from Adler PrivatBank and then, by transfer to this client, as security for his investment with the bank. It was a little unusual but not remarkably so, just a little fun really. Fun, as it is understood, by the staid community of Swiss bankers.

The Directors of the Adler PrivatBank became quickly, but confidentially, aware that the Senior Partner's wealthy client, was none other than Eduardo Roni, one of Italy's richest men. Such news, with its attendant ringing of cash registers or the gushing of oil wells, is the life blood that sustains the economy of Switzerland, and the deal was completed with corresponding alacrity.

The Adler PrivatBank's Directors became considerably alarmed, naturally, when they learned that the Proprietor of the business to which they had, only one day earlier, advanced a substantial loan, was being pursued on fraud charges. This was considerably more concerning than the other fact that another Director of this same business had been arrested in England on a murder charge. Murder is only the taking of a life, fraud is the taking of MONEY, Switzerland's only and all-powerful God.

These same Directors now beseeched their colleague, the Senior Partner of the Legal firm, to contact his wealthy client and express their dismay and condolences that these dreadful things had come to pass so early in their relationship with this wealthy client. They wished his client to know that Adler PrivatBank stood ready to assist in any manner that it was able.

Eduardo, after receipt of this message, could not resist replying that these events had in fact been unfortunate and distressing made even more so by the fact that he had been acting on the bank's advice. He did not specify which bank, but the thought of the dyspepsia that this comment would have created in the digestive systems of the Adler PrivatBank's Directors, was the highlight of his morning.

This communication though, made him realise that he needed to protect the asset that, at the completion of the bankruptcy process, would revert to him. He called his friend Chen Chin-Lung in Taiwan and asked him to arrange security for the land buildings and plant of the Intercontinental Precision Engineering Company (IPEco). During the phone call with Chen, he learned that all the stock seized by the Civil Aeronautics Administration of Taiwan, valued at in excess of US$50 million in the books of IPEco, were in fact worthless, as they were all illegally manufactured. They had now been dumped, beneath several thousand tons of concrete, as part of the runway extension at Taiwan International Airport.

Eduardo had recently had an interesting idea about the future use of these buildings and plant and he now discussed this with Chen. Chen was indeed interested and suggested that he would like to be part of this new plan himself. They agreed to discuss this further at the next meeting between them in Tainan.

Eduardo had called DCI Warbrick the day he learned of Morales' arrest and remand. Warbrick was delighted and mentioned a celebration. "My friend we will indeed celebrate, all of us, it will be at my pleasure but let us have a little more patience and wait for the conviction. I understand that the trial will commence six weeks from now. I do not believe that it will be a lengthy trial."

Warbrick had agreed, "I also have heard that the trial for the four involved with Aileen Colquhoun's murder is set for two weeks following your date of the rape trial in South Africa. It would be fitting if we could bring this whole thing to a close around the same time for the benefit of the families who have suffered so much. Celebrations then, would be certainly worth having."

Eduardo agreed and was about to hang up when Warbrick continued, "I had a call from DCS Goddard two days ago. He has been in contact with our colleagues in the South African Police. It seems that when Morales was admitted to the remand centre in Cape Town he was subjected to a mandatory medical examination. Goddard tells me that he is somewhat less of a man than he was when he taught at ICE. He wanted to know if I knew anything about it. I naturally told him the truth, that I didn't. I just want you to know that I liked you, considerably, beforehand, but I love you like a brother now, well done my friend."

Eduardo replaced the phone, he smiled, that call had meant more to him than he thought that it would have. Clearly Lindsay would have done the same thing had he been able to. First Greta now Lindsay, perhaps he wasn't such a disreputable man after all.

42

The trial of Dacian Jiminez/ Ramiro Morales began on a Monday in Cape Town. The preliminaries had been gone through, the defendants name stated, and the charges read out. The defendant had been asked to re-state his plea and he had replied "Not Guilty."

Defence and Prosecuting Counsels had outlined their cases, Defence Counsel submitting that the defendant did not deny that sex had occurred between the defendant and the alleged victim, but that it had been consensual. Prosecuting Counsel submitted a far different scenario, one involving the production of unknown and non-consensual films of a pornographic nature, purely for the commercial gain and sexual gratification of the defendant, rape, sexual abuse and extreme humiliation.

The trial was being held, in Camera, before a jury of seven women and five men. The Judge, the Honourable Amahle Kotze, instructed the jury that as the trial was being held in Camera, all evidence presented was and would continue to be regarded as confidential. Any breach of this confidentiality, at any time, now and into the future, by any member of the jury, would be regarded as Contempt of Court and charges brought accordingly.

Yvette Botha, Counsel for the Prosecution rose.

Although Jiminez had previously agreed to his stated name, he was asked to state his name again.

"Dacian Jiminez," he replied.

"Do you have a passport in that name?"

"Yes."

"From which country?"

"Panama."

"Is Dacian Jiminez the name you were given at birth?"

"No"

What was your given name at birth?"

"Ramiro Morales"

"Where were you born?"

"Buenos Aires Argentina"

"Do you have, or did you have a passport in that name?"

"I no longer have one."

"Mr Jiminez, I asked you if you had one, did you?"

"Yes"

"From which country"

"Argentina"

"Mr Jiminez, when did you change your name and your nationality?"

"2012"

"Mr Jiminez, why did you change your name and your nationality in 2012?"

No answer

"Mr Jiminez, I ask again why did you change your name and your nationality in 2012."

"I fell out with my mother."

"You fell out with your mother, why did you fall out with your mother, Mr Jiminez?"

"She is a strange woman."

"She is a strange woman, in what way is she strange Mr Jiminez?"

"I don't know, just strange."

"Just strange, I find that answer just strange, but we'll return to it later."

You have a Bachelor of Economics degree from the University of Buenos Aires?"

"Yes"

"And a master's in economics from Columbia University in New York?"

"Yes"

"You were a lecturer in Economics at Columbia University from 1991 to 1992?"

"Yes"

"Why did you leave Columbia University in such a hurry in 1992 Mr Jiminez?"

"I didn't leave in a hurry from Columbia University in 1992, I was wanting to move to London, there was a job on offer there.

"I have a letter here, exhibit 1 in your bundle my Lady, from the Dean of Columbia University that Mr Morales, as he was then known, departed his role as Lecturer at Columbia University, midterm, on 13th September 1992, and without notice."

Mr Morales/Jiminez let's call you Mr. Morales, that was how you were known back then, and I don't wish to confuse the jury. Do the names Mary-Jean Walford and Marylin Monckton, known as Maisie Monckton, mean anything to you?"

"No."

"Really, that is a little surprising Mr. Morales given that Mary-Jean Walford and Maisie Monckton had both reported you to the police in New York, for sexual assault. You were due to appear in court to defend these charges, oh let us see, oh here it is, on 15th September 1992. Two days after you departed your job, without notice, at Columbia University. Is that why you were in such a hurry to leave Mr. Morales?"

"No"

"Did you defend these charges brought against you in court?"

"No"

"No, so these charges are still outstanding, don't worry Mr Morales, the statute of limitations has now probably expired, so you possibly won't be arrested if you should ever return to New York. Pity about those poor young women though, Mary-Jean Walford and Maisie Monckton, they never did receive justice, did they?"

The interrogation of Ramiro Morales continued for the best part of that day. By the time Judge Amahle Kotze called for a recess, at the end of the day, the jury had heard from Loraina Beyers as the main witness who had described in graphically horrific detail about how she had been ensnared by Morales and her revulsion when he had shown her the films he had taken. They had been shown ten of the worst photographs of those taken of Loraina and Morales with several showing his grinning face between her legs and wielding a cucumber. Both her parents had given evidence on her behalf describing the nights of hysteria they experienced with their daughter as she relived her experiences with Morales through her nightmares.

The Defence Counsel attempted to claim entrapment, stating that Morales had been brought to South Africa under duress. Prosecuting Counsel, then produced the British Airways boarding pass for his flight from London to Cape Town, the letters to his secretary requesting her assistance in booking both flights and accommodation, and the letter to the real estate agent regarding inspections of industrial type properties. But the real clincher was the letter to the South African based aircraft repairing company, requesting a contract and countersigned by a senior member of a well-respected bank in Switzerland. The claim of entrapment had been thoroughly refuted.

They had also learned of the suicide of Loraina's friend, Anika Kampfert from Port Elizabeth, when Morales had sent photographs of his activities with his daughter, to her father, having been begged by Anika not to, as her father was a Minister in the Dutch Reform Church.

Yvette Botha had returned to his comment about the strange behaviour of his mother. She produced evidence which consisted of his mother, Isabella

Morales, publicly describing him as the spawn of the Devil and roundly disowning him. This was following receipt of a letter and a video disc. from one of two of his victims, named Maria Olivares, in 2004, prior to his dismissal from ICE. In this letter, Maria Olivares, had begged Morales' mother to first read the letter and then watch the video of her shame. The two victims had subsequently suicided. The author of the letter by an overdose of barbiturates and the younger via the opening of her veins in the bath following receipt of a video of her with Morales by the Mayor of the town where she lived with her deeply religious family. Her father had subsequently shot himself which had led to the 18-year-old Juanita Mendez, ending her life.

The following morning was the turn of the Defence Counsel. The young male lawyer had been horrified to hear all that he had heard during the previous day, and he knew without a shadow of a doubt, that his client could not be more guilty if he had raped someone before a thousand witnesses. He tried to defend his client. He had recalled Loraina Beyers to the stand attempting to prove that her role in all of this had been consensual. Loraina Beyers had heatedly denied this. When his cross examination had ended the Prosecuting Counsel had risen again.

"Members of the jury, I had wanted to spare you from this, I really believe that you have seen and heard so much horrific detail of the victim's experience that it would be un-necessary to show you more, but my learned colleague has stated that these acts were consensual."

She asked the consent of the judge to show another video, it was given.

Yvette Botha stood again, "This video runs for 40 minutes, it is disgusting. I only intend to show you five minutes of it simply to disprove my learned colleagues' assertions."

The video commenced, the plaintive cries of Loraina Beyers could be heard sobbing, "Stop, oh please stop." Then a long wail reaching a loud scream, "Oh Stop, stop. please oh please, stop. Loraina had remained in the witness box, and she broke down into convulsing sobs.

"Stop it, stop it NOW,' ordered the Judge.

It was now time for Counsels for the Defence and Prosecution to summarise their cases. The Defence Counsel rose, "I have nothing further to add my Lady." He had been so shocked and outraged following those few minutes of the last video that he deeply regretted implying that the relationship had been consensual. He intended to apologise to the victim when the trial was concluded, which he was sure would be later that day.

Prosecuting Counsel then rose. "Ladies and Gentlemen of the Jury, this has been, by far, the most horrific and traumatic case of rape and sexual assault that has fallen to me to prosecute. I apologise for subjecting you to just a little of the horror that the victim, and many more like her, have been subjected to at the hands of this man. There can be no doubt in your mind now that this man, is evil. There can be no doubting his mother's grief when she described him as the spawn of the Devil and disowned him. There can be no doubt, that what you have heard over these past two days, is not just the pain, the shame, the humiliation of a single woman. Many more have suffered this same fate that she has. And why, because he appeared to be charming, he told them that they were beautiful, and to show themselves to him, and he then, without their knowledge or consent, he filmed them. He told them that he loved them, and he lied, and he destroyed their lives with it."

"I would dearly like to address this court and request the death sentence for this man, for he has murdered the hopes and dreams of so many young women. They had every right to believe that in a university environment they would be safe. They had every reason to trust their lecturer who was supposed to be guiding their young minds along the paths of fulfillment and success. Instead, he was simply exploiting their young bodies for his own sexual gratification and commercial gain. Yes, I would dearly like to ask for the death penalty, but I cannot. It is not permitted under the laws of our Republic to sentence someone to death for rape and sexual abuse, no matter how extreme, no matter how many victims, no matter how ruthless the methods of the rapist were."

However, I can ask, that when you find this man guilty, as you most assuredly will, then I ask that you recommend that this man is sentenced to be imprisoned for the maximum term possible, 18 years."

She sat down. The judge then offered guidance to the jury to consider in their deliberations and asked them to retire to consider their verdict.

They returned less than fifteen minutes later. The Forewoman of the jury rose.

"Had they reached a verdict."

"Yes."

"Was it a unanimous verdict."

"Yes."

"Did they find the defendant guilty or not guilty"

"Guilty," my Lord

The judge, the Honourable Amahle Kotze had been an eminent civil rights lawyer prior to her elevation to the judiciary. She had been particularly prominent in defending the rights of women.

She now addressed Morales in a mood of controlled outrage at the despicable things that this man had done to so many women. She was measured and she was careful, and she provided no outlet for anyone to appeal on the grounds of judicial bias, and she sentenced him to the maximum term possible. 18 years at the Maximum-Security Prison of Pollsmoor in Tokai, Cape Town

The judge thanked the jury, and they were dismissed. The young defence lawyer sought out Loraina Beyers and apologised to her, but he didn't believe that his reasons for doing so had been fully understood and he remained angry with himself.

Ramiro Morales was taken away to begin his long-term incarceration in one of the toughest and most violent prisons in the world.

As he entered the prison compound thousands of prisoners lined the chain wire fence that enclosed it. The cry of 'Vars Vleis' began to echo around the compound. The guards grinned.

Morales didn't speak nor understand Afrikaans, so he didn't understand what was being called out so loudly.

He would soon enough though, Vars Vleis means Fresh Meat.

43

The news of Ramiro Morales' conviction and extensive prison term was a source of great delight in Wilmslow police station. It had also been similarly received in the offices of DCS Goddard who came on the phone early in the day following the decision, "Great news Lindsay," he said," my congratulations to you all, to you, to DS Fellingham and that young hard working copper DC Proud, he is well named that lad. No doubt you are planning a huge celebration?"

"Not so huge, at least not yet, I want to see Aileen Colquhoun's murderers convicted and sentenced before I will be completely satisfied," he had replied.

"Yes, I do understand, not much doubt about that happening though is there?"

"You know, better than I David, what smart-arsed lawyers can sometimes do. I'll keep my single malt aging for just a little longer before I throw my hat in the air."

"There's no money though, is there, to pay for smart-arsed lawyers and I can't see any of our more celebrated Pro-Bono performers stepping up can you. Not for three South American hoodlums?"

"No, I know all that, I'll simply sleep easier when we have finally nailed all these bastards. When does our obnoxious 'would be Lord Lichfield's case come up?"

"Not for another couple of months, but put your mind at ease on that one, he's changed his plea to "Guilty'. He now claims that Morales put him up to it, that he never wanted to photograph those poor girls, as he put it, in the first place."

"Oh really, and his explanation for raping several of them himself, did Morales put a splint round his dick?"

Goddard laughed, but not with any humour, "Don't worry about it, Lindsay, Mr Guvara is going down for a very, very, long time. He has admitted to rape, he says that he did so under duress, tell me how that works heh. He has been charged with rape alongside the other charges that he faces, and when convicted, he will be sent to a sexual offender's prison, there are eight of them now, as you probably know, in England and Wales. It is also likely that it will be recommended that he be placed on a rehabilitation programme involving the injection, four times annually, of the Zoladex agonist drug which is a Luteinizing Hormone Releasing Hormone (LHRH) most often used on patients suffering from prostate cancer. This decision won't be made until after his conviction and his admission to prison where he will be seen by a psychiatrist."

"We should just castrate the bastard."

"I don't disagree Lindsay, but it is the most that we are able to do under the circumstances."

"Have you charged your Bluebird yet with her chick, the DC.

"Not yet, the CPS are reluctant to progress a case of 'Accessory,' they don't think that they can make it stick. They think that we should pursue a 'Perverting the course of Justice," but she'll only receive eight years max for that and she'll be out in 4-5. Not enough in my book. She is also now claiming temporary insanity."

"For thirteen years, you must be joking?"

"Apparently not, there is no limit on for how long you can have been insane without anyone noticing."

"On an entirely different note, after you have achieved your conviction of Miss Colquhoun's murderers, I had planned to suggest that you and I meet up and share a good malt between us. But not anymore, I am planning to resign at the end of this week. I have talked to Jane about it, and she understands. I let her down Lindsay. I let Aileen Colquhoun and her family down and I must live with that for the rest of my life."

"I know that you are planning to retire soon, and I have heard that a wedding is on the cards, so I realise that you won't have a great deal of time. I think that I should simply say Goodbye now and say that it has been a real pleasure for me to have known you."

Warbrick paused for a moment or two, "I don't think that you should retire David, not like this, you have been a fantastic copper for nigh on forty years and been an inspiration to us all throughout that time.

Speaking as a friend I would like to ask you not to do it."

"Decisions made my friend, be happy with your new wife and your retirement Lindsay, you're a damn good cop yourself," and Goddard ended the call.

DS Fellingham wanted to call Duncan and Isla Colquhoun to give them the news, but she had an idea that would help to make the news more special. She rang Liverpool University and asked to speak to Dr Rory Colquhoun. The deep voice of Rory filled her earpiece, "Rory," she said, "what chance would there be of you travelling up to see you parents any time soon?"

"I was thinking of going there in a couple of weeks, but I suppose I could try to make the trip sooner, why do you ask?"

Susan then told him the news about Morales, he erupted in delight, "The thing is that I promised to call them when I knew, but it wouldn't be fair to make them wait for another couple of weeks. You see, I think that you should be there when I tell them, and you should be ready to take them somewhere to celebrate."

"What a brilliant idea Susan, I have a few days owing to me, I'll speak to the Prof, he'll release me I'm sure and I'll try to fly to Inverness early tomorrow. I'll call you back when I've booked my flight and give you my arrival time in Inverness. You can call them any time after an hour following my arrival. I'll make the arrangements for the celebration; I know exactly where to take them."

Rory called back two hours later, "I'll be arriving in Inverness at 11.15am, are you able to check arrival times in Inverness airport, my flight number is," and he gave her his flight number. "If it's on time call them any time after 12.30pm."

Now that the matter of calling Duncan and Isla Colquhoun had been settled her mind turned to the most vexing problem facing her now. Alex had asked her to give him some dates for their wedding.

He had been pressed to accept a lecture tour to the United States in the early part of the New Year, he was required to be in Rome in October of this year and the Belgian police were asking him to fly to Brussels to give an expert opinion on a work of Italian art which was suspected of being a forgery. If it turned out to be so, he would then be required to attend the trial of the forger, currently under arrest on an unrelated matter, with the trial being expected to be conducted in September. He was an extremely busy man.

She had received her invitation to Gina and Lindsay's wedding on the third Saturday in September. Oh God, she thought, Alex just HAD to be home for that. Terri and Gary had not yet set a date for their wedding. Gary was determined to be wearing his Sergeant's stripes before they did so.

Her parents could probably travel north almost at any time, but her dad did like receiving several weeks' notice of any planned event.

She knew that she didn't wish to wait until the winter months, she disliked the cold at the best of times and thought that her Christmas Party Polar Bear suit would not be the best choice as a Wedding Gown. They hadn't settled on a honeymoon destination, that too would be affected by their chosen wedding date.

She rang him, he answered, "How about the last Saturday in July?" she said.

"Perfect," was his unthinking response, "can't talk now, Venus needs a little more examination, ring you later."

"Oh, don't let me keep you from examining your Venus, is this one a virgin too?"

But he had gone.

Unfortunately for her, DC Proud was passing her office at the time of her outburst, his grinning face appeared around her door, "I must say Sarge, you are an extremely tolerant Detective Sergeant. If I was to tell Terri that I was examining a virgin named Venus, I'm sure that she wouldn't be nearly so tolerant as you."

She threw her stapler at him.

They had now both sat their respective examinations necessary for promotion. The results of both exams were due within the following two weeks, during the trial of Aileen Colquhoun's murderers. She was feeling upbeat about the trial. George Stubbins had decided to stand as a witness for the prosecution of Juan Aiza, he had never met the Torres brothers previously so clearly could not do the same thing there. He was hoping that his appearance in such a capacity would impact on his own trial and sentencing as an accessory to murder, before the fact. Warbrick had made him no promises, but Fellingham believed that he would agree to a more lenient sentence than the one which would come the way of the Torres brothers.

They were facing charges of being accessories to murder before AND AFTER the fact. She was hoping that they would receive identical sentences to Juan Aiza. The precedent had been set several times, where accessories to murder had received identical sentences to the actual murderer. It would not be too long now, before she knew.

Alex called her back, "What was that you were babbling on about the last Saturday in July?"

"Oh, nothing much," she said coldly, "I was just wondering whether you might be free on that day to marry me, that is if I'm not disturbing any plans that you might have of examining further virgins named Venus, or Delilah or Mata Hari, or whomsoever?"

"I do believe that Delilah and Mata Hari had lost their virginity long before they were ever portrayed on canvas." Then he began to laugh. "I do love it when you become so grumpy, I'm sorry that I was distracted, examining virgins is a distracting business, but to answer your question, I would love to marry you on the last Saturday in July. Do you have a particular venue in mind?"

She softened then, "I was thinking of St Peter's Church in Prestbury, if it's not fully booked would you like me to check?

"I can, if you prefer, it's the least I can do after my transgressions with Venus. Would you happy for me to keep the honeymoon location secret and make the booking, or would you like to be involved in the selection.

"That sounds perfect, thank you. I love the idea of the honeymoon location being a secret. You wouldn't do anything crazy would you, like booking a bed beneath the ceiling of the Sistine chapel so that you might better explain Michelangelo's brush strokes?"

"What a great idea, but no, the strokes I have in mind won't need any explaining."

She squirmed, deliciously, on her seat.

44

The trial of Juan Aiza, Emilio Torres and Pasquale Torres was held in the Central Criminal Court of England and Wales. It is the court where most of the country's most serious crimes are held. It is also more popularly known as The Old Bailey.

As murder trials go, it was not particularly interesting. There were no titillating crimes of passion. The only matter in this regard emerged when Gladys Roxie Brown gave her evidence of the night of the 5th of April when she 'entertained' Mr George Stubbins at the Hilltop Country House Hotel in Prestbury, Cheshire. Even this was tame by Old Bailey standards and the Press representatives present gave it scant notice. Neither was Mrs George Stubbins present, so there were no photographs to be had of the slighted and angry wife. She had long since commenced divorce proceedings against her husband and was demanding that he forfeit his share of the marital home.

Neither were any of the defendants British with any relatives or connections in Britain. They were, all three, from Central or South America, and so there was no interest there. They were not even known terrorists, a couple of less experienced and optimistic journalists hung around for a while hoping that something juicy might be revealed such as a torrid affair with an 'A' list celebrity, but their waiting was in vain.

There was a slight stirring of interest when it was revealed that Mr George Stubbins, whilst also facing charges of accessory to the murder, before the fact, of the victim, Aileen Colquhoun, would be appearing as a witness for the prosecution.

Prosecuting Counsel was Sir Wilton Smethwick, an eminent Queens Counsel specialising in Criminal Law, who was so confident of an early result that he had booked a fly-fishing holiday in the Grampians three days hence.

Defence Counsel was Ms Phoebe Cunningham, appearing in her fourth murder trial. Her previous three had all resulted in a victory for the prosecution.

George Stubbins gave his evidence on behalf of the prosecution and clearly identified Juan Aiza as the man who had introduced himself as John Stone and offered him 5000 pounds to allow Mr Stone to test a revolutionary underwater design of a boat to be trialled at Trentabank Reservoir. He then added that he had not seen the boat to be trialled nor in fact viewed any drawings of said design. He also admitted that as the Manager of the facilities and RSPCA protected Heronry at Trentabank Reservoir he did not possess the authority to grant access to the reservoir. He had done it solely for the money he said.

Whilst in the witness box he was asked to view the enhanced photograph of the three defendants in the act of murdering Aileen Colquhoun. He was asked how such a photograph had come into existence? He had answered by saying that Mr Stone had asked him to ensure that the particular security camera was turned off, but he was not able to do so without alerting his Head Office. He admitted that he had not told Mr Stone of this fact. When asked why not, he answered by saying that he really needed the money. He was then asked to identify the three persons in the enhanced security photograph, and he pointed to the three prisoners in the dock.

He was cross examined by Defence Counsel who asked if Mr Stone had specifically asked him to stay away from the reservoir on the night of the 5th of April and he had answered by saying, 'Not Specifically No.'

When asked to elaborate, he had admitted that he had asked Mr Stone if he wished him (Stubbins) to remain at the reservoir. Mr Stone had replied 'not at all no,' Defence Counsel had then said, "No further questions my Lord."

Prosecuting Counsel had then risen and asked, "Is that all Mr Stone said Mr Stubbins?"

Stubbins had blushed and said, "No, he laughed and said, 'No,' again 'go and enjoy your night, go and give your girlfriend one.'

"So, he knew about your girlfriend, Miss Brown?"

"Yes, I had told him about her."

"So, he knew there would be little chance of you returning to the reservoir that night."

"I suppose so, yes."

Dr Audrey Mathieson was then called to the witness box. After confirming her credentials and occupation, she informed the Court that she had known the deceased for many years, since she had been a young child. She then added that Aileen Colquhoun suffered from chronic aquaphobia and had done so, all of her young life. She was asked to describe aquaphobia and she did so. She was then asked to describe the last moments of Aileen Colquhoun's life. She did so in graphic detail. Every member of the jury was made to visualise the high level of distress that Aileen experienced. How she would have been defenceless and unable to extract herself from her predicament. How her body, under stress would have released excessive amounts of adrenaline and norepinephrine and how these hormones would have extended her suffering by struggling to protect her life.

Two further psychiatrists were called to give evidence, both confirming what Dr Mathieson had said. One of them a professor in Forensic Psychiatry at St Bartholomew's Hospital, who also happened to be Jewish, added that the Nazis had experimented with this form of torture, in the second World War. The records that they kept indicated that patients whose adrenaline and norepinephrine levels had reached excessive levels remained alive for many minutes longer, following the receipt of a fatal stab wound, if they had been physically crucified with nails driven through their wrists and ankles. This was when compared with prisoners who had simply received the fatal stab wound.

The Defence Counsel, Ms Phoebe Cunningham was slumped in her seat. She had no Psychiatric witnesses to refute any of the evidence given. The latest piece of information supplied by the Forensic Psychiatrist had shaken her to her core, all she could think was, 'that poor woman.'

DCI Warbrick had then taken the stand and described what he believed the security photograph indicated. That Aileen Colquhoun had been brought to the reservoir with the perpetrators understanding fully her condition and absolute fear of large bodies of water. Why else would they have paid George Stubbins 5000 pounds to have access to the reservoir. They could have murdered her in a hundred different ways, without having to come near to any water. No, they had done it deliberately, in full knowledge of her condition.

What happened when they brought her there, Aileen would have been totally and absolutely terrified incapable of raising an arm even to protect herself, as Dr Mathieson has so vividly described. She was placed in a canoe and the canoe paddled a short distance from the reservoir bank. The Torres brothers then held her so firmly that she was unable to move, and Juan Aiza then forced her head beneath the water, for several minutes.

He had then added, "Although I am unable to prove this next statement but having listened to the evidence of the three eminent doctors, I believe that they forced her head beneath the water several times. She took a long and painful time to die. When they were able to confirm that life was in fact extinct, they paddled the brief distance to the side of the reservoir, disembarked, then capsized the canoe to simulate a drowning. That, in my opinion, is what these thoroughly despicable men did."

The Defence Counsel tried to dismiss Warbrick's evidence on the grounds of speculation but everyone in that courtroom believed that what Warbrick had said was the most likely version of the truth and the expert witnesses appeared to confirm it.

Both Defence and Prosecting Counsels presented their submissions to the jury. Defence pleading that they return a verdict of Not Guilty whilst the Prosecuting Counsel insisting that only one verdict was possible, Guilty. The judge offered his advice to the jury on issues of reasonable doubt and the obligations of the Prosecution to prove BEYOND reasonable doubt. He then requested the jury to retire to consider their verdict.

They were back inside two hours, and the unanimous verdict was Guilty as Charged.

Before sentencing the Judge reflected on the horrific circumstances of Aileen Colquhoun's death. He reminded the convicted prisoners of their complete and utter heartlessness over the manner in which they had murdered this young woman. They were amongst the most evil men to have ever been tried at the Central Criminal Court. He sentenced all three men to a complete life of imprisonment to be served at Her Majesty's Maximum Security Prison in Bellmarsh, South-East London.

The three prisoners stood, totally stunned; Dacian Jiminez/Ramiro Morales had told them before they had travelled to the UK to murder Aileen Colquhoun that they wouldn't be caught, and even if they were, prison life in Britain was easy, they'd get twelve years max, and be out in six, with a huge lump sum of money to come home to. What had happened, they were now about to be incarcerated in a Maximum-Security Prison for the remainder of their miserable lives.

George Stubbins began to shake when he heard the sentence. Life in prison, the rest of his life in prison all over five lousy grand and him wanting to get his leg over. What an absolute idiot he had been.

The case was over inside two days, Sir Wilton Smethwick would not need to disrupt his fly-fishing holiday. Ms Phoebe Cunningham departed the Court determined to find a different occupation.

George Stubbins managed to have a few words with DCI Warbrick before he was taken away, "Does that mean I'm going to prison for life as well Mr Warbrick, please tell me that I'm not."

"Your case hasn't yet gone to trial Stubbins. Maybe you'll have a nice female Judge who falls for your boyish good lucks and has a passion for Heron's eggs."

As it turned out, George Stubbins didn't go to prison for life, he was sentenced to 12 years, to be served at a Medium Security Prison in Doncaster. He would be released after a period of six years, wifeless, homeless, girlfriendless, jobless, and hopeless. Plenty of time remaining for him to reflect on his stupidity.

45

DS Fellingham had rung Duncan and Isla Colquhoun at 1.00pm on the day of Rory's arrival in Inverness. He was in the home of his parents. When she had given Duncan the news he had gasped, "Give me a minute lassie, thank you but please give me a minute?' She had heard him call Isla and as Isla could be heard shuffling toward the telephone, Duncan had gasped again, "The lassie's done it, he's in jail, that bastard is now in jail, in South Africa, and please God, let him rot there."

Isla had then taken over the phone, she sounded strangely calm compared to her husband, "Susan, my dear, thank you so much for letting us know. Rory is here, I suspect that you had something to do with that also. I know that it wasn't you alone who has achieved what has been achieved, but I know that you have played a major part. We shall be forever in your debt for bringing us to this point where we can now say our goodbyes to our beautiful daughter and find some peace in God's good time. Thank you, my dearest Susan, and may God bless you."

Rory took his parents to the Dores Inn on the banks of Loch Ness, south of Inverness. The restaurant, with its grounds, are located at the edge of the loch and is highly regarded for both its location and its cuisine. Before sitting down for a meal, the remaining members of the Colquhoun family gathered at the edge of the loch. Isla threw a single bright, yellow rose into the loch and all three lowered their heads. Isla spoke, "Beautiful Aileen, let this rose be a symbol of the joy and sunshine that you have brought into the lives of all that have had the privilege of knowing you. You are so precious to us, and you were so cruelly taken from us, but I know that you will understand that you will live in all our hearts forever. Sleep softly and in peace our precious Aileen."

They returned to the dining room of the Dores Inn; the mood was sombre. Although no one knew the reasons for what had just been witnessed, they all believed that they should be silent, out of respect. It was Duncan who lifted the mood, "Good folk, we have just said goodbye to our wonderful daughter, and I know that she would not have wanted sadness to have accompanied her departure, please drink up, the next few rounds will be from the purse of Aileen Colquhoun."

Back in Wilmslow, as everyone was preparing for the huge 'knees up' that DCI Warbrick had promised, DS Fellingham and DC Proud each received a letter. Susan called Gary, "have you received a letter?"

"Yes," whispered Gary.

"Have you opened it?"

"Not yet, I'm scared to."

"I have one too, shall we open them together?"

"Yes, I'd like that."

DC Proud came to her office, clutching his letter.

"Open yours," she said.

"No, lady's first," he had replied.

She did so, and fell back in her chair, "I've passed, oh my God I've passed, I'm a Detective Inspector. Quickly open yours."

DC Proud did as he were told, his reaction was completely different to that of his sergeant. He leaped four feet off the ground with a single roar of "Yes."

They hugged one another and then read one another's letters. "My God Gary, you passed with a High Distinction, well done, really well done."

"I have to thank Terri for that, she sat with me for weeks helping me swat and asking me questions over and over again."

Gary's roar had brought several other people into DS Fellingham's office, including DCI Warbrick. The sea of smiling faces told him all he wished to know, he hugged them both, first Gary and then an especially long and loving one for DS Fellingham. He then pulled them to him and with one either side of him he threw an arm around each of them and announced to the now completely full room, "These two are the two best detectives it has ever been my privilege to work with in my forty years in the force. We really have the best possible reasons to celebrate now."

The party began then, it would continue long into the night but before the afternoon was over DCI Warbrick slipped quietly to his office to call his co-conspirator and now good friend Eduardo. "I'm calling to give you the news."

"I can tell from your voice that it is good."

"Yes, my friend, it is the best, we now have Morales in that hellhole of Pollsmoor, Aiza and the Torres brothers were found guilty yesterday and have been sentenced to life, and I do mean life, in another hellhole we call Bellmarsh Prison outside London. It is a Maximum-Security Prison like Pollsmoor, but it also houses the worst terrorists that Britain has ever been able to capture and jail."

"To top it all though I am delighted to tell you that my two colleagues DS Fellingham and DC Proud have both passed their examinations and will be promoted. Fellingham will now become Detective Inspector Fellingham and Proud, Detective Sergeant Proud. I am delighted and can now begin to think seriously about my retirement."

"And your marriage, don't forget your forthcoming marriage to the delightful Gina."

Warbrick began to laugh, "Not just my marriage Eduardo, my whole bloody team is marrying, Susan to Alex of course and Gary Proud to the lovely Terri Ryan who I have not yet had the pleasure of meeting, it must have been those oysters you served the last time we were at the Villa Giustiniani."

"That cannot be so," protested Eduardo, "DC Proud was not here then, but we must correct that. I insist that Gina and you, Susan and Alex, and Gary and Terri be our guests at the villa for an extended weekend, ten days from now. I will have the travel arrangements made, you pull rank Lindsay and order your subordinates to attend."

Warbrick laughed again, "You're a hard man to refuse and Gina would never forgive me if I did. I will also need to clear it with DCS Speers to ensure that he is comfortable with his junior officers being so generously treated. I'm sure that he will be though, he has been delighted with the result that we have achieved together. I also have to add that there must be a way I can thank you for all your help and generosity to us on this case. I have no idea what it could be that I could do, but if it is at all possible, I would gladly do it."

"Lindsay, you have already done more for Lucia and me than mere words could ever convey. Our hearts are still sad, but you have brought peace to them. Is there a more beautiful gift that someone can give to others, than a peaceful heart, I don't think so. Let us join, now all eight of us, in the joy of celebration."

And so it was that Eduardo's 12-seater Lear jet took off from Manchester airport the following Friday morning for Verona with six extremely happy aboard, none more so than Terri and Gary. Terri had now met all of Gary's colleagues, she had been impressed with all of them and could well understand how Winston Macauley had been smitten by Susan Fellingham, her fiancée Alex McQualter was also pretty dishy.

It would be fair to say that her feelings were fully reciprocated by all of Gary's colleagues, with DCI Warbrick commenting to Gina Moretti, "Gary Proud never ceases to impress me, he's a first-class copper and he obviously knows how to pull the stunning birds, on a DC's pay as well."

Gina had looked at him over her glasses and whispered, "Down boy down," leaned over and hugged him and then a few minutes later, "ooh, maybe not."

The weekend was wonderful in so many ways. Lake Garda continued to weave its magic, the chef excelling himself again with culinary creations that brought gasps of pleasure from everyone. Eduardo had chosen the very best of his wine from his extensive cellar. Lucia, and Gina, had re-connected like the close and longstanding friends that they would become. Alex and Susan had taken to long walks along the banks of Lake Garda, Gary and Terri had been taken into Verona by Vanessa to view items for their forthcoming nuptials. At the end of each day, they would meet on the terrace for pre-dinner drinks.

Eduardo and Lindsay had found a lakeside spot where they could sit quietly and share thoughts and experiences which had been kept secret within each of them for many years. Eduardo found Lindsay's perceptiveness and wisdom a refreshingly stimulating aid to his own deliberations and found himself opening up, more and more to the discerning comments of his newfound friend.

Lindsay found Eduardo's ease with his money, fascinating. He had never met, with the possible exception of a brief meeting with the Duke of Westminster on an earlier case, anyone who possessed so much, yet remained so humble. He sensed the supressed desire in Eduardo to one day return to clinical practice. Had he had a son, perhaps that might one day might have been possible, but the empire that he ran with Lucia was as demanding as it was unrelenting. He had loved his daughter very deeply, she was for him, the embodiment of the passion that he shared with Lucia, but perhaps now he might find peace.

They were sitting quietly in their favourite spot on the Sunday morning, when Eduardo said, "Do you remember a few months ago when you quoted Cicero and the ancient Greeks to me?"

Lindsay had smiled and replied "Yes."

"Well, I have found a new mentor, a Russian author, teacher, and philosopher, who lived in the United States. His name was Yevgeny Yevtushenko."

"So," continued Lindsay.

"He once wrote, 'Justice is the train that is nearly always late'. I think that he should have added, 'and is so much more welcome when it does finally arrive."

THE END

If you enjoyed the Aquaphobic Canoeist why not try a sample of Richard Butler Glenn's next book:

"THE FALL OF THE FACELESS MEN"

Pre-order your copy now through our website:
richardbulterglenn.com

THE FALL OF THE
FACELESS MEN

1

Sabine collected her cards for yet another hand of whist, but her mind was not on the game. The train was approaching Crewe station and although she had felt quite comfortable at the outset of her journey from Glasgow Central to London's Euston station, the presence of the two men who had subsequently boarded the train, one in Carlisle, the other in Preston, had disturbed her more than she would have cared to admit.

They were both policemen, she was sure. The first guy had taken his seat on the aisle of the first row of seats closest to the exit door that was clearly visible from her position midway down the carriage. He was dressed in clean but well-worn working clothes of the type worn by construction workers, but what she could see of his hands failed to confirm this illusion. They were far too well cared for and the manner in which he folded his newspaper was more reminiscent of an accountant than a carpenter.

He had studiously avoided looking in her direction. Far too studiously she had thought. She was well aware that she was an extremely attractive woman, and most men would have found it almost impossible to take their eyes of her and she dressed, deliberately, to stimulate this affect. The suit she was wearing, in a deep emerald green, clung tightly to a body that only the many hours that she had spent in the gym could have possibly created. The skirt, lying just above her knee gave only the slightest hint of her inner thighs but there was no hiding the shapely contours of these same thighs as they seductively stretched her skirt like a second skin.

Her jacket cut in bolero style emphasised the narrowness of her waist and the fulsomeness of her breasts with just the briefest tantalising glimpse of cleavage. As if to test her impressions she moved languidly in her seat, revealing slightly more of her inner thigh, but her 'carpenter' failed to be stirred.

The second man had boarded the train in Preston. This man, dressed in a cheap ill-fitting suit had looked hard at her as he passed and taken up his seat two rows behind her and on the opposite side of the carriage. She had been around enough policemen in her time not to be able to pick this type for what they were. There were several indicators, but the most obvious one was the shoes they chose to wear. It was though too many years plodding a beat had made it necessary for all of them to wear well worn, comfortable shoes. She wondered briefly if they all bought their shoes at the same supermarket.

Dennis and Irene Brown had boarded the train shortly before she had done so in Glasgow's Central station. She had initially sat on the opposite side of the carriage from the Browns, but before she had been able to fully settle, Irene Brown had crossed the aisle and sat down opposite her.

"Do you play whist dear?" she had said, "it's a long journey to London and Dennis there,' she indicated her companion, "is a boring whist player. As well as which it's never much fun with only two playing."

Sabine's first reaction was to decline but some inner instinct whispered to her that there was probably increased security in being seen to be travelling with two others. Three people travelling together attracted far less attention than a single woman travelling alone, so she had smiled and said that she would love to join them.

Dennis reacted as most men did when she moved over to his side of the carriage with Irene. His face beamed as though all his Christmases had just come at once and he spluttered, "Gosh sweetheart, has anyone ever told you that you're bloody gorgeous."

Irene glared at him and Sabine gave him her sweetest smile thinking, "This is going to be the longest five and a half hours of my life."

The train pulled into Crewe station, a man and a woman entered their carriage. He was quite good looking and smartly dressed, she looked to be several years older than him with a lived in face, but what took her breath away was that she knew that they were also police officers.

They did not give her a second look as they walked past her seat to take up two seats several rows behind her, but she dared not look where, exactly.

How the hell had they got on to her so rapidly. She had been her meticulous self, or so she believed. She had booked the two rooms, both with queen beds, as instructed. She had checked in the day before she was due to meet her 'date,' also as instructed. She had taken possession of both room keys having smilingly told the receptionist that her sister, with her partner, would be joining her and her husband later. She visited both rooms but was careful not to touch anything, despite wearing gloves. She left the Grosvenor Hotel to stay overnight at the Blossoms Hotel, also in Chester.

The following lunchtime she met with her two accomplices, Mike and Mary Turner, and gave them the key to one of the rooms. She then had only two hours to wait for her 'date's' train to arrive at Chester station. She returned to the Grosvenor Hotel and to the café in the foyer area, ensuring that she was seen to be alone throughout this time. One hour later she received a text message on her phone which said simply "In position." Thirty minutes later she asked the concierge to call her a cab, which he did, and she instructed the driver to take her to Chester station.

She had been told by her employer's representative, Giles, that Mike and Mary Turner were present primarily for her protection. Mike, just in case either of her 'dates' became violent, Mary, to dampen any worryingly level of ardour which her naked body might arouse in Mike. A secondary requirement for their presence was to install the necessary photographic equipment required for the photographic session, and to remove this same equipment, post photographic session. They were then to leave the card advising her 'date' that he was now a star of a video, together with two selected photographs which graphically displayed his activities, check over and clean the room, whilst still leaving her sufficient time to quietly dress and exit the hotel.

Her 'date,' Alan Johnson, arrived fifteen minutes later and they took a cab back to the Grosvenor Hotel. Alan Johnson tried to appear nonchalant and in control, but she could feel his pulse racing as she took his hand and entered the hotel. She had told him in the car that she had already checked them in, but she expected him to settle the account when they checked out. He had been happy with these arrangements and so they bypassed reception and walked to the lifts, arm in arm.

She took him to her room, opened the door and they moved inside. Alan Johnson was immediately on the attack, but she fended him off, laughingly saying, "Patience Alan, we have all night." She spun him around, and she reached up to kiss him on the mouth.

"Would you like to view my goods first?" she laughed. He nodded enthusiastically. She firstly donned an ornate facial mask, the type seen at the many Venetian balls which were held throughout the year. It completely obscured her face. She then pushed a small button on the side of her watch which alerted Mike to commence recording on all four video cameras. She then removed all of her clothing and pushed Alan Johnson back onto the queen-sized bed. Simultaneously, Mike activated the remote control of the four hidden video cameras, and the first of four monitors clearly showed the naked Sabine's masked face and breasts as she straddled him. She had been aware that she would have to participate in some actual sex in order to provide both pre and post coitus photographs, but she was confident that she could keep it to a minimum. The second monitor reflected the ecstatic face of Alan Johnson as he sampled her wares, and the third, a rear view of Sabine's undulating hips as she appeared to sensuously copulate with her willing partner. The fourth monitor later showed him swallowing, in its entirety, the refreshing drink which she had set out on the bedside table.

This refreshing drink contained a syrup of Midazolam, its bitter taste disguised by the bourbon and coca cola which he had told her was his favourite tipple. Midazolam belongs in the family of benzodiazepines which is conventionally used by anaesthetists when participating in an endoscopic gastrointestinal procedure. It is usually kept under strict medical supervision during the entirety of this endoscopic procedure. In this case though, the people who had arranged for the supply of this Midazolam cared little whether or not the recipient survived the ingestion of this anaesthetic. They just wanted him unconscious, or dead.

The video cameras having provided the evidence, the anaesthetised body of Alan Johnson slumped back on the bed. Mary Turner tapped on the door to enter and placed the card and two photographs which informed and illustrated for Alan Johnson that he had just performed on candid camera with the cheerful wish that "He enjoy the headlines." She also instructed Sabine to urgently dress herself and leave the hotel discreetly. This Sabine did whilst Mary checked over the room before she finally admitted Mike to the room to check if Alan Johnson was still alive. He was.

Sabine had worn clothes that were fully reversable, and her soft case opened out in a backpack, she removed her blonde wig, donned large sunglasses, and left the hotel. No one noticed her leaving. She had been in the hotel for less than one and a half hours. She returned to the Blossoms Hotel and collected her overnight bag and changed into a different outfit. She caught a cab to Chester station and was quickly on her way to Glasgow with a change at Crewe.

Acknowledgements

My continuing gratitude goes out to the following people who have maintained their support of my literary efforts and continue to provide their very welcome encouragement. Karen Clarke, Irene Wolff and Nicole Wolff, Michael Thain, Teresa Hargrave and Cecily Chittick.

My daughter-in-law, Eran Naylor continues to provide her unstinting advice on all social media matters, and she was recently joined, here in Ballina, by Benjamin H. Clarke who astounds me with his superior knowledge of this contemporary form of communications. I am in awe of their ability to make sense of publishing algorithms and these influences on publishing success.

Nick Caya and his team at Word-2-Kindle continue to offer their enthusiastic support and I have been greatly encouraged by the many kind and positive comments of my readers, and I continue to be grateful to them for taking the time to read my book.

I express the hope that this, my latest effort, will stimulate your interest, and excite your imaginations, with the exploits of the Warbrick/McQualter team in East Cheshire. Your reviews provide the stimulus to my imagination, and I am continually grateful for your efforts in writing them. Your positive comments really are the oxygen which fuels my efforts and my desire to create an exciting narrative for your enjoyment.

I also wish to once again to acknowledge the major contribution of my wife and editor, Virginia Glenn. Her quiet and constructive comments contribute, massively, to the final product and I am truly grateful for her unlimited love and support.

About The Author

Richard Butler Glenn is the author of the Warbrick/McQualter Crime Thriller Series mostly set in Chesire, England with frequent forays in Italy, which feature the same team of detectives.

He has also written The Symphony of Friendship Chronicles, which follows the lives of four families from quite disparate cultures who come together in Australia.

Richard is married with four children and lives in Ballina, New South Wales, Australia, with his wife.

Visit Richard Butler Glenn Website:
www.richardbutlerglenn.com

Follow us on social media

Also By Richard Butler Glenn

Check my website: www.richardbutlerglenn.com for upcoming publishing dates for the following books:

The Warbrick/McQualter Crime/Thriller Series:

The Aquaphobic Canoeist (Book 2)

Then Fall of the Faceless Men (Book 3)

Death before 'I DO" (Book 4)

Coming later – Books 5 & 6

The Symphony of Friendship Chronicles:

The Symphony of Friendship (Book 1)

Days of Wrath and Wonder (Book 2)

Coming later – Book 3

www.ingramcontent.com/pod-product-compliance
Lightning Source LLC
Chambersburg PA
CBHW030804260626
47169CB00001B/187